Hide and Speak

Everly Summers

Happily Inked After

Published by Happily Inked After

ISBN: 979-8-9985244-0-0

For more information about the author and upcoming releases, visit:
www.authoreverlysummers.com

First Edition
Printed in the United States of America

Contents

Dear Reader

Hey, there my glorious reader!

Before diving headfirst into the emotional rollercoaster that is this book, here's a little heads-up from your friendly neighborhood romance author:

This story contains themes that may be distressing to some readers, including references to:

- childhood trauma

- kidnapping

- physical and emotional abuse

- PTSD

- and mental health struggles

While it's wrapped in banter, sass, and a healthy dose of swoon, some scenes dig deep into darker territory.

Your mental health matters more than any plot twist. If today isn't the day to read this kind of story, that's okay. We'll be here, pages waiting, whenever you're ready.

Now that we've covered that, let's turn the page and meet the emotionally repressed hero who's about to have his whole life upended by one hell of a woman.

Oh, but before you do you boo, don't forget your handy guide (*or warning*) to the spicy chapters that are in this book. You can avoid these if you prefer a more closed door approach, or skip ahead to them. This is a judgment free zone, my friend.

Spicy chapters include: 25 (a touch of spice, but not full on), 26, 33, 34, 43, 47 (a few hints), 55 (just a bit), 56, and 59.

With love and caffeinated chaos,
Everly

Prologue

Rico - Age 13

Being kidnapped blows.

I had plans today—solid plans.

It's summer, and I should be at the park with my cousin, hitting on the junior high girls who rollerblade around in shorts that leave little to the imagination.

But no. Thanks to Marco and his complete inability to run, here I am.

No clue why I'm surprised by this.

The last time I chased him down, it was embarrassingly easy. He's two years older, taller, and supposedly stronger, but his speed rivals a buffering dial-up connection on its best day. So now I'm sitting here, tied to a chair, because these geniuses thought I was Marco, and I didn't correct them.

Better me than him.

Marco would've folded five minutes in and spilling family secrets all for the low, low price of a Capri Sun and a participation trophy.

Me? I have standards. And a backbone. My idiot cousin, lacking even a fraction of our family's survival instincts, caused a preventable hostage situation, and I'm stuck watching it unfold.

And when I get out of here? That nose I broke last year? Oh, it's due for a follow-up appointment. Because thanks to Marco's inability to run—or, let's be honest, function as a useful human being—I'm missing out on bubblegum-sharing, swing-set-sitting, Cali McAllister time. Cali McAllister, whose white shorts are beyond short, and whose heart-patterned underwear are practically a public service announcement with how well you see them through those infamous white shorts.

Justice will be served. And by justice, I mean Marco's face meeting my fist.

The basement air is damp and reeks of mildew. It's cold, but I refuse to shiver—gotta keep up appearances. They twisted my arms behind me, binding them tightly enough to make my shoulders burn worse than when Marco hog-tied me after watching Uncle Tony.

Only instead of the real bullets Uncle Tony *likely* used, Marco opted for Nerf bullets. Didn't matter. Once I was loose, I chased him down and broke his nose. Best day ever.

Doubt I'll write this one up as the same.

Adjusting to the darkness takes time, and every wiggle in these ropes makes me hate Marco's cement feet a little more. The ropes bite into my wrists, the rough fibers grinding against my skin until I feel the warm trickle of blood dripping down my fingers. Great. That'll definitely ruin my chances with the girls this summer. "Hey ladies, check out my abduction scars"—yeah, real smooth.

Everything hurts, but I'm not about to let it show.

Uncle Tony drilled it into us—Bennetti boys don't break. No fear. No weakness. Doesn't matter if they're holding a gun to your head or threatening to cut off your fingers, you hold your ground. Our family isn't just powerful; we own this city. The mayor, police chief—hell, half of New York's top brass are on Uncle Tony's payroll. They look the other way, and they're well compensated for their selective blindness.

The biggest lesson drilled into us since we could talk? Don't do it.

Bennetti boys always notice more than we admit. We collect details—tuck them into the corners of our minds until the perfect moment to use them. Just like the guy I saw Uncle Tony haul out of his basement one day. Trust me, he wasn't napping.

Words get you favors, words cash in favors. Words are worth more than cash. Words can also save your life—*if* you know how to use them.

"Tell me, *ragazzo*," says one of the goons ruining my summer. He's about Uncle Tony's age, with slicked-back gray hair, dead fish eyes, and teeth yellower than my morning piss. A cigarette dangles from his cracked lips as he paces back and forth, flicking a Zippo lighter open and shut, the flame dancing for a second before disappearing with a metallic clank. I focus on the sound. Anything but him.

When he finally lights up, he takes a long drag, blowing smoke right in my face. My insides twitch. A cigarette would hit the spot right now, but asking for one would mean talking. And, as we've established, that's a no-go in these situations.

He crouches down, his face too close for comfort. His breath? A mix of cigarettes and something that crawled in there and died. Ever heard of a toothbrush, dude? Clearly not.

"Where is your Papa hiding his shipments?"

I stare straight ahead, silent. My heart might pound harder than Marco's drum set—an unfortunate Christmas gift from Uncle Tony—but they don't need to know that. I won't make a sound.

They've already ripped my favorite navy blue polo, the one Mama just bought me. Bruises bloom across my torso and arms, dark and spreading in angry, uneven patches. Sure, my brothers and I spar and take boxing lessons, but let's be real—taking a fist to the gut from a full-grown man is a little different from scrapping with my lanky twin brother, Dom.

No matter how many punches, kicks, and even the occasional slap from their meat hooks, I stay quiet. Tears sneak out, but I don't acknowledge them. The fat one in the corner, the one who threw the hardest punches, cracks open a beer, gulping it down while watching me with disinterest. I can still feel the phantom pain from his last hit—probably bruised my kidneys. Pissing blood tomorrow should be fun.

Assuming I even see tomorrow.

The old man sighs, ashing his cigarette onto the floor. "You're stubborn. That's not good for your health."

Neither is smoking, but I keep that one to myself.

I don't talk. Not to these idiots.

It's not about loyalty.

It's about survival.

Because there's one fundamental truth about the Bennetti family that no one ever says out loud: you can survive a lot of things. You can survive a few broken bones. A few bruises. A night in a freezing, piss-scented basement.

But you won't survive betraying the family.

And I don't plan on dying today.

These geniuses think I'm Marco—the golden boy, son of Tony, heir to the Cosa Nostra.

When they pulled up in their creeper van and asked which one of us was Marco, I didn't hesitate. If Marco opened his mouth—and he would, because the moron never shuts up—he'd be the one getting shoved into the back, and he wouldn't last ten minutes. His bones crack with sharp, brittle precision, and his reputation for never shutting up is practically legendary at this point.

So I did what any good cousin would do.

"I am Marco," I said. Simple. Effective. *Idiotic*.

Next thing I knew, someone tossed me into the back of a van that smelled of vomit, pee, and wet dog.

If they figure out I'm not Marco, they'll come back for him—or worse, my family. Yeah, not happening. They're too dumb to even have a photo to compare.

So not only am I spending a perfectly good summer day tied to a chair in a damp basement, but I'm dealing with idiots.

I might be thirteen, but growing up a Bennetti and hanging around my cousin Marco has made me more aware than most kids my age—though Marco missed the memo.

A sharp right hook slams into my ribs, sending my insides clattering around with the chaotic rhythm of a dryer full of loose change. I swallow down the coppery tang of blood and mentally note to ask Alex to hit me a few times next time we spar. Gotta build up my pain tolerance because damn, that one stung.

The Fat One—every kidnapping crew has one—pushes off the wall, sauntering over. A single bulb swings above me, flickering. It's the scene straight out of one of those B-rated mob movies, except this one sucks, and I'm the unwilling star.

Piss Teeth takes another drag on his cigarette, blowing smoke in my face. "Thought Tony's kid never shut the fuck up." His teeth are an insult to dental hygiene.

"The boy will talk," Fat One says, chucking his empty beer bottle against the wall. Glass explodes, brown shards skittering across the floor, beer fizzing in a slow, pathetic pool. His meaty hands yank at what's left of my shirt while he pulls out a switchblade. Idiot flips it open way too close to his hairy nostrils. Seriously, dude, trim that jungle.

The cool metal glides down my cheek, and I tell myself *don't flinch, don't flinch, don't flinch.*

I don't.

A sharp twist of the blade nicks my skin, and warmth dribbles down my face. Great. I appreciate my face. The girls enjoy my face. And the last thing I need is my twin brother looking better than me.

"Gonna tell us where the shipments are?" Fat One drags the blade across my ribs, right over the spot he kicked earlier. The crackling sound still echoes in my head. He slices deep, slow, and I feel warmth seep down my side. Not a fatal stab. Yet.

My brain drifts, latching onto details that don't matter but do. *The stains on the wall are green like puke, like zombie flesh, like the goo you blow out of your nose when you're sick. Brown like Lola's dog crap. Gold like my brother's ridiculous bumblebee bike.*

"Tony's kid is fucked up," Piss Teeth mutters, shoving the cigarette against my skin. Burning flesh smells like a whole new kind of hell. I lock my jaw, focus on the wall. *Green moss, green kelp, green scabs.* Anything but the fire searing into my chest.

Time blurs. They leave. They come back. They hit me, ask questions, leave again. I stop keeping track. Hunger gnaws at me. Thirst burns my throat. But I wait.

Because no matter how many punches they throw, they won't get a damn word out of me.

Then footsteps echo outside the door. Voices. A man crying—no, sniveling louder than a toddler lost in a grocery store—then a loud crack before the metal door swings open. Fat One crumpled onto the floor, crimson pooling from a neat hole in his forehead.

Red like stop signs. Red like Nonna's marinara.

A man in a three-piece suit steps over the body, pausing in front of me. I know him. I've seen him at Uncle Tony's house, but he's not family.

Uncle Tony once said he had this guy "in his pocket." I didn't realize Tony's pockets could hold an entire human being, but hey, who am I to question the physics of the Cosa Nostra?

Piss Teeth shuffled in behind him, lighting another cigarette. "Kid won't talk. Won't give up Tony's shipments." He shrugged. Apparently, torturing a thirteen-year-old was just another Tuesday.

Suit Guy snorted, eyes scanning me. "Why the hell would he? He knows nothing." He stepped closer, circling me before grabbing my chin, tilting my face up to his.

"How dumb are you fuckers?" His accent was thick—not Sicilian, not Russian. Boston, maybe. I could see him worming out of the hell of Southie.

A beat of silence.

Green like your puke after eating way too much Halloween candy.

"No, you idiots. This isn't Tony's kid. This is Ricardo's. And if you think Tony's a psychopath, wait 'til Ricardo finds out you snatched his son instead of Marco." He let go of my chin and turned toward the two morons by the door. "You grabbed the wrong Bennetti, you dumb fucks, and I'm not gonna be the one to explain it."

"So... what do we do?" New Guy asked, while Piss Teeth eyed me.

Suit sighed, slow and tired, reaching into the back of his waistband. In one smooth move, he drew his gun and put a bullet in each of them. Piss Teeth groaned, a wet gurgle, but Suit just stood over him and fired two more rounds before holstering his gun and yelling into the hallway. Guess stupidity only takes you so far in life.

Red like my boxing gloves. Red like the color of tomatoes. Red like a cherry slushie that I'm craving right now. Only I'll never want to eat or see red again after this.

Two more guys appeared, eyes flicking from the bodies to Suit to me. Suit stepped over the corpses, careful not to scuff his shiny shoes. "Get rid of the boy. Do not kill him. Do not put another scratch on him. Drop him somewhere he will be found, but not the hospital." He glared at them, his tone sharp. "Do. You. Understand. Me?" They did their best bobblehead impression while nodding. "If you add one more scratch, even a little, I will personally gut you and wear your intestines as a belt."

Then he turns to me, his pale skin and green eyes glowing under the dim light. Irish, maybe. The type that burns instead of tans. "Tell your Papa it was a misunderstanding. Tell your uncle..." He smirks. "My apologies."

Yeah, somehow I don't think they'll accept his *oopsie*.

I meet his gaze, my voice hoarse but steady. "You're dead."

He laughs.

Then he walks out as if executing three people in a basement were just another item on his to-do list.

A few hours later, I was back in the van, the stench of wet dog and stale beer making me gag. My stomach was empty, and my ribs screamed with every pothole we hit. They finally tossed me out into a filthy alley, the cold asphalt biting into my skin. Rain pelted down, each drop stinging against my bruised and broken body.

"No hard feelings, kid," one of them said before hopping into the passenger seat and slamming the door. The van rumbled off, leaving me in the trash and darkness.

I lay there, sprawled in the filth of a forgotten alley as rain hammers down in cold, relentless sheets. Every shallow breath sends a bolt of pain through my ribs, each inhale sharp and jagged, swallowing glass with every gasp. Blood, warm and sticky, spreads beneath me, merging with the downpour until there's no telling where I stop and the concrete starts.

The world blurs—lights flickering in the distance, the hum of traffic far off, the occasional slam of a car door—but none of it feels real. None of it belongs to me. *I don't belong to me.*

The idiot who thought he could take Marco's place? He's gone.

The boy they dragged into that basement? He's dead.

Something darker took his place. Something hollow. Something that understands what pain really is now.

They beat me. Cut me. Burned me. Left me to rot in the gutter like garbage, but that wasn't what broke me. It wasn't the pain or the blood or the suffocating knowledge that, for a while, I was sure I wasn't getting out of there alive. It was this—this. The silence.

No one's coming.

No one knows where I am.

No one will find me unless I crawl out of here myself.

A laugh tears out of me, raw and broken, swallowed instantly by the storm. The only person who can save me is me, and that realization burns hotter than any cigarette pressed to my skin.

I press my forehead against the cold, wet pavement, my mind looping the same thought over and over again.

Words are useless.

Words get you hurt.

Words betray you.

The people who speak the most? They're the easiest to break. The easiest to manipulate.

I should've never spoken up for Marco. I should've never taken his place. I should've stayed silent.

And I will.

From now on, words belong to the weak. They belong to people who believe in second chances, in rescue, in salvation.

But I know the truth.

No one is coming.

No one saves you.

You either survive, or you don't.

Allie

WHEN I WAS A little girl, I had big princess dreams. The kind where I wore an over-the-top ballgown, met my prince on a white horse, and got whisked away to some magical kingdom where I was blissfully happy. After all, I was Papa's little princess.

"*Principessa*," he called me, Italian for, you guessed it, "princess." And he meant it. But let's be real—fairy tales missed a crucial detail with my kind of royalty. Because I don't live in a castle with turrets and singing woodland creatures. No, I live in a prison. A lavish, marble-covered, gold-trimmed prison, but a prison nonetheless.

Sure, I wake up every day and slip into custom Italian designer clothes directly from the runway, swipe my black Amex without a second thought, and bask in the constant stream of groveling from people who know exactly who my father is. Whatever I want, I get.

Except for the one thing I actually want.

Freedom.

I am a princess, but a mafia princess. A title that comes with all the luxuries of a high-society socialite and none of the autonomy of an actual human being.

My father is a Capo in the Cosa Nostra, working directly under Don Bennetti. That means he's a boss, and as his only daughter, my future was sealed the second I was born, whether or not I wanted to follow that future.

And, shocker, I do not.

People assume a mafia princess spends her days shopping, her nights clubbing, and her life smiling for cameras. Been there, done that, got the overpriced exclusive Hermes handbag.

None of it's for me.

You know what I actually dream about? Cooking. Not for show. Not to impress some future husband with my ability to make pasta from scratch. But because I love it. Because food brings warmth and joy. Because creating something with my own hands feels real in a world where everything else is fake.

But mafia princesses don't cook.

We don't do chores. We don't get our hands dirty. We don't work.

God forbid one of us joins the actual workforce, let alone dares to go to school after high school. The horror.

A mafia princess is a spectacle. A showpiece. We're meant to be admired—draped in perfection, praised, and paraded as if we're blue-ribbon trophies up for bidding. We're the pretty birds locked in gilded cages, groomed to smile, wave, and accept our fate.

And the number one rule? There's no leaving the Cosa Nostra. Ever.

Which, if you ask me, is a pile of absolute bullshit.

I didn't choose this life. I didn't choose my father, my last name, or the suffocating expectations that come with it. Do I love my parents? Of course. But do I love what they represent? Not even a little.

The Cosa Nostra isn't all bad, though. They operate in the gray area, toeing the line between illegal and morally questionable. Papa talks about the donations they make, the schools and homes they rebuild, how they take care of their own. In this life, family extends far beyond blood. Technically, I have hundreds of siblings, aunts, and uncles. We live and die by the rules of family loyalty.

And my role? My entire existence has been leading to one thing: marriage.

I'm meant to marry someone in the Cosa Nostra. To produce heirs while my husband does whatever the hell he wants. Rarely are mafia wives treated as equals. They're placeholders. Vessels for children. Lavish spenders of their husband's wealth. Expert socialites.

And above all else? They must pretend to be happy.

Some of them are. Most of them aren't.

It doesn't matter, though. Because we don't get a choice.

Standing here right now is stupid. And yet, here I am, because I refuse to roll over and accept that this is my only option. That this is the only path carved out for me. I refuse to believe it until I've exhausted every alternative. Until someone tells me there is no way out.

"He's going to say no," Vinnie mutters, his massive frame practically blocking out the light as we stand outside the office door.

Vinnie has been my shadow since I was a little girl, assigned as my personal bodyguard. All mafia princesses get one. Not solely for our protection—God forbid a single scratch appears on our flawless skin—but because our virtue is apparently a national treasure that must be guarded at all costs.

The irony? Our future husbands will be anything but virtuous. They'll keep swinging their dicks around long after the ink dries on the marriage certificate. Hypocrisy at its finest.

"Your brother got out. You told me yourself he said we had a chance if we asked Bennetti."

"A chance," Vinnie frowns. "But, as I warned you, there's a price. Antonio got out, but he had to pay the price. He lucked out and is happy with his price, but you might not be. He might not even give you the option. He could say no, or worse, he could go straight to your father, tell him what you're asking, and how do you think that's gonna work out for you, *bambolina*?"

I shoot him a snarl. He's called me that since day one. And sure, it tracks. I've been styled within an inch of my life for as long as I can remember—fresh outfits, pristine shoes, hair always camera-ready. Case in point: today's fashion disaster. I'm wearing a shiny vinyl dress that has me feeling straight out of the Madame Barbie collection. Toss me a whip and a spiked choker, and I could moonlight as a dominatrix.

For the record, vinyl is not comfortable. It sticks. It clings. On the upside, it's currently waxing away hairs I won't have to pay a salon to rip out later. Silver linings.

Mr. Bennetti's assistant—a woman so slim she could double as a coat rack—taps her crimson nails against the desk, each click dripping with judgment. Her blood-red lips curl into a venomous smirk as she tosses her glossy black hair over one shoulder and scans me with the disdain of someone spotting gum on their Louboutins.

"We have an appointment," I say, my tone all sugar-coated steel. This bitch thinks she can intimidate me. Clearly, she doesn't realize who my father is or what I've seen. Her nasty sneer is about as threatening as a wet napkin.

She taps a pen against the desk, unimpressed. "I see that, but just because you have an appointment doesn't mean Mr. Bennetti will meet with you. So, I'll ask again—what is your reason for requesting this meeting?"

Vinnie shifts beside me, silently asking if I want him to handle it. I shake my head. If it were anyone else, I'd let him strong-arm them into doing what I want, but this is Marco Bennetti's assistant. And something tells me that if Vinnie so much as sneezed in her direction, her skeletal frame would snap in half, and Bennetti wouldn't be pleased.

People say he's crazy. Then again, all men in the Cosa Nostra are varying degrees of insane. And considering what I'm about to do, I probably belong in a padded room myself.

I lean in, flashing my best Mafia Princess smile. "Can you please tell Mr. Bennetti that Alessandra De Luca is here to meet with him? And if he refuses to see me, I'll be leaving the Cosa Nostra without his permission and he can go fuck himself."

Vinnie stiffens beside me, and the assistant's lips part in shock, her gaze flicking up and down as if reassessing every decision that's led to this moment.

Vinnie leans down, voice low. "I thought I told you not to poke the bear."

I nod toward the assistant, still gawking like she's never seen a woman in heels before. "That look like a bear to you?" I hiss. "More like a half-starved hyena. Someone get her a sandwich. Or better yet, a sandwich with a surprise ingredient. Preferably arsenic."

Without a word, she picks up her phone, pressing a button before her voice turns sugary sweet. "Mr. Bennetti, it's Francesca. Your new assistant, sir. I started six months ago..." She trails off, immediately dropping her pen. "Yes, of course, sir, I know I've worked here long enough to know better. I know you asked not to be interrupted, but—" Her dead, soulless eyes flick to me. You know what, I take it back. A wet napkin *is* more threatening.

"Yes, sir. I understand, sir. Your appointment is here. Miss De Luca." She clears her throat, and I watch the color drain from her face at an alarming rate. I may be dressed one whip-crack away from a new career, but she's wearing a skin-tight white dress so sheer I can see the outline of her nipples through the fabric.

And somehow, even in this absurd outfit, I've still outclassed her.

I believe this is rock bottom.

"Yes, sir, I know. But Miss De Luca has said that if you do not meet with her..." she chews on her blood red painted lip, clearly debating if she has the nerve to repeat what I said. "She will leave the family without your permission." *Chicken.*

Francesca's voice barely makes it past a whisper before she jerks back with a shriek, dropping the phone just as the office door swings open, kicked in by the wrath of God himself.

Marco Bennetti, the Don himself, steps out, and the room shifts—air sucked clean, gravity bending around him in that silent, terrifying way only true power manages. His secretary practically launches from her chair, all but swooning in his direction, teetering between full-blown worship and hormonal freefall. I mean, fair. The man's objectively hot. Annoying, but hot.

The man is a living, breathing, villainous fantasy. Dark brown hair, sharp liquid fire amber eyes missing all the warmth, an angular jawline and basically rocking the look of a man carved by an ancient sculptor with a god complex topped off with a silk-lined designer suit. No wonder the women of the Cosa Nostra fan themselves into heatstroke whenever his name comes up.

But let's be real—he's also the devil in Armani, which, for me, significantly dulls the shine.

His gaze drags down my body, slow and assessing, before he nods at Vinnie. "You stay out here."

"I prefer not, sir," Vinnie says, standing there with the unwavering resolve of a man who clearly skipped the self-preservation gene. Bold choice. Especially from the guy who told *me* not to poke the bear.

Marco smiles—and not the charming, let's-share-a-glass-of-wine kind of smile. No, this one's colder. The kind of smile that makes your stomach plummet and your survival instincts shriek *abort mission*. Goosebumps crawl up my arms, but instead of bolting, I dig my heels in. Because unlike the other silk-wrapped mafia daughters who faint at confrontation, I was apparently born with a steel spine. One my Papa never tires of reminding me is a pain in his ass.

"Are you insane?" I whisper at Vinnie through gritted teeth.

He doesn't answer. Just keeps staring down Marco, who now stands there with his arms folded over what is definitely a chest carved from punishment and protein powder, watching us both with all the casual menace of a lion deciding whether the snack in front of him is worth the calories.

I muster up my confidence, which at this point is hanging by a very thin, very frayed thread, and flash my best fake smile. It's about as convincing as a politician's campaign promise, but it's the best I've got.

"Fine," Marco says, gesturing for us to follow.

I swallow the ten-pound lump lodged in my throat and step into the office, brushing past him. That's when it hits me—his scent. Sharp, expensive cologne layered with something darker. Dangerous. Now I know exactly what the devil smells like. And no, it's not brimstone. It's sin in a bottle with a designer label.

The office is stark, almost clinical. A single mahogany desk, a laptop, a phone, and one file folder. There's a small sofa in the corner and two chairs across from the desk, but nothing personal. No photos, no art, not even a stray coffee cup. It's like the man doesn't actually live in any of the spaces he owns, which, given his reputation, makes complete sense.

The only other living presence in the room is a man built from concrete with a chip on his shoulder for charm. He's posted up against the wall, exuding bouncer energy—the kind who's seen too much and trusts no one—but there's nothing casual about the way his nearly black eyes follow my every step. Even more telling is how closely they're watching Vinnie.

I know exactly who he is. Marcello.

Comically called "Marco" for short—because creativity died years ago in the Cosa Nostra.

He's the bodyguard. Bennetti's personal shadow. Which means two things:

1. He could kill a man with a toothpick.

2. He probably already has.

People don't hire men like him; they're chosen, and any man trusted to guard the most powerful boss in New York isn't someone you cross unless you've got a death wish and a funeral plot picked out.

I try not to stare too long because he radiates, *I'll snap your spine like a breadstick vibe.*

"Sit," Marco Bennetti barks.

I take one chair while Vinnie takes the other. Marco slowly lowers himself into his seat, unbuttoning his jacket before clasping his hands together on the desk. His amber eyes pin me in place and the confidence I had outside his office is now puddling at my feet.

Do I speak first? I have no idea. I've never been in a room alone with the Don before. Papa meets with him all the time, but that's business. This? This is something entirely different.

"Miss De Luca," he purrs, his voice smooth as sin, but those sharp, calculating eyes go straight to my chest. Fantastic. "To what do I owe the pleasure?"

I glance at Vinnie, who gives me a silent nod, which is no help at all. Great. Apparently, my spine abandoned ship between the hallway and this chair.

I clear my throat, clasping my hands in my lap. "Well, Mr. Bennetti, first, I want to say that I love my family, and I appreciate all you and your father have done for us—"

He holds up a hand, cutting me off. "Miss De Luca, you don't need to stroke my ego. I've been told it's big enough already. And I doubt you made this appointment just to tell me how wonderful I am. So, let's skip to the part where you tell me what you actually want."

I take a breath, square my shoulders, and meet his gaze head-on.

"I want to leave the Cosa Nostra."

Rico

LIFE, WHEN YOU STRIP away the Hallmark card sentiments and Instagram filter bullshit, boils down to two irreplaceable commodities: words and time. And like most idiots in this world, people waste both with the reckless abandon of drunk frat boys tossing hundred-dollar bills in Vegas.

Take my family, for example—a masterclass in controlled chaos. Every Sunday, without fail, they gather for what they call "family time."

What it actually involves is inhaling food as if we're preparing for a natural disaster, talking over one another because silence is apparently forbidden, and pretending our last name doesn't come with enough emotional baggage to sink a cargo ship. The table stretches longer every year, Bennettis multiplying at a rate that would concern most scientists. Conversations clash, kids scream, babies wail—an unfiltered, high-volume symphony of dysfunction.

And here I sit. Every damn Sunday.

Why? Because the noise drowns out the demons. The nonstop chatter, the clink of glasses, the scrape of silverware—it's a static hum that, for a few hours, keeps everything else at bay. Temporary peace is still peace, even if it comes wrapped in loud Sicilians and unsolicited life advice. The only other time I get that kind of relief is the rhythmic clicking of my keyboard when I work.

To my left, my cousin Eddie—who has the intellectual depth of a kiddie pool—chews with his mouth open, shoveling food in with all the grace of a farm animal at feeding time. Honestly, that's insulting to farm animals. Across from me, Valeria *tap, tap, taps* her nails against the table, auditioning to become the next Morse code prodigy. The red polish catches the light, and because I'm a glutton for punishment, I glance. *Red*. It doesn't send me into cold sweats anymore, doesn't clamp my chest shut with steel-jawed precision, but it lingers at the edge of my vision, a ghost that refuses to leave.

Hands under the table. Fists. Open. Close. One... two... three. *Red like marinara. Red like the Cabernet I clearly didn't drink enough of.* By the time Valeria's nails tap out another round of passive-aggressive irritation, I've convinced myself I'm fine. Fine-ish.

"Well, we have an announcement!" My twin brother, Dom, grins from across the table, his arm around his wife, Sienna. Sweet girl. Talented. Gorgeous. I still have no idea how my brother landed that one.

"We already know you knocked her up," Eddie, the village idiot, interjects, proving once again that he has the self-preservation instincts of a lemming. He registers my glare, swallows hard, and looks down at his plate. "Sorry, Dom. What's the news?"

Unfazed, my brother looks toward our parents at the head of the table. "Yes, we're having a baby." He pauses because the drama gene runs strong in this family. "But we just found out—it's twins."

The collective gasp is unnecessary. Nobody needs to be shocked. Bennetti twins are about as predictable as the Manhattan gridlock. We breed in bulk.

My jaw tightens, so I rock it back and forth, ignoring the warning creak of my molars. I could replace them, but I'm not in the mood for oral surgery.

"Well," Mama starts, but Dominic holds up a hand. She grins, folding her hands in front of her, letting him have his moment. If I did that, I'd get slapped upside the head, but apparently impregnating your wife earns you a free pass. I suppose that's one perk to look forward to.

"Twin girls," he announces, beaming as he kisses Sienna's hand, gathering votes for the role of *Devoted Husband of the Year*. My gag reflex considers activating. I rather enjoyed Nonna's eggplant parmesan, and I'd prefer to keep it down.

"Girls?" Papa, who has an army of grandsons, looks as though he just hit the genetic jackpot. He's out of his chair before his brain fully processes the news, moving with the agility of a man half his age, crushing Dom and Sienna in a hug. "Baby girls!" He's practically glowing.

I'd like to take a moment to thank Nonna for her eggplant parmesan, which is currently staging a mutiny in my stomach.

Across from me, my older brother Alex sits with his wife, Violet, and one of his sons strapped to his chest in a ridiculous baby backpack contraption that makes him look like a combat-ready marsupial. The kid, a tiny dictator with a head full of chocolate-brown hair, is blissfully unaware of his father's dignity dying a slow death.

Two of Alex's boys inherited his blue eyes, while the third got Violet's striking green ones. Genetics did them a favor. The other two kids are inside, no doubt being force-fed espresso-dipped biscotti and whatever else Nonna has deemed suitable for infants. Their fault for leaving them alone with a woman who considers bedtime a social construct.

I nod at Dom, my way of saying congratulations. He knows what it means. No need to waste breath stating the obvious. I *am* happy for him. He spent years raising his now six-year-old son alone, met Sienna, decided she was it, and permanently anchored her to his side with an iron-clad pregnancy contract.

Unfortunately, thanks to Dom and his overachieving sperm, all eyes—specifically Mama and Papa's—are now firmly on me.

Perfect.

As I sip my wine, my gaze drifts toward the garden, but I can feel the burn of their stares.

Thanks, Dom. Really. Couldn't have timed this announcement for a day I conveniently "forgot" to show up?

My future is no longer a mystery. In thirty minutes or less—about the time it takes for everyone to finish fawning over Dom's twin revelation—Mama will rise from the table, conveniently leave Papa behind, and set him loose on me with a carefully curated list of why it's time I do my duty and get married.

It doesn't take a genius to know where this is heading. I am the only unmarried Bennetti at thirty-seven. Our family doesn't believe in divorce, only long, emotionally suffocating love stories. Not that anyone has ever been miserable enough to test the system.

But as the last remaining Bennetti bachelor spawned from my parents, Dom might as well have taken a freshly plucked cactus and jammed it straight up my ass. Because now, the expectation isn't just that I get married—but that I impregnate some poor woman and dedicate the rest of my days to diapers, bottles, and ungodly amounts of screaming at all hours of the night.

I love my nephews. I babysit them.

Babysit.

Keyword.

I watch them for a few hours—hell, sometimes even an entire night—so Alex and Violet can get some sleep. Then I kiss them goodnight, hand them back, and return to my blissfully quiet, child-free life.

Fatherhood? That's a whole different beast. Kids of your own don't come with an off switch. They're permanent. An eighteen-year (or more) prison sentence, especially if they turn out like my idiot cousin Eddie, who, at thirty, is still living in his parent's basement, working for his papa, and coasting through life with the drive of a sedated sloth.

Yeah. No, thanks.

Do I want a family? Sure. But not for the bullshit reasons that make Dom look at Sienna—apparently she's single-handedly keeping the Earth from spinning off its axis from the way he worships her. I don't care about love, soulmates, or whatever cosmic nonsense makes people think destiny plays matchmaker. I want an heir. Someone to carry the Bennetti name. *That's it.*

So, I raise my glass to Dom, who smirks because he knows exactly what he's set me up for, and down the rest of my drink in one gulp.

I'd give my left nut to punch him right now, but something tells me I'm going to need my nuts to reproduce.

"Another set of grandbabies," Papa announces, his eyes locking on me while he says it. "Just one of you left to go."

Subtlety has never been one of Papa's strong suits. Marriage and children rank about as high on my to-do list as hiking Mount Everest. I don't do nature, and if forced, I'd rather be mauled by a mountain lion halfway up the incline.

I always figured I'd get married—eventually. Preferably after forty. Thankfully, men don't have that ticking clock my cousins are always whining about in their wombs, so I've got time. Or at least I *had* time until Dom dropped his twin-baby bomb. Now, the countdown has officially begun.

Sienna clears her throat, resting her hand on her already swollen belly. She's due in two months, and why Dom waited until now to share the twin news is beyond me. What I know is that thanks to my brother's prolific sperm, I'm about to be fast-tracked into "marriage and kids" territory faster than I can blink.

My parents will insist. No *demand*. Find a wife. Knock her up. Keep the family legacy rolling, and now there is a looming deadline.

Not sure where I'm going to find a woman crazy enough to marry me.

And even if I did, I'm not convinced I'd survive the experience.

Rico

MY BROTHER IS DEAD to me.

Okay, maybe that's a little extreme.

But still. Because of him, I'm now planted in *this* spot, in *this* study, with *this* glass of whiskey in my hand, waiting for my inevitable execution like a man on death row whose last meal was force-fed to him. The leather couch under me is worn from decades of Bennetti men sitting in the same position, probably having the same conversation, staring at the same man who believes his word is law.

Papa's study is designed to intimidate. Dark wood, rich leather, shelves stacked with books he has actually read and aren't there solely for aesthetics. Every single Violet Hart novel ever printed sits on one shelf—signed, of course—because my sister-in-law is the woman notorious for giving every other woman in Manhattan a misguided idea of relationships.

I forgive her for that though, because she's also the only woman on the planet capable of making my older brother *somewhat* tolerable, and even then, it's questionable. A massive mahogany desk sits in the center, its surface perfectly organized because clutter gives Papa a migraine. An old-school globe that doubles as a hidden bar cart looms in the corner because a normal liquor cabinet isn't enough.

And then there's the smell—whiskey, old paper, and a faint trace of cigar smoke, even though Mama would set this place on fire if she ever caught him smoking inside. The air is thick with it, clinging to the walls, the furniture, my clothes. Hell, it might as well be woven into the very fabric of the Bennetti DNA at this point.

Papa sits upright in his armchair, relaxed in that *I'm-about-to-drop-a-bomb-on-you-and-you-can't-do-shit-about-it* kind of way. His glass sits untouched on the table between us, ice melting, condensation pooling around the base.

That's the thing about Papa. He sets the stage for conversations that aren't really conversations. This isn't a discussion. This is a verdict.

After dinner, I thought I was in the clear. Plates cleared away, the noise faded, and no one uttered the dreaded words: *We need to talk.* I was already halfway out the door, my freedom within reach, when I made the fatal mistake of stopping to give Nonna a goodbye hug.

I turned around and almost smashed face-first into Papa's chest. For the record, the man is built like a marble statue. He's pushing seventy, but he could still bench-press a truck. His salt-and-pepper hair is the only indicator he's over the hill. Wrinkles? Mythical creatures in the Bennetti gene pool. Sicilian blood has its perks.

And now, here we are.

At least he gave me a drink first. Small mercies.

I bring the glass to my lips, take a slow sip, and let the whiskey burn all the way down, hoping it dulls the irritation clawing at my insides.

It doesn't.

"Rico," Papa says, his voice calm and steady, like he's about to tell me I have cancer, but it's the *good kind* — also known as marriage. "We need to talk about your inheritance."

I blink, caught off guard. I'd mentally prepped for the *wife, kids, and settle down* lecture. Not this. I lean back, nursing the whiskey. "My inheritance?"

In case you're wondering, we all have trust funds. Generous ones.

Papa made a lot of money before any of us existed—most of it was not exactly legal. The kind of money that required creative accounting and a strategic mix of businesses to launder it. Think dry cleaners, nail salons, pizza joints. He diversified like a mobster Warren Buffett. Toss in a few charitable donations for good measure, and voilà—he's practically a saint. The rest of his cash went into the pockets of people who could arrest him. I believe the technical term is *payoff*.

My oldest brother, Alex, inherits the family estate—because, obviously, the eldest son gets the house. Dom inherits all the real estate investments, mostly commercial properties and warehouses. God only knows what's stashed in them, considering Uncle Tony has been known to use a few for "storage."

And me?

I inherit the *businesses*. Papa's little empire of small companies scattered across the city. Nail salons. Dry cleaners. Diners. Leave it to him to bestow the one son who approaches human interaction with all the enthusiasm of a root canal with businesses that require me to interact with a shitload of humans. Every day.

Humans. Daily.

I down the rest of my whiskey, already mourning my solitude.

"Rico, I can't let you inherit the family businesses if you don't have an heir to pass them to."

Ah. There it is. The sales pitch, also known as my bitch slap of reality.

Papa leans forward, clasping his hands together like he's presenting a well-rehearsed PowerPoint. This isn't my first rodeo. So, I settle in. "Each of you boys have inheritances because we wanted you to have something, be comfortable, and carry on the legacy."

Love how he conveniently leaves out the part where that *legacy* started with a lot of blood, a few offshore accounts, and enough creative accounting to make the IRS have a collective stroke. But sure. Hard work and perseverance for the win.

"Alex has the boys, Dom is about to have his girls, and he has Luca. You?" He levels me with a look. "You're not even married. I'm getting older, Rico, and without an heir, I can't leave the family businesses with you not knowing if they'll stay in the family. Without an heir, you have no one to pass them to."

"I'll leave them to one of Alex or Dom's kids." Hell knows they'll have plenty. Alex treats knocking up Violet like it's an Olympic event and peacocks about how he broke the genetic code and got three kids in one go instead of the highly predictable twins us Bennetti's are known for.

Papa scowls. "No, *you* get these businesses so you can pass them to *your* children, who will pass them to *their* children. That's the entire point of a legacy, Rico."

Ah, yes. Silly me. How could I forget the sacred Bennetti tradition of breeding future restaurant and dry-cleaning moguls?

"Are there any women in your life?"

I blink at him. *Seriously?* The entire family knows the answer. *No.* And not for lack of opportunity. Even when I was younger, I'd take a woman out, let her talk to me for an hour about the latest diet trends or why her best friend was a *total bitch*, and five minutes after she stopped talking, I'd forget everything she said. The date would end in awkward silence, and I'd make a mental note to never bother again.

By twenty-five, I came to an undeniable conclusion: the only way to get exactly what I needed from a woman was to pay for it. Remove the variables, eliminate the unnecessary, and streamline the process. Efficiency at its finest.

For the last three years, I've had a standing appointment with the same escort. She only sees regulars now—something about being married. How her husband sleeps at night knowing his wife is treating matrimony like a side hustle is beyond me, but people have justified worse. Every Wednesday, fifteen minutes. In, out, done. A transaction as routine as renewing a domain subscription.

My family, in their infinite talent for selective blindness, calls it *therapy*.

Their way of skirting reality with the kind of grace only those with old money and deep denial can pull off. Since what they now refer to as *the incident*, they've opted for willful ignorance, as if slapping a polished euphemism on my habits makes it any less damning.

Therapy sounds a hell of a lot better than *Rico pays a woman through Venmo, complete with emoji-coded transactions that give our mother heart palpitations.* I keep my payment history public just to test if they check. A little weekly reminder that yes, I'm still attending my sessions.

Escorts don't require conversation. No pretense, no tedious small talk, no listening to someone recount the latest plot twist in their coworker's love triangle. She doesn't talk. I don't talk. It's all very... surgical. And that's how I prefer it.

"You know the answer to that."

I push up from the couch, moving to the liquor stash in the corner, and pour myself a generous three-finger measure of whiskey. I sip it slowly, mindful of how much I drink. Unlike my brothers, I don't have a driver waiting outside to ferry me home like I'm some delicate prince. I drive myself.

The idea of someone else in control while I'm on the road? No. My skin crawls just thinking about it.

My brothers' drivers aren't just chauffeurs, anyway. They're guards. Vetted, cherry-picked by Uncle Tony before Marco took over.

I don't need a guard.

Ever since the *incident*—the family's adorable euphemism to avoid saying *the time Rico got kidnapped and nearly executed*—I've spent my life ensuring that no one gets the drop on me again. Boxing. Krav Maga. Training with Marco's best men.

The only downside to not having a driver? Nights like this. Nights where I'd rather get blackout drunk and forget this conversation ever happened, but instead, I have to sit here. Stone-cold sober(ish). Listening to my father lecture me about a wife and kids I don't have and don't want.

If I ever do get married, she better be mute.

And ovulate on command.

"You have six months, Rico."

Mid-sip, I pause, glass hovering near my lips, and turn to my father. "Six months?"

He nods, entirely too pleased with himself. "I'll give you six months to find a wife on your own, or your Mama and I will choose one for you."

Fuck. That.

I know exactly what that means. Any time I've been forced into a "date," it's been with a woman hand-picked by Mama. Always some friend's daughter. Always someone with too much personality, too much enthusiasm, and the ability to monologue for hours without requiring air.

No sane woman would willingly marry me. Which means whatever desperate soul my mama picks will be absolutely *unhinged*. The kind of woman who sees nothing wrong with baby talk, demands matching Christmas pajamas, and is one nervous breakdown away from naming our future children after the herd of cats she already owns.

Hard pass.

Papa's sharp gaze flicks to my fist, clenched tight at my side. It's a habit. Open. Close. Open. Close — all the while my eyes focus on one solid object in the room, defining color and what it reminds me of — it's that or another rage fit. I've kept the fits under control for almost twenty-one years and not about to break the streak. It's my body's version of buffering when my brain is trying to process too much bullshit at once.

I focus on the antique clock in Papa's office that has been there longer than I've been alive. Perched on the mantel, watching, waiting, judging. It's an aged brown, though brown is a gentle way to describe the decay it's settled into.

Brown like the damp earth after a rainstorm. Brown that reminds you of libraries filled with books and yellowed pages. Browned wood left in the sun too long, dried, cracked, and clinging to life.

I force myself to shake it out and place my glass down on his desk. "Going now."

I don't even make it two steps before Papa moves, blocking the door. His hand lands on my shoulder, heavy, warm—weight with something I don't want to name.

"Rico, I'd prefer you find a wife on your own. Someone you'd be happy with. Someone you could love, like your brothers do. Have kids. Be settled."

He means it. I know he does.

But that's the problem.

He thinks love is something I'm capable of.

The thing he still doesn't get after all these years? I'm not built for that. Never have been. There's never been a woman who's piqued my interest, and I'm pretty sure that thing in my chest people call a heart is either dead or cryogenically frozen—either way, no plans to thaw anytime soon.

Feelings? Emotions? A foreign concept for me.

The odds of me being happy, let alone loving someone, are about as likely as me adopting a rescue cat and naming it Fluffy.

My soul kicked the bucket twenty-four years ago, and last I checked, there's no CPR for that.

Allie

ONE HUNDRED EIGHTY TWO days ago, I sat across from Marco Bennetti and told him I wanted out of the Cosa Nostra.

Bold, right? Brave, even. Except it felt less *brave* and more like volunteering to stick my hand in a garbage disposal.

Considering I've grown up surrounded by men who treat problems like piñatas—whack them until something breaks—that's saying a lot.

Sure, women leave the family all the time. But not *mafia princesses*. No, we're groomed for one purpose: to be bartered off like rare Pokémon cards. My dad's been shopping around to various "upstanding" families for years. Each one as appealing as strolling barefoot over broken glass.

The Romano family? *Filthy rich but dull enough to bore me into a coma.*

The Bianchi family? *Lots of political connections, zero personality.*

The Contis? *Handsome. But charming? Eh, if you're into sociopaths.*

Papa hints at these families over Sunday dinners with the subtlety of a jackhammer. *"Oh, you'd be so lucky to marry into one of these families, Principessa."* He and I have different definitions of lucky.

My papa doesn't get the final say. That honor belongs to Marco Bennetti, the Don. He's the one who has to approve any marriage arrangement. And the Don doesn't often say no. So, there I was, sitting across from him, tossing my dignity on his desk like a last-second Hail Mary pass.

Did he say yes? *No.*

Did he say no? *Also no.*

He said, *"In my time. Not yours."*

And just like that, I entered the world's most excruciating waiting game. Every time my phone buzzes, my heart jumps, thinking maybe it's Marco finally setting me free. Spoiler alert: it never is.

The worst part? I begged him not to tell Papa. If my family knew I wanted out, they'd feel betrayed. They think I'm the perfect daughter. *Principessa*. Sweet, spoiled, but loyal. They have no idea.

I feel awful keeping it from them, but I know the reality of what would happen if Papa even thought I was leaving. I love my family. They're not bad people—well, relatively speaking. But I don't want to marry one of these Cosa Nostra Ken Dolls and spend my life popping out heirs while my husband gallivants around with his mistress of the month.

I definitely don't want my kids waking up one morning to the FBI raiding our house and freezing our bank accounts, because *surprise!* all our money is technically illegal. I lived that life. I know what it's like to wonder if the unfamiliar car down the street is a neighbor—or someone sent to make us disappear.

I might be twenty-four, but I've got the soul of a sixty-something woman, and honestly, I'm one *you should be grateful speech* away from slipping into orthopedic shoes and moving to a retirement community.

Maria lets me into the kitchen to help cook, which is basically the equivalent of giving a kid the keys to the candy store. Why? Because Papa's at "work"—which, in our world, could mean anything from laundering money to burying a body—and Mama is probably out single-handedly keeping Gucci in business. The coast is clear.

I'm elbow-deep in dough, kneading it with a little too much enthusiasm. Therapy? Overrated. Dough between your fingers? Highly underrated.

Next to me, a pot of marinara simmers away on the stove. Not just any marinara—my marinara. This baby is my Frankenstein sauce, the product of weeks of experimenting like some mad scientist in an apron. Marinara is usually just marinara. Tomato, garlic, a pinch of basil. Boring.

But mine? A masterpiece.

Well, slowly crawling its way there if I can fine-tune the right mix of ingredients and get the flavor that pops right just the moment it slides onto your tongue.

Forget sugar—I've subbed in ground carrots and their juice to sweeten the tangy kick of fresh tomatoes. Anchovy paste for a rich umami punch, and, the pièce de résistance, a whisper of cinnamon. Sounds questionable? Sure. But trust me, it's a little taste of magic in a pot.

"Smells delicious, Allie." Maria strolls back into the kitchen, wiping her hands on her apron.

Her dark hair is twisted up in a messy bun, the kind that looks effortless but probably took three hair ties and a whispered prayer to keep in place. There's a streak of flour on her cheek, and she smells like garlic, basil, and the underlying confidence of a woman good at her job and content in her life. I envy that.

The kitchen in our home is warm and rustic, a space that's been lived in for generations and a stark contrast to the gaudy features that decorate the rest of the house. Dark wooden beams stretch across the ceiling, and the cabinets—handcrafted by my Nonno decades ago—are worn smooth from years of use. Copper pots hang above the stove, their surfaces dulled by time but well-loved. The scent of simmering tomatoes lingers in the air, mixing with fresh-baked bread cooling on the heavy oak table at the center of the room. This is my heaven.

Maria peeks over my shoulder before going back to the pastries she's rolling out for dinner this evening.

I grin, rolling the dough one last time. "Thanks! Just a little experiment." I don't mention it is helping relieve the growing tension of knowing whether or not I will be here tomorrow.

Maria laughs, oblivious, as I silently bask in the dream of *one day*—a day where my life doesn't revolve around negotiating family alliances and fake yoga classes.

Twice a week, I'm not in downward dog but in a cramped community college kitchen, learning the finer points of French cuisine. As far as Mama and Papa know, I'm busy finding my Zen. The truth? I'm up to my elbows in béchamel and perfectly diced mirepoix.

The plan is simple. Leave the Cosa Nostra. Work the line at a restaurant. Live in a shoebox apartment. I'll trade fancy clothes and personal shoppers for late nights, aching feet, and minimum wage. And it'll be worth every second.

"*Principessa!*" Maria hisses, snapping me out of my daydream. She rushes toward me, eyes wide with panic. "Your Papa just came through the gates."

My heart jackknifes. I glance at the clock. "Crap. Why is he home so early?"

I'm already yanking off my apron, tossing it onto the counter, and scrubbing my hands clean. In ten seconds flat, I'm out of the kitchen, my hair flying out of its bun as I sprint down the hall toward the study. I don't even bother checking for flour smudges; there's no time for a mirror. I throw myself onto the couch with a book in hand just as the front door swings open.

Heart racing, I force my breathing to slow and flip the book right-side-up—because, yeah, it was upside down—and paste on an innocent just-a-girl-reading expression.

Papa walks in, his footsteps deliberate, his gaze scanning the room.

"Reading again, *cara mia?*" he says, smiling.

"Of course, Papa." I flash a sweet smile, casually flipping a page. "You know how much I love Tolstoy." I am so glad he didn't realize that I was, in fact, not reading Tolstoy.

He nods, satisfied, as I internally high-five myself for the flawless save.

"How was your day, *principessa?*" He asks.

"Good, Papa. You're home early." I snap my book shut and rest it on my lap, giving him my best dutiful daughter smile. I'm hoping he can't read between the smile lines and see I'm hiding something.

Let's set the scene: I'm sitting here, pretending to be a delicate, well-behaved mafia princess in my designer prison uniform—a gaudy black Prada pantsuit. Sure, it's tailored within an inch of its life and costs more than a small car, but the only redeeming quality is that it's a pantsuit, which means I didn't have to shave my legs. Small mercies.

Of course, that's where the convenience ends. I still had to cake my face in foundation and bronzer, glue on my fake lashes, and top it all off with a spritz of my signature perfume—a custom blend of lilac and vanilla that Mama's been forcing on me since my sixteenth birthday. Sounds elegant, right? Wrong. It smells like a floral assault, and if I have to inhale one more whiff of vanilla that isn't baked into a cupcake, I might hurl.

But perfection is the family brand, and as a *principessa*, I'm expected to look flawless from the second I wake up until the moment I dramatically collapse onto my bed at night. Cozy yoga pants? Not in this house. Instead, I'm currently sweating bullets in my peach silk blouse and five-inch torture devices masquerading as heels.

Over the years, I've at least mastered walking—hell, even a light jog—across our marble floors without breaking an ankle. Impressive, I know. Sadly, that's the pinnacle of my talents. Well, that and piano, which I loathe with the fiery passion of a thousand suns. Every time Papa insists I play at one of his functions, I fantasize about taking a sledgehammer to that smug, shiny grand piano. *One day, Steinway. One day.*

"We're dining with the Romanos tonight," Papa announces, his deep brown eyes locking onto mine like a sniper zeroing in on a target.

Oh. No.

Fighting the urge to roll my eyes so hard they get stuck, I force a smile. "Oh?" My voice is a little too chipper like I'm genuinely thrilled about this not-so-delightful surprise.

Carlo Romano.

The ick in human form. He's attractive, sure—in the way a well-dressed serial killer might be—but he's also fifteen years older than me and gives off major *you'd-look-great-served-on-a-platter* vibes. Every time he looks at me, I can practically hear him mentally adding a pinch of salt and a garnish of parsley.

Creeper.

Papa unbuttons his jacket and takes his usual spot in the armchair across from me. The study—unlike Papa's hard edges—is all soft cushions and cozy furniture. Thank Mama for that. Built-in bookshelves line the walls, filled with everything from *The Art of War* to *Pride and Prejudice*. Papa likes to think his collection makes him a well-rounded intellectual. I prefer to think of it as a visual reminder that he could easily switch from negotiating business deals to quoting Mr. Darcy. Terrifying.

Meanwhile, I safely stashed my collection of Violet Hart novels under my bed. Papa calls them "smut." I call it self-care. Or more accurately, living vicariously through women who aren't trapped and—bonus—have mind-blowing orgasms. Not those half-hearted, participation-trophy kinds I've experienced. No, these heroines get the gold-medal Big O's—the kind I'm still waiting for in real life.

According to Papa, however, I have no clue what the Big O is. Why? Because in his world, mafia princesses are supposed to be untouched, wrapped in a perfect little bow for their future husbands. Virginity: the Cosa Nostra's most prized currency.

Yeah, about that...

Let's just say I cashed in my V-card years ago. No way was I going to save it like some wedding night surprise gift for my future husband. I took matters into my own hands—or rather, into the hands of a particularly talented guard with a tongue that deserved its own Michelin star. Laundry room. Ten minutes. No regrets.

But since that one rebellion-fueled night? Nothing. Nada. Three years of forced celibacy. What happens to a vagina that's out of commission for that long? Do cobwebs form? Does it shrivel up like an old sponge? I wouldn't know because my virtue—aka my social life—is constantly monitored.

So yeah, I live vicariously through heroines who run their businesses, wear sweatpants, and get the occasional toe-curling orgasm.

Papa clears his throat, bringing me back to reality. "What do you think of Carlo?"

I think he's a pit viper that figured out how to squeeze into a three-piece suit.

"He's... alright, I suppose." You thought I was going to say that out loud? Cute. Mafia princesses don't just go around insulting potential suitors. We have tact.

"He's shown interest," Papa says, quirking one of his perfectly waxed brows. Yes, waxed. My terrifying mafia boss of a father gets his eyebrows professionally groomed every other week.

I carefully place my book beside me on the couch, ensuring the spine faces away from Papa. No need for him to see my contraband. He hides illegal firearms; I hide spicy romance novels. We're both rebels in our own way.

"He's rather..." How does one politely say a man is slimier than an oil slick? Every time Carlo touches me, I feel like I need to bathe in bleach. "Papa, don't you think he's a little... old for me?"

He snorts. Bad argument. Age gaps in the Cosa Nostra are as common as over-gelled hair. A fifteen-year difference isn't scandalous here—it's standard. One of my "friends" recently married a man twenty-three years older. No thanks. I'm not marrying a man who has Papa on speed dial for poker nights.

"*Principessa*, it's not that big of a difference. You two have a lot in common."

If by "a lot in common" he means we both breathe oxygen, then sure. Otherwise, the only thing we share is being related to people with criminal records.

"He's very wealthy," Papa continues, his tone all practicality. "He could give you a good life. A nice house, whatever car you want, as much clothes as you can buy."

Ah yes, the Holy Trinity of Happiness: a house, a car, and unlimited clothes. Never mind that I can't buy $26 yoga pants because I don't have $26 of my own, and even if I did, Papa would rather die than see his daughter in yoga pants.

I shrug, keeping the cringe from reaching my face. "We've talked, Papa. I just... don't feel anything."

What I *don't* say is that Carlo gives off serious Dateline vibes. I'm fairly certain he'd take out a fat life insurance policy on me and light our house on fire for the payout. Not exactly the recipe for a dream marriage.

With the worst timing possible, my phone lights up on the side table. The screen reads *"Nonnatus."* My code name for Marco Bennetti. Because, let's be real, I can't have *The Don* casually flashing on my phone when Papa's around. Too many questions. Zero good answers.

Nonnatus, by the way, comes from St. Raymond Nonnatus—the guy who volunteered to take the place of Christian captives and got locked up himself. I'm not technically a captive, but this life is suffocating enough to feel like I'm on some medieval hostage exchange program.

I hit the ignore button on my phone with my brain scrambling for an excuse to escape Papa's study and call him back. Preferably from the furthest, most forgotten corner of the vegetable garden—where no one would think to find me unless they were actively searching for a runaway.

"I think I'll take a walk," I say, already halfway out of my seat and smoothing down my ridiculous pantsuit.

Papa eyes me like he's deciding whether I'm really going for fresh air or plotting my next act of rebellion. He adjusts his cufflinks. "Wear the new Valentino tonight for dinner."

Ah, the dress. The one with more cleavage than fabric. Just perfect for an awkward dinner with Carlo, who absolutely strikes me as the secret-basement-playroom type.

Holding in a full-body shudder, I nod, grab my phone, and power-walk out of the study. I turn down the hallway, ducking beneath the grand staircase, my heels click-clacking against the marble with each hurried step. I'd run, but that would draw attention.

The second I reach the patio doors and step outside, I immediately regret this idea.

Outside is humid. Sticky. Hot. The kind of heat that makes your clothes cling to you like a desperate ex who can't take a hint. Even though it's technically spring, New York's weather is about as reliable as my excuses when Papa catches me sneaking off. Greenwich is usually lovely—if you like spending your days sweating in pantyhose while pretending you're living some glamorous life.

And speaking of pantyhose...

"Oh, hell!" My heel sinks into the grass like a stake through Dracula's heart. See? Another reason dressing up is stupid. What if I needed to make a quick getaway? Death by stilettos is not how I plan to go.

I yank off my heels, my toes wiggling in sweet relief. If feet could sigh, mine would sing a hymn of gratitude. I clutch my heels like weapons and make a run for it, my pantyhose absorbing all the lovely green dye from Papa's precious, spray-painted lawn. Yes, you read that right—*Papa dyes the grass*. Eco-friendly? Not so much. Obsessive about appearances? Absolutely.

The vegetable garden is in the farthest corner of the estate, tucked away behind the manicured hedges, the infinity pool, and the waterfall—because naturally, every mafia estate needs a waterfall. The whole area is fenced in with black iron and topped with those delightful pointy spikes of death for anyone feeling acrobatic. It's quite the trek, which is why only Maria and the gardener ever bother coming back here.

The second I reach the garden, the scent of fresh soil and ripe tomatoes fills my lungs. Basil leaves stretch toward the sun, herbs beg to be picked, and the air smells like a farm-to-table dream. The dirt calls to me, practically begging me to plunge my fingers into it and feel like an actual human for five seconds. I'm tempted to do just that—to crouch down, sink my hands into the soft soil, and pretend that I'm not a mafia princess but *just Allie*, the girl who likes to prune tomato plants and doesn't have to answer to anyone.

Once I'm sure I'm alone—no lurking Capos or nosy housekeepers—I pull out my phone to see a text waiting from Marco. Of course, the man can't just call once and let it go. Nope. Text follow-up required.

> Nonnatus: I don't appreciate my calls going unanswered.

He might be *The Don*, but seriously? Not everyone can leap into action the second he graces their phone screen. Then again, Papa does exactly that—family dinners, church, business meetings. If Marco calls, the man practically backflips to answer no matter where he is or what he's doing.

I click on his contact and call back, muttering a quick prayer and crossing myself for good measure. Let's hope he picks up and doesn't go full petty on me by letting it ring just to teach me a lesson.

"About time," Marco mutters by way of greeting. No *hello, no how's life?*, just straight to condescension. "You realize I'm a busy man, Alessandra. I don't have all day to wait around for your call."

I bite my lip to keep from pointing out that he clearly *does* have time, considering how quickly he answered. "I was with Papa," I explain. "I couldn't exactly pick up while sitting in front of him."

"Ah, right. Because he doesn't know..." His voice dips in that *you've made my life a pain in the ass* way. "You do realize that helping you leave the Cosa Nostra isn't exactly easy when I can't tell one of my most trusted men about it, and worse, it's his own daughter?"

"I know. I'm sorry." I offer a half-hearted apology, though I'm not really sure what for. Needing to escape this life? That feels like something he should apologize for, honestly.

"I've found a way for you to leave," Marco says, cutting through my thoughts.

My brain barely registers the words before my heart starts doing flips. Free. *I'm going to be free.* My toes curl into the soft grass, pantyhose forgotten, green dye seeping into my skin, and I have the sudden urge to break into a full-on *Sound of Music* moment and twirl around singing about hills and freedom.

"But," Marco continues, snapping me back to reality with the most dangerous word in the history of language.

Nothing good ever starts with "'but."

"As I told you before, there will be conditions."

Right. The conditions. How could I forget?

Not only does he get to decide *when* I leave, but *how.* I'm desperate enough to agree to just about anything at this point. My list of hard no's has shrunk significantly in the last few months, and with Carlo Romano showing up for dinner, that list might catch fire by the end of the night.

"Yes, of course," I say, nodding furiously even though he can't see me. "How soon? Carlo Romano is coming for dinner tonight. Papa seems... eager." *Eager* being code for practically salivating over the idea. The Romanos are powerful, influential, and just the kind of family Papa would love to marry me off into—while I'd rather hurl myself off a Manhattan skyscraper.

"I'm well aware Carlo wants to wed and bed you," Marco says flatly.

I'm mid-sigh of relief when he drops it.

"But..."

Dammit. There it is again. *But.*

"When can we meet? We need to discuss terms."

There's a crunch of grass behind me, and I spin around to find Vinnie standing there with a shrug. I swear he's a shadow reincarnated as a person. I can't go anywhere without him finding me, and he never apologizes for it.

"Any time," I say quickly, well aware my voice borders on desperate. "I can meet before dinner. Whenever you want." *Please, for the love of everything holy, rescue me from Carlo and his creepy basement eyes.*

"Be in my office in two hours," Marco commands.

I freeze, doing quick mental math. "But I live out in Greenwich."

"Guess you'd better get moving." The line goes dead.

I stare at my phone for a second, blinking, and then turn to Vinnie. "How did you know where I was?"

He just gives me that deadpan stare. No response needed. Of course, he knew where I was. He's my personal shadow. I wouldn't be surprised if he waits outside the bathroom every time I pee, just in case an assassin decides to jump me mid-stream.

"We need to get to Manhattan. Marco wants to meet in two hours," I tell him, already making my way across the grass barefoot, pantyhose shredded, heels swinging from my hand like weapons.

Vinnie rubs his beard, thinking. "That's pushing it with traffic, but if we leave now..."

"We. Have. To. Be. There." I don't need to explain the reasons, the top being Carlo Romano for dinner and all that.

"I'll get the car ready. Tell your Papa I'm taking you shopping."

Shopping. The foolproof excuse. Papa never questions my shopping trips. Never.

Allie

We're ten minutes early.

Normally, that would feel like a win. Early is punctual. Early is responsible. Early means I didn't leave the Don waiting—which is good because leaving Marco Bennetti waiting sounds like a fast track to cement shoes.

But no. Instead of relief, I now have ten long, excruciating minutes to sit outside his office, spiraling internally while my anxiety tap-dances all over my sanity.

Six months.

That's how long Marco's kept me dangling over the edge of freedom sitting on ice until he's ready. And not the fun kind of ice—you know, sipping a frozen margarita on a beach somewhere while bronzed men fan you with palm leaves. No, I've been kept on ice *mafia-style*, which is a lot more like living in a freezer with no end in sight, waiting for the door to finally swing open.

Today's grand meeting is at a strip club.

Because where else does a respectable Don conduct life-altering business?

It's midday, and yet the place is alive—if that's what you call half-naked women in pasties and thongs grinding on poles while middle-aged men, some of whom I recognize, sip whiskey and shove dollar bills into places no fabric should ever cover. Oh, and they're all wearing wedding bands.

Hypocrites.

In this family, wedding vows mean about as much as a carnival prize—a fun trinket until you're bored with it.

But when I get married, it'll be *real*. No strip club escapades. No "business lunches" with women named Cinnamon and Destiny. Nope. My future husband will love me, adore me, and definitely not spend his afternoons licking salt off another woman's navel.

"Come," Marco's voice barks from behind the closed door.

Vinnie opens the door, nodding for me to enter first. The office looks like a time capsule from 1975—a beaten-down metal desk, peeling wallpaper, and carpet that probably has more stories than the club itself. The only modern things in the room are the wall of security monitors and Marco's sleek laptop. Everything else is straight out of a sad garage sale.

"Sit," Marco commands, waving toward two rust-covered metal chairs that look like they're barely holding on to life in this decade.

I glance at the chair, then at Vinnie, wondering if it'll survive his weight. Probably not. Still, I sit, crossing my legs and trying to seem composed while I resist the urge to bite my nails down to stubs. The car ride here was pure torture and judging by how tight my jaw feels, I've probably ground my molars down to nubs.

Marco leans back, steepling his fingers across his chin, and studies me with unnerving focus. "So... you can cook, yes?"

I nod eagerly. *Is he going to set me up as a chef?* Butterflies take off in my stomach. This could be it—the dream. A life of sauté pans and stainless-steel counters.

"Do you know how to clean?"

I blink. "Clean?"

Okay, that's not exactly what I expected. "I mean, sure. I *could* figure it out." Cleaning in cashmere isn't exactly practical, and Mama shrieks like I've burned down the house every time I so much as touch furniture polish. But I'll scrub toilets all day if it gets me out of here.

"And you're twenty-four?"

I nod again, darting a glance at Vinnie, who just cocks his head like a curious golden retriever.

"And... you are untouched?"

A chill runs down my spine. *Normal people* don't ask about virginity. But in our world, it's about as private as the weather report. Only this? This is giving me a very bad feeling.

Clearing my throat, I sit up straighter. "Mr. Bennetti, where exactly are you going with this?"

His fingers stop their steepling. My pulse stops right along with them. *Shit.* Why can't I just keep my mouth shut? It's not like I wasn't raised to speak only when spoken to.

"I'm assessing if my current idea will work for you," Marco says, casually, like he's plotting brunch plans, not life-changing decisions. "You came to me wanting out of the Cosa Nostra, and the only way to leave is to either change your identity or marry outside the family."

Those butterflies in my stomach? Full-on riot. It's like they've organized into warring factions and are battling it out for control. Meanwhile, my heart is racing like it's auditioning for NASCAR.

I glance at Vinnie, hoping for some kind of lifeline. Maybe a wink, a blink—*something*. But no. His face is as blank as a fresh sheet of printer paper. Super helpful.

"Then," I say, lifting my chin, "I'd like to change my identity." Simple. Logical. Done.

Marco laughs. Not the jolly Santa Claus kind of laugh. No, this is deep, gravelly, and teetering dangerously close to a mad scientist unveiling his evil plan. His smile is all menace, the kind that sends a shiver down your spine, and his amber eyes lock on me like I'm an insect pinned under glass. I'm seeing where his reputation comes from. Just a solid look gives you a glimpse of his infamous "crazy" hiding under the surface.

"You don't get to choose," he says, leaning back in this chair. "The only choice you had was wanting to leave. I told you there would be stipulations. So, do you want out or not?"

I swallow hard.

Marco checks his Rolex, tapping his finger on it impatiently. "I've got a family meeting in a few, so I'll cut to the chase. My cousin, Rico, needs a wife. *You're going to be that wife.*"

My mouth opens. Words try to form, but all that comes out is a tiny squeak. I sound like a dog toy.

Marco raises a hand, silencing me before I can get my bearings. "Not done. You'll marry him. No questions asked. Be a good little wife. Cook, clean, do whatever it is housewives do. If you want to work as a chef, fine. I'll make it happen, and Rico won't object. Honestly, he won't give a flying fuck what you do. He just needs a wife to bear his children, and you're young, untouched, and not too shabby to look at."

I sit there, stunned. Processing. *Rico needs a wife to bear his children.* I'm running from the Cosa Nostra because I don't want to be used as some heir-producing machine. I've spent my whole life dreaming of something more—a husband who loves me, a partner who actually gives a damn, someone who won't measure my worth by my fertility.

And now?

To earn my freedom, I have to give up that dream by doing the one thing I dreaded most of all. Irony is a real bitch.

Marco's words hang in the air so thick I could chew them. I'm pretty sure I blinked twice and stopped breathing somewhere between *"wife"* and *"bear his children."*

I've been given some pretty questionable offers in life—like that time Tori Valencia suggested I get matching lower-back tattoos with her—but this? This is a whole new level of insanity.

"You don't have much time to answer, Miss De Luca," Marco says, checking his Rolex again. "I meet with my uncle and cousins shortly, including Rico. If you accept, you'll come over for dinner tonight to meet your fiancé." His eyes flick toward the ceiling as if the right words are hiding in the water-stained ceiling tiles above him. His jaw ticks, and then, with a resigned sigh, he mutters, "Rico is...difficult. Yeah, let's go with that. Unique creature. Not very sociable. Hates people, really. Prefers to sit in his little office dungeon and code." He waves a hand vaguely in my direction. "You'll only have to deal with him when it's time to, you know... consummate and produce an heir. Other than that, he'll probably leave you alone. You'll be provided for, no worries there. My cousin is loaded. You can work, follow your dreams, chase rainbows or whatever it is women like to do. Just, you know, raise some kids in between."

Consummate and make an heir. Fabulous.

He hates people. Fantastic.

And *a unique creature?* Could he sound any more like the Beast from Beauty and the Beast? Only, there's no enchanted roses here.

"He doesn't like to talk?" I ask, my brain still catching up to the verbal train wreck I just witnessed. "What does that even mean? Like... antisocial? Or mute?"

Marco shrugs. "Talking isn't really his thing. You'll get more grunts and snorts than full sentences. Honestly, I think you'd have a better conversation with a brick wall. The man has zero interest in socializing, which makes finding him a wife... tricky. Easier to just pick one for him."

I glance at Vinnie, who's covering his mouth to hide a smirk. *Traitor.*

Why is this funny? This is awful. I'm running from one arranged marriage with a man who would ignore me to end up in another arranged marriage with a man who... will ignore me. The difference is, in this scenario, I can work. I can have a life. A say in things. A glimmer of freedom that one path would never give, while the other does...but with conditions.

"I can work?" I ask, needing confirmation.

Marco nods.

"He won't stop me from having friends or doing what I want?"

Another nod.

Marco leans forward, resting his elbows on the desk. "After tonight's dinner, you'll sit down with the family lawyers to draft the wedding contract. Terms, conditions, all that legal crap. If there's something specific you want, speak up. Rico won't care. He only cares about one thing—a woman who can have his kids."

Oh. Good. I'm being reduced to a walking uterus. My inner feminist just died a little.

I slump back in my chair, the hope I clung to moments ago deflating like a cheap party balloon stabbed with a toothpick. *Will I really be free if I'm stuck in a loveless marriage with a man who barely acknowledges my existence?*

Marco stands, his chair scraping against the floor. "You've got ten minutes. I'm going to get a drink. Coffee, no... fuck that, scotch. I'll need it to survive my family dinner. When I get back, give me your answer, or I'll find another woman for Rico. Simple as that."

The door clicks shut behind him, leaving me alone with Vinnie. I turn toward him, and tears sting the back of my eyes. The burning sensation is real, but I can't cry—I'll ruin the three pounds of makeup on my face, and waterproof mascara is a damn liar. One tear and I'll be sporting raccoon chic for the rest of the day.

Vinnie gives me a sympathetic look, the kind that says *Yup, you're screwed, but this is what you wanted.* Meanwhile, my brain has officially left the building, chasing after the rapidly fleeing shreds of my sanity.

"So... just to clarify," I say, because apparently, I hate myself, "I'm supposed to marry this socially awkward tech hermit who doesn't enjoy talking or physical contact, yet we'll somehow make babies in complete silence?"

Seems doable. Totally. Maybe I should start practicing my *Monk of Silence* routine now.

Vinnie is not even pretending to hide his amusement. "Yeah, sounds like you've got it all figured out.""Figured out?" I scoff. "I'm basically walking into an episode of *Married at First Sight.* Except no roses, no champagne, just a family full of overly curious Sicilians waiting to assess my reproductive potential."

Marco chuckles when he enters the office, swirling his scotch like a man with zero sympathy and a lot of alcohol tolerance. "Don't worry, *principessa.* The family is *mostly* harmless. Just steer clear of Nonna. She'll pinch your cheeks, interrogate you about your virginity, and then whisper wildly inappropriate advice into your ear. She once told my cousin's new wife to 'keep things spicy by wearing lace and a smile'—at the dinner table."

So we've got Nonna the Ninja who moonlights as an X-rated fortune cookie.

"What time am I supposed to be there?" I ask, already regretting that I'm actually considering this.

"Six. I'll send Vinnie the address," Marco replies, downing the rest of his scotch like it's a shot of water. "I'm headed over now to break the news to Rico. Fair warning—don't expect a warm reception. Rico doesn't do enthusiasm." He stops at the door, glancing back at me.

"Oh, and Miss De Luca, a little tip: introduce yourself, but don't bother blabbering. He'll tune you out. Avoid touching him. He doesn't like to be touched."

My mouth falls open. Avoid touching him? He doesn't like to be touched?

"How does he plan to have babies, then? Psychic conception?" I mutter as Marco walks out, knowing he won't answer.

Vinnie chuckles. "Guess you'll find out soon enough."

"Soon enough?" I whisper-shout, following him out the door. "I need a crash course in *How to Seduce a Man Who Hates Humans.* Is there a manual for that? Because if so, I missed the memo."

Vinnie just grins as he holds the car door open for me. "Relax, Allie. You'll be fine. Rico's... unique, sure. But it beats Romano, right?"

He's right, but I'm still not convinced. At least with Romano, I'd know what I'm getting—a total creep with wandering hands. With Rico, I'm walking blind into a marriage with a man who might not speak to me for days on end and could very well text me instructions when it's time to "do the deed."

But...it's a way out.

Rico

IT'S NOT A SUNDAY. I have shit to do. So why am I here?

We're all seated in the living room at the family estate like it's some kind of Bennetti summit. Mama and Nonna have claimed the couch like it's their throne, Papa's in his armchair, and my brothers—Alex and Dom—are parked on the loveseat. None of their wives or kids are in sight, which is always a bad sign.

And then there's Marco, lounging in the other armchair like a kingpin with nowhere better to be. Casual as fuck, legs crossed, the hint of a grin tugging at the corner of his mouth. It's been a while since I've punched him, but right now my fist is itching like an allergy I can't scratch.

Is this an intervention?

It better not be. I'm well aware that I'm a brooding asshole. I don't need a committee to tell me that warm and fuzzy isn't part of my DNA.

But no one's smiling. Not Mama, not Nonna, not even Papa. And my brothers—who usually find something to smirk about—look dead serious. *Shit.* This is worse than an intervention.

"It's been six months, Rico," Papa says, as if I don't know how time works.

Yeah, it's been six months. I've spent the past four weeks holed up in my office, working on security updates because some hacker decided to breach my system. Not because I care about stocks or quarterly profits—God, no—but because no one beats me at my own game. Time moves differently when you have no windows, a bank of monitors, and a keyboard that feels more like an extension of your body than a tool.

My sanctuary.

Hell, I felt like a vampire dragged into daylight when Dom pulled me out of the office this afternoon. The sun stung my eyes like it held a personal grudge for me ignoring it the past month as it seared straight into my retinas. I didn't bother asking questions; I just followed, assuming this was another routine family ambush. Which, for the record, happens every other month.

Wrong.

"So," Papa continues, his voice steady but loaded with landmines, "you know what that means..."

I glance at him, then Mama, then my brothers. Dom looks confused. Good. I didn't tell them about Papa's little six-month threat, and it appears he didn't share it with them either. Rare. No one holds secrets in this family.

"Six months for what?" Dom takes the bait.

"Rico had six months to find a wife," Papa explains.

Alex folds in half, howling. Full-on choking for air like Papa just told the greatest joke of the century. "Oh shit, that's a good one," he gasps, tears streaming down his face while I contemplate how best to wipe that smirk off without leaving a bruise. "You could've given him twelve months. Wouldn't have made a difference."

Papa doesn't even spare him a glance. He doesn't need to. Mama, his ever-loyal enforcer, locks onto Alex with the precision of a sniper, and just like that, all the color drains from his face faster than a gambler watching their last chip slide across the table.

I sink back into my chair, suddenly grateful that those eyes aren't aimed at me. At thirty-seven, Mama still scares the ever-living hell out of me. And Nonna? She's the real threat. Forget needing a bodyguard; if Nonna ever decides I've stepped out of line, I'll lose my balls faster than I can say *ciao*.

Alex clears his throat, coughs once, and stands upright like a soldier at attention. His hands tuck into his jean pockets—*jeans*. When the hell did he start wearing jeans? Marriage and babies have turned him into a different species. This, right here, is why I don't need a wife. Women change you, mold you like pliable Play-Doh until you're unrecognizable. My brothers may be soft and squishy, but I don't bend.

I'm wearing jeans too, but it's nothing new. Unlike my suit-obsessed brothers, who spend thousands tailoring their Brionis, I stick to the basics—jeans, a T-shirt, sneakers. Efficient. Comfortable. Cheap. Sometimes I throw on a dress shirt or sweater for good measure, but only when it makes logistical sense and not fulfilling some societal check box. Why the hell would I spend a small fortune on a suit when I can keep my money in the bank collecting interest? Flashing cash requires human interaction and small talk, and I'd rather slowly untangle my own intestines.

"Okay, so it's been six months. What does that mean now?" Dom asks, throwing me a lifeline since Alex is too busy clamping his mouth shut like a toddler trying not to laugh. Man's been spending way too much time with his kids. He's picking up their habits—like acting four instead of pushing forty.

"It means he can either marry the woman we've chosen for him or..," Papa says, fingers gesturing between himself and Mama like the 'we' wasn't glaringly obvious, "Well, there is no 'or.'" His lips curl into a smug smile, head cocking to the side in that *go ahead, fight me* way.

Truly, I didn't think Papa would follow through on picking out a bride. One, he has to find someone willing to marry me, and despite my bottomless bank account and what I've been told is a good-looking face, those two things don't make up for the miles of items I don't have to offer a wife. So, I figured being disinherited was the only real consequence of blowing off my six-month gift, which I was totally fine with. Let my brothers inherit the businesses. They're already knee-deep in family life and cranking out kids like it's a competition. They can have the empire. I've got my keyboards and peace of mind—or at least, I did.

Then Nonna grins, and it's the kind of smile you see in horror movies right before the sweet neighbor turns out to be a serial killer.

"We found you the perfect bride," Nonna says, her smile fixed and eyes disturbingly unblinking. I'm fucked.

Marco clears his throat and leans forward, elbows on his knees, all casual-like. "Technically, *I* found her."

Correcting Nonna? Bold move. Man clearly has a death wish. Nonna gives him the *look*, the one that sends grown men running, but Marco doesn't even flinch. Dude's certifiable. I may be an asshole, but at least I'm not clinically insane.

I haven't spoken a word since I walked into this house. A glance at my watch tells me I've been here for thirty minutes. In that time, I could've stress-tested the new code I implemented, but nope. Here I am, about to be auctioned off to the highest bidder.

Could I say no? Sure. But Papa plays the long game, and he plays it well. It's not about the inheritance—he knows I don't give a shit about that. What I do care about is family. And he knows how to twist that knife just right.

Besides, arranged marriage? Possibly the best life hack ever. No dates, no wasted time, and no pretending to be interested in someone's vacation stories. Efficient. Like a business merger with wedding cake.

"Doesn't matter who found her," Nonna waves off Marco's correction. "We found the perfect woman. You'll meet her tonight, get to know her over the next few weeks while your Mama and I plan the wedding."

I arch a brow. Few weeks? Please. Mama and Nonna planned Dom and Sienna's wedding in under a week. If they've already picked a woman, the wedding is probably booked, catered, and floral arrangements are already en route.

"It has to be a big wedding," Mama chimes in, as if I needed more reasons to break out in hives.

Big wedding = a lot of people.

I don't do people. If there's such a thing as a human interaction allergy, I have it. Benadryl won't help. My skin will break out, and I'll go into anaphylactic shock just thinking about small talk with second cousins twice removed.

A sharp sting pulls me out of my spiral. I glance down at my hand, where my nails have bitten half-moon indents into my palm. One hard enough to draw blood.

Mama's icy-blue eyes flick to my hand, then back to my face. Calm. Controlled. Dangerous. "This is for the best, Rico. You might not see it now, but you'll thank us later."

Yeah. Doubt it.

Arguing would take more energy than I'm willing to waste.

"Don't you want to know who you're marrying?" Alex asks, his earlier grin wiped clean. Now it's all business.

I shrug. Do I care? Not even a little. Whoever Mama and Nonna picked is the woman I'm marrying. Whether her name's Susan or Gigi, whether she has brown hair, blonde hair, or collects taxidermy squirrels as a hobby—it makes no difference. The paperwork's already being drafted, so why waste my time worrying about trivial details like her name, appearance, or, God forbid, personality.

What does concern me is that I'm now stuck here for dinner to meet her. My plan was an hour—two, max—at the family house. Enough time to sit through the meeting, check the boxes, and bounce. Now, I'm recalculating my entire day like a GPS rerouting through hell's scenic route.

I'm mentally reorganizing my calendar when I feel a hand clamp around my arm.

Dom's standing next to me, nodding toward the formal living room—aka the Museum of Untouched Furniture. "Let's talk," he says.

The formal living room is a museum for furniture that no one's allowed to sit on. Gray and cream sofas that are graced with an ass cheek sighting as often as the world sees an eclipse, a fireplace that's decorative at best and depressing at worst, and a massive family portrait hanging above it. Dom's wife painted it two months ago. Sitting for that portrait made me want to gouge my eyes out with a spoon, but I survived it. Barely. Still, a few hours in that room were enough to convince me that a big wedding—complete with hundreds of guests and endless small talk—would probably land me in prison after I punch the third person who asks me if I'm excited to marry whatever poor woman agrees to this unholy union.

I drop onto the biggest sofa in the room, sprawling out in the middle like a king. No dust cloud, so I guess the housekeeper earned her keep this week. Dom and Alex squeeze onto the loveseat across from me, their knees bumping awkwardly.

Could I have taken the smaller sofa to be a decent human being? Sure. But they butted into my life, so here we are.

I expect Alex to lecture me first, but a voice from the doorway cuts in.

"Don't worry, boys. I picked him a good one," Marco says, strolling into the room before dropping onto the sofa next to me, patting my thigh like I'm his golden retriever.

My fingers twitch with the urge to break one—or two—of his. I don't like being touched. This isn't news to anyone in the family. But Marco? Marco doesn't care. Marco doesn't do boundaries or sanity.

Marco's the Don of the New York Cosa Nostra, which technically makes him terrifying, but I've known him long enough to recognize that his crazy outweighs his scary by a solid 70 percent. I saved his ass years ago. He owes me.

Unfortunately, that doesn't stop him from being *Marco*. He's also somehow the only person who is close to me. Not my brothers. Nope. I make nice with the crazy one in the family. Not sure what that says about me.

Nothing good.

But Marco—aside from Papa—is the only one in the family who's seen the darker side of humanity up close and personal. The kind of shit that changes your internal wiring to see the world differently than those still sporting blinders. I guess that makes us kindred spirits. We've both stared death in the face and flipped it the middle finger.

Dom pinches the bridge of his nose, already exasperated. "Rico, look. I get it. You hate dating, but do you really want to marry some stranger?"

Technically, she won't be a stranger after I meet her tonight. Problem solved.

"Bennettis don't do divorce," Alex reminds me. "If you don't like her, you're still stuck with her."

I glance at their wedding bands—Alex's a classic gold, Dom's some sleek black metal. They've got wives they love, kids they dote on, and they're the epitome of domesticated. If you listen closely, you can almost hear the leash snap when their wives call.

"Oh, speaking of..." Marco reaches into his suit pocket and hands me a small black velvet box. "What? Like you'd buy one yourself? Open it, you moron."

I tuck the box into my jeans pocket without bothering to look inside.

"Wow. Romantic," Dom drawls.

"I mean, it's Rico. Did you expect him to get on one knee? I'll be impressed if he doesn't chuck the box at her across the table and tell her to put it on," Marco says, giving me a nudge.

I close my eyes, silently praying for patience. "How long?"

"Until she gets here or until you're married? The marriage thing's forever, you know. Death 'til you part. Although... she might kill you once she realizes that's her fastest way out."

I arch a brow at him. So do Dom and Alex. Mama and Nonna may be terrifying in their own right, but Violet—Alex's wife—while pregnant was a walking horror show of hormones and death threats. Even Marco learned to tread lightly and that crazy bastard cowers at nothing. Except for a hormonal woman apparently.

"What do you mean by that?" Dom asks.

Marco shrugs, completely unfazed. "None of you asked where I found this gem of a bride for this one." He grins, thumbing in my direction like I'm some rare exhibit at a zoo.

"Do tell." Alex crosses his arms, settling in.

"She's in the Cosa Nostra," Marco starts. Both my brothers groan, but he raises a hand, silencing them. "*But* she wants out. She asked me a while ago, and I was debating how to let her leave without causing waves. Then Nonna mentioned this situation,"—he twirls a finger around me—"and *ta-da*. An idea was born."

I remember when I used to like my cousin. You know, two minutes ago. Life changes fast.

Alex pinches the bridge of his nose this time. "So, let me get this straight. You're forcing some poor woman to marry our brother to escape the mafia?"

"Well... when you put it that way, I can see how it *sounds* bad." Marco offers.

"And *looks* bad," Dom deadpans.

"She wanted out. No money, no job, no family. This way, she gets security, and Rico's problem is solved. Do you know who your mama was setting him up with if he didn't produce someone on his own?"

The three of us exchange glances, mentally scrolling through every woman Mama's mentioned in passing.

"Tori Valencia."

We all shudder in unison. Tori Valencia makes Marco's brand of crazy look like a mild case of road rage in rush-hour traffic.

"So..." Marco stretches the word out as he leans back into the sofa, the cushions groaning at the fact they are in use. "You're welcome. Because otherwise, your blushing bride and future mother of your children would have been Tori and her *tics*." Literally, the woman twitches when she's angry. It's like watching a computer glitch in real-time.

"So, what's the plan? Shake hands, hand her the engagement ring, and what? What will her family say?" Alex is speaking to Marco, but his eyes are on me. If he's expecting some sort of reaction, even in this asinine situation, he'd be wrong. I wouldn't even catalog this as mildly irritating. In fact, I'm seeing a light at the end of a rather dark and dreary tunnel.

"She can't go back home after tonight. She'll meet Rico, and if she agrees, I'll put her in one of my properties until the wedding. I'll let her papa know she left the family with my blessing to marry my cousin. They won't challenge it, but if she goes home, they'll likely lock her up."

"This is ridiculous." Alex glares my way. "Rico, talk to Papa. Hell, I can talk with him. Let's buy some time. Give you a chance to find someone on your own. Not tie you to a woman who's marrying you because you're her only option."

"Or yours," Dom adds. "That's not a marriage. It's a business merger."

It's almost poetic how this setup is perfect for both of us. We're here for the same reason: to sign a piece of paper and reap the mutual benefits of this little arrangement. No hearts. No flowers. No bullshit. Just a legally binding contract wrapped up in a designer wedding dress.

We don't need love. Hell, we don't even need to like each other. We don't have to share a bedroom, meals, or even oxygen for more than five minutes at a time. I'll knock her up—strictly business, no conversation required—and once the heir situation is handled, we can comfortably exist in mutual indifference. Blissful, separate, yet entirely functional lives.

I like kids. I'll raise mine, make sure they're educated, respectful, and can throw a punch if necessary. The woman who helps me breed them can handle the rest. We won't co-parent; we'll co-exist. And if we play this right, we'll barely have to speak.

Dom breaks into my mental planning session, looking far too concerned and likely sprouting another gray hair or three for me to admire and know I'm their cause. "You do realize you'll have to talk to your wife, right?"

"Do I?" I deadpan.

He blinks, rubbing his temple. "Rico, marriage—even an arranged one—is a partnership. You'll need to build *some* kind of relationship with her. You're going to be raising children together. That requires communication. Decisions. Actual human interaction."

Dom clearly believes this nonsense. He's in love, so his version of marriage involves joint decisions, heartfelt conversations, and matching coffee mugs that say *His* and *Hers*.

Me? I believe marriage is a contract. An agreement between two consenting adults. No emotions necessary. No speeches. And absolutely no talking if we can avoid it. Played right, it's a simple transaction. I didn't have to date, endure mind-numbing dinner conversations, or listen to a woman drone on about horoscopes or her third cousin's gluten allergy. I bagged myself a wife, and a guaranteed heir. Efficient and to the point. Besides, my family will have no reason to lecture me on life choices, so I'll finally have some sliver of peace.

"I'll be fine," I mutter before the two lovesick fools in front of me spout sonnets about the miracle of love. That speech traumatized me before, and I'm still recovering.

Alex leans back, rubbing his jaw. "A woman who's *okay* with an arranged marriage... to *Rico*." He winces. "No offense, but... did you tell her Rico doesn't exactly love words?"

"Or human interaction in general?" Dom adds.

Marco grins, completely unfazed. "She's aware that Rico's... a bit closed off."

Something tells me she's *not* aware of the full extent of that statement. Like, *at all*.

Both of my brothers gape at Marco as if they just found out he's harboring a fugitive. The woman could be fleeing a cult or plotting her own escape plan for all I care. Her backstory, personality, or even her name? *Irrelevant*.

Petty details, much like emotions, don't matter.

Allie

THE SECOND WE STEP inside, it's clear that Marco's family subscribes to the go big or go home school of home decor. Marble floors, towering ceilings, and a chandelier the size of a small spaceship hanging above us. Subtlety? Never heard of her.

"Welcome to the Bennetti madhouse," Marco says, his voice syrupy smooth, with just enough bite to make me question his sobriety. He waves us in like we're contestants on a game show. "The blushing bride-to-be," he adds with a grin, eyeing my black dress. "Dressed for a funeral, I see. Fitting, considering Rico's personality."

I stare at him for a second, debating whether to respond or just let him think he's clever. I opt for the latter, adjusting my "death dress" and following him into the house, heels clicking against the marble with every step. Vinnie stays close behind me like the human shadow he is, silent but observant.

Marco leads us through the glittering foyer and into a living room that is opulent and yet doesn't have the stuffy vibes you'd expect, considering the grand entrance and all. The couches are plush, the lighting is low, and the air smells faintly of coffee.

It's not until we step into the room that I notice the Bennetti family staring at me like I just crash-landed a spaceship in their living room. All eyes are wide, on me, and blinking. I'm now rattling through reasons to feel self-conscious. Is it my dress? Should I have worn something more conservative? Were they expecting someone older? Younger? Skinnier?

Two older women sit primly on a couch, eyes sharp and assessing. Across from them, three men occupy another couch—two of them sporting matching smirks. And then there's the third man sitting all broody and no facial expression.

"You must be Alessandra." An older man stands up from an armchair heading toward me. His dark hair sports a few flecks of silver, and his amber eyes remind me a lot of Marco's. Without a chance to answer him, he's wrapping me in a hug.

Uh...what now? Hugging? From a stranger? My eyes dart to Vinnie for help, but the traitor is holding back a laugh, clearly enjoying the show.

"Pleasure to meet you," I manage, my voice a little too high-pitched from the sheer awkwardness of being swallowed by this man's overly enthusiastic embrace. I have not been introduced, but I'm going to assume this is Ricardo Bennetti.

"Ricardo, release the poor girl!" One woman on the couch scolds, swatting at his arm until he finally lets me go. She steps in, immediately pulling me into another hug. Her perfume wraps around me—something warm and floral, like lavender with a kick. "I'm Cecilia," she says, mid-hug, her voice a lilting blend of Italian and something else I can't quite place.

When she pulls back, her hands grip my shoulders, holding me at arm's length while she looks me up and down with the scrutiny of someone evaluating an antique vase at an auction.

"Well, you're a pretty one! Marco didn't mention you were so gorgeous."

I blink, not really sure how to respond. "Uh...thank you, ma'am."

"Mama," she corrects with a tsk, waving me off. "'Ma'am' makes me feel ancient. Come, come."

Before I can process what's happening, she tugs me toward the couch. Marco gives me a thumbs-up and disappears with Vinnie to find drinks. Asshole.

Cecilia nudges me onto the couch next to another older woman. This one studies me, only she's looking at me with the same intensity as a doctor about to deliver a diagnosis. Her eyes sweep from my face to my hips, and she nods in approval.

"Alessandra? Yes?" she asks, still giving me the once-over.

"Yes, but most people call me Allie."

Her eyes light up. "Oh, I like that. Very pretty." Before I can thank her, she continues her visual assessment plus narration this time.

"Excellent hips," she declares to no one in particular. "Good for babies."

I nearly choke on air. Babies? Did we just skip straight to my reproductive capabilities?

Cecilia nods in agreement as if my hips just passed some secret fertility test. My cheeks burn as I try to decide if I should say *thank you* or bolt for the door.

I glance at the three men on the couch. All three are tall, dark, and devastatingly gorgeous, but that's where the similarities end.

One of them—sharp features, dark brown hair perfectly combed, and piercing blue eyes—grins at me like this is the most entertaining thing he's seen all year. His eyes practically dance with amusement. I never realized eyes could dance and sparkle, but this man's eyes do. He looks familiar. Why?

The other two are easily identical twins, but their vibes are anything but identical. One is warm and inviting, flashing a charming smile that feels genuine, like he'd help an old lady cross the street just because.

The other... well, he's all sharp lines and blank stares, his amber eyes boring into me with an intensity that makes me think he'd more likely shove the old lady across the street. If human interaction were toxic, this man would take out the entire room.

Regardless, there is way too much hotness on one couch right now. It's distracting. Even if one of them is looking at me with all the warmth of a January storm.

I clasp my hands in my lap, trying to ignore how awkward the silence is. It just hangs there, heavy and uncomfortable, like the world's worst group interview.

"Mama," the Blue-Eyed Man God speaks. "Don't you think you should do the introductions before we pick out china patterns?" He turns to me, smiling, and I blush like a teenage girl.

"Oh! Gosh. I'm so sorry, dear. This whole situation has me a little... unprepared."

You and me both, sista.

With a bright smile, she turns toward Blue Eyes. "This is Alexander, my oldest son. His wife is at home with their three boys. Triplets."

Triplets? The man doesn't look sleep-deprived enough to have three small humans running around or old enough to have the words "wife" and "kids" tied to him. Alexander stands, shakes my hand firmly, and flashes a grin that says *welcome to the family, also sorry for your loss.*

"And this," Cecilia continues, pointing to one of the identical heartbreakers, "is Dominic. His wife is at home with their newborn twin girls and their son."

So... apparently the Bennetti men specialize in mass-producing children. Good to know that my hips probably play a role in pushing out children in multiples, and my uterus is screaming to run. Stretch marks and a lot of long nights in my future.

Dominic steps forward, his handshake combined with his lips twisting in amusement, and a low whisper I swear sounds like "My condolences."

By now, I'm bracing for the third act.

"And this," Cecilia's voice pitches up like we're about to meet royalty, "is Enrico. Rico, where are your manners? Get up and meet your future bride."

I gulp. *Oh shit.*

Rico, as it turns out, looks about as thrilled to meet me as I am to marry a stranger. I was prepared for a troll under a bridge—someone with bad teeth and a questionable cologne habit, considering he needed help to find a bride.

But this man? He's tall, broad-shouldered, with dark hair and eyes that gleam like molten amber. He's stupidly handsome in that *brooding antihero with secrets* kind of way. The kind of hot that makes your body betray you on sight. Suddenly, it's a sauna in here, and my internal temperature is creeping toward full meltdown. How on earth does this man need an arranged marriage?

He stands, gives me a slow, dead-eyed nod—like we're strangers passing on the street—and sits back down. That's it. Not a word. Not even a *hey, welcome to this weird new life we're about to share*. I'm starting to see why finding a wife himself is not easy.

Cecilia beams as if his silence is perfectly acceptable. "Rico's always been a man of few words."

Oh, fantastic. My new husband might actually be a statue. Maybe he's one of those *blinks once for yes, twice for no* types. This should be fun.

"Let's go eat." Cecilia pats my thigh and nudges me to stand. "Break the ice while we break bread."

Pretty sure no amount of bread—or wine—can fix this level of awkwardness, but I nod and follow her lead.

Nonna, the tiny but mighty older woman from the couch, links her arm with mine. Her grip is surprisingly strong for someone who looks like she spends her days knitting doilies. "I'm so happy you agreed to this, my dear." She pats my arm affectionately.

I glance at Marco, who casually salutes me with his glass of liquor. Is he saluting my new future or downfall?

Nonna keeps walking and talking as we go. "Rico has always had trouble meeting people, especially women. But you are so pretty. So much more than we expected."

More than they *expected*? What did they expect? A swamp creature? A gargoyle?

Rico's amber eyes are locked on me as I make my way into the dining room. Dominic leans over, mutters something to him, then rushes around the table to pull out a chair for me, planting me directly across from my very own mute anti-social fiancé.

"Sorry," Dominic murmurs as he pushes my chair in, and I can safely assume he's apologizing since his brother made no effort to do so himself. I smooth out my dress, trying to keep my cool, but the second I look up, my eyes lock with Rico's.

Nothing.

No smile. *No* frown. *No* spark of life. His face is a blank canvas, and I'm wondering if his vocal cords are part of some underground witness protection program.

Marco takes the other head of the table. I'm seated between Nonna and Ricardo—front and center in what is quickly turning into one of the more awkward dinner experiences of my life.

A housekeeper brings out dishes, and the table buzzes with light conversation—mostly Nonna drilling me like I'm a contestant on *Jeopardy*. Only this one involves every personal fact about me. *My age? Do I read? Play piano?* Apparently, Nonna knows all about the life of mafia princesses, but I feel like some regency era chaste doe on the "marriage mart." It's like she watched *Bridgerton* on repeat but skipped the sexy parts with the Duke of Hastings. Shame. That was some good eye candy to use when times were bleak.

And then it happens.

"And you are a virgin, too?" Nonna drops the question with the casual grace of a hand grenade.

Cue choking.

I nearly die on a rogue piece of rigatoni while Alexander chokes on his wine. Across the table, Vinnie unsuccessfully hides a laugh behind a cough, while Marco raises a brow looking at me with a *you were warned* eyebrow wiggle.

"Mama, now is not the time," Ricardo says gently, throwing me an apologetic smile. The only smile I've seen so far, and it's wasted on trying to smooth over his mother's insanely inappropriate question.

"Well, why not? Rico needs to know if he's getting himself a virgin bride or not."

Who *is* this woman?

Horrified, I glance at Cecilia. She just sips her wine and waits, as if this is the most natural dinner topic in the world. My eyes dart to Marco, who—oh, look—knows I'm *not* a virgin and is enjoying watching me squirm.

"Maybe we can let them talk about that in private," Alexander offers with an awkward smile, trying to salvage what little dignity I have left and I shoot out a silent thank you.

Nonna waves him off. "We're all family here. So, you're twenty-four? Never had a serious boyfriend?"

"No, I haven't had any boyfriends," I say, hoping this conversation dies faster than a bad first date. I would know. Been on plenty of those.

Technically true. I was forbidden from having relationships. God forbid a boy tried to hold my hand and accidentally steal my virtue. Heaven knows that would be catastrophic.

"So inexperienced then," Nonna huffs, tapping her chin. "We'll have to teach her some things."

Teach me... *things*? Oh god. Do I look like I want to be taught *things* by a group of relatives I've just met?

I put my fork down, deciding food is now a choking hazard. Breathing feels risky enough.

"Apologies for my Nonna," Dominic interjects, shooting his grandmother a look. "You'll quickly learn that our family has no filter. We ask and answer questions people wouldn't normally discuss—especially at the dinner table with a complete stranger."

He smiles at me like we're in this together. Spoiler alert: We are *not*. Then his eyes flick to his brother, who's still sitting there with his arms folded, eyes locked on me like he's mentally categorizing my every reaction. He hasn't touched his food, but I'm guessing that's because he's too busy plotting how to survive this dinner without engaging in human conversation.

"So, is that a yes on the virgin thing?" Nonna blinks at me expectantly.

This woman is relentless.

And apparently, we are not dropping this topic.

Rico

DINNER WENT AS EXPECTED. Nonna prodding, poking, and extracting enough intel from my future wife that I didn't have to lift a finger—let alone speak.

Age? Twenty-four. Preferred name? Allie. Loves to cook, and wants to be a chef. Oh, and the cherry on top? She might be a fucking virgin. So the first man she has sex with will be me. I might prefer code to people, but I'm not a prick. Well, not entirely. The idea of *me* being her first experience makes my stomach coil.

Now here I am, trapped in Papa's study, alone, with my fiancée.

She's perched on the couch, hands folded, while I'm sprawled in the armchair, making myself comfortable for however long they expect us to sit here.

Fifteen minutes drift by, blissfully uneventful. She fidgets—smooths her dress, twists her fingers, glances at the clock, the bookshelves, the floor, and me — only when she thinks I'm not looking. Meanwhile, I keep my eyes locked on the door, willing it to open. I feel like a kid in timeout, waiting for someone to open it and ask if I've learned my lesson before I'm set free.

Marco had to pick a woman who ticked every box on Nonna's dream-wife checklist. And to make matters worse? She's fucking hot. From the moment she walked into the house, all glowing skin and long legs with hair that belonged in some slow-motion shampoo commercial, I wanted to run. Olive skin. High cheekbones. Full lips. Dangerous as hell.

She's gorgeous and that sure as shit is going to make ignoring her a hell of a lot harder when she's in my orbit.

It changes nothing, but now I have to train myself not to notice the way her dress hugs her curves, how her tits are the perfect handful, or that her face is annoyingly symmetrical. Huge hazel doe eyes that catch the light with gold and green flecks practically winking trouble.

One thing is for certain as she sits there, long toned legs crossed, I realize I might have to insist she wear floor-length skirts and turtlenecks.

Why couldn't I get an ugly wife?

I don't ask for much. Hell, I don't ask for anything—mostly because I don't talk to anyone long enough to make a request. So why the hell am I saddled with a wife I'm going to avoid staring at the rest of my miserable life?

Smoothing out her dress, Allie turns to me, doe eyes steady. "So, is there anything you want to know about me?"

Only if your uterus is functioning and how quickly I can toss a kid in there to get the world off my back (also known as Mama). I have a feeling that very thought isn't the best way to kick off a marriage. Not that I have an alternative. I don't do relationships. My longest commitment is my Wednesday appointment with my therapist—fifteen minutes in, fifteen minutes out. Get in, get off, get out. That's my level of dedication, and there's no relationship. It's a contracted agreement.

"Nope."

Her forced smile deflates, a slow collapse of bravado.

"I see." She bites her bottom lip, tucking it beneath her teeth—and my cock twitches in betrayal. *Traitor.*

This interlude needs to end. Now.

Not only is it a monumental waste of time—time I should spend on something productive, basically anything other than what I'm doing right now would count—but this woman is eliciting a physical reaction from me. And that is unacceptable.

My body functions on logic. Cause and effect. I decide when and where it reacts. Yet here I am, experiencing a wholly unsanctioned physiological response—my dick stretching awake like a house cat after a long, indulgent nap, all because of *her.*

She turns toward me again, those absurdly big eyes locking onto mine like she has any right, and I make the rookie mistake of looking back.

Fuck. Me.

I need to get out of here. Immediately. Preferably before my self-control officially flushes itself down the toilet.

She lets out an exhale and her cheeks flush—scarlet, not pink—a reaction so immediate it makes me wonder how that breathy little exhale of hers would sound in other, less PG contexts. And just like that, I mentally kick myself in the proverbial balls for even entertaining the thought.

I don't look at women like this. Ever. My mind isn't a breeding ground for carnal distractions; it's a well-oiled machine, efficient, pragmatic, entirely devoid of hormonal interference. And yet, with her in my breathing space, it's like my subconscious has run a beta test using my body against me.

Unacceptable. Illogical. Infuriating.

Worse, I'm not exactly doing anything to stop it, am I? Not when I'm idly considering what those long legs would feel like wrapped around me. Odd, considering I've never entertained that particular geometry before.

Apparently, some things come naturally—like intrusive, thoroughly uninvited thoughts and an inconvenient desire to test just how flexible she really is.

"Listen, I know I'm not what you expected. You probably figured you'd be marrying someone your age, not some spoiled, naïve woman who's never worked a day in her life." She swallows, eyes briefly shutting, and when they open again, they're glossy. Shit. If she cries, I'm out. "I was raised to be a trophy wife, someone to pop out heirs. I know this isn't normal, and obviously neither of us want this, but maybe we could at least try to get to know each other. Make it easier. It's not like you're oozing with a bunch of warm and fuzzies about this arrangement, but would it kill you to talk to me even a little?"

Yes, actually. It would.

I scrub a hand down my face, silently cursing Marco. Speaking of that asshole, I reach into my pocket and pull out the black box I haven't even bothered to look in. "Here." I hold it out to her.

She blinks at it. "What is that?"

Really? The size of the box. The entire damn situation. Come on.

"A ring." I wiggle my hand, and she plucks it from my palm.

I refocus on the door, willing it to swing open and for someone to announce my time is up. From the corner of my eye, I watch as she slowly opens the box, staring at whatever monstrosity Marco picked.

Does she not like it? Not that I give a shit. She can replace it, buy ten if she wants. As long as I don't have to be involved. Knowing Marco, it's probably gaudy as hell, something rivaling Sienna and Violet's obnoxiously large rings—beacons warning any man within a ten-mile radius that they're off the market.

"It's beautiful."

Her voice is soft, almost reverent, and it irritates me. I don't like the way it trails up my spine like a ghost of something I refuse to acknowledge.

"Did you pick it out yourself?"

"No."

She snaps the lid shut. "Yeah. Didn't think so."

Not a mutter. Not under her breath. Direct. Clear. Loud enough to make me reassess if having a wife with opinions she doesn't mind voicing is a good idea. I'm still undecided on whether I hate it or if it's the only tolerable thing about this conversation. My dick, apparently, has an opinion, because it twitches at the sass she wields, and freely might I add.

"Marco mentioned you're good with computers. That you work at the company you and your brothers started?"

Did Marco give her my entire life story? I hope so. It means I won't have to sit through a tedious 'get to know me' session. I nod.

"I don't know much about computers. Wasn't allowed to use them much."

A snort escapes her, and she slaps a hand over her mouth like she's just giggled at a funeral. "Sorry."

I glance over. Is she laughing?

She's trying to smother it, but her shoulders shake like she's holding in something unholy. When she finally removes her hand, her eyes stay locked on the velvet box in her lap.

"It's just funny that I'm marrying a guy who works on computers all the time, and I barely know how to use my phone."

Christ. She's joking, right? Because I sure as hell won't be tech support.

"I know how to cook," she adds, perking up like this applies to my existence.

I internally groan. If she's getting comfortable, she'll keep talking. If Papa hears any conversation, he'll assume we're bonding and leave me in here longer. Which is ridiculous because I do not bond. I barely tolerate.

"Good," I say, but should have kept my mouth shut because now she's still going.

I should shut this down, but I'm focused on how her laugh is like honey—smooth, warm, and entirely unnecessary for my survival. And yet, I'm listening. Does she have some cheat code to my internal systems? In this whopping thirty-minute torture session, this woman has already pulled out more physical and mental reactions from me than my brothers have in a month of poking at me. It can't be a good sign.

"I always wanted to be a chef. Our housekeeper, Maria, used to let me help her when I was younger. I still cook when my parents aren't home. But now that I'm older, I'm not allowed in the kitchen."

Great. So she can cook but probably doesn't do dishes. Can't use a phone. Likely has no concept of a dishwasher. What else am I going to have to teach her? God bless YouTube tutorials—I'll send her the links and let her figure it out.

She exhales, long, and heavy, like she's gearing up to make another point. "That's one of the reasons I'm leaving the family, you know. I wanted to be something. Someone. I've been taking classes at the community college's culinary school, though, so maybe I can get a job. I can't do that if I stay, or if I marry Carlo Romano like my father wants me to."

Her voice trails off as the door handle flicks.

Papa steps inside, eyes bouncing between us. "How's it going in here?"

He's smiling, but his gaze is pinned on me, which means he's not pleased. Probably assuming I've been my usual anti-social self. He's not wrong.

From my periphery, I see Allie glance at me before facing him. "Fine. I think we got to know each other a little better."

Yeah. In the last thirty-four minutes, I've learned she likes to cook, and wants to be a chef, but can't use a phone or do dishes. Not that I need her to. There's only one part of her I need to function, and that hasn't come up for discussion yet. What's a good segue into asking if she can pop out a kid or two?

Papa grips the door handle tighter, his knuckles whitening. "Cecilia wanted to discuss some wedding details before you leave... that is if you decide you want to do this."

Oh, she gets a choice? Must be nice.

Then again, her options are me or going back to her father and Carlo fucking Romano. Not sure I'm the better alternative. I might be emotionally unavailable, but Carlo Romano is a human hemorrhoid who thinks he's a Sicilian god. He comes to the boxing club where Marco and I spar, and the guy fights like a toddler throwing a tantrum.

Allie's eyes flick to the black box, and Papa follows her gaze before turning his back on me.

Please, as if I went shopping for a ring. I just hope part of the wedding planning includes her picking out her wedding band, because I am not lifting a damn finger for that. My role here is to show up, mumble whatever vows Father Alberti recites, and not make the old man keel over at the sight of me getting married.

"Do I have to decide right now?"

My head snaps toward her. She has to think about it? She'd rather go back home and marry Carlo Romano? I may be as emotionally available as a concrete wall, but that guy is about as appealing as an expired can of Spam—dull, questionable, and guaranteed to give you regrets.

I unclench my fists, flexing my fingers, forcing them to stay loose. Apparently, the idea of her saying no stresses me out. Maybe because if she does, I'm stuck with Tori Valencia, and at that point, I'll need witness protection.

"Of course you don't." Papa steps further into the room, his gaze burning into me. There's a lecture brewing behind those eyes, and I will not like it. "It's a lot to take in." *That's an understatement.* "But we'd like to know in a day or two."

Allie nods and places the black velvet box on the coffee table. Watching her set it down makes my fists tighten again.

Black like the coffee that keeps me from committing homicide before noon. Black like my soul and tolerance for stupidity. Black like the screen of my phone when I ignore calls. Peaceful. Silent. Perfect.

"Let's call it a night, yeah?" Papa says.

I'm on my feet before he finishes the sentence.

"Well, thank fuck for that." I mumble, heading straight for the front door. No good-byes. No pleasantries. I fish out my keys, climb into my Porsche, shift into drive, and peel out of the driveway.

I need distance between me and Alessandra De Luca. She'll accept. Carlo Romano isn't the better option.

Rico

I'm in my office—though calling it an office is generous. It's a glorified cave. No windows, no clocks, no trace of the outside world. Just four walls, my screens, and the low hum of servers like a machine's heartbeat.

Technically, this was a storage closet when we bought the building. Now it's my domain. Let them keep their glass-walled corner offices where sunlight streams in like it's supposed to make them happy with all that vitamin D. I'll keep my cave. At least shadows don't ask you to smile or make polite conversation.

It was two in the morning when I came in and who knows what time it is now, but I don't care. I woke up wired, pissed off, and fully aware that sleep would be a lost cause. So, naturally, I came here—my sanctuary, where people don't exist and problems are solved with code, not conversation.

The blue glow from the monitors casts sharp shadows across the room, washing over me like some twisted imitation of a halo. The irony isn't lost on me.

For the last four hours, I've been tearing apart my code, dissecting how some hacker—a little digital parasite—bypassed my latest security update. He's not even stealing anything. Just poking around like a kid testing the strength of an electric fence, and that somehow pisses me off more.

I don't play games. I dismantle them.

But here I am, engaged in a game of hacker chess with some faceless idiot, while another far more aggravating problem worms her way under my skin—Allie fucking De Luca.

Somehow, she's set up camp in the back of my mind, making herself comfortable. And the worst part? The idea that she might say no to this arranged marriage? Laughable. Yet, here I am, irritated that she might.

Apparently, I have an ego. How pedestrian of me.

Or maybe it's my survival instincts kicking in. If she says no, I'm stuck with another bride—a woman so unhinged she'd marry my corpse just for the inheritance.

I crack my knuckles and dive back into the code, fingers flying over the keyboard like I'm trying to exorcise her from my brain one line at a time. The click of the keys is sharp, relentless, echoing in the empty room. Mechanical keyboard—blue switches. Maximum tactile response. If I'm going to type my way into an early grave, I may as well enjoy the ride.

Somewhere in the background, white noise fills my headphones, drowning out reality. The only light in this cave is from my screens—cold, blue, and merciless. They say blue light ruins your circadian rhythm.

Sleep is for the weak. Or the dead. Not sure which category I'm inching closer to.

Then, warm yellow light pours in from the hallway, cutting through the darkness. I squint against it, hating how it stings my eyes—like acid poured into my skull.

A figure steps into the doorway, arms crossed, posture sharp and perfected. The tailored suit is overkill, especially at this hour. Who gets fully dressed in a three-piece suit at six a.m.? Psychopaths. Or, in my case, my brother.

With the way the light hits him, he could pass for an angel.

Except angels don't haunt you at ungodly hours.

"What the fuck are you doing?"

His voice is a whip crack across my carefully constructed peace.

Doesn't this guy have a life? I thought he stepped down from CEO to COO for work-life balance. Yet here he is, standing in my doorway. He should go live his *balanced* life and leave me the hell alone.

"Work," I mutter, waving vaguely at the glowing monitors, because what else would I be doing? Starting a knitting club?

The only reason this company thrives, literally, is because of me. Instead of hiring ten subpar coders, they get one world-class asshole who does all the updates, development, and security implementations while avoiding office birthday parties and mandatory happy hours.

Coding is my safe place. My fortress of solitude. Until now, when some troll of a hacker keeps tapping on my back door for shits and giggles—right in the middle of a merger talk with the Locke brothers.

And the Lockes? They won't merge with a cybersecurity firm that has even a whiff of hacker baggage. Can't blame them. A hacker worming around your systems isn't exactly a worthwhile investment.

Not that I want the merger to happen. More employees mean more people to dodge in the hallways. More coders means I'll lose control of my cave and—God help me—have to talk to people.

As if that isn't bad enough, I'm also supposed to tie myself to a woman I barely know. A sassy mouthed woman with hazel eyes and a disarming face. Memorable enough, I had to jerk off this morning just to clear my head. The first time I've ever done that. Ever. Not even when I was a horny teenager with unlimited internet access. Porn and my hand were never my thing. So what the hell is wrong with me that in my late thirties I'm now embracing it?

To top it off, my brother—Saint Alexander, the smug prick—kills my vibe by flipping on the overhead lights and my eyes nearly melt out of my head.

"Fuck!" I hiss, covering my eyes.

The door slams behind him, and when I crack one eye open, I see Alex leaning against it with his arms crossed, ready to settle in and lurk there until I grant him a minute of my time.

"What?" I ask without looking up, fingers already flying over the keyboard. I lost half my weekend to a family dinner, sitting across from Allie De Luca, waiting to see if she'd agree to marry me. Now I'm behind on everything, and I'm not in the mood for interruptions. Let alone my big brother and one of his glorious lectures.

Alex pushes off the door and strolls over to me, oozing that confidence that he only puts off when he's about to fuck up my day. He leans against my desk—my desk—and wiggles his ass on it just to piss me off further.

Then, because apparently his goal is to die today, he hooks his stupidly expensive shoe against the edge of my chair and pushes me back from the keyboard, yanking my headphones off with a sharp tug.

My older brother is dangerously close to earning himself a black eye.

"Fuck. Alex. What?" I drag the words out, already bored. Patience is a virtue, but I'm far from virtuous.

"Congratulations. That woman was crazy enough to agree to marry you," Alex says, grinning like he just handed me a winning lottery ticket.

So, she agreed. Interesting. Though, let's be honest—a woman willingly signing up to marry someone like me can only be so sane.

Sure, she seemed more put together than Tori Valencia (who twitches like a glitching robot when she's pissed), but for all I know, Allie De Luca has skeletons in her closet. Real ones. The kind that probably have names and unfortunate last breaths, considering her background and the fact she comes with a stamp of approval from Marco, our resident nut.

"She agreed?" I ask, shoving Alex's polished shoe off my chair as I reach for my headphones. I don't really expect an answer.

Before I can slip them back on, Alex smacks them out of my hand. We both watch in silence as they fly across the room, hit the wall, and land in the corner.

A normal human would be pissed. Maybe even throw a tantrum. I'm not normal.

I lean back in my chair, lacing my fingers behind my head. "Are we done here? Or are you planning to monologue on about a solid relationship?" If I had the ability, or care, I'd roll my eyes. But that's more effort than what I'm willing to give.

"Are you really going through with this?" He acts as though he hasn't seen how low the bar is for me.

I nod once, slow and deliberate. Cute that he thinks I have options.

"Papa called," he frowns down at his Rolex. Meanwhile, I glance at the space on my screen where a clock should be. I turned them off months ago. Time is irrelevant. I work until I'm done, or until I get bored and move my operation to my home office.

Alex waits, probably hoping for a reaction. He gets nothing. I may have blinked, but that's as generous as I'm willing to be. Part of me worries that blink was a twitch from the mounting stress in my life, but I'll dissect that one later.

Finally, he sighs in defeat and slides off my desk. I mentally note to disinfect it after he leaves. Only coffee cups and keyboards on my desk. Tom Ford wool-covered asses not allowed. "You need to be in the conference room at ten. Wolfe will be there. So will your blushing bride. Time to go over the paperwork."

Shit. I have to see her again?

The fewer times I see her, the better.

I need at least seventy-two hours—bare minimum—to reprogram my brain, to over-write the way her scent clings to my lungs like a damn virus and the way she looked at me like she could see through every carefully constructed defense I've spent years building.

If I were a machine, I'd call it a system breach. One I can't patch fast enough.

What I need is distance. Space to scrub her from my mind, to forget the shape of her mouth when she talks back, or the exact shade of her eyes when she stares me down.

Brown with flecks of gold like the color of old whiskey in a glass — smooth, dangerous and a reminder that things can look good but be dangerous. Brownish gold like a tarnished brass antique. Gold like the kind you find in flames, which are guaranteed to burn you if you get too close.

Clearly there's a problem and I need time to figure out where it starts so I can make sure it ends. Seeing her only makes it worse.

Isn't that the whole point of this arranged marriage? We don't have to deal with each other until we're forced to stand at the altar and mumble vows that tether us together like inmates in a chain gang.

Apparently, I was wrong. I don't enjoy that feeling.

Allie

I'M SITTING AT THE conference table, the cold stone surface biting into my palms while I try to decipher the legal mumbo-jumbo spread out in front of me. Words like "*equitable distribution*," "*transmutation*," and "*elective share*" blur together, blending into one long-winded spell conjured by some evil law wizard. The only phrase I halfway recognize is "*full disclosure*." Lovely.

Full disclosure: I have no clue what I'm signing.

Vinnie sits in the corner scrolling on his phone like this whole marriage agreement situation is just another day for him. Meanwhile, Marco sits beside me, officially playing the role of life coach in this brave new world I'm about to step into—unofficially, my guide out of mafia life and into whatever the hell this is.

Take the deal, Allie. Your freedom is calling, and it's offering unlimited data and a clean slate.

"None of this makes sense," I mutter to Marco, leaning over just enough to whisper. I pointedly ignore Rico, who's sitting across from me with his arms crossed, radiating nothing but glacial energy while Jaxon Wolfe—the Bennetti family's lawyer and apparent overlord of everything legal—drones on about the agreement we're about to sign.

"It will when I'm done explaining it," Jaxon cuts in. He throws me a glare that gives me middle school flashbacks. "The purpose of today is to go over the details—non-negotiable items that protect both of you—then gather input for what you'd like to include in your marriage contract."

"Marriage contract?" I blink. Isn't *I do* the contract? You know, the vows, the priest, the whole *till-death-do-us-part* thing?

Jaxon's lips twitch in what I'm guessing is supposed to be a smile, but it's closer to a condescending smirk. "Because this marriage is arranged, there's a contract in addition to the prenup. It outlines what's expected from the marriage. If either party violates the agreement, it allows for a clean break. Compensation terms are already built into it."

Compensation? Wait—if we don't follow the rules of this marriage, someone gets a payout? Interesting. But what happens if *he* doesn't follow the rules? And compensation from where? I have exactly zero dollars, no assets, and a suitcase filled with designer clothes I can't afford to dry-clean.

The closer I get to this *arrangement*, the further away from my dream of a loving husband, kids, and domestic bliss drifts. Instead, I'm stuck with *him*—the man who's currently staring at me like I'm a bug pinned to a board for examination.

He doesn't speak. Not to me, anyway. I'm not even sure I've heard him utter a full sentence since this whole circus started. Just a series of grunts and half-snorts. But I've *seen* him talk—to his brothers, to Marco. Actual words. Short sentences, yes, but still. So, he *can* talk. He just doesn't waste words on me.

Right now, his side of the table is so cold I half-expect to see my breath when I exhale like we're in some Arctic tundra.

How am I supposed to marry this man, let alone raise children with him? Children need warmth, laughter, and I'm pretty sure some actual human interaction. I'm not entirely sure he even knows how to smile, much less hold a conversation that doesn't involve stony stares.

I stare at him. He stares back, completely blank.

This isn't a fiancé.

It's an iceberg in a dress shirt and jeans. A very attractive one, but rather than send heat throughout my body, I'm holding back shivers.

"Miss De Luca, do you need a minute?" Jaxon's voice pulls me out of my thoughts, and I suddenly realize I've been locked in an intense staring contest with Rico.

I blink, shaking my head. "Nope, I'm good. Continue."

"As I was explaining, I have Mr. Bennetti's terms here, but I'll need yours. These terms can be personal, including your preferences regarding marital relations."

My face instantly catches fire. Did he just—?

"The marriage contract talks about...sex?"

The words come out strangled, like my throat just decided we're done here and blocked any chance of oxygen. Am I hearing this right? There's a legally binding sex clause in this contract?

I sneak a glance at Rico. No reaction. He's sitting there, probably scheduling our sex life in his head with all the enthusiasm of a dental appointment.

Look, I'm not clueless. I know how sex works, thank you very much. I've been there once—okay, once is generous—but it happened! Still, how does one phrase that in a legally binding document? *Required to deliver orgasms on demand?* I could totally get behind that clause. But judging by his current *I'm-dead-inside* expression, I'm guessing he's not exactly a passionate, rip-your-clothes-off kind of guy.

"This might help." Jaxon slides a piece of paper across the table toward me. "These are Mr. Bennetti's terms. We'll draft the official contract once I have yours."

I glanced at the paper, and my mouth hung open.

Term #1: Live with your husband.

Wow, what a privilege. I'm required to live with him. Great. But wait...

Term #2: You will have your own room.

Oh. Okay. So, not even the *illusion* of a normal marriage. Fabulous.

It keeps getting worse.

Term #3: Monitor ovulation and notify your husband accordingly for procreation purposes.

I'm sorry, notify him accordingly? Should I send a formal email? Maybe a Google calendar invite: *Tuesday at 8 p.m.—Baby-Making Time. Please RSVP. Please click "yes," "no," or "maybe" if you will be attending.*

The next few terms blur together—something about responsibly cutting back work hours when I get pregnant, a no-drugs clause (easy), and a responsible-alcohol-use clause (uh, might be trickier after today). But one thing stands out like a flashing neon sign: There's nothing in here about fidelity.

Not a word.

My blood pressure spikes. I may not be a lawyer, but even I know that if it's not in writing, it's not enforceable. Translation: Rico Bennetti doesn't give a damn about fidelity.

Nope. Over my cold, dead body. *Or his.*

I didn't dodge an arranged marriage in the Cosa Nostra just to end up with a husband who views me as nothing more than a breeding machine while he plays out his *real* sex life elsewhere. If this man thinks he's getting away with some convenience marriage arrangement where I pop out heirs while he frolics in someone else's bed, he's got another thing coming.

I glance at Rico again. He's inching his chair back from the table as if I'm the carrier of some rash he can't risk catching.

"I have one stipulation already," I say, trying to sound calm, even though my body is on fire. My skin feels like it's hosting a spontaneous bonfire, and my heart is doing a full percussion solo in my chest. If this is what they mean when they say your blood is boiling, I'm practically a human teapot.

I lock eyes with Rico. His expression doesn't change—not even a flicker of curiosity or concern. Just that same unreadable mask he's worn since the moment we met.

"There will be no extracurriculars," I announce, feeling pretty damn proud of my fancy word choice.

Confidence, meet Allie. Please stick around. I'm going to need you.

"Extracurriculars?" Jaxon lifts a brow.

"No sex with anyone outside our marriage. It's not in the contract, but if I'm expected to wave an ovulation flag every month, then I'm not sitting around while my husband waves his wiener at other women."

Jaxon's eyes dart from me to Rico, then to Marco. The silence stretches, and the pit forming in my stomach grows bigger by the second. Why does this feel like such a controversial request? Shouldn't fidelity be a given? Or...does Rico already have someone? Is there a secret girlfriend waiting in the wings? Am I going to be *that* wife—the placeholder while he keeps someone else on the side?

My pulse thunders in my ears as I wait. Rico's dark eyes stay locked on mine, his face giving away absolutely nothing. But then, finally, he nods at Jaxon. Relief rushes through me—until Marco clears his throat.

"No therapists either," Marco adds.

My head whips toward him. "Wait, what? Why no therapy?" I glance between Marco and Rico, their gazes locked in a silent, intense standoff. What is happening? Why is therapy a no-go? Therapy is great. It could even help this man learn to express more than a grunt or two.

"Yeah, Rico," Marco drawls. "Why no therapists?" He tilts his head in that *I'm about to stir some shit* way that's clearly designed to provoke a reaction, and surprisingly he does.

Rico's jaw tightens, the muscle in his cheek feathering as he clenches his teeth hard enough that I half expect a molar to crack and skitter across the table. Rico still doesn't speak, but Marco turns to me instead.

"It's fine. I got it. Well, you see, my dear—"

"Fine. No therapists," Rico interrupts, his eyes locking on mine for a fleeting second before turning to Jaxon. "No other partners, no therapists. Of any kind."

My spidey senses tingle. I've never been to a therapist myself, but something tells me that Rico's *therapy* sessions weren't about working through whatever issues he has with guided breathing exercises.

"Okay then," Jaxon scribbles a note on his legal pad with the same enthusiasm one might use while ordering a latte. "Anything else come to mind?"

"I can request anything I want?" I ask, tilting my head.

"Yes, and you should," Jaxon replies, surprising me with his sudden tone of advocacy and the odd look he shoots toward Rico, as if he's all in on me demanding more. "This is your marriage, too."

My marriage. The words feel strange, like trying on shoes two sizes too small. Ideal marriage? Yeah, that ship sailed the minute I agreed to marry this statue. Still, if I'm stuck here, I might as well make some demands. Think of it as negotiation.

"Dinner together every night," I say firmly.

The silence that follows is deafening. Rico's eyes narrow, sending a frosty glare my way. But I don't look at him. Nope. Best to avoid making eye contact when your husband-to-be looks like he's mentally flipping through *101 ways to kill you with a spoon.*

Besides, he may not find me attractive, but I'm not blind. The man is ridiculously good-looking. I'd rather not get lost in that right now. Confidence is a limited resource, and I need every drop.

Jaxon nods, scribbling furiously on his legal pad. Encouraged, I lean in, the heat of confidence filling my chest like a helium balloon. I'm floating now—might as well see how high I can go.

"And on the nights we... have sex," I pause for dramatic effect, locking eyes with Rico, "you have to sleep in my bed. I'll have my own room, fine, but I'm not going to be treated like some escort you toss a few bills at before you vanish into the night."

Jaxon's pen stills. "That might be a problem..." His gaze flicks toward Rico.

At least Mr. Stone Statue is no longer wearing his usual blank expression. Nope. His jaw clenches so tight I'm pretty sure I can hear his molars screaming for mercy. His eyes? Wolfish. Cold. Predatory. The kind of look that a normal person would run from, but a normal person wouldn't be here negotiating marriage terms with a robot. So, there's that.

I blink at him, refusing to back down. "Why would that be a problem?"

Marco taps a line on the paper in front of me, his finger practically burning a hole through the contract. I follow his gesture, rereading the clause I hadn't fully absorbed earlier.

No touching or kissing.

I arch a brow. "So how exactly are we supposed to have sex if we can't touch each other? Do we high-five from opposite sides of the bed and hope it counts?"

"Minimal touching," Rico grits out, his voice as sharp as his cheekbones.

"Fine, then you can *minimally* touch me while you sleep on your side of the bed. Deal?" I fire back.

His lips press into a thin line, his eyes still locked on mine like we're in a staring contest neither of us plans to lose. "Fine," he bites out.

Jaxon clears his throat, clearly ready to move on, but I'm just getting started. The balloon is still rising, and I have plenty of air left.

"Once a week, you're taking me out on an actual date," I announce, my voice steady.

"Fine." Rico's voice is low and dangerous.

"And in public, you have to hold my hand."

Jaxon's brow lifts, the corner of his mouth twitching in what can only be described as barely concealed amusement. Clearly I'm making his day.

"Fine."

Is he programmed? Like some human Siri, with preloaded responses? Because if I hear *fine* one more time, I'm going to throw something.

"Every morning," I continue, "you have to tell me something about yourself. Something that isn't work-related. And once a week, share a secret with me. Something only a wife would know about her husband. I'll do the same."

"Mr. Bennetti might need some time to consider these conditions."

"Does Mr. Bennetti have a reset button?" I ask, cocking my head. Looking at the man who hasn't so much as blinked at me. "Because I think he's frozen and needs a reboot. Care to point me toward the reset button?"

Marco snorts, coughing to cover the laugh, while Rico remains as stoic as ever. He doesn't flinch. Doesn't even blink. I'm almost convinced the robot theory is closer to reality than I thought.

"One last thing," I say, ignoring the looks from Jaxon and Marco.

"You," I point directly at Rico, "are contractually obligated to spend time with me. Act like a real husband. Treat me like a wife." That's right. I used fancy legal terminology. In my defense, it was right there on the paper in front of me.

Jaxon leans forward, clearly entertained. "Care to specify what *acting like a real husband* entails?"

I shrug. "I'll leave it open. Rico can work his way toward his comfort level. But I will not be some random breeding mare in his stable. He needs to show up and act like my partner, or you can take these contracts and—" I pull off my engagement ring and slap it down on the papers — "keep this."

I push back my chair and stand, my pulse racing. Marco stands with me, buttoning his jacket as he glares at Rico.

Vinnie is already at the door, holding it open, but before I step through, I glance back at Rico, whose expression remains as blank as a sheet of paper. Jaxon still looks mildly entertained.

"When you're ready to agree to my terms, come find me. Like a real man who wants a wife—not a uterus for hire."

And with that, I walk out, holding in the trembles trying to shake my body, and hope that it comes off confident like I hold the power in this room.

Rico

ALEX AND DOM LOOK at me like they've just won the lottery of blackmail material, their eyes lighting up as they read Allie's list of demands for our marriage contract. If Allie had sprouted wings and breathed fire during the meeting, it would've been less surprising than the barrage of conditions she threw at us. And yet, it wasn't her sudden transformation into a demon queen that threw me. No, it was the way my body betrayed me—my cock hard as steel at her little power play.

Unideal reaction.

"Jesus," Dom chuckles, holding the paper like it's the funniest thing he's read in years. "No therapists? How the hell did she find out about *that*?"

"Marco," I say flatly, already plotting how to make him pay for that little betrayal.

Marco knew exactly what he was doing when he mentioned therapy, like a cat batting at a mouse just to see what happens. He knew damn well I wasn't cheating—*technically*. Therapy, in my world, has always been code for scheduled, no-strings sex with a woman who gets it. No feelings, no foreplay, no pillow talk. Just clinical, detached efficiency.

My weekly 15-minute sessions were part of my survival strategy. Some people meditate, others take up yoga. I have a standing appointment with a woman whose last name I don't care to know. There's no kissing, no undressing. Scheduled and controlled, like everything else in my life. *No complications. No emotions. No mess.*

But now, thanks to Marco, Allie wants it *all*—complete fidelity, no loopholes. Cute.

Alex's shoulders shake with laughter. "Man, you're really in it now. So when's your last *session*?" He practically spits out the word "session," mocking the ridiculous euphemism my family has embraced for years. God forbid anyone in this family just say what it is: I've been banging an escort once a week for years.

"Tomorrow," I say, running a hand down my face. "I'll cancel it after that."

Dom smirks. "Sure you will. Going out with a bang?" He pauses, his eyes glinting with something far too amused for my liking. "Or no bang at all?"

I roll my eyes, refusing to dignify that with an answer. My brothers have no boundaries, and yet somehow the words *Rico fucks an escort* can't pass their lips without adding quotation marks or pretending it's an alternative therapy. The irony is astounding, considering our family's habit of openly discussing everything from childbirth to favorite sexual positions at family dinners.

"She's married anyway, right?" Dom asks, his tone turning slightly more serious.

"Yeah. Not that it matters. It's over."

It's not a lie. Ending it is logical. Allie wouldn't understand—hell, I don't expect her to. My "therapy" was never about infidelity or affection. It was about control. Control over my needs, my desires, my dark corners that no one, least of all my wife, should ever have to see. Allie's the kind of woman who expects hand-holding and confessions under the stars. She doesn't need to know that my version of sex is cold, calculated, and devoid of anything resembling intimacy.

And now, I'm expected to figure out how to be a husband without relying on the only routine that's kept me sane. Just me, my hand, and a lot of creative thinking is my bleak new future.

"You're really not going to share a room or a bed? You just want her to what—holler when she's ovulating?" Alex leans against the table, frowning down at the contract in front of him.

I shrug. They act like it's a reckless move. It's not. It's damage control. For her. For me. For whatever's left of my grip on reality. Sharing a bed is a risk I don't need to take—too much room for error. She rolls over and touches me in her sleep? Could be fine and I just flinch away, or I might swing first, wake second. Hasn't happened in a while. Not since I started keeping my stress levels in check. But with what's coming, I'd bet good money on a relapse.

From my research, she'll ovulate once every 28 days (give or take). Her fertility window is around five or six days, but the two golden days before ovulation and the day of are the jackpot. That's it. Two to three nights of hell every 28 days. Manageable. I've survived on less sleep for worse reasons.

Eventually, once she realizes there's no misunderstood prince buried beneath the layers of my dead exterior, she'll stop asking me to share her bed. She'll take what she needs and then let me retreat to my corner of the world. We'll both be better for it. Trust me.

"Rico," Alex's voice drops the usual mockery. He's no longer grinning like a jackass. His eyes flick toward Jaxon, who takes the hint and steps out of the room, shutting the door behind him.

"What?" I snap, knowing damn well where this is heading. If he dares compare me to him or Dom again, I swear I'll lose it. We are *not* the same. Never have been, never will be.

"You're not just signing a contract. Yeah, you've got your terms laid out to keep everything under control, but you're about to make a family. You can't control everything, Rico. How's this gonna work when you have kids? Are you gonna keep your wife in a guest room while raising your kids like roommates? What are you gonna teach them about relationships? That parents barely speak, sleep in separate beds, and interact only when absolutely necessary?"

I don't see the issue with that way of thinking, but that doesn't stop him from continuing with his lecture.

"When she gets pregnant, she's gonna need help—support. You can't just hide in your office, tapping away at code while she figures it all out alone. I don't know her well, but she seemed nice. Sweet, even. This setup? It's gonna hurt her. If you're dead set on not having a real relationship, marry someone like Tori. You know she'd be happy swiping your credit cards and living in different wings of the house."

Tori? *Absolutely not.* That woman is one screw loose away from going full-blown apocalyptic crazy. She's not raising my kids. Hell, she can barely raise her voice without it turning into a banshee-like wail that makes dogs howl. Seen it myself. I'm still traumatized.

"Allie knows what she's getting into. She's seen the demands." I nod toward the contract she might as well have lit on fire this morning.

"Seeing them and living them are two different things, Rico. What happens when she realizes the reality is ten times worse than what's written on that paper? What if she's unhappy?"

Then she can join the 99% of us in this world who aren't happy, unlike these two unicorns sparkling across from me.

"I'll make sure she works, follows her dreams, and has everything she needs to be happy."

Dom snorts under his breath, but leaves the lecture to Alex.

"Sure, Rico," Alex says, pushing off the table. "Just know, when this whole thing backfires and she's either miserable or ready to stab you in your sleep, I get to say *I told you so.*"

"Good," I deadpan. "You can have it engraved on my headstone."

He chuckles as he heads for the door. "I might just do that."

Rico

I think my fiancée is trying to kill me.

Papa insisted we exchange numbers, like this was some *real* relationship where we'd text goodnight and talk on the phone until one of us fell asleep.

Not happening.

He and the rest of the family are acting like this marriage is a love story, as if I actually got down on one knee and asked this woman to strap herself to my emotional baggage for the rest of her life.

The reality is I sent the ring back with a courier and a note: *I accept.*

That's the best she's getting. Congratulations, sweetheart—our grand proposal story.

Can't wait to see how Vi spins that into some swoon-worthy moment in one of her books. I heard she placed a bet on my wedding being the inspiration for another one of her spicy bestsellers. The woman churns out smut faster than the rest of my siblings produce offspring. Not a bad thing, but knowing Violet, there's a high probability I'll be the inspiration for her next book.

They need to accept reality. I have.

Everyone knows what this is. Just like they knew about my... *therapy.* Just like they knew what happened years ago. And just like that incident, they're pretending it's something else, turning it into whatever makes them feel better.

Fine. Let them have their delusions. Who am I to stomp on false joy?

Now, I have a woman I've been actively avoiding texting me. A lot.

She tried calling a few times before realizing I didn't answer the phone. Not just for her—for anyone. Phone calls require talking. Talking requires effort and time. You can't nod and grunt over the phone. That's time I could spend doing something productive, like staring at lines of code or contemplating my own mortality.

Send me a text? Sure. I'll probably ignore it. But at least you've gotten whatever nonsense you needed off your chest.

Unfortunately, she hasn't given up. Instead, she's become relentless.

Cake flavor.

Wedding colors.

Suit preferences.

Do I look like I care?

Peonies or roses? *Couldn't give a shit.*

Lemon or raspberry filling? *Don't care. Won't eat it.*

Lilac or blue-violet for the accent color? *That's the same damn color.*

She's sitting with Mama, Nonna, and half the family, planning this circus, and she still insists on dragging me into it. For what? A shared experience?

The only experience we need to share is her ovulation schedule.

She's wasting her time and stealing precious minutes of mine. If I was going to pretend to be an invested husband, I'd at least have the decency to pretend in person.

The woman's a thief.

No mask, no gloves, no dark alleyway where she lurks waiting to strike. Just a phone, an arsenal of emojis, and an unholy ability to steal every ounce of my attention. She stole my therapy, three weeks' worth of it.

So, in the past three weeks, all I've had to occupy my thoughts is a woman texting me, the reminder of how she smells, looks, and continually makes my fists clench while I perform breathing exercises that do jack shit.

I should refine my firewall against the hacker who keeps slipping through my system like a cockroach that parades on even after a nuclear fallout. Instead, I'm sitting here, staring at my screen, rereading the last text she sent as if it contains some sort of hidden algorithm I need to crack.

The wedding is in three days.

I have done my part. I sent the ring. I agreed to the terms, and even broke off my weekly arrangement with Em, via text. She wasn't devastated. There was no dramatic exit or desperate plea to reconsider. Just a quick, *Got it. Thanks for the notice.*

No emotions. No attachment. No complications.

And yet, I have spent the last three weeks in a living hell of forced socialization.

Allie has traded wedding planning texts for post-nuptial inquiries, each message chiseling away at the safe, structured life I've built like a sculptor hacking into marble.

I've buried myself in work, the only thing that keeps me from setting my entire life on fire at the moment.

Are we going on a honeymoon?

She can go. Pack her bags, pick a destination, and sip overpriced cocktails on a white sandy beach. But I'm staying here. I have work to do. Besides, the agreement states I only have to be present during her ovulation window, and I have no interest in playing tour guide in some overpriced romantic getaway where I pretend to care about scenic views.

Is there furniture in the guest room?

Shit. No. Hadn't thought of that.

So, at Sunday dinner—because my family is oblivious to my needs and demands for my weekly suffering—I handed her my card, told her to buy whatever she wanted.

"But I haven't even seen the room." She blinked at me, as if this was some huge oversight.

What does she need to see? It's four walls, a door, a closet. She wants to pick out her own furniture? Great. Use my money and do it. Problem solved.

Should we go to dinner before the wedding?

Hard pass.

I've already agreed to the absurdity of a weekly date night, but that clause doesn't activate until after the vows. So, until then, I'm keeping my ass right here in my office.

No candlelit dinners. No long walks through Central Park. No pretending we're two normal people embarking on a happy little love story.

She wants romance? She can buy that with the same credit card I just gave her.

My office is soundproof. A necessity.

Dom had wanted glass walls for "transparency," but even he knew better than to suggest that shit for me. I need walls. I need silence. And, most importantly, I need a door that never stays open.

When he took over as CEO, he gutted the entire office space, ripped out the glass walls, and made everything sleek and modern. Whatever. Didn't matter to me. My space remained exactly as I wanted it—dark, quiet, and uninviting.

Right now, the rhythmic click of my keyboard is the only thing keeping me from losing my mind.

The closer I get to the wedding, the more my panic meter spikes.

I can't handle people in a normal setting. How the fuck am I supposed to handle a wedding? Just attending my brothers' weddings required a borderline alcohol-induced coma to numb the itchy feeling of human interaction. Sadly, I can't be blackout drunk at my own. At least, I don't *think* I can.

Maybe Allie wouldn't mind? A husband with a drinking problem is probably preferable to one who looks like he'd rather get waterboarded than be in the same room with her.

My phone pings.

I don't have to look at it. I already know who it is.

Allie.

I haven't, for the record, responded to a single text in the three weeks since Papa handed over my number. Our text thread is nothing but her talking to herself—an eerie preview of what the rest of our marriage will probably look like.

Yet, she keeps texting.

Seventy-four messages deep, and she *still* thinks today is the day I reply.

Admirable.

Also, infuriating.

"Are you going to ignore your fiancée until the wedding?"

I glance up, spotting Dom standing in my doorway, arms crossed like some moral authority on marriage.

Since this woman bulldozed into my life, my brothers have been interrupting my work more than in all the years we've worked together. I don't like it. They meddle—sure, they always have—but not with me. My engagement has apparently given them a free pass to barge into my office like it's their personal confessional.

I didn't even hear the door open. That sneaky bastard.

I check my watch.

Five in the morning.

Shit. Did I stay here all night?

Better question: *Why is he here?* Dom doesn't stroll in until eight, sometimes nine.

"It's easier for her if I do." I mutter, eyes locked on my monitors.

I don't keep extra chairs in my office—deliberate design choice. No one feels inclined to sit, which means no one overstays their welcome. The only chair is mine.

"How so?"

I keep typing. "Shouldn't you be at home with your wife?"

"I had emails to get through. I'm off the rest of the week."

Right. For Sienna's gallery exhibit. My brother bought his wife an art gallery, which keeps her busy, and when she has an exhibit, he disappears.

Both of my brothers work from home more, take more days off, make more time for their families.

I will *not* be that kind of husband.

I'll still be here. Working. Drowning in code. Blissfully unreachable.

Maybe I should buy Allie a restaurant. That way, she'll be too busy to bother me. She never shuts up about her love of cooking—perfect. Keeps her occupied. Keeps her out of my hair.

Otherwise, what the hell happens after we're married?

Right now, she's busy with wedding planning, but what about after? What will my text messages look like then?

A daily interrogation of my whereabouts?

A request for a spreadsheet of my emotions so she can track progress?

A picture of a dog at a shelter with the caption *He needs a home, Rico. Let's be good people?*

Or worse...

Hey, babe.

I hadn't planned that far ahead, too preoccupied with the immediate disaster looming over me.

"Tell Sienna I said good luck," I offer, just to get him out of my doorway.

Dom ignores the hint. "Did you stay overnight again?"

"Maybe."

"Rico—"

"Dom—"

He groans.I smile. Internally, of course.

I love how little effort it takes to irritate him.

"I assume you're not going on a honeymoon?"

I cut him a look. "Do you have to ask?"

Dom shrugs, his shadow stretching across my desk, disrupting my workflow. I don't stop typing. If I stop, he'll assume it's an invitation to keep talking.

"So you're going to what? Get married, head home, drop her off, and come back to work?"

He says that like it's a bad thing.

People really don't respect a strong work ethic these days.

"Rico, what about the wedding night?"

Fuck. Forgot about that.

No. *Ignored* it. Neatly folded that disaster and shoved it into the mental junk drawer labeled *deal with later*, which in this case meant *never*. I spent an entire day debating how to handle it before concluding the best course of action was simple: postpone, avoid, and hope for a miraculous asteroid impact.

Consummating the marriage isn't the issue. Well, it is. A massive, glaring, neon-flashing issue. But so is the fact that unless she miraculously ovulates on cue, it'll be a complete waste of time, effort, and—most importantly—a waste of perfectly good sperm, which I hold rather dear considering my current circumstances. Technically, she only said we *have* to do it, but luckily for me, she never specified *when*.

Details, cara mia. Details matter.

I shrug. "I'll figure it out."

Dom pushes off the doorframe, hands stuffed in his pockets, wearing that brotherly face that makes me want to throw something at him. "Sienna's been talking to Allie. She likes her. Hell, I think I've spoken to your fiancée more than you have. I like her too."

"Good," I snarl. *Now you all can keep her entertained while I spend the rest of my life in blissful silence.*

"Sienna also mentioned that Allie's nervous about the wedding," he continues, undeterred by my general lack of giving a fuck. "She mentioned that you, unsurprisingly, haven't spoken to her *at all*. Rico, I know you don't like to talk. The rest of us tolerate it. But you're about to marry this woman. You have to come out of your shell, even just an inch. Be human for a millisecond. Whether she divorces your ass down the road and remarries or not, this is her first wedding. If she's crazy enough, it might even be her only wedding."

I stop typing.

Divorce?

That particular *D* word doesn't exist in the Bennetti vocabulary. Divorce isn't an option in our family. Not because of some outdated cultural belief—no, it's much worse. It's because every single one of these assholes is disgustingly, nauseatingly happy. No one in this family is unhappily married. Not a single miserable bastard in the bunch.

Except me. And it's no fun having a pity party for one.

"You really think she's going to stay married to you if this is how you are?" Dom shakes his head, looking at me like I'm some wounded dog who still bites the hand trying to feed it. "Papa's already told her that if she doesn't feel it's working out after a few months, he'll give her his blessing to divorce you."

My fingers freeze on the keyboard. My pulse stutters along with said appendages.

Divorce means freedom. Isn't that what I wanted?

"She knows that?"

Dom nods. "Papa feels bad. She wanted out of the Cosa Nostra, and this was the only option given to her. He doesn't want her escaping one miserable life, only to be shackled to another permanently."

Miserable life.

If only they really knew.

"That's if she even makes it down the aisle."

Dom smirks, because he's a bastard who enjoys getting a rise out of me. I squint at him, waiting for the punchline.

"Yeah, did it occur to you that in the past few weeks of planning her own wedding, only seeing you at Sunday dinner, your fiancée might not be excited about this marriage? I believe her words to Violet were that she's *'made a mistake.'"* He pauses for dramatic effect, the asshole. "Wouldn't be surprised if she runs back home. A woman opting for the mafia over a life with you, Rico. That's a new low."

Leaning back in my chair, I cross my arms and stare him down. "What do you suggest?"

I don't miss how he practically chokes on his own breath. I don't ask for advice. I don't offer it, either. Everyone else can weave in and out of traffic, find their own damn route. I stay in my lane. Only this isn't something I can research. I tried.

Google was fucking useless.

I typed *how to keep a wife happy when you don't talk to her* in the search bar, and the first result was to *communicate with your spouse*. So much for artificial intelligence. Maybe Alexa has better answers.

This is simple. She needs to show up at the wedding. That's the only hurdle right now. Once we say "I do," I assume her good Catholic values—drilled into her little mafia-princess brain—will make it hard for her to opt for divorce. Sure, Papa dangled it in front of her, but divorce is still a naughty word in devout Catholicism.

I go to church on Sundays. No offense to the Big Man upstairs, but I don't believe in religion. I don't voice that, either, in case that whole smite you where you stand thing is real.

But divorce? That's the ultimate bad omen.

Once she's married, she won't be so easily swayed. She'll take those vows seriously. *Until* death, *do us part.*

Fuck. I hope she doesn't kill me. I have code to write.

And fine. I can *try*—and I use that word loosely—not to be a complete asshole for a few days. That's about all I can offer, though, because I am an asshole, and if this woman is stupid enough to marry me, she needs to accept *exactly* what I am.

Even if I have to dangle a bit of hope in front of her first. Just enough to get her to chase the carrot.

Until she's mine.

Legally, at least.

Allie

I TAP MY PEN against my notepad, staring at the latest crime scene that is my recipe.

Cocoa powder? Check. Still tastes like disappointment? Double check.

The list of ingredients before me is a war zone—crossed out, rewritten, rewritten again because it's not right now matter what I try.

Maybe it's time to wave the white flag.

Or maybe, just maybe, I'm not exactly in the right headspace to be testing new recipes.

Could have something to do with the fact that I'm getting married tomorrow. *Married*. As in legally tied to another human being until death do us part, and if things keep going the way they are, that death part is looking real enticing. His, not mine. I have things to do, places to see, people to meet. None of which I would assume he has tucked under "life goals."

Right now, I'm free. Kind of. Sure, I'm in the Don's kitchen, but at least in here, I can pretend I have some semblance of control over my life.

Meanwhile, my future husband—the human embodiment of a walking *Do Not Disturb* sign—avoids me like I might literally carry The Black Death.

I haven't even seen the house where I'll be living. That little fun fact punched me right in the pride when Sienna—Dom's wife, the actual personification of a Disney princess—tagged along while I shopped for bedroom furniture. For *my* bedroom. Singular. Not *ours*.

She frowned the entire time, and I knew why. She kept asking—*Why separate rooms?*—and I couldn't lie to her, not outright, so I danced around the topic. Why they hadn't told her this was an arranged marriage I'll never know, but I would not break her heart. She was too sweet and giddy about the fact Rico found a wife.

The real humiliation came when I went to pay, and they asked where to deliver it.

I had no answer. Not a clue. Didn't even know my address.

So there I stood, my soul physically leaving my body, while Sienna—bless her sweet, all-knowing heart—stepped in and provided the address to my *own* future home.

Is this my future? A lifetime of playing twenty questions with myself because my husband won't even text me back?

Oh yeah, let's talk about that.

Rico, my dear fiancé, has yet to respond to a single message, including my very reasonable suggestion that we go to dinner before, you know, legally binding ourselves together for the rest of our natural-born lives.

To get to know each other.

To talk like normal people who are about to merge tax returns.

But no. Apparently, Rico has bigger things to do, like being a cryptid and communicating exclusively through short, passive-aggressive stares.

I can't stop thinking about the vows. How we won't even be saying our own. Just the standardized, paint-by-numbers wedding vows the priest will make us repeat.

We even rehearsed the wedding already. *Without* Rico.

His entire family didn't look shocked. Not even a little. But the pity? Oh, the pity was real.

Each of them gave me the same tight-lipped smile, the kind that said, *Sorry it's like this*, their eyes flickering with a sympathy I didn't want or need as I walked down the aisle—practicing my wedding to a ghost—while Rico's cousin stood in for him.

Tonight is the last rehearsal, but what's left to rehearse? I'm marrying a man with all the warmth of a high-functioning Roomba. This wedding isn't a romantic celebration—it's a glorified business transaction with vows thrown in for legal purposes.

I planned everything down to the molecular level. My dream wedding, the picture-perfect event I always imagined.

As long as I mentally edit the reality of him out of my future, I can stomach this. I picture myself in a beautiful home, taking care of it how I want. Maybe working a job I actually enjoy. Having kids. Creating a life on my own terms.

It's all perfect—until I remember I don't get to do any of it solo. He'll still be there in some form, lurking around the edges of my peace, the unwelcome spirit of a relative who refused to move on and now haunts the hallways muttering about duty and heir production.

And then there's the part that's been eating away at me, slowly eroding my resolve like the ocean chipping away at the cliffs. Mama isn't here.

Not once has she shown up to help me pick a dress, argue over cake flavors, or offer unsolicited motherly wisdom I would pretend to ignore but secretly take to heart. The version of my wedding that lived in my head for years had her in it, and now, she's not even taking my calls. Neither is Papa.

Not even Rico's parents—who have the patience of saints, considering they raised him—could convince them to answer the phone.

I knew they'd be mad, but this? Their only daughter is getting married, and their response is radio silence? That's cold. Even for Papa, a man who has spent most his life making legally questionable choices.

It makes everything feel even less real.

Not only do I not have my parents, but let's be honest—my husband won't really be a husband.

Violet, ever the optimist, keeps telling me Rico is a good guy, even if he doesn't know how to show it.

Yeah. I'll believe it when I see it, sista.

And then there's Papa Ricardo's generous six-month escape clause. *"If you're not happy, you have my blessing to divorce. I promise."*

Instead of relief, that statement hit like a brutal dose of reality.

Because let's be honest—I won't be happy in six months.

I'll have my freedom from the Cosa Nostra. No longer Alessandra De Luca. No longer a pawn in my father's power plays. I'll be Alessandra Bennetti, a woman who can get a job, leave the house when she wants, make real friends.

But will I be happy?

No.

I scratch out the latest failed addition to my recipe and shove the notepad aside.

The clock reminds me I have an hour before I need to be at the church. A gorgeous church, white and grand, complete with towering pillars and breathtaking stained glass. The reception will be just as stunning. The wedding of my dreams.

Except for the minor detail that I'd rather have a root canal without anesthesia than actually go through with it.

A knock at the front door pulls me from my downward spiral, and I already know who it is—Violet.

Over the past few weeks, I've grown close to both her and Sienna, two of the few people who haven't looked at me with pity eyes while trying to convince me that Rico's behavior isn't personal—it's just him.

Great. So I'm marrying a man-shaped glitch in the Matrix.

Violet offered to go with me to the rehearsal tonight, probably because she's seen the defeat on my face every time I send Rico an invitation, hoping he'll actually show up this time.

He doesn't.

So I go alone. Again.

I stand there like a loser, running through the motions while Rico's cousin Eddie fills in for him because even attending the rehearsal is too much of a commitment for the man I'm about to marry.

I try not to let it get to me.

Just get through the wedding.

Get the job.

Things will get better, Allie.

That's what I keep telling myself.

"One second, Vi!" I yell, scrambling to grab my clutch and dig through the black hole of my purse for my phone. I don't know why I bother checking. Seven messages. *Seven*. And Rico hasn't responded to a single one today or any day for that matter. Not a thumbs-up, not a *k*, not even an emoji to mock me.

At this point, it's on me. I'm like one of those tragic romance heroines who refuses to learn her lesson, clinging to hope when the very silent man she's about to marry has made it abundantly clear that texting me back is not, nor will it ever be, on his to-do list.

With a deep sigh, I shove the phone back in my purse and make a beeline for the door, reveling in the fact that I'm wearing normal human clothing for once. Goodbye designer dresses and ankle-snapping stilettos. Hello, skinny jeans, cozy sweater, and flats that don't make me contemplate sawing off my feet at the end of the day.

I fling the door open. "Sorry, I know I said I'd meet you downst—"

My words die a quick, unexpected death because the shoes in front of me are not Violet's. Nope. Those are leather loafers. And they belong to someone far too tall and way too male.

My gaze travels upward in slow motion, like I'm in a horror movie realizing the call is coming from inside the house. And then—boom—all the air is violently ejected from my lungs.

Rico.

Standing at my door. In the flesh.

"What the—" I blink. "Are you real? Or did I inhale too much cocoa powder earlier and now I'm hallucinating?"

I glance around the hallway, half-expecting a gotcha moment, like my life is some elaborate prank show and any second now a camera crew is going to pop out.

But no. It's just Rico, standing there with his usual blank, emotionally bankrupt expression, scanning me from head to toe.

Great. If he actually spoke to me, he'd know I switched up my wardrobe weeks ago. But I don't say that. What's the point?

"What are you doing here?" I fold my arms, aiming for my best *oh, now you acknowledge my existence?* look.

His jaw tightens for half a second before relaxing. And then—is that a smile? No, it can't be. But there's something suspiciously close to one flickering on his lips. Like he's trying, but it's painful. Possibly life-threatening.

"Taking you to the rehearsal."

I stare at him. Blink twice. "The rehearsal?"

The corners of his mouth twitch again. Okay, what the hell is happening? Rico Bennetti, trying to smile? If I had a bingo card for this engagement, I never would have marked this box.

"It's in an hour," he says, glancing at his watch, then back at me, looking confused. Which is ironic, because I am the one who should be confused. "Right?"

"Right." I nod slowly, stepping out into the hall and closing the door behind me, still waiting for him to answer. "But why are you here?"

He tilts his head like I'm the one not making sense. "We're getting married tomorrow."

He says it so matter-of-factly, like it's just another calendar reminder. Trash day, oil change, marry the woman I've barely spoken to.

I squint at him. "Wow. I'm honestly surprised you knew."

I push past him toward the elevator. I'd be thrilled to know anything about where we'll live after tomorrow, but that would require my fiancé to communicate, and I'm guessing his words-per-day quota maxes out at ten.

He falls into step beside me, all tall, silent, and broody—which is apparently his brand—and that's when it hits me.

The scent.

Woodsy. Citrus. A little sinful.

He smells like a forest took a shower in luxury cologne, and it's completely unfair. I glance sideways, instantly irritated that he's both infuriating *and* smells like temptation bottled.

Seriously?

Out of all the things he could be good at—like, I don't know, talking to his future wife—he nailed "smelling like sex and secrets." Meanwhile, I'm over here mentally sending hate mail to Marco Bennetti for marrying me off to a man who won't make eye contact, barely speaks, and *still* somehow smells like the beginning of toe-curling mistakes.

"Could this elevator be any slower?" I groan, practically vibrating with frustration. If there was ever a time for an elevator to drop a few floors faster than usual, it's now.

Why is he here? No, really—*why?* I spent the last two weeks begging the universe, praying to whatever wedding gods exist, and throwing pennies into fountains, hoping he'd acknowledge me. And now that he has?

I hate it.

Rage bubbles up inside me because I finally realized how pathetic I've been. *Twenty* days of waiting. *Twenty* days of checking my phone. *Twenty* days of hoping my fiancé—the man I'm legally binding myself to tomorrow—would remember I exist.

What does that say about my future?

Nothing good, that's for damn sure.

"Why are you here?"

"Rehearsal." Truly, a robo caller's voice would be warmer than his right now.

"I know we have a rehearsal. But you haven't shown up for anything before this, so let's try again. Why are you here? Here, at my apartment. Here, talking to me. Hell, why are you even going to the rehearsal? Do you even know what time we're getting married?"

The elevator dings, and I launch myself inside, slamming the button for the lobby—only for his arm to move past mine, hitting it before I can.

That's when it happens. His arm barely brushes against mine, and the man jerks away like I'm some radioactive mutant he accidentally touched and now needs to schedule an emergency decontamination.

Tears prick at the corners of my eyes. Nope. We are not doing this. I will not cry over a man who gives me the warmth of an Excel spreadsheet.

I press my lips together, willing myself to swallow down the lump in my throat. *I can't do this. I can't.*

He doesn't talk to me. He doesn't look at me. And now, apparently, the thought of touching me is too much for him.

Maybe I am that hideous. Maybe I've been lying to myself my entire life.

At least back in the mafia, I was wanted. Sure, not for good reasons, but you don't realize how much weight you put behind people wanting you—until no one does.

It hurts.

Like a slow, festering wound that won't heal.

"I can't do this." The words tumble out, barely above a whisper, but they feel final. Like a decision I should have made weeks ago.

Beside me, Rico freezes. Which is impressive, because I already thought his default state was a motionless statue. But now? He's really not moving.

I see him turn his head slightly in my peripheral vision, but I keep my eyes locked on the floor numbers, willing this elevator to hurry the hell up. Ten more to go.

"Vinnie's waiting for me downstairs," I continue, my voice steadier than I feel. "He'll take me to the rehearsal. There's no need for you to go."

Because why would he? What's the point? We could just sign the damn marriage certificate and call it a day. I could stand up there alone, in my dream dress, and at least that would be less humiliating than standing across from a man who refuses to see me.

He probably won't even grab my hand during the vows. Definitely won't kiss me.

And that's just the wedding.

A nice little preview of what my actual life will look like: empty, silent, alone.

"It's my wedding too," Rico says, almost offended. As if this jerk cares.

That asshole.

I whirl on him, not even caring that the first tear has finally broken free, sliding down my cheek. Screw it. Let him see what it looks like when you treat someone like a damn ghost.

"Why now?" My voice cracks, but I push through. "You haven't given a single shit about this wedding. Your cousin had to stand in for you at the last rehearsal, and honestly? He was more appealing to be around than you. At least he smiled—even if it was a pity smile. Do you know how embarrassing it is to have my fiancé ignore my texts? To not even know where I'm about to live?"

I wipe at my cheek, frustration morphing into something raw. Something I don't want him to see, but here we are.

"You avoid me. You flinch when you touch me. Do I really disgust you that much?"

Silence.

Just... silence.

I shake my head. "Yeah, fine. Don't answer. Don't bother coming tonight either. There's no point in you standing there looking at me like you regret everything. I can do that all by myself."

Rico

FUCK.

I wasn't avoiding her specifically. I avoid all people. It's a full-time job. But if we're being honest—and we are, because lying to myself would be redundant—I've made an extra effort to sidestep Allie De Luca like she's a landmine with a countdown timer.

Not because I care. No, that would imply feelings, and I don't do those. It's just that every time she's within a ten-foot radius, my body—traitorous and downright stupid—reacts in ways I have no interest in analyzing.

A single glance, a stray thought, and suddenly, I'm experiencing foreign sensations, like tingling and shuddering. Not exactly a symptom of repulsion, which is *exactly* the problem.

So, I've chosen the reasonable solution: avoidance. Until my body regains its senses and remembers that I am, in fact, not interested, she needs to stay the hell out of my airspace.

She doesn't know my past, and my family hasn't told her. They never do. It's one of those unspoken rules—like never asking Nonna how much wine she's had or questioning Alex's life choices when he broke it off with Violet. We refer to it as "the incident," then promptly move on to happier topics, like real estate acquisitions, and why Luca should never be allowed near the kitchen.

But then I touched her. By accident. Instinct. And the look on her face when I recoiled made me want to kick my own teeth in. I rarely regret how people react to me—it's a survival tactic—but the flash of hurt in her eyes made me, ever-so-briefly, feel like an epic ass.

Now I have to at least pretend to be pleasant so she doesn't run before we make it to the altar. Then again, maybe I should let her go. Maybe she should reconsider. I am who I am, and there's zero chance I'm changing, and this woman has that flicker of hope that she could be the one to change what will never bend.

Alex suggested I marry Tori instead. She's batshit crazy enough to say yes without me having to fake a personality to coax her down the aisle. Just flash a black Amex, and she'd be picking out napkin colors before I could blink. But the thought of sharing a bed with Tori Valencia? Yeah, no. Some crazy women have that appeal—the kind that makes you overlook the insanity because the sex is worth the psychiatric bills. Tori isn't one of them. She's all lunatic, no reward.

And now my fiancée is crying.

I don't handle crying adults. Babies, sure. They have an excuse—they're helpless. Adults? No idea. Normally, I'd walk away, but we're trapped in this fucking elevator with six floors to go and an entire evening ahead, where my family will look at me like I've joined the circus because I'm voluntarily showing up to this rehearsal.

For her.

So, I do the only thing I can think of. I grab her hand, lacing my fingers through hers. Her skin is soft, her hand warm, and the contact sends an unwelcomed jolt right up my forearm. I clench my free hand into a fist, flexing and releasing, forcing myself to stay in control. I've never held an adult's hand. My nieces and nephews little sticky hands? Sure. But not a silky, warm hand like hers.

You have to touch her, you jackass. She's your fucking wife. Besides, the contract literally says to hold her hand in public. Quit being a coward and deal with it.

Her body stiffens, her fingers lying limp in mine, and I can't decide if she's trying not to flinch or waiting for me to let go. I give her hand a light squeeze, inhaling slowly, steadying myself even as my chest tightens.

She's alive. I'm barely breathing.

And I need to figure out why the hell that bothers me.

"I'm taking you to rehearsal." I say for no other reason than to fill the silence. Again, not something I normally do, but here I am holding hands and speaking to someone I would rather be at least three states apart from.

The elevator doors slide open, Vinnie standing there like a human roadblock. His gaze immediately drops to where my hand is wrapped around Allie's. Yeah, I get it. I'm surprised too. Desperate times and measures and all that bullshit going on.

She tries to pull away, but I tighten my grip and tug her back. Her hazel eyes dart between our hands and my face, searching for an answer. For once, she doesn't seem to have one. Interesting. If this is all it takes to shut her up, I might start holding her hand every minute.

"Uh... I suppose we're ready to go?" Vinnie's looking at her when he says it, not me. Like I've got her on some kind of hostage transport, and he's waiting for the signal to take me out and stage a rescue.

Vinnie, much like his brother, is a beast in human form—massive, dark-haired, built like he was sculpted in a war zone. But unlike his brother, he only offers smiles to one person, and it's not me.

Allie starts toward him, but I tug her back. "You're riding with me."

Those wide, Bambi eyes squint while she's trying to decode some hidden agenda. *Good luck with that, Princess.* I've spent years ensuring people only see what I allow them to, and what I allow is nothing.

"Riding with you?" Her enthusiasm is what you'd expect if I offered her a seat on a roller coaster built by a drunk contractor. Can't tell if she's horrified or intrigued, and I'm not invested enough to find out.

"Yes. My car's out front."

"You drive?"

I nod.

"Vinnie will follow."

She stops short, tries to yank her hand away again. Tiny little thing, as if my hand doesn't swallow her fingers entirely. I don't let go. Does she not get that I'm making a point here? Jesus.

"Vinnie goes with me," she argues.

"Only two seats."

Her head tilts, baring the long, delicate line of her throat. Would she like my hand there? Or would she knee me straight in the balls? My money's on the balls. This one may be a princess, but she's no pushover.

Hell, she requested to leave the Cosa Nostra. That alone gives her more balls than ninety percent of the men still loyal to it. Maybe even ninety-five.

"How do you plan to take our kids around in a two-seater car?"

I'll worry about our metaphorical kids and the logistics of driving them as soon as you're knocked up. I shrug.

I glance at my watch and grunt.

I should be anywhere but here. Preferably in my office, hunting down the hacker who's fucked with me like an irritating mosquito that won't die. Instead, I'm about to waste an entire evening surrounded by people, pretending to give a shit about a rehearsal for a wedding that feels about as real as my interest in socializing.

We're going to be late. Late to something I already don't want to attend.

"Let's go." I tug her toward the door where the doorman holds it open for us. I nod as we pass through and kick myself. I never nod. I just don't give a shit to bother with it, and here I am nodding. What's next? A *"thanks man,"* with a shoulder pat for good measure?

Vinnie gives us both a once-over. Not because he's worried I'll hurt her. He trusts me about as much as I trust the general population—not at all. No, he trusts his brother's opinion of me. Antonio has been my older brother's shadow for years, and we all knew he had a younger brother in the Cosa Nostra, but I never thought it would come full circle like this. Vinnie, out of the mafia, now playing watchdog for my soon-to-be wife.

Open the door for her like Mama taught you. Even if you think it's stupid.

I yank the passenger door open, and those wide, curious eyes blink up at me. Yeah, I know. Didn't expect me to do it. Her instincts are correct—I don't normally. Women want equality in every way unless it comes to opening doors or carrying groceries. The equal opportunity act mysteriously expires in those moments. *Yes, I'm that much of an asshole, but at least I admit it, unlike 99.9% of the male population.*

She slides in without a word, the city lights catching the amber flecks in her irises. Green and gold and brown—pearlescent, almost. A rare beauty, pure and untarnished.

Pearlina.

I nod at Vinnie, who looks like he'd rather chew glass than leave her alone with me, but he still gets into his black sedan rental.

I round the car and slide into the driver's seat.

My car is a sanctuary—one of the few places I think clearly. You have no choice when you're stuck in Manhattan traffic for hours. It's think or develop a savage urge to commit vehicular manslaughter.

Checking my watch again, I exhale sharply. Five minutes late. Unacceptable.

I start the Porsche, letting the purr of the engine settle in my chest. My grip tightens on the steering wheel as I inhale a slow, measured breath before pulling into traffic.

Allie sits stiffly beside me, her hands clasped so tightly in her lap that her knuckles go bone-white. She doesn't speak. Doesn't look at me. The silence stretches, and I try to convince myself I like it.

I don't.

Not because I want to hear her voice, but because silence lets my mind wander. And my mind? Not a safe place to be.

I flick on the sound system. The fast, erratic rhythm of a piano solo floods the car. Not that flowery classical bullshit that sounds like a lullaby—this is the piano playing that belongs to a man with a death wish, pounding the keys like he's on a caffeine overdose or in the middle of an existential crisis. Chaotic. Angry. Perfect.

I don't turn to look at her, but I feel the weight of her stare burning into the side of my face.

Yeah, I get it. Not what she expected.

Her expression flickers with something I can't place. But what sticks with me is that the moment I let go of her hand, my fingers didn't immediately flex and unclench the way they usually do after touching someone.

Instead, my palm felt empty. Cold.

And for a split second—one I refuse to analyze—I wanted it back.

Allie

THE MOMENT RICO PULLS up to the church, he sticks his hand in my face.

I blink at it. What is this supposed to be?

A high-five? A weird power move? A poorly executed magic trick?

Assuming it's his caveman way of telling me to stay put, so I lean back in my seat and let him do...whatever this is. He jumps out, stalks around the front of the car like a man on a mission, then yanks my door open and—boom—there it is again.

The hand.

Silent. Insistent. Suspiciously polite.

What is this? A thing now? Are we suddenly a couple that holds hands in public? Because last I checked, the man gripping my fingers like a contractually obligated lover had spent the last three weeks ghosting me harder than a bad Tinder date.

I hesitate. His face is its usual blend of cold indifference, an emotionless wall of 'fuck off' energy, so I have zero clues about what's happening here.

Fine. Two can play this game.

I slide my hand into his. It's no big deal. Sure, I *don't* feel that jolt of something traitorous up my arm, and no, I *will not* think about what it means. I have enough to decode this evening as it is. The moment his fingers curl around mine, warm and strong, my stomach turns into a cage fight between a hundred caffeinated butterflies. I need a bouncer in there, stat.

But then—*oh no*—he doesn't let go.

Instead, Rico shuts the door, locks the car, and keeps holding my hand like we're a *normal* couple who do *normal* couple things. We are so far from normal it doesn't share the same zip code as us. What's his game?

I'm convinced I'm hallucinating. It's not like I've gotten much sleep lately—thanks to him and the stress levels he's cranked up times ten. So maybe this is my little crazy mirage, or I'm dreaming. I'd pinch myself, but my hand is occupied.

Just to test my reality, I decide to not hold back. I don't let my hand go all limp-noodle like in the elevator when he pulled that unexpected squeeze maneuver. Nope. I engage. Give it a little flex. Rub my pointer finger across one of his, even if it's making my skin ignite. He doesn't enjoy being touched. So why not see if he notices?

He does...and he still doesn't let go.

What is happening?

I keep walking, but the man's legs are the length of a commercial airliner's runway, and I'm out here hustling just to keep up. Three steps to his one. I might as well be power-walking. If this were three weeks ago, I'd be sprinting in stilettos and praying my ankles didn't file for divorce. Flats? Best decision I've ever made. My feet, previously plotting a coup, have now called off their revolution.

Unfortunately, I seem to be faster clicking away in heels than running in ballet flats. Go figure.

We reach the stairs of the chapel, where we're supposed to get married, and Vinnie is already lingering behind us, watching and waiting for whatever might leap out — like my fiance's personality.

And suddenly, it all hits me.

I'm standing outside a church, hand-in-hand with my fiancé, a man I've barely seen in the last three weeks, heard from even less, and exchanged fewer words with than my distant cousin in Italy—who, by the way, only calls once every two years.

And now, we're supposed to stand in front of a priest and pretend like this whole thing isn't absolutely absurd?

The urge to break into hysterical laughter is strong.

But I swallow it down because if I laugh, I might not stop.

Father Alberti stands at the door, looking every bit the part of a man pushing eighty—gray and white hair slicked back, sterling-gray eyes, and a face full of wrinkles that somehow glow when he smiles. Except right now, he's not smiling.

Nope, the moment his gaze lands on Rico, his entire body stiffens like he just saw a ghost, eyes wide, mouth slightly agape.

"Rico..." he starts, but the sentence dies somewhere between his throat and the pearly gates.

It's not fear. No, it's shock. Pure, unfiltered *Rico Bennetti is voluntarily at a church shock.*

Welcome to my world, Father. No one knows how to handle it. Least of all me.

"I am glad you came, son." His voice is gracious, full of sincerity, as he lifts a hand to pat Rico's shoulder.

Rico jerks back rapidly, recoiling like he just got hit with a cattle prod. Father Alberti barely reacts, just gives him a knowing nod. "Apologies. I forget sometimes."

"It's fine," Rico says, though his tone makes it clear it's not.

My mind, however, is now a runaway train of questions. *Why doesn't he like to be touched? Trauma? A lifelong aversion to human interaction? Was he programmed this way, a mix of half-robot, half-statue, with just enough humanity to be annoyingly attractive?*

Because let's be clear, this whole brooding, cold, untouchable thing? Way too hot for my sanity. Then again, I'm thinking I'm not all that rational to begin with.

I always imagined my future husband would be adoring—whispering sweet nothings in my ear, bending over backward to treat me like a queen. Instead, I've somehow ended up handcuffed (*figuratively*, not yet *literally*, but there's still time) to a man who broods for sport, talks in monosyllables, and looks like he has an allergy to physical contact.

"Thank you for hosting us one more time," I say to Father Alberti, who beams at me and then pats my cheek. Like I'm five. Like I'm some adorable little princess instead of a fully grown, tax-paying adult. Okay, so I've never paid taxes, but I also never had an income.

I ought to be agitated. But honestly? It's more warmth than I've gotten from the man holding my hand, so I'll take it.

Apparently, you can leave the Cosa Nostra, but you'll still forever be treated like a delicate little mafia princess. Even by the neutral ones, like Father Alberti. Sure, he's *technically* Switzerland, but let's not pretend the "family's" generous pockets did not n't fund him.

The moment we step inside the chapel, I come to a sudden stop—so fast that Vinnie, who was walking right behind me, smacks into my back. Hard.

I let out a startled *oomph*, Vinnie's arm instantly circling my waist to keep me from face-planting in the house of God. And Rico? Oh, he notices.

His hand tightens around mine, grip firm, gaze laser-focused on exactly where Vinnie is touching me.

A flicker of something—something sharp, something possessive—crosses his face before Vinnie mutters a quick, "My bad," and lets go.

Jealousy? Doubtful. But a girl can fantasize.

The chapel is dead silent. And not in the holy, reverent kind of way.

His entire family is looking at him like he just grew a second head, which means this is *not* normal behavior for him.

But let's not kid ourselves—he didn't come for me.

Nope. This isn't some grand romantic gesture. He's just making sure I don't bolt before the wedding. Probably caught wind that I'd been having second thoughts and slapped some metaphorical handcuffs on me in the form of showing up. It will take better manipulation tactics than that. I grew up in a world where you learned to exploit things in your favor by four.

The more significant worry here is Violet or Sienna definitely blabbed.

Never drink four glasses of wine and then tell your two newly minted best friends you might not go through with a wedding. Because one of them is married to his brother, and apparently, loose lips sink my plans.

Sure, I've entertained a few escape fantasies involving a stolen motorcycle, a fake passport, and a discreet relocation to a country where no one knows my name. But after drafting an extensive pros and cons list—complete with a gray area column, because Violet swears by it (seriously, she used the same method to name her kids)—I concluded.

The pros? *Freedom.*

The cons? *Being legally tied to a man who avoids me like I'm a telemarketer calling about his car's extended warranty.*

The gray area? That held the strength of a high-powered Dyson sucking up most of my list items. Which, frankly, was not helpful.

So, here I am. Marching toward a future that may or may not include a divorce, but at least it means I get out. And if Ricardo—er, Papa, because apparently, that's what I'm expected to call him now—is serious about giving me an out after six months, then I have a safety net.

I don't love Rico. I don't even *like* him. Hard to like a man you barely know.

Favorite color? No clue. Food preferences? Who knows? Blood type? Well, in the Cosa Nostra, that's kind of important since, you know, gunshot wounds happen. Not *if*, but *when* situations.

But one thing I know?

Rico Bennetti will *never* love me. And that's a reality I need to get cozy with now.

"Rico!" Rico's mother clutches her chest like she's *this close* to fainting, then barrels through the small crowd and flings her arms around him like he's been lost at sea for a decade.

And here's the kicker: the man flinches. *Actually flinches.* Like physical contact burns him, but he's too polite (or dead inside) to yank himself away from his mother. He barely returns the hug, one arm stiffly patting her back, while his other hand crushes mine in a grip so tight I'd like to remind him that bones are fragile.

Regardless, even though he's incredibly uncomfortable, the man *can* and *will* hug. Under the ideal circumstances, at least.

Cecilia—whom I've also been told to only call Mama—pulls away, pressing a hand to her heart. "Right, sorry, Rico. I just got so excited when I saw you."

Excited? Really? Is this man a rare sighting? Should we alert National Geographic?

It's not just me. He avoids touching everyone.

And no one will tell me why.

Violet and Sienna swear it's something he has to tell me. That it's not chatted about in the family. That I'll understand when he's ready to share.

Which is adorable, truly, because this man doesn't share. He barely speaks. At this rate, I'll learn his tragic backstory from a carrier pigeon before he voluntarily tells me himself.

And just like that, he drops my hand and walks off.

Not a single word.

Not an ounce of shock from me either while we are at it.

Violet and Sienna creep up beside me.

"Did you bribe him?" Violet whispers.

I snort. "Nope. I answered my door, expecting you, and *boom*, there he was."

Which reminds me. "Where were you?"

"Alex told me you were riding with Rico, so we came alone."

"Okay, no bribes," she allows, "but, like... he *doesn't* come to things. Wedding-related or otherwise."

She winces, then promptly plasters on a smile like that somehow softens the truth, even if we both know there's a high probability he doesn't show tomorrow.

"Sorry! I just meant... he's not really a family gathering kind of guy. But I promise he'll be there tomorrow. I mean, he comes to family stuff, but not all of it. The kids' birthdays he never misses, but there are times he's just...Rico. But for your wedding, he will be there. I promise."

Only now her voice wobbles a little. And that wobble sparks one very troubling thought:

Is there a chance he won't show up?

Am I about to be the bride who gets left at the altar by the silent man?

Oh, that would officially be rock bottom. No coming back from that one.

"But!" Violet chirps, chipper as ever, like a woman who did not just say my fiancé is a habitual no-show. "He came tonight! Sooo, progress, right?"

She pops her shoulders up, smiling—forcing it, if I had to guess—while her eyes dart between Rico and me like she's trying to manifest good vibes.

Father Alberti shuffles up behind us, placing a cold, frail hand on my shoulder. "Ah, seems we're all here."

He moves between us, making his way toward Rico, who's already deep in conversation with his brothers — again, only more evidence the bastard *can* talk. But...not to me.

"Let's begin," the priest announces, then fixes a pointed look at Rico, lips pressing into a thin line. "And remember, after tonight, no seeing your bride. It's bad luck."

Oh, please.

I barely hold back a snort, but thanks to years of being trained to be gracious and proper in public, I keep it bottled up.

Because let's be real: Rico has zero plans of seeing me tonight, or any night after this, unless enforced.

Hell, I wouldn't be shocked if someone has to tow him to the wedding tomorrow.

Because that's what this is. A transaction. A deal.

I get my freedom.

He gets to please his parents with an inheritance bonus.

That's it.

And that's all it will ever be.

Rico

Now I KNOW WHY I avoid rehearsals. Or, more accurately, why I avoid groups of people altogether.

My brothers had rehearsals for their weddings, and despite being a groomsman, I conveniently neglected to show up. What's the point? Walking is a skill most toddlers master before their second birthday. Standing still? I've been perfecting that art for most of my adult life. I don't need a practice run.

And yet, here I am.

We made it through the rehearsal, my pulse ticking up every time I had to touch Allie. Holding her hands while the priest droned on from his little book, repeating vows like a script from a play I never auditioned for. Pretending to place a ring on her finger. Pretending that any of this is authentic.

My eyes linger on the engagement ring Marco picked out for her—gaudy, yet elegant. Not the ring I would have chosen, but then again, I didn't *choose* any of this, did I?

I didn't even pick out the wedding bands. I skipped every opportunity to give my input, too uninterested to care. Now, I'm kicking myself. I should be indifferent. And yet, I wonder what they look like. What it'll feel like sliding it onto her finger. The more I touch her hands—since apparently, getting married requires far more physical contact than I was led to believe—the less my insides shudder.

Then comes the part that makes my stomach turn.

Father Alberti wraps up with a *yada, yada fill-in-the-blank* speech and reminds me that, tomorrow, I will kiss my bride.

Right.

A few glaring problems with that.

First—crowds.

I hadn't really considered how many people would be here until now. Someone fully decorated the church with flowers, ribbons, and runners. They've set up the pews, and judging by the looks of it, someone will occupy every single one I don't care to know or talk to. Allie's immediate family might be a no-show, but that doesn't mean we won't have a full house. Bennettis. Friends. Business associates. A nightmare buffet of eyes. *On me.*

Second—the *kiss.*

Why the hell does a kiss seal a marriage? Who came up with that? I've signed business deals worth billions with nothing but a handshake, and yet I'm supposed to stamp a lifelong contract with a kiss?

After the priest finishes, I exhale heavily, then I look at Allie.

Her face is unreadable. That serene smile she's been forcing all night? Gone.

"Right, well, thank you for coming. I'll see you tomorrow."

And then she turns—walks away—straight over to Violet and Sienna.

And just like that, I get two simultaneous death glares from my sisters. The look that would make their husbands sweat through their expensive suits.

I don't sweat. I have a spine.

Still.

They're pissed. Which means *she's* pissed.

And if Allie's pissed...

Was tonight not enough?

I get a quick bump on the shoulder, but my brother knows better than to go for a full clap-on-the-back moment.

"So, you came." Dom steps in front of me, completely blocking my view of Allie.

"Yeah."

"Care to tell me why you finally showed up?"

"Had to."

"No, you didn't. You haven't shown up for a single thing. Not a single meeting, not a single tasting, not a single decision. Hell, I helped plan this wedding more than any man should. I'm permanently marred by Pinterest idea boards, just so you know. So, I'll ask again. Why. Are. You. Here?"

My eyes flick past him. Allie is smiling. Not the polite, awkward, *why-am-I-here smile* she reserves for me, but a real one. Genuine. Warm. My sisters are eating it up, surrounding her like she's a new puppy they're adopting.

She doesn't beam like that around me.

They make her happy. They fill the gaps where I sure as hell can't. And I just need to keep up this act for a few more days. Get through the wedding, get through the wedding night, then break it to her that this is it—this is who I am. There's no grand revelation, no hidden romantic underbelly, no secret longing to be transformed by love.

"You said I needed to." I answer.

"And since when have you given two shits about what I think?" Dom stares me down. "Or Alex? Or literally *anyone*?"

Good question. One I don't have an answer for. "I want her down the aisle."

Dom scrubs a hand down his face, exhaustion settling in the fine lines around his eyes. The twin girls are kicking his ass. His fault for spoiling them rotten, one of them already a certified daddy's girl who refuses to sleep unless she's in his arms. He made that monster.

"So, let me get this straight," he starts, and I internally grumble for inviting yet another brotherly lecture. "You're pretending to be someone you're not just to get her to show up at the altar?"

I shrug. "Seems to work."

"Rico..." He sighs, shaking his head. "She's not dumb. She's not going to suddenly think you've had a personality transplant just because you showed up once. She's not gonna fall for it."

She doesn't have to fall for it. She just has to show up.

Good thing this performance is short-lived. I'm already mentally exhausted from the effort, and I'm counting down the minutes until I can return to my usual evening routine: silence, work, and pretending the world doesn't exist.

Last I checked *until death do us part* is the most prominent vow in this whole charade. *Sickness and health* comes in a close second. And I'm already halfway to the emotionally unavailable terminal case, so she's going to have to accept me as is.

Do I feel guilty about faking it just to get her to the altar?

Nope.

Do I want her to at least enjoy her first—and if I have any say in it, *only*—wedding?

Yeah.

I also don't want her to look at me like I'm a complete demon when she realizes she married me.

"It'll be fine." I roll my shoulders back. "She knows who I am. Twenty-four hours of this won't change her mind."

Dom mutters something under his breath, but I ignore it, moving toward Allie.

Violet shoots me a glare that would make most men cower. Too bad for her, I'm immune—unlike her husband.

"Allie."

She turns, eyes meeting mine. I extend my hand, avoiding the obligation hanging there to say something.

Sienna beams while Violet squints at me. She knows this is bullshit.

Allie hesitates for a second, then excuses herself from my sisters and places her hand in mine.

I don't waste time. I lead her to the doors.

"Wait, we can't leave yet." She tugs back slightly, wide-eyed. Almost pleading.

Begging. Pleading. Tears—none of that works on me. She'll figure that out, eventually. Save herself the energy.

"I need to get back to work." I've handed out all I can for tonight. "Besides," I add, like I actually give a damn about tradition, "we can't see each other before the wedding. Right?"

Then, because I figure I might as well commit to the act, I pull her close and press a light kiss to her cheek.

Bad idea.

Her skin is warm. Soft. She smells like vanilla and something floral I can't place, and yet I want to lick it off her and taste it on my tongue.

She sucks in a breath, and for the first time in my entire existence, I nearly forget myself. I nearly let it linger.

Nearly.

Quickly, I pull back and meet her gaze. "See you tomorrow, *Pearlina.*"

Her brows crunch, like she's trying to unscramble my sudden shift in behavior.

Will she show up tomorrow?

She nods. Looks sure about it. But *nodding* and actually *showing* up are two different things.

I release her hand.

My palm feels empty—a-fucking-gain—and I officially despise how holding her hand for mere seconds creates a loss.

Without another word, I turn and stroll out.

Allie

I'M GETTING MARRIED TODAY.

For most brides, this is supposed to be the most joyous day of their lives, right? They're all giddy and glowing, leaping around like caffeinated bunnies, counting down the minutes until they can pledge eternal devotion to the love of their life—or at the very least, a man they like.

Me? I've thrown up three times and am well on my way to a fourth. At this rate, I'm losing more weight than a contestant on a survival show.

Violet, bless her, has somehow pinned my hair into a sophisticated updo despite my repeated sprints to the bathroom. Every time I move too fast, she curses under her breath, threatening to glue my curls in place if I mess them up one more time.

When I'm positive I have nothing left in my stomach, my so-called "bridal squad" forces me into my wedding gown. My bridesmaids—my soon-to-be sisters, Sienna and Violet, and my soon-to-be cousins, Valeria, Gloria, and Alena—are all smiles and sunshine, chattering excitedly as if I'm actually marrying a man who wants to be married to me. They're sweet, welcoming, and warm. The exact opposite of my fiancé.

But hey, if he insists on keeping a ten-foot pole between us at all times, at least I'll have them. That's something. It's just not a marriage.

"Here," Gloria shoves a champagne flute in my hand, the bubbles rising like tiny cheerleaders tormenting me. "You're gonna need liquid courage to make it down that aisle."

She's not mistaken. But unless this flute magically morphs into a full bottle of tequila, it won't be sufficient.

I chew on my lip, staring at the glass, then look up at Violet. "Is my...Papa and Mama out there?"

Her ever-present smile falters. "Not yet," she murmurs.

Not yet.

Which means they presumably aren't coming.

I knew this might happen, but it still stings like hell. Papa was supposed to walk me down the aisle, but ever since I chose my future, they've all but disowned me.

I get it. I do.

Papa operates on a very simple rule—his daughters are his leverage, and I just burned my contract. The second I asked the Don for a way out, I secured my fate in his eyes.

I knew I was betraying him the moment I spoke the words.

But this betrayal? It started long before I had the nerve to ask.

I told Papa when I was twelve that I didn't want to be a mafia princess. I wasn't stupid—I knew the deal. I knew that the moment I turned of age, I'd be married off like a prized mare, my future locked in a handshake between men who'd never asked what I wanted.

And I played along. Because I *thought* I had to.

Until I realized I didn't. Until I found the courage to ask for something different.

And here we are. I'm still walking down an aisle. Still sealing my fate with a ring.

Only instead of Carlo Romano—the greasy, leering substitute—I'm marrying Rico.

Rico, the man who barely looks at me, barely communicates with me, and yet somehow, is still the better option.

Freedom comes with a price tag, right? Well, here's mine.

I chug the champagne, ignoring the way my stomach protests, like a tenant filing a formal complaint with management. No time for digestion concerns—if I'm going through with this wedding, I need something to take the edge off.

Rico was...nice yesterday. *Sort of.* He looked at me. Spoke in actual sentences. Touched me—granted, only in the way a doctor might check a pulse, but progress is progress.

And because I'm a nitwit with a heart that refuses to listen to reason, a flicker of hope keeps trying to bloom in my chest. Maybe once he's forced to be around me—sharing a house, eating dinners together, suffering my presence during our mandatory weekly dates—he *might* thaw. He agreed to my terms, after all. This means at some point, he thought about spending time with me and didn't immediately burst into flames.

Progress. Right?

"I still can't believe this is Rico's wedding," Valeria says, tipping back her fifth flute of champagne with an ease that makes me think she might be immune to alcohol.

I narrow my eyes. "Yeah, well, neither can he."

Gloria adjusts the train of my gown, her fingers smoothing the endless fabric layers. I still can't believe I found *the* dress. The ivory fabric cascades in soft, shimmering waves, catching the light every time I move. The bodice hugs my figure perfectly, with lace appliques trailing like whispers across the fabric. The subtle sweetheart neckline gives it that romantic fairytale touch.

Too bad the man waiting for me at the altar is less *Prince Charming* and more *stoic cyborg with emotional Wi-Fi issues.*

The skirt flows in delicate layers of silk chiffon and tulle, pooling at my feet like something straight out of a bridal fever dream. Tiny hand-sewn pearls and beads glisten like morning dew, and the whole dress sways when I move, a masterpiece of elegance.

It's the dress.

But it's not *the wedding.*

And I'd be a buffoon to pretend otherwise.

"You can still back out, you know." Violet plants herself in front of me, grasping my hands like she's about to stage an intervention. Which, honestly, she should have done three weeks ago.

I force a smile. "Nah. I already paid for the cake." Okay, *Rico did*, but his money is my money in about twenty minutes, since that elegant marriage contract had a rather careless prenup — odd for a man with his wealth.

Her lips press into a flat line, and I don't miss the way she studies me—like she's analyzing an emotionally compromised heroine in one of her novels. Which, to be fair, she is.

She keeps pausing mid-conversation to jab a finger in the air, eyes going wide. "Wait! I need to add this to my notes. This is gold. How did I not think of this before?"

And then she rambles, typing at warp speed, already plotting how to turn my marital horror story into her next bestselling romance minus the horror.

Not sure how I feel about that one.

"Is he... mean?" The words choke out of me before I can stop them. They've been festering in the back of my mind since the moment I met Rico. His entire family keeps their distance. No one touches him, and the man never smiles. I have to know—am I walking into a life of silence, or something much worse?

I'll walk down that aisle. I'll marry him to get out of the Cosa Nostra. I'll say I do to my freedom, not the man standing next to me. But I refuse to escape one prison, only to be locked in another.

Violet's green eyes nearly swell out of her skull. "What?"

I hold her stare, refusing to let the question hang between us. "Is Rico mean? Will he hurt me?"

Silence.

The kind that makes my stomach turn, the champagne I just downed sloshing around like it's looking for an exit.

These women didn't grow up like I did—where husbands *do* beat their wives and the men around them turn a blind eye. Marco Bennetti doesn't tolerate it, but that doesn't mean it *never* happens. It just means no one snitches. No one tells him what he doesn't want to hear. Maybe Rico is the same. Maybe his family keeps their mouths shut because they don't want to admit what he *really* is.

Because every time I've been in his presence, his hands clench into fists, so tight the skin turns bone-white, like he's resisting the urge to snap something. *Or someone.*

Violet tightens her grip on my hands. Gloria stops fussing with my dress. The air clots with something unspoken, and the longer they all stare at each other, the more the panic builds, snaking up my throat.

"No," Violet finally says, her voice tender as silk. "He's not mean. He's just... *Rico.*"

I blink. "What the hell does that mean?"

She looks at the others. Sienna gives me a strange look, as if I should already know the answer to this before asking. But she doesn't seem to understand this is an arrangement, and I'm not about to correct her.

Finally, Violet sighs. "All I know is that there was an... *incident* when he was younger. Alex says it's why he is the way he is, why the family doesn't push him. Except now." She waves at my dress, at the room, at all of *this*, as if I needed a reminder that Rico is being forced into this just as much as I am. "But they give him space because that's what he needs, and he doesn't enjoy being touched, so they make sure not to."

I open my mouth, about to ask how the hell am I supposed to consummate a marriage without touching my husband? But she keeps going.

"Rico's been around my kids, and Sienna's. And he's never been unkind. He may not talk much, or at all, but he's amazing with them. I trust him with my children. They love Uncle Rico. Swear he talks to them, though I think they mistake his grunts and occasional snorts for words." She giggles, then snorts, then stops, realizing now might not be the best time.

Gloria speaks up next. "He's not mean. He's just... detached. And he's been that way since he was a kid. But I've never seen him violent. Outside of the boxing ring with his brothers and Marco, that is. So no, he won't physically hurt you."

Physically.

I don't miss the significance.

"But he could still hurt me in *other* ways."

Violet tugs on my hands, forcing me to look at her. "What she means is that Rico might hurt you unintentionally. If you get attached to him. Because he's not capable of feelings or emotions, at least not in the way you want him to be. If you go into this expecting him to change, expecting him to love you back, you're the one who's going to end up hurt."

I didn't quite picture my wedding day including a *Will my husband hurt me?* discussion, but here we are.

Still, I'm not stupid. I don't plan to fall in love with a man who doesn't want me. I know exactly what I'm signing up for.

And yet...

There's this naïve pinhole in my laboriously constructed walls.

A tiny, troubling speck that refuses to let me believe he's as empty as they say.

Because for all his coldness, all his silence, he gave me *something* yesterday.

There's a knock at the door—soft, hesitant, almost like the person on the other side knows they're walking into a room full of estrogen-fueled nerves.

Dom steps inside, and I take a second to remind myself that *no*, this is not my almost-husband suddenly deciding to show up and be charming. Because that would require emotions and facial expressions, and we all know Rico doesn't do either of those.

Dom? Smiles. Laughs. Uses actual words instead of terrifying blank stares. He's basically a living alternate reality version of what my future husband could be if he wasn't, well... *Rico.*

"You look beautiful, Allie."

I don't know if it's the sincerity in his tone or the fact that, for once, a Bennetti man is looking at me with something other than indifference, but I nearly tear up. Instead, I keep it together and brandish a smile. "Thanks, Dom."

"You ladies ready to waltz down the aisle in fifteen?" He turns to Sienna, but his gaze flicks back to me. Everyone glances at me.

I don't miss how they're all collectively holding their breath, like I'm a spooked horse they're trying not to startle. And sure, I could make a run for it. Could yank up my dress, throw off my heels, and take off down the street like some runaway bride—except this isn't a movie, and Julia Roberts isn't here to help me figure out my life after I take off sneakers and all.

But here's the thing: Rico *is* my ticket out.

And yesterday... he touched me.

A man who allegedly doesn't like to be touched, who flinches when people get too close, held my hand.

It wasn't much. It wasn't love. Hell, it wasn't even affection.

But it *was* something.

And maybe, just maybe, that something is worth walking down that aisle for.

Rico

"You're unbelievable," Alex mutters, fingers tracing the rim of his untouched drink like he's debating whether to hurl it at my face. "A real, genuine prick." My money is on him throwing it in another minute if his attitude doesn't shift.

I glance up from my scotch, indifferent.

Tell me something I don't know. Though, I didn't expect name-calling to be part of the pre-wedding toast. Especially not when I'm already more enthusiastic about undergoing a root canal without anesthesia than standing at the altar, pretending this farce means something.

I fixate on the wall behind Alex—cream-colored, old, the kind of old that comes from slapping paint over outdated wallpaper during a botched budget reno.

Cream like the overpriced ribbons strangling every pew in the chapel. Cream like the espresso foam I drown in coffee to tolerate mornings. Cream like my sanity slowly curdling in the heat of this suffocating room.

I unball my fists, stretching stiff fingers, but the dull ache barely registers. My nerves are taut, frayed like the ancient blue-and-yellow carpet underfoot. It's threadbare, patched in places with what looks like duct tape, like someone figured the groom's waiting room didn't deserve even basic dignity.

Probably the same genius who thought hanging six pictures of Baby Jesus and an ominously large wooden cross would soothe a man investigating every life choice that led him here.

The air is thick and stagnant, like the room itself is holding its breath, waiting to see if I'll bolt. One window, cracked and useless, leaks just enough light to make the dust motes dance. Papa blocks the only exit, seated like a kingpin overseeing a hit, glass in hand, eyes sharp. No fresh air, no escape. Just four walls, one exit, and the crushing weight of tradition and expectation.

Maybe this is God's final exam. Stick the reluctant groom in a windowless box, surround him with judgmental relatives, and see if he cracks. Will he bolt? Pass out? Stand there like a moron and go through with the vows? I hate tests. But I always ace them. Though, in this case, I'm not sure which outcome counts as passing—marriage or escape?

Papa, Alex, and Marco consume the air circulating in this room from hell. Dom left to make sure my bride hadn't bailed. Smart. If anyone was fleeing this circus, the odds were always on her. Alex, though, has apparently appointed himself my personal morality officer, which is laughable coming from a man who once tried to convince me scotch counted as a balanced dinner back when we were younger and our issues didn't involve brides and babies and family commitments.

He crosses his arms, leaning in like proximity will make me care. "I know what you're doing, and I don't like it."

"Doing what?" I take another sip, overlooking the heat of Papa's gaze from the corner.

"Giving that girl false hope. Holding her hand? Showing up for the rehearsal? You either grew a heart overnight—which means hell froze over and the apocalypse is likely—or you're playing nice just to make sure she shows."

Can't fault his logic. Even Marco gave me the side-eye when I walked into the church last night. They know me too well. A man who actively avoids human interaction voluntarily taking part in anything remotely social? Absurd. And yet, there I was, standing beside my bride-to-be, pretending to be halfway decent while my brain screamed at me to get the fuck out.

Lines were crossed last night. Personal boundaries eliminated. I'd touched her—twice. Willingly. And not in the perfunctory, *let's-get-this-over-with* way I'd planned. Her skin had been soft, warm, the touch that messes with your head. It made little sense, and I hated it.

I grit my teeth, jaw tightening as the memory creeps back. If holding her hand for ten minutes made my pulse spike like I'd run a marathon, what the hell would a week of marriage do? A month? Twenty-four hours already feels like a stretch.

When I left rehearsal last night, I spent an hour in my gym abusing the heavy punching bag until my knuckles split. The skin's raw today, irritated and tight. Good. It should be. If I don't exorcise the tension deliberately, it festers, rotting from the inside out until it explodes. And explosions? They don't end well—for me or anyone caught in the blast radius.

The worst part? Holding her hand *wasn't* awful. It was almost comforting, like she thought we were on the same team. Only one issue: I don't do teams. I prefer a functionally detached lifestyle.

Am I giving her hope? Enough to get her down the aisle? Absolutely. Does that make me a bastard? Probably. But survival isn't about kindness. It's about strategy. I needed her facing me, not the door. Mission accomplished.

"You just gonna flip the switch and go back to yourself tomorrow?" Alex drawls from the corner, arms folded like some brooding high school principal gearing up for a lecture.

That was the plan. Obviously.

"She knows who she's marrying." I don't look up from my glass, swirling the amber liquid until it catches the light. "She's not stupid. The way she looked at me last night—like she wanted to throw that gaudy-ass engagement ring at my head—tells me she's under no delusion this is love. I gave her crumbs. Just enough to keep her from bolting. That doesn't mean I'm setting the table."

My options are limited. So are hers. This isn't romance. It's survival with a diamond band.

Dom strolls back into the room, grin fading the second he catches the hostility clotting the air. He clocks Alex's scowl, my stretched-out sprawl on a couch older than me, and the unspoken challenge floating between us.

"How's she holding up?" Alex asks, like I'm not sitting right here. Like it's not *my* fiancée he's checking on.

I *should* be the one asking. But I'm me. So, I don't.

"Nervous," Dom says, gaze snapping between us. "But she said she'd be ready."

His words hang there, waiting for someone to catch them. Neither of us does.

"Problem?" Dom pushes, eyes narrowing.

"Yes," I said deadpan, pushing off the sofa with all the energy of a man heading to his execution. "He's wasting my last minutes of freedom."

Alex doesn't recoil. He's spent years developing immunity to my bullshit. "I'm making sure you understand what you're walking into. You're not just tying yourself to someone. She's tying herself to you. She's moving into your house tonight, Rico. *Your* space. *Your* time? *Gone.* You'll have someone to answer to. Someone who—whether you love her—deserves your respect and protection."

My gaze slides past him to Marco, who's lounging like an emperor, scotch in hand, pompous smile firmly in place. He salutes me with the glass. *Asshole.*

"You're really selling this marriage thing," I mutter, jaw tightening. "I won't disrespect her."

I might be a bastard, but I'm not heartless. I'll respect her. I'll give her space, keep the house running like clockwork, and stay the hell out of her way. But the reminder that she'll be living under my roof, eating meals across from me, expecting a conversation, date nights—*dates, for fuck's sake*—makes my skin itch.

I've never willingly gone on a date in my life. Every single one was Mama-orchestrated, fueled by elaborate guilt trips and cloaked threats about disappointing the family name. And now? Now I'm willingly signing up for a lifetime of them.

Sure, I conceded to her terms. Dinners together. Weekly dates. Occasional, *limited* affection. But *agreeing* doesn't mean *enjoying*. And I never promised words. She can fill the silence, talk until she's blue in the face, and have entire debates with herself while I nod, maybe grunt, and certainly exist — even if it's against my will.

Being a husband doesn't require dialogue. It requires presence. I can do presence. Silent, detached, efficient. Like a ghost in my home. She wanted freedom. I wanted peace.

Let's see which one of us suffocates first.

The fact that my brothers think indifference equals disrespect pisses me off. I might not give two shits about anyone in the romantic sense, but I'm not a complete sociopath. I don't kick puppies or trip old ladies—two things I'm not entirely convinced Marco doesn't do. I'm just chronically selective about who gets access to the mess in my head.

But disrespecting a woman who voluntarily shackled herself to me? Not happening. I'm already miserable enough for both of us. No need to spread that shit around like glitter—impossible to clean up and aggravating as hell.

Marco winks from the corner, swirling his scotch and completely at ease as he grins like a smug bastard my way. The man lives to poke bears. If he ever ends up in a zoo, he'll be the boob dangling a raw steak through the bars, laughing his ass off when the bear inevitably swipes at him. Like he's doing now, daring me to lose my cool.

I won't. My fists might be clenched tight enough to cut off circulation, but I won't give him the pleasure of a broken jaw. He'd wear it like a badge of honor.

"Let me worry about my wife." The word feels foreign, like trying on someone else's clothes. Doesn't itch, and doesn't fit quite right, but it's wearable. Functional.

There's no immediate urge to vomit, which I suppose is a favorable sign.

It also doesn't thaw my cold, dead heart. But I assume you need an actual working one for that first.

Alex scoffs, sharp and humorless. "You do that." Three words, five million meanings, and I catch every damn one. His eyes, glacier-blue and equally wintry, drill into me, judgment wrapped up in brotherly concern. Or disappointment. Hard to tell with him.

Dom glances at his watch like the coward he is. "We should, uh, head out there?" He thumbs toward the door, already inching toward escape.

Papa's faster. He's at the door, hand on the handle, watching me like I'm a ticking bomb and he's the poor bastard assigned to cut the wire. Every man in this room is staring at me, waiting for something—meltdown, revelation, spontaneous combustion. Take your pick.

My stomach churns. Not from nerves. From inevitability. Out there, behind that flimsy wooden door, is a crowd. Pews stuffed with family and acquaintances. *Not friends.* I don't do those. Too much upkeep. Family's exhausting enough, and I can't opt out of that subscription.

Even through the closed door, the hum of conversation leaks in—laughter, soft chatter, the unmistakable buzz of people enjoying themselves. Must be nice. I glance at my glass, the whiskey inside now an amber memory. I down the last, welcoming the burn as it scorches its way down my throat.

It's the only warmth I'll feel today.

Pushing off the couch, I button my jacket, never breaking eye contact with Alex. *Stare all you want, big bro. You won't find a soul to judge in here.*

He's the first to look away. Victory, however small. I tuck it away, savoring it as I stride out the door and into my personal purgatory.

Father Alberti stands at the end of the aisle, decked out in his ceremonial robes, smiling like he's about to baptize a baby, not officiate the union of two people with less chemistry than distilled water. Behind him, a wedding planner's dream board seems to have mushroomed all over the altar—flowers, candles, and unnecessary fabric drape from every conceivable surface.

"Happy day for you, son," Alberti beams.

I glance at him. We clearly have different definitions of *happy*.

Dom, Alex, and Marco fall into place beside me. Dom's tense, Alex looks like he's preparing a bullet point list on why I'm an asshole, and Marco—smug bastard—grins at the fact he's here.

He's in my wedding party and I'm the only one to grant him the honor. The family lunatic standing beside me, while my "normal" brothers watch like they're attending a funeral. Fitting if you think about it.

The thing is, Marco gets it. He understands me better than they ever will. Probably because his moral compass broke years ago, and no one bothered to fix it.

Not sure what it says about me that the most unhinged man in the room is the one I trust most.

Probably nothing positive.

Allie

THE DOUBLE WHITE DOORS leading to the chapel stare me down like they know something I don't. All filigree and stained glass, framed by enough freshly cut flowers to make a florist retire early. The air reeks of roses. Or is that my impending doom? My dress, once light and floaty—like a whimsical, ethereal dream—now feels like it's made of lead.

In front of me stand my bridesmaids, all dressed in lilac. They're smiling, but it's the smile you give someone about to bungee jump without checking the cord. And every single one of them keeps scanning at the exit behind me.

Yeah, same, ladies. Same.

I've side-eyed that door at least five times. How hard would it be to pull a full-on *Runaway Bride?* Dash out, barefoot, veil flying, straight into the limo I know is parked outside. But Julia Roberts had somewhere to run. I don't. The last time Violet checked, my parents weren't even here and I have nowhere to go. That's my reality.

I snort, the sound so loud and unladylike that all five heads whip toward me. I can't help it. Laughter bubbles up and spills out, wild and lawless. The wedding planner looks like she's seconds away from hitting me with a tranquilizer dart. Honestly? I'd welcome it.

I'm crazy. That's the only explanation. Certifiably deranged. I'm about to marry a man who treats conversation like a hostage negotiation and offers touches like they're tax deductible. All for the grand prize of not being shackled to the mafia.

Violet, scribbling notes into her phone like my breakdown is prime content for her next bestseller, wasn't wrong. This is a great story. A genuine mafia princess escapes one prison only to chain herself to the world's grumpiest human in the name of freedom. Someone get Hollywood on the line and I sure as hell better see a royalty check. I'm taking one for the team here.

"I'm sorry," I wheeze, wiping away tears while trying to breathe through the laughter. "I'm fine. It's fine."

"How much champagne did you give her?" Violet hisses at Valeria as if I'm a toddler who got into the liquor cabinet.

"Not enough," I groan, still half-laughing. I should've polished off the entire bottle. Hindsight is a bitch. Liquid courage might be cliché, but clichés exist for a reason. Insert my current situation.

Sienna leans in, eyes wide. "Did someone slip her a happy pill?"

The wedding planner clears her throat, clipboard clutched tight, and she's two seconds from snapping it with tension. "They're... uh... about to start."

Right. Showtime. I suck in a breath, straighten my spine, and face the firing squad.

"Well," I say, flashing the girls a grin that probably borders on unhinged, "let's get this circus on the road."

The music starts, and I step to the side, waiting for the double doors to swing open like I'm a contestant on *The Price Is Right*. Except, instead of running toward a brand-new car, I'm strutting into a marriage with a man who views me like I'm as valuable as an expired coupon.

I glance to my left, to the spot where Papa should be standing. His arm should be out, solid and secure, ready to walk me down the aisle. Instead? Empty. Just me, a fistful of nerves, and the realization that my family officially RSVP'd *hell no* to my wedding.

It's not amusing anymore.

The sarcastic little giggle I'd been holding onto dies a quick death, replaced by the cold slap of reality. This is it. My only trip down the aisle, and I'm doing it solo. No Papa. No Mama. Not even a rogue second cousin who only shows up for free booze and Instagram photo ops.

The pews are packed with Bennettis, all smiling like this isn't a sham stitched together with forced vows and mutual indifference. They're whispering behind programs printed with *Enrico & Alessandra*, like we're some fairytale couple and not two strangers playing house because life backed us into a corner.

And my family? Nowhere. The people who raised me to be the perfect mafia princess bride couldn't be bothered. No handbook, no pep talk, no "Here's how to fake a smile while legally binding yourself to a cyborg." Just radio silence and a gaping hole where familial encouragement should be.

Violet, ever the opportunist, is standing near the front, not-so-discreetly jotting notes on her phone with that stupid little iPen. *I see you, Violet.* Don't think I've missed the way your eyes flick from me to Rico, like we're live-streaming the plot of your next bestseller. If the title ends up being *Married to Mr. Miserable,* I want a cut of the profits.

A knot forms in my throat, but I swallow it down. Tears won't change anything. The doors creak open, and the music swells. But the dream I had as a little girl—the one where my Papa kissed my cheek and told me how proud he was? Gone.

So, I do what De Lucas do. I straighten my spine, lift my chin, and step forward. Alone. Because if my family won't show up for me, I sure as hell will.

Violet goes first, smile glued on like she's trying to assure herself this isn't a slow-motion train wreck. She peeks back one last time like she expects me to yank up my skirts and bolt. Can't blame her. I'd place that bet, too.

Then a deep voice rumbles beside me. "May I?"

I blink, because I've clearly lost my mind. Ricardo Bennetti, the Ricardo, stands there in a tuxedo, hand outstretched. My *almost*-father-in-law. The man I've exchanged maybe a dozen words with since signing my life away.

My throat closes up again, but this time, it's not bitterness clawing its way up. It's something delicate. Warmer. My Papa isn't here, but this man—this almost stranger—is offering to walk me down the aisle.

"You're walking me down?" I manage, voice splintering. I really can't afford to burst into full-out waterworks — not with how long this makeup took.

His smile is soft but sure. "No woman should walk down the aisle alone."

And just like that, my vision blurs. Because if my real father won't stand beside me, maybe the man giving me away should be the one whose name I'll be stuck with. The one whose son I'm about to marry. For better, for worse, and presumably in silence.

I clear my throat, swallowing down the bile creeping up my esophagus like it's late to the party, but determined to make a debut. Best not to dwell on the future. A future where I'm legally bound to a man who treats conversation like it's a finite resource, and I've already maxed out the monthly allowance.

I slide my hand through Papa's arm, and the music shifts to the wedding waltz. Romantic. Sweeping. Like I'm about to step into the happily ever after part of my life, not an arranged marriage with a human version of airplane mode.

Just as I'm about to take that first, life-altering step, Papa tightens his grip, snapping me back. The wedding planner—poor thing—goes pale. She looks one deep breath away from hyperventilating into the floral arrangement beside her.

Papa turns me to face him, brows squeezed in doubt, mouth set in a grim line. "Do you want to do this?"

I blink up at him, confused. "I...uh...bit late for that question, don't you think?" My laugh comes out sharp, brittle like glass cracking under pressure. Seriously, what is wrong with me? Stress-induced hysteria? Is the champagne hitting faster than expected?

Papa doesn't budge. "Do you?"

His voice stays soft, but his eyes? Stone cold serious. Like he might actually lug me out of here if I so much as wavered. Meanwhile, the wedding planner looks like she's mentally updating her resume. *Expert crisis manager. Can corral brides with minimal casualties.*

"Why does it matter?" I ignore the tension in my throat that makes it come out like a croak.

It's a logical question. This man helped orchestrate the arrangement. He's the reason Rico's even wearing a tux instead of sitting in his soundproof office, happily ignoring the existence of humanity. Why the sudden concern for the lamb about to marry the emotionally suppressed wolf?

Not that Papa's an evil man. Quite the contrary. He's been nothing but kind, accommodating, and oddly chill about the fact that I have a *get-out-of-marriage-free* card if I'm miserable. *Divorce him if you want*, he'd said, like it was *that* simple. As if the Big Man Upstairs would just shrug and let me walk away from it all.

But we both know the truth. Vows aren't poetry. They're shackles. In sickness and in health. For better, for worse. Til death do us part. And death? In this world? It's not a metaphor.

I lift my chin, swallowing around the knot in my throat. "I'm not walking down that aisle unless I'm sure."

"And are you?" He combs my face like he's trying to read between the lines of a contract. "Because I will not be able to live with myself if you're doing this out of obligation."

Obligation. That word tastes bitter.

I've always wanted marriage. Kids. A home with laughter, disorder, and the occasional sock stuffed between couch cushions. Did I picture getting there through an arranged marriage with a man who stares at me like I'm background noise? Absolutely not.

But life doesn't care about plans. If anyone knows how quickly dreams can sour, it's a woman raised in the Cosa Nostra. We adapt. We survive. We smile while the world burns and pretend we don't smell the smoke.

"I'm fine," I say, squeezing his arm. "I want Rico to be my husband."

The words hang there, massive and hollow. They don't suffocate me like I thought. Don't delight me, either. I feel...*nothing*. A dull, numbing acceptance. Great. Rico's indifference must be contagious. Can apathy spread through prolonged exposure?

Papa studies me a moment longer, while the wedding planner shifts from foot to foot like she's two seconds from throwing herself between us, shrieking *Think of the timeline!*

I pat his hand. "We're ready," I announce, more for her benefit than his. Papa clears his throat, visibly resigned, and together we step toward the double doors.

The chapel is packed. Not just *oh, it's a big wedding packed*, but Coachella headliner packed. Bodies stuffed into pews like sardines, all decked out in designer clothing. Hundreds of faces turn to look at me like I'm the halftime show they didn't know they signed up for.

Holy hell. I knew it was going to be a big wedding—family, business associates, friends of the Bennetti empire—but standing here under the glare of crystal chandeliers and judgmental side-eyes? It's suffocating. Like someone wrapped me in a cashmere blanket, only it's on fire.

My stomach twists into a sailor's knot, the kind you'd need a YouTube tutorial to untangle. Four hundred pairs of eyes, all dissecting my dress, my hair, my entire existence. I can practically hear the whispers. *Is she nervous? Is that the girl Rico's marrying? Do you think she's being blackmailed?*

I keep my chin up, pretending I don't want to turn around and sprint out the door. *Focus, Allie. Eyes forward. One foot in front of the other.*

Father Alberti comes into view first, standing at the altar like he's about to preside over the social event of the season, his smile a little too enthusiastic for a wedding that has all the warmth of a business merger. He beams at me like I'm the embodiment of true love and not a woman speed running her way to freedom.

My gaze shifts to Rico.

Stone-faced. Hands clasped in front of him, ready for his trial and not waiting for his bride. His dark hair is swept back, not a strand out of place, and his jaw—freshly shaved, sharp enough to slice through my last shred of sanity—locks into its default setting: brooding. He stands tall, broad, and impeccably tailored, the black suit hugging every inch of his gym-earned muscles. Italian James Bond, minus the charm and martini.

And damn it, my stomach flutters. *Actually flutters.* Like a lovesick teenager spotting her crush in the cafeteria. What the hell is wrong with me?

But there's no ignoring the fact he's infuriatingly, sinfully hot. From the powerful lines of his shoulders to those cold, unwavering amber eyes, he's the man romance novels warn you about. The *"don't fall for the emotionally unavailable billionaire"* type. Only plot twist—I'm not falling. I'm marrying him.

And that scowl? Should be off-putting. Should make me want to moonwalk out of this chapel and into witness protection. Instead, it's a turn-on. Full-blown, heart-racing, why-do-I-hate-myself level attraction.

I walk forward, bouquet clutched like a lifeline, and for a split second, I swear his jaw twitches. A smile? No. Couldn't be. Gone faster than a decent man on a dating app. His eyes sweep down my body, slow and deliberate, like he's memorizing every inch of the dress I obsessed over for weeks. Like he approves.

Every nerve in my body screams run, but his gaze pins me in place. I don't hear the music. Don't notice the hundreds of eyes watching. It's just us, locked in a silent standoff that feels more intimate than it should.

Never thought I'd buy into that whole "eyes are the windows to the soul" nonsense, but Rico? His exterior might be carved from ice, but those eyes...they burn. Golden flecks glint in the sunlight streaming through the stained glass, like embers refusing to die. There's heat there, buried deep, under layers of indifference and avoidance.

I'm used to men looking at me—usually with an expression that spells out their intentions in neon lights. Rico doesn't need an expression. He could wear a ski mask, and I'd still feel it.

He wants me.

Rico

IT'S OFFICIAL. BESIDES EVERYTHING else this woman has done in the few weeks I've known her—and actively avoided her—she's solidified that one assumption: she steals shit.

A gorgeous, cunning thief currently rewiring my internal circuits with the finesse of a world-class hacker.

And I can't look away.

She stole my breath and refused to give it back. Tiny pinpricks crawl up my spine, the familiar warning of overstimulation. Too *much* eye contact. Too *much* exposure. My nervous system waves the white flag, but she's got me cornered. Thief and kidnapper, apparently. Because I sure as hell can't escape, and my lungs remain stubbornly empty.

I'm not blind.

I knew she was beautiful when we met. It's hard to miss when every inch of her is perfect. But I blamed my sped up heart rate and blood pressure on the involuntary celibacy this marriage has shoved me into, not her specifically. It's biology. A glitch in the system. Nothing more.

Then she stepped onto the aisle, and I immediately wondered how many engineers it took to glue her into that dress. No way something that fitted that smooth—that damn sparkly—isn't held together by sheer willpower and industrial adhesive.

She moves like she holds the world. Chin up. Shoulders back. Striding toward her future with a confidence that makes the room shrink around her. Unfortunately, that future includes me.

Her dress is white. Obviously. Because this entire spectacle is built on traditions that hold about as much weight as a politician's promise. Worse, the fabric doesn't just cling to her curves; it reveres them. Soft, flowing lines interrupted by lace that snakes up her body like elegant armor. Fitting. Can't blame her for suiting up, considering she's about to marry a monster.

Her dark hair is pinned back, but long, loose tendrils escape, curling around her face. And her eyes—hazel, intense, locked onto mine.

My pulse picks up. Faster. Louder. I know the fix—look away. Stare at the wall behind her. Focus on the sea of bodies packed into the pews, all here to witness the Bennetti family's latest business merger. But I don't. I hold her gaze like a drowning man clasping to driftwood. Because the substitute is facing the reality crashing down around me.

Hazel like fall leaves that can't decide if they're clinging to summer or surrendering to fall. Green like grass untouched by lawnmowers or drought. Hazel like the aged pages of an antique book, fragile but enduring. Gold like dusk, that fleeting moment when the sky forgets its color and hangs in limbo, caught between light and dark.

My fists clench and unclench, tendons straining as I attempt to override my inner malfunctioning. How long does this damn aisle have to be? Does no one else feel like we've slowed to half-speed?

Her lips press together, vacant expression betraying nothing. Is she seconds from a smirk or a scowl? Could go either way. But her eyes never leave mine, not even when Papa hands her over. My soon-to-be wife.

And she's not scared of me.

Which is the best thing that could happen—or the worst.

Knowing my part—thanks to last night's colossal waste of time disguised as a re-hearsal—I extend my hand. Her gaze flicks down to it, brows pulling together like I've just offered her a live grenade.

Take it, Pearlina. As if telepathy works now. If it did, I'd be somewhere far from here in heavenly silence, not standing in a church with enough floral arrangements to prompt an allergy epidemic.

After what feels like a full five minutes, but is likely a few seconds, her fingers slide into mine. Soft. Small. Like everything else about her—deceptively delicate, until you realize the core's pure steel. She glances up, meets my eyes for a beat, then flicks her gaze at the priest, already checking out of this moment.

I'm barely registering whatever poetic drivel Father Alberti's spewing. The man's practically glowing. Maybe he missed the memo that we'd both rather face a firing squad.

The vows start. Repetitive. Predictable. Words people toss around like confetti, pre-tending they're more than air. *Honor. Cherish. Forsake all others.*

Empty, for most. But not for me. I don't speak often, but when I do, I mean it. Efficiency of language. If I promise something, I will keep it. Which makes reciting these vows less absurd and more... binding.

Allie's eyebrows creep higher with every word I echo, like she's questioning my grasp of the English language—or my sanity. Both are fair assessments. Her lips part soft and plump, a shade of pink that looks more like temptation than makeup.

What the hell did she put on them? I'm seconds away from leaning in, biting that bottom lip, and seeing if it tastes as good as it looks. For a man who made his soon-to-be-wife sign an agreement on no kissing, I'm sure thinking about doing the opposite more than is necessary.

I tighten my grip on her hand, grounding myself in skin-on-skin reality.

She inhales calmly before her turn, and something sharp lodges itself into my chest. Not irritation—I know that intimately. Not anger, either. This is different. Heavier. As if someone stacked bricks on my ribcage while I wasn't paying attention.

There's a tightness in my throat, and my stomach feels like I swallowed a boulder. It's just sitting there—heavy, immovable, and smug about it. I'm holding her hands, parroting vows I barely registered, while every nerve in my body paces like it knows something I don't.

The logical part of my brain—what's left of it—is already running diagnostics. Heart attack? No. Stroke? Unlikely. Emotional malfunction? Christ, let's hope not.

Then I make the mistake of meeting her eyes.

She shifts, bracing for impact, and there it is—a flicker. Quick, but loud enough to drown out everything else. The weight in my chest doubles down, pressing like a debt collector who doesn't take rain checks.

I *should* say something. Do *something*. But I just stand there, suffocating on a feeling I can't name and already hate. And the worst part? She's the reason for it, all wide-eyed innocence, utterly unaware she's disabling me from the inside out.

She recites her vows, inhaling between each word like oxygen might be the only thing keeping her upright. When she stumbles over "forsaking all others," my hand tightens around hers before my brain even catches up to my body. She gasps, eyes darting to mine, but she doesn't let the pause stretch.

But why the hell did I do that? Comforting someone isn't exactly my brand. And yet, her nerves were so thick in the air they might as well have been secondhand smoke curling around me, dragging me under. I squeezed her hand the same way I had last night, like muscle memory kicked in before common sense could hit the brakes.

Father Alberti's voice yanks me out of my thoughts. "You may now kiss the bride."

Right. Kiss. Wedding. Marriage. Shit.

Her eyes snap up to mine, wide but incomprehensible. Fear? *No.* Excitement? *Please.* The woman's about as thrilled as someone volunteering to hand out flyers on the corner for minimum wage and twelve hours in the sweltering summer sun.

I step forward, one hand instinctively finding her waist while the other cups her jaw. It's such a cliché move that I almost laugh. Where the hell did I pick this up? Certainly not from personal experience. My usual MO involves an obligatory nod, and a strategically timed exit. Maybe Violet's books — which, for the record, I read purely to support my sister and for no other reason—taught me more than I ever wanted to know about seduction by proximity. God help me if I'm subconsciously channeling one of her book boyfriends.

I pull her closer, my lips brushing against hers in the barely-there kiss meant to check a box and avoid any lawsuits. Done. Complete. We can move on now.

But we don't.

Because the second our lips meet, something stalls out in my brain. Heat licks up my spine, acute and searing like someone poured gasoline on my nerves and flicked a match. Without thinking—because thinking would involve realizing how fucked this is—I tighten my grip and crush my mouth to hers. A gasp escapes her, high and breathy, before I swallow it whole.

My lips move against hers, demanding, taking, consuming. I angle her face, fingers threading into the silky strands at her nape, while my tongue sweeps across her lower lip. And when she opens for me? Game over. Her tongue meets mine. Not shy, not hesitant, but wild. She kisses like she fights—no holds barred, nothing left behind.

I don't kiss women like this. Hell, I don't kiss women at *all*, not outside the sterile obligated pecks on the cheek to my Mama and Nonna and literally no one else. But this? This is a fucking war. And I'm losing. Worse, I think I might be okay losing.

My cock hardens to the point of agony, pressing against the soft planes of her body. There's no way she doesn't feel it. No way she doesn't realize exactly what she's unleashed. Don't worry, Pearlina. It's a biological reaction. Chemistry, not poetry. Science, not sentiment. Nothing more.

The hoots, whistles, and scattered applause from the pews rip through my skull like a warning siren, shattering the moment. I break the kiss fast, thumb already swiping the smudged lipstick from her swollen lips. Her breathing's ragged, chest heaving against mine, and I'm not doing much better. My lungs burn, my pulse races, and I can't tell if I'm lightheaded from the lack of oxygen or the fact that this woman, this thief, just stole every breath I had.

Selfish woman.

Father Alberti chuckles and the old bat offers some lame-ass joke to the crowd. I want to punch him. The man just witnessed a kiss that could set off a nuclear war and thinks it's the perfect time to crack a joke. The crowd eats it up, laughter rippling through the pews.

But I'm not paying attention to the priest or the congregation. My focus stays locked on Allie. Her eyes, wide and unblinking, remind me of someone waking from anesthesia, unsure if the world around them is real or just another hallucination. One blink. Two. And just like that, the spell shatters. Her cheeks flush, and she drops her gaze, severing the connection like she just realized she'd been kissing her cellmate, not her soulmate.

I grab her hand because that's what I'm supposed to do. Husbandly duty and all. Together, we pivot toward the crowd, descending the altar steps in synchronized, robotic strides. March down the aisle. Smile. Wave. Pretend you're not shackling yourself to someone out of pure necessity.

Next...photos. Of course, there would be photos. Why wouldn't my family want a glossy 8x10 reminder of their little matchmaking victory? The perfect shot of the bride and groom, not beaming with joy, but looking like we just sealed a corporate merger neither of us wanted. There's no reception—small mercies—but there is a party at my parents' estate. Nothing says felicitations on your arranged marriage like a bunch of people getting day drunk while pretending they believe in love.

Outside, the limo waits, and the driver, ever the optimist, offers a cheerful *"Congratulations!"* like we didn't just recite vows with all the warmth of a hostage video. I nod, resisting the urge to correct him: *Condolences would be more appropriate.*

Allie hesitates, the layers of tulle and chiffon swallowing her in a tragic bridal marshmallow. She tries to maneuver into the car with dignity, but dignity died the moment we agreed to this charade. I have to nudge—okay, shove—her inside, practically folding her into the seat while the skirt poofs up like a deflated parachute.

The door clicks shut. The car glides forward, and silence impregnates the space.

I crank the air conditioning, aim the vents at my face, and yank off my tie that's more of a noose than fashion accessory. Still, she says nothing. Just sits there, drowning in designer fabric, hands fighting with the layers from hell.

Somewhere between the altar and the limo, the thief returned what she stole—my breath. I can finally inhale without feeling like my lungs are on strike. Oxygen floods my system, and with it, clarity. No more endorphin-induced haze. No more misfiring neurons. Just cold, hard logic snapping back into place.

Until she lifts her hands to her hair.

One pin. Then *another*. And *another*. They drop to the floor, each one freeing another perfect curl from the intricate updo. Long, dark strands stream down her back, cascading over bare shoulders and brushing against the neckline of her dress. Her skin—silky, sun-kissed olive—gleams under the dim limo lights, every exposed inch caressed by strands that have no business being that seductive.

My cock hardens again, like it missed the memo that the show's over.

I shift, adjusting myself with the casualness of a man deeply aware of how screwed he is. *Look out the window. Quit staring at the problem, and the problem goes away. Basic logic.*

But the problem isn't the hair, or the dress, or that her mouth still looks kiss swollen and sinful.

The problem is my *wife*.

And thanks to a few well-rehearsed vows, I'm stuck with her until one of us dies. Judging by the way she steals my air without trying, I'm betting she'll have me six feet under before our first anniversary.

Allie

THE WEDDING PARTY AT Rico's parents' house was lovely—if you're into unwilling smiles, cold handshakes, and pretending your brand-new husband isn't silently plotting his escape the entire time. I'd swapped the bridal marshmallow dress for a sleek white silk gown, smooth as butter and blessedly free of fifty pounds of tulle. The beaded lace straps gave it just enough "bridal" without screaming I just signed away my independence in glittering rhinestones.

My new sisters-in-law, bless their optimistic hearts, had already stuffed the wedding gown into a garment bag, promising to have it cleaned, pressed, and sealed so I could "treasure it forever." As if I'd gaze fondly at it one day, reminiscing about the time I married a man who treated conversation like a limited commodity.

Everyone was kind, though. Congratulations here, warm smiles there. Rico hadn't left my side, but I'd bet my new wedding band it wasn't out of devotion. His eyes kept flicking toward the door like he was mentally calculating how fast he could bolt without Mama Bennetti launching a shoe at the back of his head.

We stood to greet guests as they arrived. We sat, side by side at the long dining table, like two mannequins on display. We stood again as people left, nodding and murmuring *thank you and yes, it was beautiful*, like an automated call center.

I'm not entirely sure how long it takes for sleep deprivation to trigger full-blown hallucinations, but I was getting close. Since I hadn't slept the night before—because, you know, wedding to a stranger—I was pretty sure I'd reached the point where I was technically asleep while standing upright. Functioning purely on autopilot, like a zombie in heels.

I was stuck in a daze looking over a vase of flowers when a warm, firm hand pressed against the small of my back.

"It's time." Rico's voice rumbled low in my ear, his breath brushing my skin and warming me from the inside out.

Time.

Time to leave. Time to go to a house I'd never seen, a bedroom I'd furnished through emails and catalogs but never stepped foot in.

And, oh yeah—time to consummate this forgery of a marriage.

I was grabbing my bag when Violet and Sienna swooped in like intrusive fairy godmothers, yanking me into a side room just off the foyer.

"Are you...good?" Sienna asked, her voice pitched somewhere between concern and *do we need to stage a rescue?*

Good? No, I was about three seconds from crawling out a window. My stomach had been tying itself into increasingly complex knots since we cut the cake, each knot labeled impending doom. But I smiled anyway because that's what you do when you're the bride. *Grin and bear it, sweetheart.*

"Sure. Why wouldn't I be?" Pretty sure the two or three octaves too high pitch on my voice says otherwise.

They swap a look. The kind sisters give each other when they're mentally preparing for an intervention.

Violet leans in, brows arched like she was gearing up for a birds and bees refresher. "Your wedding night. With Rico..."

Ah. That.

"You mean the night where I fulfill my contractual obligations like I'm checking off a to-do list? Can't wait."

It wasn't like I hadn't been thinking about it. The countdown had been ticking away in my head since the final *I do.* And while the kiss at the altar had been amazing—hot enough to make my knees wobble and my brain misfire—I wasn't delusional. That was theatrics. A performance for the crowd. Tonight would be different.

Mechanical. Dutiful. Transactional.

I'd prepared for that reality. What I hadn't figured out was how one consummates a marriage with a man who explicitly added a *minimal touching clause* to the contract.

"Listen," I sigh, "I'll be fine. He's my husband. I have to face the demon, eventually." Not sure if I'm calling Rico the demon or just the situation. Both, probably.

"Did you guys...talk about it?" Her brows wiggle like we're teenagers at a sleepover, dissecting crushes. "You know. *It.*" When I don't immediately reply, she adds, "I mean, that kiss was *hot.* So maybe it'll be...fun?" There's an actual question mark hanging at the end of her sentence, like she's asking me if my wedding night will be enjoyable.

My cheeks flame, and for once, I can't blame the champagne. "I'm sure it'll be an experience." Because memorable doesn't always mean good, and this already feels like one of those awkward, cringe-worthy stories you tell after several margaritas. *Oh, you think your wedding night was weird? Hold my tiara.*

I leave out the fact that I've only had sex once. Underwhelming and over faster than a bad Netflix show that gets canceled before the credits even roll on episode two. Not exactly a benchmark experience. What worries me isn't the act itself—it's doing it with a man who treats human contact as if it might trigger the apocalypse.

"Some women don't enjoy it at first," Violet muses, gnawing on her lower lip. "But I can always offer you tips."

Tips. From my sister-in-law. On how to enjoy sex. With her brother.

"And it takes time to figure out what feels good," Sienna adds, ever the dreamer. "Even if the first time is a little...weird. Though, with Dom, it just felt right."

Of course it did. They were practically eye-screwing each other from the moment they met. Chemistry everywhere—sparks, heart palpitations, all the gooey stuff people write bad poetry about. Meanwhile, my husband handles me with the enthusiasm of someone stuck caring for a pet he never wanted but is too guilty to rehome.

"I'm attracted to him," I mutter. "I'm not blind. But pretty only gets you so far when your conversations have the emotional intensity of a grocery list."

Sienna winces, clearly realizing my marriage isn't following the happily ever after playbook. No, my husband and I have a notarized document detailing *when* and *how often* we'll have sex. At the pace outlined, I'll need a flowchart to track progress. Three years from now, I might finally figure out what I like—right before Rico checks reproduce off his life's to-do list and officially retires from marital duties.

"It's fine," I lie, smoothing the nonexistent wrinkles on my silk gown. "I knew what I was signing up for."

Even if that means a marriage without speaking, touching, or orgasming. *Jesus, what the hell did I do?*

The car ride home is exactly what you'd expect from a man who probably views eye contact as an invasion of privacy. Silent. Tense. Like sitting in an elevator with a stranger, only the stranger is your husband and you're contractually required to share a bed tonight.

Rico doesn't look at me once. He just opens the door, waits for me to slide in, and shuts it behind me.

The silence lengthens, the hum of the engine the only sound until he pulls into a garage. I jerk upright, blinking out of whatever mental spiral I'd fallen into. When the car stops, I reach for the handle, already over this entire evening.

Rico's out of the car before I can blink, rounding the hood quickly. He pauses, clearly irritated when he sees I've already opened my door and stepped out.

I lift my chin, meeting his miffed gaze head-on. "What? Thought I'd sit there and wait for my chivalrous groom to escort me? Please. If we're not speaking tonight, I can at least open my damn door."

I follow Rico into the dark house; the silence widening between us like an awkward third wheel. He flicks on the lights, revealing a mudroom that's as uninviting as the man himself. Gray tile floors. A couple of coats and shoes lined up with precision. Nothing out of place, nothing remotely warm. It's the house that looks like a showroom but feels like a holding cell.

I slip off my shoes, clutching my bag like a lifeline. My things were moved here while I was at the wedding, but God knows where, because the pathetic truth is already settling in: this is *his* house, and I'm just a glorified houseguest. No welcome mat. No shared space. Just a contract and an address change.

The mudroom opens into the kitchen—modern, sleek, and completely devoid of personality. Stainless steel appliances. A massive center island. Exposed brick walls that scream *rustic chic,* except there's nothing chic about it. The whole vibe is "luxury Airbnb where the owner doesn't live here." No fruit bowl. No magnets on the fridge. It's a kitchen that's never seen a midnight snack or a lazy Sunday pancake session.

The living room? Same story. Charcoal gray sofa, single floor lamp, wall-mounted TV. No bookshelves, not even a clock. Just...blank. Like someone googled *minimalist aesthetic* and hit add to cart without acknowledging the fact that people are supposed to live here.

Rico stalks ahead, wordlessly assuming I'll absorb the floor plan like I'm touring a model home. I follow, half-expecting a PowerPoint presentation to project on the walls. *Here's where joy goes to die,* slide one says.

We reach the second floor, where there are only three bedrooms. He opens the first door and nods inside. "Nursery."

I blink at the empty room, as barren as my zeal for this marriage. A bare bulb dangles from the ceiling, casting pathetic little shadows across vacant walls. Just space. Like he's planned but couldn't be bothered to, you know, *actually* plan.

Nothing like an entire room devoted to reminding me that my womb is now part of a five-year business strategy.

Without waiting for my opinion, Rico crosses the hall and pushes open another door. "Guest room."

The room is about as encouraging as a dentist's office. Single bed. Beige comforter. One sad little pillow, like even it gave up. Guest room, huh? Not my room? I glance at Rico, but his face is a perfect mask of disinterest.

Finally, he moves to the double doors at the end of the hall and swings them open. "The master bedroom."

My furniture. The stuff I picked out. The bed frame I agonized over. The bedding is still sealed in plastic like a crime scene. The dresser wrapped tighter than leftovers in cling film. The room itself is huge, with vaulted ceilings and massive windows, but it's as hollow as the rest of the house. A showroom, not a sanctuary.

My room. Not *our* room.

To the right is a walk-in closet. My suitcases sit on the carpet, unopened. Beyond that, an en suite bathroom—marble flooring, walk-in shower, oversized jetted tub that looks like it's never seen a single bubble bath. It's pristine and clearly untouched.

"Where do you sleep?" I ask, frowning at the sheer emptiness.

Rico scrubs a hand down his face, already exhausted by my presence. "Downstairs."

Right. *Separate* floors. *Separate* lives. *Separate* everything. I shouldn't be surprised, but the confirmation still stings like paper cuts from the contract we signed.

I step back into the bedroom, eyeing the still-packaged bedding. "I'll need to wash the linens first." The words are informal, but the implication? Not so much. If we're doing anything tonight, it's not happening here, buddy.

He follows my gaze to the untouched bed, and I swear I can hear the gears grinding in his head. Is he calculating the spin cycle time?

"Will we be spending the night in your room since mine isn't ready?"

His eyes flick from the bed to the plastic-wrapped comforter, then back to me. He exhales sharply. "Follow me."

Not exactly the victory dance I was hoping for, but I'll take it.

Chasing behind him, we head back down the stairs, through the sterile kitchen, and into a side hallway I hadn't noticed before. Three closed doors line the hall. He skips the first two without comment—because why would he communicate like a normal human—and stops at the last set of double doors.

He pushes them open, and I instantly understand why he didn't offer the grand tour.

The room is dark. Not just dim. *Dark.* The walls are painted black, like he walked into a Home Depot, found the brooding billionaire section, and said, *Yes, this will do.* The massive bed in the center is covered in black bedding, neatly made. Two nightstands flank the bed, empty except for a single phone charger. No art. No plants. No personality.

Just walls, a bed, and the crushing weight of isolation. Color me amazed — oh wait, color dies here.

It's another master suite, complete with a walk-in closet and an en suite bathroom, mirroring the setup upstairs. Same layout. Same size. Just...darker. Lukewarm. Like he moved in, stripped the room of anything remotely comforting, and called it a day.

Separate rooms weren't enough. We're on separate floors. The man might as well have a bunker under the house to put an entire six feet barrier of concrete between us.

"My room." Rico glances around like he's just now noting where we are.

Right. Fantastic. How am I supposed to sleep with a man—hell, *have sex* with a man—who treats me like an unwanted giveaway mug from a company picnic? Barely used, shoved in the back of the cabinet, only pulled out when everything else is in the dishwasher... and definitely not the first pick.

We both stand there. Silent. The awkwardness thickens, settling over the room like a San Francisco fog. If this is a preview of married life, I'm screwed. Him, a marble statue with issues. Me, a bundle of nerves, barely held together by champagne and denial.

Rico nods toward the bed. "Sleep there tonight."

"With you?" The words flop out before I can stop them.

"No."

I blink. Did I black out and skip the part where we mutually agreed to be Amish about this whole thing? "Wait, seriously? It's our wedding night. You're not even gonna pretend to fake romance me?"

Nothing. Not a twitch of emotion. He's already walking past me, heading into the master closet. I hear hangers scrape across the rod; the light flicking on and off like he's performing some half-assed magic trick. Five minutes later, he emerges in jeans and a plain black T-shirt, looking like he's about to run errands, not celebrate his legally binding commitment.

I stare at him. "Where the hell are you going?"

Adjusting his watch, he finally meets my gaze, as if I'm the one being irrational. "Office."

The word drops like an anvil, flat and unmerciful.

"You're...going to work. *Now*. On our wedding night?"

He doesn't wait for my inescapable meltdown. He just heads for the door like I'm invisible. My brain scrambles for words, for something sharp enough to cut through his apathy, but the room is so devoid of throwable objects I'd have to hurl the whole damn nightstand to make an impact.

"Rico!" My voice cracks.

He pauses, hand on the doorframe, turning his head just enough to acknowledge my existence. *Barely.*

"It's our wedding night."

"Well aware." His voice flat and emotionless.

"We're supposed to consummate. You agreed."

Slowly, he pivots, and those amber eyes rake over me, cold and calculating. Like he's assessing a business deal, not his wife. And damn it, I know what I look like—silk gown, hair tumbling down, makeup still intact despite the day's marathon. I'm objectively attractive. But his expression doesn't shift. Not a flicker of want. Just...detached.

"We agreed."

I glance at the bed, then back at him, gesturing between us like I'm explaining the birds and the bees to a particularly dense high-schooler. "Well? What's the hold-up? Clothes off. Lights out. Let's get this done." God, I never pictured that as my foreplay, but here I am.

His lips twitch. Not quite a smile—Rico doesn't smile—but close enough to make my blood pressure spike. "Well..." he mimics, voice low and taunting.

My hands flutter in exasperation. *"It's. Our. Wedding. Night.* We're supposed to consummate. How many more facts do I need to spell out? Should I draw you a diagram? You here, me there, penis meets vagina—boom, deal sealed."

Aaaannndddd, this is rock bottom. Welcome Allie.

This time, I swear I catch the ghost of amusement flashing across his face, but it's gone before I can confirm it. "I'm going to work."

My jaw unhinges. "You agreed!"

"I did." He shrugs, plucking an invisible piece of lint from his shirt as if he couldn't make it any more obvious about how fatigued he was with this conversation. "But you're the one with the problem, *Pearlina*. Not me."

I sputter. "Of course I have a problem! We agreed to consummate!"

"Didn't say when."

The room tilts. I grab the bedpost for balance, my entire body vibrating with the rage usually reserved for tech support calls. "Are you kidding me? It was implied we'd consummate on our wedding night. What else would consummation mean?"

Another shrug. This man shrugs like it's an Olympic sport and he's gunning for gold. I snap. "So, are we having sex or not?"

Never in my wildest nightmares did I imagine standing in my future husband's bedroom, wearing the world's most impractical lingerie riding right up my ass under this dress, begging for sex. The woeful note in my voice makes me hate myself a little.

Rico tilts his head, more animal than human. "Are you ovulating?"

"W-what?" It's all stutters at this point. "No...I don't think so."

"No? Then nope." He pops the *"p"* like a bubblegum-blowing brat and strolls out, leaving me standing there, speechless and seething.

On our wedding night. While he goes to work.

I glance down at my wedding band, the small pearl glinting mockingly in the dim light. Pretty. Pointless. Just like this marriage.

Allie

I SLEPT IN MY *husband's* bed.

Not *our* bed.

His.

The clock blinked 5:13 a.m. when I cracked my eyes open, the sun still deciding whether it gave enough of a damn to rise. Rico's side? Empty. What did I expect? Not rolling over to find him there peacefully asleep. The man all but ghosted me the second we said *I do*, so why would he suddenly start practicing marital bliss now?

Slipping out from under the ridiculously crisp sheets—because God forbid a wrinkle exists in his cold, soulless sanctuary—I tiptoed into the hallway. The house is silent, dark and eerily still, like its owner. Even the air felt...indifferent. It's as if the walls had decided they were done trying to be lively and welcoming.

I peeked into the first door, half-expecting to catch him brooding in a corner. Nope. Home gym. If you could call it that. A weight bench, a rack of dumbbells organized by size, and a worn boxing bag hanging in the corner.

Closing the door, I moved to the next room. Office. And by office, I mean a sad, cavernous space with a single desk, an ergonomic chair, and six oversized monitors mounted to the wall. The whole thing resembled the control room of a spy movie more than a workspace. The desk, though impressive, seemed swallowed by the sea of empty square footage—no plants, no pictures, not even a rogue pen. Just screens and an almost eerie kind of silence.

Also, no Rico.

Back to the kitchen, then the living room. Same minimalist aesthetic, though "aesthetic" might be giving him too much credit. More prison chic than modern luxury. Sure, there was a center island, new appliances, and some exposed brick for that rustic touch, but not a single sign of life. No mail stack. No rogue coffee mug from the morning before.

Just...emptiness. The kind of sterile, soulless setup you'd expect in a staged home—meant to impress, not to live in.

And the living room? Even colder. A large couch. Two matching armchairs. Glass coffee table with sharp metal edges, as if to say, *Sit here, but don't get comfortable.* No blankets. No throw pillows. Not even a freaking candle. The man didn't just dislike coziness—he'd declared war on it.

I sighed, about to retreat, when something caught my eye. The mantle. Among the brick veneer and sterile decor, there were—wait for it—picture frames. Actual, personal, non-stock-photo picture frames. I hadn't noticed them last night in the darkness.

Curiosity piqued, I wandered over, heart doing a weird little lurch. The first frame held a family photo, though calling it that barely did it justice. The Bennettis didn't take family pictures—they took crowd shots. At least forty people were crammed into the frame, all dark hair, olive skin, and sharp features. Genetics obviously ran this family.

My eyes snagged on the familiar faces. Alex and Violet, looking annoyingly perfect. Sienna, very pregnant, standing next to Dom, who held a small boy with the same amber eyes as his dad. Marco stood off to the side, wearing his signature *I'd rather be anywhere else expression.* And there, in the back, towering over the rest, was Rico.

Holding a baby.

Not just holding—cradling. The infant might as well have been made of spun sugar and dreams. His face was vacant, of course, because an emotional expression would probably send him into anaphylactic shock, but something about him had softened. The intensity had been dialed down. He didn't look miserable. He didn't look bored. He almost looked... content?

I snorted. Rico Bennetti. Content. Sure. Maybe the light hit his face just right, and I was mistaking shadows for sentiment. His "happy face" probably had the same energy as a DMV employee who just told you the system's down—neutral bordering on hostile.

The other frames held more photos of kids—nieces, nephews, little Bennetti spawns grinning. A few pictures of his parents, all formal, as if they were posing for a classy couple's calendar. But not a single photo of Rico alone. Not one shot of him outside that lone group picture.

Of course, the man probably believed cameras stole souls. If that's the case, the wedding photographer must've robbed him blind. We stood through at least an hour of forced poses. Poor guy looked ready to toss his camera into traffic by the end. "Smile," he'd gritted out more than once, willing my husband's face to show a single emotion.

Try to look happy, they'd said.

Try to be happy, they'd meant.

I walk over to the three oversized windows in the living room and flick open the roller shades. Sunlight streams in, golden and affectionate, stretching across the floor, reclaiming its territory. The sky's a swirl of buttery yellows and soft oranges, blending into streaks of pale blue. The sunrise Instagram influencers would slap a motivational quote over and call it self-care.

I smirk, peering around the barren living room. I wonder how often—if ever—my husband opens these. My guess? Somewhere between never and when hell freezes over.

Fueled by pettiness and caffeine withdrawal, I make it my special mission to banish every shadow from the house. Living room? Shades up. Foyer? Sunshine, baby. Kitchen? Let there be light. Dining area? Boom, it's bright now. I stride down the hall into Rico's cave of a bedroom and yank open the floor-to-ceiling window coverings too.

And that's when I see it.

The backyard.

It's perfectly manicured, the grass trimmed to an obnoxiously uniform length, as if he hired a lawn service with a clinical obsession for symmetry. A massive concrete pad sits smack in the middle—empty, sterile, and about as inviting as a hospital waiting room. No patio furniture, no fire pit, not even a sad little folding chair pretending to care. Just wet concrete, glistening under the morning sun, probably courtesy of sprinklers on a timer because heaven forbid Rico actually enjoy something as simple as watering grass.

If backyards reflect personalities, my husband is officially labeled as vacant of joy.

I head back toward the kitchen, passing the mudroom. On a whim, I crack open the garage door and flick on the light. His car's gone.

And with it, my last shred of patience.

Where the hell did he sleep?

The same slow, simmering rage from last night starts bubbling up again, red and prickly beneath my skin. He could've slept at the office—fine, whatever, workaholic—but something tells me Rico doesn't just work loopholes in contracts. He lives for them. The man probably gets off on technicalities. Which means there's a chance he snuck off to see his so-called *"therapist."*

Therapist. Right.

Violet practically choked on her words when she finally confirmed what that actually meant. My future sister-in-law, bless her heart, had winced and cringed her way through the confession, like telling me her brother frequented escorts was on par with announcing a terminal illness.

Should I be reassured I'm not the other woman? Sure. In theory. But knowing he preferred transactional intimacy over literally any human connection doesn't exactly scream husband of the year.

Neither does going to work on your wedding night, but here we are.

Escorts aren't rare in the Cosa Nostra. They're practically an accessory. Most married men have an arrangement: wives for appearances, mistresses for pleasure, escorts for fillers. Lavish apartments, unlimited credit cards, first-class flights to nowhere special—just in case their "employers" needed a little company. They're spoiled, pampered, and ready at a moment's notice, legs spread and loyalty guaranteed—because emotional attachment isn't part of the contract.

That's the part that gnaws at me. Rico Bennetti has *never* formed a connection with anyone. Not romantically, not emotionally, not even in a *let's be civil and tolerate each other's existence* way. He's set up for isolation, like one of those AI boyfriends TikTok keeps trying to sell me—except less chatty and way more broody.

And now he's legally tied to me. In marriage. You know, the ultimate "let's share every part of our lives" situation.

How is this supposed to work when my husband treats intimacy like a business takeover? He expects me to sign on the dotted line and keep my feelings locked up tighter than a Swiss bank account.

Once I'm sure Rico isn't lurking in this sterile, serial-killer minimalist "home" of his, I make a beeline for the kitchen, eyes laser-focused on one thing: coffee. Survival comes first.

But my caffeine mission screeches to a halt when I spot what's waiting on the counter. A set of car keys, dealership tag still dangling—a pompous reminder that money solves everything. And next to it? A shiny black Amex card, my name—Alessandra Bennetti—stamped across the front as if I'm some freshly gained luxury item.

A shiver snakes up my spine. *You've just been bought and paid for, sweetheart.*

Because that's what this is, right? I'm no longer a De Luca pawn. Now I belong to *one* Bennetti.

I tap the card against the marble countertop, mulling it over.

Unlimited funds in the hands of an enraged wife? Bless his bitter, detached little heart.

I'm about to make this mausoleum look like Joanna Gaines got drunk on pumpkin spice lattes and went on a shopping spree. Throw pillows? Everywhere. A floral arrangement in every room? Yes, sir. The man will sneeze himself into submission before I'm done.

But then I see it. A pale blue Post-It, sitting innocently under all the wealth, the cherry on top of my rage sundae. I pluck it up, expecting—what? Directions to the nearest coffee shop? Maybe a list of things I'm not allowed to touch?

Instead, I get this gem:

Rico: *Every Tuesday, I eat a grilled cheese sandwich for no other reason than it feels right.*

I squint at the note.

I flip it over, fully expecting a punchline or, I don't know, a secret code that will unlock his personality. But no. That's it. No context, no explanation. Just a grilled cheese confession from my emotionally stunted husband.

And the kicker? There's coffee already brewed in the pot.

What is this? Am I in some Twilight Zone marriage? He won't talk to me, won't touch me, but make sure I have coffee and a note like we're part of some emotionally distant pen pal club?

I pour a cup, because caffeine is the only thing keeping me from lighting this place on fire, and lean over the counter, eyeing my new arsenal: a useless fact, a set of keys, and a credit card.

So this is his plan? Give me a car, a charge card, and a random fun fact while he ghosts me?

I glare at the note; the rage simmering under my skin, hotter than the coffee I now want to throw in his face.

Abandoning my cup, I march right back to his room, the T-shirt I stole from his closet swishing around my thighs. I'm not about to drag my ass upstairs to unpack my things when I can pillage his wardrobe out of pure spite. If he's going to disappear on me, the least he can do is lose a shirt or two.

I grab my phone off his nightstand, unlock it only to find it opens directly to the Notes app. Naturally Rico is the man who communicates solely through passive-aggressive tech.

And there it is, waiting for me like the complacent little notification it is:

Rico: *Take the card. Go shopping. Do whatever you want. I will not be home until dinner unless you miraculously decide to cancel it. The keys are for the new car. Vinnie will drive you. Don't message me for permission to buy anything. We both know I won't reply.*

I ball the Post-It in my fist before I even realize it, steam practically building behind my eyes, cartoon-style fury loading for launch.

Stomping back into the kitchen, I yank open every drawer until I find a pen shoved in the back of the last one, buried as if the house itself avoids being too functional.

I slap his stupid note down on the counter, flip it over, and write my own "fact" in handwriting that is as chaotic as my emotions right now.

Allie: *I will make grilled cheese on a Wednesday because mid-week cheese just hits better.*

Petty? Absolutely. Immature? Without a doubt. But if he wants to toss out weird facts, I'm all in. I will match his level of ridiculousness and raise it.

Satisfied, I smooth out the note and slap it back on the counter where I found it. Then I march toward the stairs, muttering to myself the whole way.

"Stupid grilled cheese. Stupid husband. Stupid, emotionally unavailable, ridiculously hot, frustrating-as-hell husband."

By the time I reach my room, I'm practically vibrating with anger. He wants to play games? Fine. Let's play. Only I plan to win. And I'll be eating my victory grilled cheese on a fucking Wednesday.

Allie

I'M ON MY SECOND cup of coffee, and I absolutely do not need it. My nerves are already tap dancing on my last shred of rationality. Across the kitchen island, Vinnie sits patiently, flipping through a paperback, his eyes flicking between me and his book.

The black Amex card remains between us, glittering under the kitchen light, mocking me. *Go ahead, Allie. Be a good little wife. Spend your husband's money. Buy shoes. Get highlights. Forget that you were unceremoniously dumped on your wedding night.*

Yeah, no thanks. If Rico thinks I'm going to pass my days as a trophy wife with a shopping addiction and a standing nail appointment, he's got another thing coming.

Since Vinnie had surfaced from the basement apartment around nine, he'd barely said a word. Just sat there reading, occasionally glancing at me, no doubt trying to assess the situation and mentally noting my status.

Day After Wedding. Female, early 20s. Habitat: Pristine, joyless mansion. Mating habits: Inconclusive.

I know what he's thinking. Why is the bride sipping coffee instead of basking in post-marital joy? Because her husband vanished without a trace, pulling a magician-level disappearing act after refusing to perform the one trick everyone expected. All because I didn't have the foresight to make that agreement ironclad. Nope—I left loopholes, and Rico has made it crystal clear he intends to crawl through every single one.

A knock at the front door jolts me from a rather glorious pity party of one. I glance at Vinnie, then around the empty house, as if expecting Rico to materialize from thin air.

"Want me to get that?" Vinnie thumbs toward the door.

"No, I've got it." I slide off the stool, my bare feet slapping against the cold tile. The knock comes again, sharper this time.

Through the peephole, I spot Sienna and Violet, both beaming, fresh off what must've been a brunch fueled by bottomless mimosas and gossip worth bottling. I'm mildly bitter

I missed it, though they probably assumed I was tangled up with my husband and too blissfully occupied to peel myself away for breakfast.

I pause. Do I *have* to let them in? Technically, it's my house now, but it still feels more like I'm squatting in Rico's cold, echoing Batcave of emotional repression.

"Hey!" Violet trills the moment I crack open the door. She's rocking skinny jeans and a floral blouse, her green eyes so bright they look Photoshopped. "Soooo... are you planning to let us in, or should we chat here like we're selling Girl Scout cookies?"

"Right. Sorry." I step aside, waving them in while mentally cursing myself for still being in this damn oversized T-shirt. I'm sporting the look of a one-night stand that overstayed her welcome, in her *husband's* bed, in *his* clothes, in *his* house.

Yup, this *is* rock bottom.

Both women peek around the foyer, their expressions varying from curiosity to mild horror. Violet frowns. "Okay, Alex always said his brother was a minimalist, but wow. This is...well, I have no words, really."

Sienna nods, walking into the barren living room. "Minimalist isn't even the right word. This is... clinically depressing. He doesn't even have a clock."

"You know Rico hates clocks." Violet breezes past the sterile seating arrangement and into the kitchen, where Vinnie looks up from his book and Violet smiles cheerfully at him. I swear the man full-on pink cheeks blushes. I didn't know Vinnie was capable of that.

It's weird seeing someone treat Vinnie as an actual human being. In my world, body-guards were essentially living furniture. You only acknowledged them when arranging someone's removal—or their untimely demise. Good times.

"Why doesn't he like clocks?" I ask, holding up the coffeepot. Sienna nods for some while Violet waves it off.

"I think it's because he doesn't want to be reminded how much time he wastes. If he doesn't look at the clock, he can pretend he's not spending all day in the work vortex."

Sienna snorts into her cup. "Pretty sure Rico wouldn't believe work is a waste of time. That man treats Java like it's his love language." Sadly, I don't know what "*java*" is, or I'd use it to my advantage.

Violet leans across the counter, manicured nails tapping a rhythm that does nothing to hide her impatience. Her gaze flicks between me and Vinnie.

"*Soooo.* How was last night?"

Vinnie's face color drains fast, with those rosy cheeks a fleeting memory at this point. "I'm gonna—uh—finish getting ready." He jabs a thumb toward the garage door, where the stairs lead to his basement apartment. The man's already dressed, keys in hand, practically vibrating with the need to escape.

"Coward," I mutter, watching him bolt the second I open my mouth—as if I just announced a dramatic live reading of *Fifty Shades of Grey*. Honestly, might not be a terrible option. Books might end up being the only source of thoughtful dialogue I get from now on. Is it bad when a paperback offers a deeper connection than the man you married?

Violet snickers. "Damn. He moves fast for a guy built to withstand a car crash." Her gaze tracks him out the door. "He really is Antonio's brother. Younger, right?"

I nod, sipping my coffee, which has officially transitioned from a morning pick-me-up to an emotional support beverage.

"Anyway." Sienna slides into the seat Vinnie abandoned, her finger landing squarely on the black Amex. "Hubby wants you to play *Real Housewives* and shop till you drop?" Her brows wiggle as she pushes the card toward me.

"That's what his note said." I shrug, because what else is there to say? My husband communicates through Post-Its and sneaky messages on my phone. I mentally add to my daily to-do list to change my phone's password. Only, I don't know how...

"Wait." Violet's brows crash together. "He left you a note? He's *not* here?"

"Nope. Went to work." I try to sound casual about it. "Last night."

Silence. Both women blink at me, synchronized brain glitch clear as day.

Sienna's gaze flicks to Violet, then back to me. "He left after you both...you know..." she trails off, cheeks adorably pink.

Sienna doesn't do crass. It's cute. She's only a year younger than me, but being married with twin girls and a stepson gives her an air of *Mom Knows Best*. Meanwhile, Violet's older, already in her thirties—not that her perfect skin or energy levels show that one bit.

Funny. I told Papa I didn't want to marry Carlo because he was *too* old for me. Now here I am, hitched to a man thirteen years my senior who has less interest in me than he does in his six-monitor setup. Karma's not just a bitch; she's a full-blown matriarch serving retribution on a silver platter.

"There was no...*you know*." Rejected by my husband. God, that is certainly going to be a fun one to unpack in therapy. My type of therapy — *not his*.

Violet gasps so dramatically I half-expect her to faint. "Wait. He just left after the wedding and went to work?"

"Yup." I pop the *p*. "Apparently, I wasn't ovulating, so he determined consummation could wait."

"But Alex said you made him agree to the contract."

"I still can't believe this was arranged," Sienna mutters, arms crossing over her chest. "How did no one tell me until the actual wedding?"

"Because you'd have staged a full-blown protest. Ranting about how marriage should be based on passion and romance and moonlit declarations." Violet offers.

"Says the woman who writes those *exact* stories for a living," Sienna fires back.

"Touché."

Sienna comes back to me, brows furrowed. "So, he already broke the contract?"

I shake my head, jaw stiffening. "No. I never specified *when* we'd consummate. Just that it *had* to happen. So, Mr. Literal took advantage of the loophole."

My eyes drift to the dining area—or what should be a dining area if my husband didn't have the interior design aesthetic of a doomsday prepper. The modern chandelier hangs above nothing, as if it's mourning the absence of a table.

Then I glance at the Amex. Just like that, an idea is born.

"You two wanna go shopping?"

Violet's eyes light up. "Are you asking if I want to spend your husband's money? Yes, Allie. Yes, I do."

If Rico wants me to be the good little wife and shop, then I'm going to shop. And this house? It's about to get an extreme makeover he'll never forget.

Rico

THEY'RE HERE. NOT BEING dramatic, just stating the facts.

I clocked their arrival the second Violet and Sienna strolled up to my front door. The doorbell camera caught every second—Violet's eyes tightening, Sienna whispering something that made Violet's grin falter. I didn't even need the audio to know they were about to rat me out. My sisters are guaranteed to run to my brothers, and especially now that I'm married to a woman that they like.

Mistakes were made.

It took precisely forty-seven minutes for my brothers to storm into my office like I'd committed a federal crime. Impressive, considering it's Sunday, and both of them have toddlers who treat sleep like a suggestion.

Alex, ever the overachiever, leads the charge, doing his best at making sure I'm aware he's irked. Dom follows, silent but simmering, the twin rage dialed to homicidal levels. It's like looking into a mirror, except the reflection actually gives a damn.

"Fast," I remark, flicking the sticker over my watch face that blocks the time when I'm deep in work. "What'd you do, teleport?"

Alex's jaw flexes. Dom just stares, his silence intenser than any lecture. Having a twin is like owning a horror movie doppelgänger—seeing your own face twisted in fury is unsettling. Not as unsettling as when he's happy, though.

I haven't smiled like that in decades. Pretty sure my facial muscles atrophied sometime around the age of fourteen.

Alex crosses his arms, the posture of a man about to hand over a TED Talk titled *Why My Younger Brother Is a Shitty Husband*. "I got an interesting text from my wife this morning. Had to leave my boys, get dressed, and come kick your ass."

Drama queen. Not my wife. No, I'm referring to my brother in front of me.

I blink at him. Once. Twice. Just enough to remind him I'm not biting. First, he can't kick my ass and we both know it. Second, I doubt Violet's text qualified as interesting by any metric I recognize.

"I left Allie a credit card. Told her to shop." I don't mention the Post-It note with my random fact of the day—something neither of these idiots knows about me. And I sure as hell don't bring up last night. My marriage, contractual or not, is none of their business.

Alex's brows lift, pure incredulity ingrained in every line of his sleep-deprived face. "You didn't even have a wedding night?"

Well, shit. So much for keeping it my personal business.

"Not yet."

Dom's gaze hones, weighing. He's quiet, but his silence demands answers like an interrogator flipping through evidence. Alex, predictably, goes for the jugular.

"You signed a damn contract, Rico."

I lean back in my chair, unimpressed. "And I'll fulfill it. When the timing's right."

Like when her body is primed to conceive. It's not rocket science. One night. One attempt. No repeats necessary. Call me an optimist, but the thought of knocking her up on the first try sounds like efficiency at its finest.

I'm not stupid. I know if I touch her—*really* touch her—I'll enjoy it. Too much. Already, she ignites something restless in me, like a live wire sparking beneath my skin. If one brush of her hand makes my gut twist, imagine what full contact would do.

And unlike my brothers, I don't have the luxury of believing in happily ever after. I believe in results. And right now, my result involves keeping my wife at arm's length until consummation is less about pleasure and more about purpose (as in knocking up said wife up).

Alex's cuts in. "You're unbelievable."

"Tell me something I don't know."

"Rico, you have a marriage contract. You might not care that you tossed your wife's first wedding night out the window, but you signed a legally binding document. A notarized contract about when you will and will not have sex. Honestly, it's ridiculous. Who notarizes their sex life?" He shudders like the concept substantially offends him, but again, he's not me. So, he will never understand.

"It says we *have* to consummate," I reply, eyes glued to my screen. "Not *when*." Okay, so that argument, at this very moment, is feeling a tad weak. Especially with these two looming over me.

Dom, ever the voice of reason no one asked for, leans against my desk. "Isn't the wedding night implied?"

Implied.

Like common sense, good taste, and that marriage requires mutual enthusiasm. They're not wrong, but they're not right either. And I'm not inclined to split hairs with men who've been brainwashed by their wives into believing love is the answer to everything.

I lean forward, tapping the down arrow on my keyboard, scrolling through the security logs I was reviewing before Dumb and Dumber held an intervention. Someone's been sniffing around our servers, and while my brothers are worried about my marital obligations, I'm more concerned about the hacker trying to break into our system, again, and booting him out before he can get through my first few protections in place. Priorities.

"I need to work now." I flick the sticker back over my watch face. I don't track time unless it's being wasted (right now, a good example of that). And I'm not keen on watching the minutes crawl while I pretend to care about their lecture. My phone, face down on the desk, vibrates quietly. I don't check it. I already know what's waiting—missed calls from these two, and probably a text or five from my wife, who I sincerely hope is out spending my money like it's her life's mission. God knows I don't spend it.

Both of my brothers are glossy-spread billionaires. Forbes cover boys with tailored suits that cost more than a used Honda and smiles engineered for photo ops. I'm a billionaire by circumstance. Investing every spare cent, avoiding frivolous expenses, and employing the same cleaning lady for the past decade—a woman who charges twenty bucks an hour and doesn't mind the fact my house is basically a glorified server room with a bed.

I should put Allie on cleaning duty. She can't shop forever. Would save me a couple hundred a month.

"You realize Mama expects an update about you at dinner tonight, and if we don't have one, she expects to see you there?" Dom grits out, clearly fighting the urge to throttle me. "She assumes—no, she *hopes*—you and your wife will do what most newlyweds do all day."

What? Avoiding each other? Mission accomplished.

"Then I won't go. Gives me time to work."

Simple. Efficient. Logical. And it means I don't have to sit through Mama's disappointed sighs while she side-eyes my now covered ring finger screams *domesticated*. Isn't that suffering enough?

My brothers should thank me, really. Here I am, on a Sunday, making sure their precious merger with the Locke brothers doesn't implode because some keyboard warrior thinks he can out-code me. I'm half-tempted to leave a backdoor open, let the hacker waltz in, and nuke the whole deal. But that would be too obvious, and while I enjoy provoking my brothers, I'm not masochistic enough to endure the fallout of that one.

"You're unbelievable," Alex mutters, running a hand through his hair like I've disturbed his moral compass.

"Tell me something I don't know."

"Locke and his team will be here tomorrow," Dom reminds me, like I need *another* reason to regret waking up. "That means lawyers. California tans. Spray-on confidence."

"Great." I deadpan. "Just what this floor needs. More noise."

Our executive suite is usually a fortress of peace—just me, my brothers, and their assistants. I don't have one. Never saw the point. If you need someone to schedule your life, you've already lost jurisdiction over it.

Dom strolls over, plopping his ass right on my desk. Because, apparently, boundaries are just a suggestion now.

How many times have these two idiots invaded my office since I got engaged? I used to enjoy peace. Silence. The comforting hum of servers and the click of my keyboard. Now, thanks to one wedding and a legally binding sex clause, my office has turned into a family lounge.

The platinum band on my left hand catches the light, tormenting me like a middle finger from the universe. Marriage isn't just a commitment—it's an open invitation for unsolicited opinions and familial micromanagement. The Married Men's Club. Perks include nagging brothers, a mother who's suddenly more invested in my social calendar, and a wife who takes up too much space for such a small person.

Dom leans in, purposefully blocking my view of the monitor. "You know I'm telling Mama tonight that you've been here all night, right? Checked the logs. You clocked in last night and never left."

I recline in my chair, scrutinizing his face. Alex bluffs like a Wall Street broker—fast, loose, and *mostly* bullshit. Dom? He's a wild card, but he has a tell when he's serious. Right now? He's beaming.

"You wouldn't."

He grins wider and I hate him just a little. "Try me."

My stomach drops. The bastard *absolutely* would.

"Fine." I snap the word out, like surrendering hurts my throat because it fucking does. "I'll go home."

Satisfied, Dom leans back and—because he's a certified menace—yanks the power cord from my monitor. If he didn't share my DNA, I'd throw him out the window.

"Not good enough." He flicks his chin toward Alex, who's still lounging against the doorframe, bored and ready to go back to his domestic paradise. "You'll go home now, do the deed—" He pauses for dramatic effect, looking back at our older brother.

Alex waves him on. Did they rehearse this shit? I'd bet this month's salary they did.

"—and spend the *entire* day with your wife." Dom finishes and I die a little inside.

It's hard to say which option sounds worse—spending Sunday with my wife or dealing with Mama after Dom tattles. Both feel like medieval torture, though Mama might actually be more fatal. Then again, my wife *was* a mafia princess. She probably has a burial site picked out. How the hell did I end up in a situation where both my mother *and* my bride qualify as threats to my existence?

Defeated, I power down my system while my brothers hover like vultures, making sure I don't escape through the vents. Dom even walks me to my car, displaying his best protective chaperon side. If he tries to buckle my seatbelt, I will crack his nose. Mercifully, he stops at the curb, watching me get in the car, then as I drive off. I wouldn't put it past him to tail me to make sure I go home.

Joke's on them. I sent the latest security logs to my home server before they even reached my office. Let them celebrate their imaginary win. I'll "spend time" with my wife the same way I spend time with my tax documents—stored neatly in the same location, occasionally glanced at out of obligation, and otherwise ignored unless there's an audit. We'll share the same three-thousand-square-foot structure while I barricade myself in my home office like a ghost with Wi-Fi. Quality time and all that.

I pull into the garage at noon. *Noon*. On a Sunday. Normally, I'd stay at the office until four, then head straight to my parents' estate for dinner. Not playing house like some domesticated Labrador. But here I am—living proof that marriage turns even the most rational men into pathetic ones known as husbands.

The Lexus I bought for Vinnie to chauffeur Allie is gone. I know she's been shopping all morning, just like I told her. My phone buzzed every hour with purchase notifications—Chanel, Bloomingdale's, some furniture store I've never heard of. No texts, though. Which, frankly, feels like a success. Maybe retail therapy is the key to a quiet life since my house is officially empty.

I almost whip out my phone to gloat—*Look, brothers, your grand intervention was a waste of time because my wife isn't even home*. But then I spot the coffee pot.

A blue, crinkled Post-it. My contribution to the required "daily fact" she ordered. I figured if I had to play the game, I'd at least weaponize the rules.

But now there's writing on the back, in neat, defiant cursive: *I will make grilled cheese on a Wednesday because mid-week cheese just hits better.*

Cute. In the same way a toddler throwing a tantrum is adorable—loud, unreasonable, and mildly entertaining if you're not the one responsible for cleanup.

Instead of heading straight to my home office, I detour to the bathroom, peeling off the remnants of the day. The shower is scalding, precisely how I like it—hot enough to burn away the evidence of a wedding I didn't want and a reality I'm actively ignoring.

Once I'm clean, I remake the bed, pulling the duvet taut—none of this loose thrown over bullshit my wife does, apparently. I'm just pleased we won't be sharing a room.

Back in my office, the monitors flicker to life, drowning me in code and numbers. It's not until the unmistakable scent of seared meat and garlic curls into the room, insidious and impossible to ignore, that I realize I've been sitting here for hours. I flick the cover off my watch. Almost seven. I hadn't bothered checking the security feed or listening for the garage door. Noise-canceling headphones—the only true marriage I believe in.

But now I look. Lexus in the garage. My darling wife is home, apparently channeling her frustration into culinary pursuits. Good. Maybe she'll burn off that sharp tongue while she's at it.

I stand, stretching until my spine cracks, and wander toward the kitchen. I stop just short of the threshold. Allie's at the stove, her back to me, stirring something that smells like it might actually be edible. But it's not the food that grabs my attention—it's the denim. Skin-tight, curve-hugging, crime-against-my-self-control jeans.

Jesus Christ.

I'm a man. Not a monk. And the way those jeans cling to her hips, framing an ass that looks like a particularly vindictive god sculpted it, is testing every ounce of my restraint. The urge to leave teeth marks along the seam is alarming. I don't bite. I've never wanted to bite. But here I am, contemplating property damage because my wife decided to weaponize Levi's.

She turns, catching me mid-ogling. Her grin? Pure sin. I'm fucked. "Oh, look who's emerged from his cave. Here to share dinner with me, or just lurking for sport?"

The arrogance in her voice is a slap and a caress all at once. My cock twitches. Annoying. Unacceptable. And yet, does it anyway.

I don't dignify her sass with a response, just nod and step into the kitchen, ignoring how the aroma seems to bypass my nose and swirl around in my stomach, which is itching for something substantial to fill it. I could say it smells good—hell, it smells like the closest thing to heaven I'll ever experience without a DNR on file—but compliments are a slippery slope. Hand one out, and suddenly people fish for more. Best to set the expectation early: silence is golden.

Still, my stomach growls loud enough to betray me. I clamp my jaw shut, mentally willing it to shut the hell up.

While she plates the food, I glance around. No plates on the island. No quick, transactional dinner at the counter, like civilized strangers. Instead, there's a recent addition to the house: a long wooden dining table, the kind you see in luxury catalogs labeled *Rustic Chic* with a price tag that could fund a small revolution. It's set for two. One setting at the head, the other directly to its right. Close. Intimate. Smack in the middle of my personal space. I detest it already.

Clever. She didn't just buy a table; she bought herself a battleground.

My gaze drifts back to her. She's wiping her hands on a towel, watching me like she knows exactly what I'm thinking. Which is problematic, considering half my thoughts involve bending her over said table at the moment.

"I figured we should eat like ordinary people. Unless you prefer to hover in doorways and silently criticize me. You seem proficient at that."

Touché, thief. Touché.

"It'll be ready in five minutes." Allie stirs something in the pan, wholly at ease in *my* kitchen. Like she didn't just move in twenty-four hours ago and start rearranging my life one overpriced dining room from hell at a time.

I glance away from her to the wall and freeze. A clock. Massive, rusty-ass clock, the size of a manhole cover, *tick, tick, ticking* like a countdown to my imminent mental breakdown. It looks like it was salvaged from the Titanic and sold to suckers who mistake corrosion for character. People actually pay thousands for this crap? Evidently, I married one.

My eyes shift to the center of the table, and I nearly choke. Tulips. Lively, cheerful, fresh. It's not enough that my wedding looked like a flower shop vomited all over it; now my house is hosting a botanical funeral. Those petals are already wilting, dying a slow, tragic death under the weight of their own beauty.

I grind my molars, forcing myself not to comment. Maybe if I stand here long enough, the furniture will vaporize. Or I will. Either works.

"Can you be useful and grab the wine from the fridge?" Allie doesn't even glance at me, like delegating tasks to her husband is already second nature. Domestic tyranny, established in record time, no less.

Wine fridge? I own a wine fridge? When the hell did I buy that? I drink scotch or whiskey. Straight. No pretentious swirling, sniffing, or notes of blackberry and oak. The fridge is built into the center island, who knew, inconveniently, between me and my wife's delicious ripe ass. Even I can't deny reality when it's standing right in front of me in skintight jeans.

I opt for the long route around the island, avoiding the temptation to admire the view. Leaning down, I open the fridge and find several bottles neatly arranged like she's been organizing this invasion for months instead of the literal hours she's been in residence.

"The merlot," she says, still not bothering to glance my way.

Nothing says celebrating a sham marriage like drinking a wine named after misery itself. I grab the bottle and drop it onto the island with a dull thud, stepping back as she turns from the stove.

"Glasses too."

Glasses. Right. I don't own wine glasses. I barely own plates. *Owned* plates, singular. One of everything—plate, bowl, fork. But now? The table's set like we're hosting a dinner party for two, complete with place mats and cloth napkins. *Cloth. Napkins. Is this what hell looks like?*

She flicks a finger toward the cabinet next to the wine fridge, like she expected my ineptitude. Sure enough, rows of red and white wine glasses line the shelves. Because apparently, drinking wine out of the wrong glass is a crime.

I grab two glasses and the bottle, hauling them to the table like they weigh more than the existential dread settling between my shoulder blades. Every step feels like I'm trudging toward domestic damnation. It's been twenty-four hours. *Twenty-four hours*, and I'm already setting the dinner table like some housebroken husband who forgot what freedom tastes like.

What's next? Weekend farmers' markets? Couples' cooking classes? Matching Christmas pajamas?

If I look like Alex or Dom—smiling, comfortable, content—I'll throw myself off the roof of our downtown office building. It's only forty floors.

Allie

I CAUGHT MY HUSBAND checking out my ass—which, frankly, was the entire point of these jeans. Not that I'd ever admit it. No, these were my freedom jeans, my official uniform for the post-marital, screw-your-dress-code era of my life. I'd been stuck in tasteful pencil skirts and stifling slacks long enough. Time to embrace the denim rebellion.

Comfortable? Hell no. Even the stretchy pair Violet swore by felt like I was squeezing into a sausage casing. I'd never thought I'd miss corporate chic—but at least a pencil skirt didn't require holding my breath, doing a full-body shimmy, and offering a prayer to the zipper gods. Fashion may be pain, but nothing says winning like a man you didn't even dress for getting caught gawking.

Skinny jeans it is.

I plated dinner with a little more flourish than necessary. Not that Rico had specific culinary preferences beyond the grilled cheese he mysteriously demanded every Tuesday—which is why I'd purposely bought ingredients for a gourmet grilled cheese this Wednesday. Because if he was going to be stubborn, I'd be petty. With extra Gruyère.

The prospect of irritating him thrilled me enough that I had to hide my grin. Which is ridiculous. I shouldn't be this entertained by passive-aggressive sandwich warfare.

And that's when I remembered: *The note.*

I'd left it smack in the middle of the coffee pot this morning—prime eye-level real estate—and now it was gone. Did he read it? Crumple it? Set it on fire? Honestly, I'd put money on the bonfire.

I lined up the plates with a perfectly seared steak, dollops of pesto, roasted potatoes, and glazed carrots. Vibrant, balanced, borderline artistic. A meal so enticing that even a heartless android might reconsider its programming. Then again, had I even seen Rico eat? Not at the wedding dinner, that's for sure—though, to be fair, I'd been too busy pushing my food around the plate. A stomach knotted with nerves doesn't leave room for much else.

Rico sat at the head of the table, naturally—because where else would the king of brooding masculinity perch? I slid the plate in front of him. His amber eyes flitted to mine for half a second. He nodded. No "thank you," no grudging compliment, just stoic silence.

I ignore the tension, taking my seat beside him, and blink at the two glasses already full of rich, deep red wine. I snatch mine up and down half in one go, topping it off without making eye contact. If he insisted on sitting there, all brooding marble statue fueled by spite, I might as well stay hydrated while watching the show.

He didn't speak. I didn't either. Not because I couldn't—I could monologue like it was my job—but because I enjoyed watching him stew. No one in his family seemed to push him, not from what I'd seen. Everyone tiptoed around Rico like he'd burst if motivated.

Well, newsflash: I wasn't tiptoeing anywhere. If he thought he'd married some docile, submissive wife who'd quietly accept silence and avoidance, he was in for a rude awakening.

I've already seen enough red flags to decorate an entire parade route, so yeah—I'm holding him to every promise he made, no matter how creatively he tries to squirm out of them. He bails on our wedding night, doesn't glance at me like I'm even mildly attractive, skips the compliments, and can't muster a "thanks" for dinner. And I'm pretty sure the recent additions to the house are eating him alive.

Just wait until the rest of my deliveries show up. Petty? Maybe. Effective? Definitely.

If Rico thinks he can ice me out and leave me marinating in a house as cold and uninviting as his personality, he's got another thing coming. He'll either adapt to my changes or move out—and honestly, if he packs his bags, I doubt I'll lose sleep.

He didn't even blink when I came home. Nope, he only emerged from his office when it suited him. Violet warned me he's the definition of a workaholic—apparently, Dom once had to physically drag him out after a 72-hour bender of caffeine and spreadsheets.

So, great. Quality time? Out the window. Emotional availability? Ha. The man uses work like a shield, and clearly, I'm no exception.

"What do you think?" I ask, eyeing him as he cuts his steak into neat little cubes—robotic, precise, like he's prepping for surgery, not dinner. He flexes his hand between slices, clenching and unclenching his fist.

He nods without glancing up. "It's fine."

Fine? This steak is a masterpiece—buttery, melt-in-your-mouth perfection with a garlicky, wine-kissed crust and a whisper of brown sugar. It's a steak that deserves poetry, not a half-assed "fine."

I watch him from the corner of my eye, afraid that direct contact might turn me to stone. Though, calling him Medusa feels off. He's less mythical monster and more... storm cloud. A cold front of doom, ready to suck me in and spit me out, personality optional.

He lifts a perfectly cubed piece of steak to his lips and pulls it off the fork with maddening slowness. No scraping teeth. No rushed bite. Just deliberate, almost sensual consumption—and, yeah, my thighs press together.

He's not trying to be seductive. After last night's rejection, it's clear he has zero interest in anything remotely close to seduction. And yet, the way he eats—so controlled, so painfully delicate—has my insides flipping and begging for more.

My throat goes dry. Sahara levels. Probably because all available moisture has migrated south. Fantastic. Why, body? Why are we drooling over the same man who basically stamped "return to sender" on our wedding night? Clearly, I'm just as broken as he is.

He doesn't even want you, and you're over here puddling like a teenager with her first crush.

I grab my wine and down half the glass, praying it drowns the tension simmering under my skin. But when I set the glass down, I catch him watching me—silent, unreadable, and definitely not "fine."

I set my fork down and delicately dab my mouth with my napkin, channeling the prim little princess I was raised to be. Then I glance at him.

"What?"

It comes out fiercer than intended, but can you blame me? I'm a woman currently waging war against my hormones, mourning the fact that I've landed myself in a wordless marriage, and—to top it all off—discovering that I find his brooding, grumpy asshole hot.

That has to be hormonal sabotage, right? There's no other plausible explanation for finding this attractive.

Unless I'm clinically deranged.

Either way, it's not looking good for me.

He just shakes his head, not bothering to grace me with an *actual* response, and goes back to cutting his carrots with the same infuriating precision he applied to his steak—perfect little orange circles, lined up and prepping for a photoshoot with *Better Homes & Gardens*. My cheeks flush, my spine prickles, and my heart pounds so loudly I'm half convinced he can hear it echoing off the walls.

And no, it's not the carrot-chopping prowess making me sweat. It's everything else—the fact that my body is betraying me, the way he's already found two loopholes around our agreement, and, worst of all, how pathetic I feel for still craving his attention after he's made it abundantly clear he doesn't need mine.

"Oh my God, enough!" I slam my cutlery down, the new china plates rattling in protest. Great—the plates have more emotional range than my husband. I probably shouldn't unpack the fact that the man I married is currently losing a personality contest to an inanimate object.

Rico freezes, fork hovering midair over a carrot like someone hit his pause button. His eyes flick up, meeting mine.

I'm two seconds away from flicking his nose just to see if he's stuck buffering when he blinks. And then—finally—his gaze drops, slow and deliberate. Down my neck, tracking the hard swallow I can't suppress, then lower... to my chest, where my traitorous nipples perk right up with an introductory wave and "nice to meet you."

I grit my teeth, willing my body to get on the same page as my brain—the page that clearly says *he doesn't want you, dumbass.*

But he keeps looking. Grazing me. Consuming me. Flaring up every inch of skin with nothing but his eyes. His fork's still frozen mid-air, but I'm the one melting—fully clothed, yet somehow feeling like he's just stripped me down and mapped every inch with his tongue.

Unfair. It's downright *unfair* that a man can wield eye contact like it's a superpower.

For half a second—half a second—I swear I see hunger flicker in those amber eyes, the same look I thought I imagined when I walked down the aisle. But just as quickly as it appears, it vanishes, snuffed out like a candle in the wind.

What—did he not like what he saw? I've never questioned my looks a day in my life, and now I'm married to a man who makes me wonder if I've been delusional this whole time. I'm sure that'll bode well for my self-esteem long-term.

But I'm done playing this game. I turn in my chair to face him, inhaling deeply, silently begging the snarky little bitch inside me to stand down. She's ready to claw her way out, talons bared and fully prepared to take his beautiful amber eyeballs as souvenirs.

"Rico. I made us dinner. I added life to this cave you call a home. I'm your wife. *Your. Wife.* And you don't even look at me like I'm remotely attractive. Honestly, I feel like a blister—annoying, inconvenient, and definitely not something you'd ever want to touch, sexually or otherwise."

He calmly sets his fork and knife down, then wipes his mouth with precision so practiced I'm two seconds from whipping him with said napkin.

"You're not a blister."

Wow. Be still my beating heart. I'm practically swooning over here.

My skin burns, and I'm positive my cheeks now resemble the merlot in my glass. Maybe it's the wine causing the flush, but no... that's pure, unfiltered rage with a dash of heartbreak.

"Rico, you only touch me when it's convenient for you and your grand plan to have kids. How do you expect me to get pregnant if you can't even pretend to find me attractive?"

"IVF, preferably."

The retort I'd cocked and charged dies on my tongue, leaving behind nothing but an acidic aftertaste. "IVF?" The word stumbles out, wobbly, like those three letters just hit me harder than a Mack truck.

He nods. *Nods.* Like he's suggesting we switch from regular to decaf.

"So you don't even want to have sex with me?" My voice cracks, and I hate myself for it. "You'd rather let a doctor handle it than..." I can't finish. The words clog my throat, held back by the sting of tears I refuse to shed.

Not here. Not in front of him. He doesn't get to see me fall apart, even if every muscle in my body coils tight and my heart shrinks like it's trying to escape this disaster of a conversation.

Pushing my chair back, I toss my napkin onto my barely touched plate. "Well, glad to know I'm so repulsive, the idea of making a baby with me sends you running to the nearest fertility clinic. I guess we'll never consummate this marriage either, huh? So what are we, Rico? Two miserable strangers sharing a house where happiness goes to die?"

I grab my wine glass, lifting it in a mock toast. "To 'til death do us part," I mutter before downing the rest in one defiant gulp. It burns—but not as much as his indifference.

The wine will kick in soon, numbing everything I'm trying not to feel. I plan to snatch the bottle off the table as I go, drown my sorrows upstairs in my room, submerged in a bubble bath with the soundtrack of my ugly sobs echoing off the tiles.

I'm two steps from the table when his arm snakes around my waist, yanking me flush against him. "The issue isn't you."

His breath scorches my ear, delivering tingles down my spine while goosebumps bloom across my skin. I shudder—*traitorous body*—and hate that I can't decide if it's from anger or desire.

"What is the issue, then?" My voice comes out breathless.

"Me."

I can't help it—I snort. "No shit. Tell me something I don't know."

Silence. We both freeze—his mouth still grazing my ear but not quite touching, like he's savoring the moment while I'm over here trying to convince my hormones to stop breakdancing. He breathes slow and controlled, the picture of calm, while I'm practically throbbing like I just shotgunned four espressos.

"I want you to find me desirable. That's the issue, right? You don't find me attractive. To you, sex would just be another item on your checklist. This won't be a real marriage.

It's just something on paper. Because you can't even bring yourself to consummate it. How unattractive am I, Rico?"

His grip loosens, and my stomach drops. Here it comes. The glorious exit.

But he doesn't walk away. Instead, his hand slides around my waist, fingers trailing down my stomach until they reach the waistband of my jeans. With one hand, he unbuttons them while the other large hand anchors me against him. I gasp—because *hello*, something very solid, very, very thick, presses into my lower back.

Well, at least that part works. I was half-convinced he needed a little blue pill or an "erection mode" button.

"I never said you were unattractive," he growls, the sound rumbling through my bones.

My jeans loosen as he tugs the zipper down, his hand slipping beneath the denim and brushing past my panties like he's done this a thousand times, and I tell myself to not think about with whom. His fingers find the heat between my thighs, and my spine arches—no conscious decision there. My body's officially running on autopilot.

I should knee him in the balls. I should spin around and give him an earful about mixed signals and emotional neglect. But I don't. Because, apparently, my internal debate team has one rational fairy screaming *Run!* and an irrational one waving pom-poms and shouting *Ride him like a mechanical bull girlfriend, yeeeeee-haaawww!*

The irrational one's winning, by the way.

"So wet and soft," he hisses, and the rational fairy officially taps out, gagged and bound in the corner.

I groan when he slips a finger inside, curling just right, and—dammit—he sighs like he's relieved. Like proving I want him fixes something inside his complicated head.

"You want me to consummate the marriage?" His voice drops lower. "Make it feel real?"

"No," I gasp, even though every nerve ending screams *Yes, you idiot!*

He slides in another finger. "No?" He pulls away, and I instinctively push back, seeking the friction I'm suddenly desperate for.

"Maybe..." My voice is barely a whisper. It's breathless, pathetic, and I don't care.

"Maybe?" His thumb circles my clit, and I'm officially gone—floating on cloud nine, ten and planning to one hundred.

"Y-yes," I stammer, heat pooling low in my belly as tension coils tighter

His other hand snakes up, fingers curling gently around my throat—not enough to hurt, just enough to keep me in place. Possessive. And *way* hotter than it should be.

I moan. *Who am I right now?*

"Fine, *Pearlina*," he murmurs. "I'll show you what it's like to be fucked by your husband."

Rico

I'VE NEVER WANTED A woman more, and that's the fucking problem.

Not her—*me*. I can't control the way my body betrays me every time she breathes in my direction. Her scent, her presence, her mere existence scrapes against my self-control like sandpaper on raw skin.

Cutting my food into perfect, symmetrical pieces is the only thing keeping me from either clenching my fists or tearing her clothes off. Apparently, precision didn't work. Because now, I'm doing exactly what I swore I wouldn't—stripping my wife like she stole something.

Which, to be fair, she did—my sanity.

The only silver lining? I'm suddenly grateful she bought this overpriced table. When I push her against it, it doesn't so much as creak. Sturdy. Well-made. Worth every damn penny, considering I'm about to christen the thing.

I pin her between the wood and my body, my hands already working her jeans down her legs. Yeah, I told her to keep them covered—I just didn't realize "covered" meant denim painted on like a second skin, showing every curve that's been haunting my thoughts. My punishment, I suppose, for assuming I'm immune.

The second the jeans slide past her hips, I bite back a groan. *Black lace.* My fingers hook the delicate string, snapping it against her skin. She yelps, and I almost smile. *Almost.*

"Did you wear this for me?" The question tastes bitter—part accusation, part possession. Because if she didn't, who the fuck was it for? I'll table the fact I even care for later.

"No." A whisper, soft as sin. It pisses me off more than it should.

I rip the thong off without thinking, some primal, irrational instinct driving the action. If it's not for me, it doesn't deserve to exist. I'm pretty sure they call that jealousy—an emotion I don't entertain. Or didn't until *now*.

Tugging her jeans off each leg, I rise slowly, hands trailing up smooth thighs, over round hips, until they find her ass—full, perfect, and *mine*. I knead the flesh, watching her brace herself against the table, spine arching like an offering.

"No?" The word coated in incredulity and something darker.

I spin her to face me, hands still roaming, cataloging every inch like I'm committing her to memory—because I am. Why the fuck is her skin so soft? Like silk warmed by sunlight. I've barely touched women before—impersonal encounters with the women I paid require as little as possible—but this? This feels dangerous. Addictive.

When my hands slip under her bra, cupping her breasts, my cock throbs against my zipper, reminding me it's here and deserves the attention. Honestly, I'm inclined to agree—but I'm not rushing this. Not when I don't know if I'll ever let myself have her like this again. Except... I know. And the awareness makes my teeth clench.

Bending down, I bite her nipple through the thin fabric of her shirt. She moans, back arching further, pressing into me like she's gift-wrapping herself and slapping on a bow. My heart slams against my ribs.

This is bad.

Touching her, feeling every curve—it's all one massive red flag. I'm supposed to fuck my wife when she's ovulating, clinical and detached, like a transaction. If I need release, it should be a quick, efficient quickie—not a slow-burn seduction where I memorize every inch of her body.

But I *can't* stop. Worse... I don't *want* to.

I'm not about to admit her tits are the first—and *only*—pair I've ever had in my hands. And fuck me if I don't want more.

Self-control? Never met the guy.

I yank her shirt over her head, flicking the bra clasp like I've done it a thousand times instead of Googling how once—for research. The bra hits the floor, and I step back, eyes dragging over her bare skin.

Mine.

She'll hate me later. Scratch that—she'll definitely hate me later. Maybe tomorrow, maybe next week. It's inevitable. But right now, she's mine. And like the thief she is, she's stolen my composure, my logic, and every ounce of my better judgment.

Without thinking—because thinking would mean stopping—I haul her into me. One hand fists in her hair, the other grips her ass, pulling her flush against my still fully clothed body. The contrast—her naked, me armored in fabric—feels wrong. Like I'm protecting her from myself. Like it'll matter.

I don't kiss. *But I kiss her.*

If you can call it that. It's not tender. I nip at her lips, swallowing every moan, every gasp, grinding into her like friction might exorcise the demons she's waking up in me. Zipper burn? Worth it. I fuck her mouth with my tongue, and she kisses me back with equal parts anger and lust—the perfect cocktail. At least now I know she'll still let me fuck her, even if she's pissed.

Again... why am I planning for a next time?

Her nails dig into my shoulders, sharp little reminders that she's not fragile. Good. I hope she leaves marks. At least they'd be scars I wouldn't mind explaining.

But when her hands reach for the hem of my shirt, I break the kiss, grabbing her wrists with a slow shake of my head. "Shirt stays on."

"What? Why?"

Yeah, why, Rico? Why the hell do I keep the armor when I'm already losing the war?

I don't answer that question.

"I have rules you need to know."

"Oh? Why weren't those mentioned when we signed our contract? You remember that little paper?"

Her sass is not helping what-so-ever, because for some odd as hell reason, I find it arousing and she's more than aware of the bulge pressing into her as evidence of that.

"First, I don't take my shirt off." Her mouth opens but I press my index finger over her lips, and when her tongue peeks out to lick my finger, sucking it into her mouth, hot and wet it gives me an all too real image of what it would look like if that sinful mouth wrapped around my cock. I'm going to pass out, but I have to tell her.

The rules are necessary. I didn't put them all in the contract, but that was poor planning. My brothers, Jaxon, no one knows my rules or how I have sex, and the idea of it on paper didn't seem right.

"Second, it's from behind."

She stops sucking, releasing my finger with a wet pop.

I've died.

Or close enough at the mere sound of her wet warm mouth releasing my finger. If I don't finish this, my cock might very well fall off at the misery it's sporting. Fuck, that was hot. *Nope, focus.*

"Why behind? You mean only from behind?" Her cheeks flush. Something tells me she's never even had sex from behind. Good. Hopefully she likes it since that's the only way I do this.

I nod.

"So, you stay fully clothed, minimal touching, from behind...Am I a dog in heat? You just romp on top of me when it works for you and then see you next time?" She smirks, and my ego deflates a bit. "You had said no kissing when we drafted the contract. Where's that rule now?"

I ignore that. Momentary lapse in judgment.

"Do you understand?"

"Yes, but I want to know why."

Instead of answering, I decide I'll just show her, make it good enough that she never argues with me about it — because it's non-negotiable. I spin her around, bending her over the table. Her ass curves up, perfect and ready, and I groan out loud. No control. None.

"I'm having my dessert now."

Jesus Christ, did I just say that? *Out loud?* Apparently, my internal monologue has gone rogue. But it's true—she looks like dessert, and I'm about to savor every bite.

I trail kisses down her spine, releasing her wrists so my fingers can follow the path my mouth blazes. When I reach the curve of her ass, I bite—gentle, but firm enough to make her choke. Worth it.

Then I find her center, teasing her entrance with one finger, then two, until desire twists into something primal. I don't just want to touch her. I want to ruin her for anyone else.

So I do the only logical thing: I drop to my knees and taste her like she's the antidote to my poisoned soul.

I flatten my tongue, licking, sucking her clit into my mouth like it's a damn lollipop. When she moans my name, breathless and broken, I practically turn feral.

Escorts fake enjoyment. This woman doesn't. She's gripping the table like it's the only thing keeping her tethered to earth and moaning in pure pleasure. And hell, if that realization doesn't make my cock ache so hard, I wonder if spontaneous combustion is an actual medical concern.

My tongue and fingers work in tandem, teasing, circling, stretching—and when her body clamps around my fingers, silky and tight, I growl. My cock's officially jealous. Ridiculous.

"So tight," I mutter, words slipping out without permission. Since when am I chatty during sex? I'll unpack that later... probably never.

She rides my fingers, ass pressing back, chasing her own pleasure until she bursts, muscles rippling, thighs trembling. The sensation alone almost makes me blow in my pants.

I don't do foreplay. It's inefficient, unnecessary. And yet here I am suddenly an expert in female anatomy, muscle memory I didn't know I had kicked in.

I stand quickly, freeing my cock and lining myself up. She's limp against the table, skin flushed, breath shallow, and I press into her wet heat without hesitation. Three women. That's my number. *Always* with a condom. *Always* transactional. When you pay for it, you triple-wrap—common sense, really. But this? This is bare, raw, and bordering on reckless. Only you can't wrap it up if you want to knock it up.

Her walls clench around me, hot and smooth, and I growl—gripping her hips like they're the only thing anchoring me to sanity. She's tight. Sinfully soft. And I'd be perfectly content staying here, buried to the hilt, until the world ends. Impractical, sure. But a man can dream.

I'm not even halfway inside her, and my spine already tingles, balls pulling tight. Fuck. I grit my teeth and start reciting lines of algorithms, sequences, anything to avoid detonating inside her before she has another orgasm.

Distance. I need distance. My gaze flickers around the room, searching for something—anything—to ground me. Instead, my eyes catch on her hair, dark as ink, spilling around her like spilled oil on polished wood.

Black like the sky before a thunderstorm. Black like the ink on our marriage license, binding me to this woman for life—and God help me, I don't hate it.

"Jesus, Rico, fuck me already."

Her voice—husky, breathless—yanks me back. She glances over her shoulder, a mischievous smile tugging at lips already swollen from my kisses. *My kisses.* "You said you were going to fuck me. So do it."

At this rate, cardiac arrest seems likely.

My heart skips—traitorous bastard—and worst of all, it moves. I'm utterly fucked, and somehow I'm the one supposed to be doing the fucking. Right? It's all fuzzy now.

I grip her hips, hard enough to bruise, and thrust to the hilt. Her eyes flutter shut, and she pushes back into me like she's trying to crawl inside my skin. I freeze.

Think about code. Think about dogs in ridiculous sweaters. Think about how kale is a government conspiracy or a Kardashian-fueled trend. Either way, it should be illegal.

She moans, rolling her hips for more friction, and I nearly lose it—ready to beg her to not fucking move, so I don't embarrass myself. Two-pump chump? Never happened. Not until now, apparently. Then again, before her, I didn't talk, touch, or know the person outside of where to Venmo and show up for my appointment. No attraction or incurable hunger.

I focus on the wall—gray, blank, impersonal. A reminder that this is supposed to be mechanical. The body under me is a vessel, not a person I need to know. Not someone I should crave.

"Fine," I grind out, jaw tight, lungs burning. One deep breath and I'll lose it. "You asked for it."

My fingers dig into her hips and I pull out before slamming back in. The table groans—so do I. Again. Again. Harder, faster, deeper. Long, punishing strokes designed to break us both.

She doesn't falter—just moans louder, palms braced against the table, pushing back to meet every thrust. I want to see her tits bounce—that sinful, hypnotic sway—but I'm not pulling out. Not now. Preferably never.

"You take my cock so well, baby." The words slip out before I can stop them. Apparently, while I was busy mentally disassociating, my mouth went rogue.

Her moan is my only answer, and it's more satisfying than any algorithm ever written.

"Rico, I'm going to come."

Her voice—breathless, raw—skitters up my spine, tightens my stomach, and probably inflates my ego to dangerous levels.

Well, that makes two of us. Thank God for small mercies.

Reaching around, I circle her clit, relentless and precise, each thrust harder, faster, like I'm trying to carve my name into her from the inside out. My molars are probably ground to dust from how hard I'm clenching my jaw, but it's the only thing keeping me from coming too soon. Then she comes—body arching, walls clamping down on my cock like a vice, and I lose it. One last thrust and I'm gone, yanking her upright, one hand around her throat, the other bruising her hip as I bury myself deeper.

My cock swells, and the spasms of her orgasm milk every drop from me, wringing me out until there's nothing left but the sharp bite of satisfaction and the dull hum of overstimulation. My hips jerk against her ass as I sink my teeth into her neck, hard enough to brand. If I don't leave a mark, what the hell's the point?

Not thinking. Because who the fuck thinks straight after the best orgasm of their life? Certainly not me. That ship sailed the moment I slid inside her.

I tilt her head, claiming her mouth, swallowing every whimper, every gasp, rocking my hips like I'm trying to crawl inside her and never leave. Well aware that not even a few minutes ago, I just told the woman no kissing and no touching and that sure as shit went away fast.

"You want to know my secret?" I mutter against her lips, her limp body practically melting into mine. "You're my first kiss."

Like I said—*not* thinking.

Her lips part, eyes widening, undoubtedly ready to demand an explanation, and because I have zero interest in that conversation, I do the only thing I know will keep her from trying to dissect it, let alone talk about it.

I take her mouth in mine, harshly, and nipping before I pull out of her. My release drips down her thighs, obscene and possessive—mine in the most primal sense. But more importantly, I'm still hard. Not the usual semi that fades post-climax, but an aching reminder that my body has officially betrayed me.

This is biological, right? Some caveman instinct to impregnate my wife. It's definitely not because she turns me on so much I can't think straight. Couldn't be that.

I spin her to face me, cutting off whatever brilliant observation she's about to make by crushing my mouth to hers. Funny how shoving my tongue down her throat keeps her quiet. I'll have to remember that.

Without breaking the kiss, I lift her onto the table, grip her hips, and slide into her again—slick, tight, perfect. This time, there's no holding back. I fuck her like she's the solution to a problem I've spent my life trying to solve—hard, fast, and brutal. My fingers dig into her flesh, hard enough to bruise, and I hope they do. Proof she was here. Proof I lost my mind over her.

Her tits bounce with every thrust, hypnotic and maddening, and her mouth falls open in a silent moan, eyes fluttering like she can't decide whether to keep watching me or let the pleasure consume her.

"Mine," I growl, snapping my hips forward, my cock sliding in and out of her like I'm trying to ruin us both. It feels better than the first time—slicker, hotter, like her body's learned how to accommodate me and doesn't want to let go and I'm quite literally so pussy whipped I will beg it to not release me.

Her eyes fly open, and just as she's about to speak, I yank her up and kiss her again. Strategy. Always strategy.

"Feel how hard you make me?" I murmur against her mouth, not giving her the chance to answer before kissing her deeper.

She nods, breath hitching.

"Then you understand my problem." I bite her lower lip, pulling it between my teeth until she gasps. "Because now all I'm going to do tonight is fuck you until you can't walk, and you're going to take every inch like the good little wife you are."

Her mouth falls open, eyes wide—scandalized, turned on, probably both—and I don't give her the luxury of a response. I swallow her protest, her moan, her everything, pounding into her like I can erase the last remnants of self-control I ever possessed.

When we both break—her body clamping down, mine emptying inside her deep and my body shudders at the sensation—she clings to me like she's drowning, arms tight, breath ragged. My mouth is still glued to hers as the kiss slows, softens, and that's when the fog lifts and the cold, rational part of my brain clicks back on.

I didn't just fuck up. I obliterated the line I swore I'd never cross. Not only did I waste possibly my sperm on a chance they'll never meet an egg—another thing she's stolen from me—but it's too much. Too close. Too real.

There's a reason I don't touch women. Why they don't touch me. Why I pay escorts to get off and send them on their way.

Because this? This is a textbook example of why I don't lose control.

And worse... because I want more.

Allie

THE MAN FLIPPED MY orgasm switch and then ran like someone just pulled the fire alarm.

One minute he's touching me like I'm the last bite of dessert he can't wait to devour, and the next, he's peeling himself away faster than a kid who's accidentally eaten a Brussels sprout disguised as chocolate.

My mouth pops open, ready to say something—*anything*—to salvage whatever's left of this moment. But Rico doesn't give me the chance. He jerks away, zipping up his jeans so quickly you'd think I'd spontaneously grown teeth down there. With one brief, clinical glance, he exits the room faster than my dignity can evaporate.

And just like that, I'm alone. Naked. In the kitchen. The door down *his* hallway slammed vigorous enough to shake the house, vibrating the picture frame I'd strategically hung just outside his precious little "private sanctuary." Petty? Absolutely. Sorry? Not even a little.

A shiver slid down my spine as I stood there—naked, sweaty, and feeling about as wanted as discount sushi on a Monday. This wasn't the post-consummation glow I'd imagined. This was awkward, sticky, and cold. Rico had walked out without a word, leaving me behind like I was a chore crossed off a list. Task done. No thanks necessary.

Scrambling for my clothes, I snatched each piece off the floor, not bothering to put them on. Why waste another second in this sterile house he clearly had given a "modern morgue chic" warmth?

Honestly, I don't know where I went wrong. One moment he's whispering things so dirty they'd make a trucker blush, and the next he's shutting down faster than Netflix when you don't click "Yes, I'm still watching." If emotional whiplash were an Olympic sport, he'd be swimming in gold medals.

The rhythmic *thud-thud-thud* of his fists striking leather echoes through the house.

"Great," I muttered, stooping down to swipe my shredded black lace panties. "Apparently, I'm married to Rocky Balboa."

The sticky reminder running down my inner thigh answered that with an unwelcome "yep," loud and clear. I swallowed hard, hating the sting of embarrassment that flooded my cheeks. *Used.* Not the fun, kinky kind of used that comes with promises of round two and a stupid grin. Nope, this was purely transactional—and detached. The used that comes with a receipt, an awkward pat on the head, and absolutely zero eye contact.

Well, never again.

I glared toward the hallway as the incessant thumping continued, fists colliding with leather like a caveman working out his feelings. Only my caveman doesn't do those.

Honestly, I hoped he punched that bag until his knuckles turned purple. Maybe it'd knock loose whatever emotional stiffness he was suffering from.

Because this time, maybe I let him bend me to his will, but next time?

Next time, Rico Bennetti would have to beg.

His *first* kiss? Ha. And I'm the freaking Easter Bunny.

There's no universe where a thirty-seven-year-old man with Rico Bennetti's skill set—particularly the filthy-talking, panty-obliterating skill set I'd just witnessed—has never kissed a woman before. Sure, he kissed me—but that wasn't romance. That was damage control. He kissed me purely because shutting me up required drastic measures. Like sticking a pacifier in the mouth of a screaming toddler. Effective, but temporary.

Maybe while he murmured those filthy promises in my ear, he was picturing someone else. A lingerie model, a celebrity, or possibly a curvy new monitor—I wouldn't put it past him. That would explain why, ten seconds after he pulled away, reality hit him like an undesirable hangover, and suddenly, he looked at me like I was expired milk he'd accidentally poured into his cereal.

His first kiss? Please. He hadn't lived thirty-seven years as a sexy-as-hell hermit. No, that was a kiss designed for damage control, a distraction from the fact he'd gone emotionally comatose halfway through sex. Like someone unplugged him mid-thrust.

And then he ran. Actually stormed off like I was the living embodiment of buyer's remorse.

Even after scrubbing myself raw in a scalding shower, I still couldn't shake the embarrassment clinging to me. Discarded napkins at a taco stand got treated with more respect.

I leaned my forehead against the shower tile, letting the scorching water rinse over me, scouring every trace of him away until my skin was pink and angry. And maybe—*hopefully*—any overachieving sperm got the message and took the express lane down the drain. A kitchen-table quickie baby? Yeah, hard pass. Talk about the universe laughing at me.

Cold embarrassment clung to my skin, chilling me from the inside out. I might have enjoyed every filthy second of it—those thrusts deserved a medal—but did that really matter when the man looked at me afterward like he'd accidentally bitten into a raisin cookie expecting chocolate chips?

Nope. I was officially done.

Wrapped in a towel and my dignity barely intact, I curled into a ball on the bed. My throat tightened, and despite the promises I made myself, tears leaked onto the pillow. At least my pillow didn't flinch or run away. Bonus points there.

Is this my future? Every time I announce ovulation like a traffic update, Rico will clench his jaw, close his eyes, and mentally retreat to some inner sanctum while doing the bare minimum required to knock me up? Then he'll storm out of the room and spend an hour going ten rounds with an Everlast—like he's training for a heavyweight championship match against his life choices.

The relentless pounding continues downstairs, rattling the floorboards beneath my feet. He must be picturing my face on that bag, because no one throws that many punches without a personal vendetta.

When we signed our marriage contract, I'd joked about being a business deal. Turns out, the joke's on me. I'm officially the other woman in my marriage. The emotional mistress he's desperate to avoid eye contact with.

He's made it clear with every punch downstairs that touching me required penance—one hit for every regret-filled thrust.

He. Didn't. Want. To. Look. At. Me.

Well, joke's on him. I'm here, I'm his wife, and avoiding eye contact will not erase me. If he thinks he can emotionally ice me out forever, he's in for a rude awakening.

Because Rico Bennetti might think he's the reigning champ of reaction lockdown, but I've never met a problem I couldn't solve—or at least annoy into waving the white flag.

Allie

I'VE BARELY SEEN MY husband since *the night*. You know, that night. The one where he finally consummated our marriage—if you can even call it that. Because nothing says "forever and ever, amen" like getting bent over the dining room table, right between a half-eaten steak and a plate of potatoes, like we were starring in an X-rated episode of Hell's Kitchen.

Romantic? Sure. If your idea of romance is staring at a crusty plate while your husband rails you like, he's trying to exorcise his inner demons.

Spoiler alert: it does not come with post-coital cuddles. Apparently, table sex isn't covered under the "spoon me after" clause.

That was a week ago. Seven full days of wedded bliss. And by bliss, I mean avoidance so extreme it should be submitted to NASA for study. Rico? He's evading me. The man moves through this house like a six-foot-three shadow, gliding silently from room to room like Batman—if Batman hated intimacy, conversation, and being legally bound to another human being.

Meanwhile, here I am, marinating in a cocktail of frustration and self-pity.

My brain knows damn well that another round of "table fun" would leave me feeling hollow—like a knocked-over wine glass that once held something worth savoring. But my traitorous body? Oh no, she's singing a whole different song. Every time he walks by, all broad shoulders and razor-sharp jawline, with those stupid amber eyes that somehow look both pissed off and devastatingly hot at the same time, my thighs go full traitor and clench.

And as if that wasn't enough, the evidence of our little furniture-based disaster stayed with me for days. Bruises blooming on my hips like abstract art. Finger-shaped marks on my ass, as if he wanted to leave a receipt. A bite on my neck was so dark I'm pretty sure even Dracula would have been like, "Damn, bro, dial it back."

So yeah. That's been my week.

The only proof Rico's alive and hasn't, I don't know, run off to start a new identity somewhere? The Post-It notes he leaves like some emotionally stunted pen pal, stuck to the coffeepot as if that fulfills his end of our very clear contract. You know, the one where we agreed to share one personal fact a day?

Apparently, I never clarified how that fact should be shared, and Rico? He lives for loopholes like a lawyer on a caffeine bender.

Today's gem?

Rico: I hate cats. Not a mild dislike—full-blown hatred. They're tiny, judgmental assassins with fur.

Wow. Deep stuff.

Naturally, I responded in kind, because two can play this passive-aggressive game.

Allie: Odd. I was just at the shelter. Saw one that could use a home.

For the record, I'm not even a cat person. But would I adopt one out of pure spite? You bet your ass I would. I'd name him Mr. Whiskers, buy him the most obnoxious glitter collar money can buy, and make damn sure he sleeps only in Rico's bed.

Yesterday's Post-It? Equally life-altering.

Rico: I don't trust people who drink sparkling water. It's an affront to hydration.

Oh. Okay. Glad we're covering the *big* issues, Bennetti.

My reply? Naturally, with all the grace and petty precision of a woman hellbent on pushing buttons:

Allie: Sparkling water with lime is delicious. Try one of the dozen I put in the fridge for you.

And yes, I absolutely stocked that fridge like I was prepping for a La Croix influencer brunch. Lime. Lemon. Grapefruit. Some weird fruit combo I couldn't pronounce but bought anyway because it looked fancy and, let's be honest, Rico probably deserves to be confused by his own refrigerator.

When Vinnie opened the fridge, blinking at the sparkling rainbow of carbonated rebellion, he looked at me like I'd finally snapped.

"Didn't he say he hates this stuff?"

I shrugged, casually tossing a lemon one onto the counter. "Yup."

Vinnie snorted, reaching in for a grapefruit. "Eh. They're not bad."

Exactly. They're not. But whether Rico drinks them or stares at them is entirely his problem. He can either hydrate like a lifestyle blogger on a cleanse or drink straight from the tap like some kind of medieval peasant. I'm flexible.

What I haven't bought? A single bottle of distilled water—aka his pretentious drink of choice—because if we're doing petty warfare, I'm about to paint my own Mona Lisa of passive aggression.

Honestly, at this point, Post-It War *is* our marriage. We don't talk. He sticks his neon notes on the coffee pot, and I fire back like a snarky game of Battleship.

B4, Rico. You sunk my patience.

It's sad, right? I've read more of his handwriting in those little squares than I've heard his voice in the entire week we've been married. And let's be real—most of the words that have come out of his mouth were moaned between my legs like I was some kind of stress-relief toy with boobs.

Romantic, isn't it?

Sure, we technically "eat dinner together" every night as agreed. If you call me asking how his day went while he grunts into his plate like a cave dweller, "dinner conversation." I sit there, trying to act normal, while he scarfs down pasta like he's in a damn speed-eating contest, barely bothering to chew. Like the faster he finishes, the sooner he can run back to whatever cave he crawled out of.

Not even a "thanks for dinner, Allie." Not a "this tastes great, Allie." Hell, I'd take a grunt of approval at this point. But no. Just a silent wipe of his mouth, a quick rinse of the plate, and his disappearing act back down the hall. Either to bury himself in work or punch his feelings out like an MMA fighter in training. Every. Night.

Honestly, it's gotten to where I eye the dining table like it's betrayed me. Because let's not forget—that was the scene of the crime. Our so-called "consummation."

First two nights after? I couldn't even sit in my chair without blushing like a nun in a strip club. And yes, I sanitized the hell out of that table the next morning, scrubbing it so hard I'm surprised I didn't take the finish right off. Pretty sure my bottle of Pledge was weeping in the corner when I was done. Fact: Pledge does not, in fact, remove memories of being railed by your emotionally stunted husband.

Maybe they should put that on the label.

But like the idiot optimist I apparently am — a title I didn't realize I was vying for — I keep trying. Because what's marriage if not a slow, painful exercise in banging your head against a wall and hoping it turns into a door?

Take last night's dinner, for example. Another shining moment in the *Allie Bennetti Attempts to Engage Her Husband* highlight reel.

"I was thinking for our date night, we could go to Via Napoli?" I say it as casually as I can, like I'm asking if he wants fries with dinner and not begging him to actually spend an evening with me that doesn't involve him giving me the silent treatment over rigatoni.

His eyes? Glued to his plate.

I push on, because apparently, I enjoy torturing myself. "It's my favorite restaurant. I've always dreamed of owning a place like that. You know, the food, the decor... It's perfect."

Nothing. Not even a blink.

Outstanding. I guess that's my daily "fact share" for the marriage contract. One-sided, as usual. I talk. He chews. The only thing we do together is chew — and let me tell you, synchronized chewing? Not nearly as fun as it sounds.

And here comes the signature move—the fist clench.

Every dinner, every interaction, the man's hands flex and tighten, like he's trying to squeeze his feelings into submission. Or maybe he's debating if now's the time to punch through the table. His knuckles? Raw. Red, purple, cracked open like he went twelve rounds with a brick wall and lost.

Because that's what it takes to survive five minutes with me, apparently—brute force and some solid upper body conditioning.

Nothing says you're *special*, like watching your husband's hands tremble from the sheer effort of not flipping the table while you chat about your favorite pasta place.

Three days ago, I officially gave up, expecting he'd text me back. And yes, I'm counting. His read receipts pop up like a middle finger from the universe. He reads them. Oh, he reads them all right. But responses? Nada. I could text him, *"Hey, the house is on fire. Grabbing marshmallows. You want one?"* and he'd probably just nod at his phone and go back to whatever weird villain plotting he does in that office.

So now, every time my phone pings, do I expect Rico?

Nope.

It's always Violet or Sienna — my honorary "Save Allie from her Awkward Marriage" hotline. Checking in, sending memes, and trying to keep me from losing my mind inside this mausoleum of a house.

Still, that tiny flicker of hope sparks every time my phone lights up, and I still text him more than aware I'll receive silence. Because apparently, my inner idiot hasn't gotten the memo yet.

I press my lips together, pushing down that knot of disappointment that seems to be my new emotional roommate. Because honestly, I knew who I was marrying. Rico didn't catfish me. He wasn't parading around like Mr. Romantic, only to pull the rug out from under me. No. He came fully packaged as Emotionally Constipated Mayor of Broodsville.

His family *warned* me. He *warned* me.

I mean, technically, I shouldn't be surprised. But just because you see the train coming doesn't mean it hurts less when it hits you.

So yeah. This is my life now.

Sitting across from a man who looks at me like I'm an unexpected meeting invite. A man who tenses up every time I speak like I'm a pop quiz he didn't study for.

And as much as I want to roll with it, pretend like I'm cool with living in a house that feels lonelier than a cemetery after hours, it sucks.

Because yes, technically, I'm not alone. My husband is here. In body, if not in spirit. But it's like living with a ghost who has excellent Wi-Fi and a gym addiction. He haunts his office, the gym, his room—anywhere but near me.

And if I didn't know better, I'd swear he schedules his entire day around not having to see me. Because every morning? He's miraculously up before me, long gone, like a puff of smoke before I can even shuffle into the kitchen for coffee.

But guess what, Rico? I'm not going anywhere. You married me. And if you think you can outlast me in a battle of stubborn, silent endurance? Well, buckle up, sweetheart. You're about to find out what happens when you marry a woman who refuses to be ignored.

My parents still haven't responded to a single call or text. Not one. And yes, before you ask, I even went full Jane Austen and wrote my father an actual letter. Like handwritten, sealed with a stamp, and probably carrying enough emotional baggage to crash a postal truck.

I laid it all out too—poured my heart out like I was starring in some Regency-era drama. It's not you, it's the life you were forcing on me, *blah blah*. I thought, surely this would melt him. Turns out, Papa's heart is apparently made of titanium.

And now? I'm not so sure I made the right call.

Marrying Carlo would've been like locking myself in a dungeon with a lifetime supply of bleach baths. The man's touch makes me wonder if full-body condoms are a thing — and if so, where can I get a 12-pack on Amazon Prime? But at least if I'd done that, I'd still have my family.

Instead, here I am, married to Rico "Emotionally Unavailable" Bennetti, whose family has—bless them—practically adopted me. Sunday dinners, Wednesday night cooking marathons, random text messages filled with unsolicited life advice from his sisters. They try. God, they try. And I love them for it. But no amount of homemade lasagna or overly aggressive biscotti-gifting can fill the mama-shaped hole in my chest.

I miss her. Like *achingly* miss her. I'd trade every shiny new Amex card, every overpriced handbag I bought to passive-aggressively fill my time, just to sit down at her kitchen table with a mug of coffee and spill my guts. I want to whine about my husband—this distant, broody blip on my radar—and hear her tell me what to do. Because if anyone knows how to survive an arranged marriage with a man who looks at you like you're a chair that keeps getting in his way, it's my mother.

Except she doesn't call. No *"hey, sweetie."* No *"you'll be fine, honey."* No *"ditch him and come home."* Just silence. No texts. Not even a "seen" notification. Radio. Freaking. Silence.

And tonight? Tonight is cooking night. Which, naturally, Rico knows. Which also explains why, like clockwork, he's suddenly forgotten where he lives. Because God forbid he show up for a family dinner and risk interacting with his wife like a functioning adult.

He hates Sunday dinners, but shows. Every time, he walks in like he's on death row, staring down the executioner. But the second one of his nieces or nephews charges at him with sticky hands and a giggle? Poof. Mr. I-Have-No-Feelings melts like butter on a hot skillet. Scoops them up, kisses their cheeks, ruffles their hair like some freaking dream dad. And my ovaries? Standing ovation. Literal applause.

And you know what? I wish I could say that sight didn't destroy me a little bit inside. Because even though I know if we ever have kids, they'll get that version of Rico—the soft, affectionate, melt-your-heart version—part of me will still sit on the sidelines, clapping with my consolation prize.

Congratulations, Allie. Your children will get the love you'll never have. Here's your emotional participation trophy!

Would I be jealous of my own kids? God, I wish I could say no. I want to say no. But if I'm being honest? Yeah. A little. Because what kind of woman marries a man who can't even look at her without acting like she's a piece of furniture he didn't order?

Oh right. This woman. The one married to a moderately attractive carved statue who runs on caffeine and unresolved childhood trauma.

Vinnie's driving me to the Bennetti estate and I don't even bother texting to remind him I'll be out for the night. Why would I? The man knows what day it is. He wouldn't care if I texted *"Off to Canada to adopt a moose. His name is now Rico Jr."* He'd probably read it, grunt, and go back to his computer.

Because that's us. Married. Sharing a house. Breathing the same overpriced oxygen. Like two strangers awkwardly stuck in an elevator, pretending they don't see each other while the walls close in.

No talking. No touching. Not even a nod. Just... *existing*.

And I'm sitting here, watching the city lights blur past the car window, wondering is this it?

Is this my forever?

Two ships passing in the night—except one ship is actively trying to avoid even acknowledging the other. And me? I'm just here, waving a giant "HEY, REMEMBER ME? YOUR WIFE!" flag, while he ducks and hides behind his walls.

Because apparently, in the Bennetti marriage handbook, page one reads:

"When in doubt, ignore your wife until she forgets she exists."

Rico

CELIBACY-INDUCED INSANITY. THAT'S THE only logical explanation for why I let myself screw my wife on the dining room table and then lost my mind over it.

Two orgasms in under ten minutes—*unquestionably* the best of my life—and now I'm hiding as if she's patient zero in a viral outbreak. Fully quarantined. No contact. Minimal eye exposure.

I show up for our scheduled dinners like a corporate drone punching a timecard, offering grunts and nods like some sort of domesticated caveman. And then there are those ridiculous notes I leave her—the Post-Its she pretends not to wait for but absolutely reads. Random facts. Useless information, I dig out of the dusty corners of my brain. Genuine enough to avoid violating the contract, but empty enough to mean nothing.

I should probably feel bad for skirting the terms of what's supposed to pass as a marriage, but guilt is a luxury for people who have emotions left to spend. My accounts are overdrawn.

She thinks those notes will create intimacy, stacking up little bricks to build some fairytale house where we hold hands and smile over pancakes. As if the broken shards of what I am—razor-edged, calcified pieces—could ever form anything functional, let alone a marriage. Hope is one hell of a drug, and I'm not about to be her supplier.

So I stick to the routine.

Sleep after her.

Leave before she wakes.

Minimal exposure. I'm radioactive and she's got a Geiger counter strapped to her chest, and it's telling us both to stay away—I'm the only one that happens to listen.

The less she sees me, the faster she'll understand this arrangement for what it is—a contract sealed with a pen, not a kiss. And certainly *not* another round of me losing control inside her. Because if my body so much as thinks about her—those curves, her scent, that damn mouth—I'll break. And I can't afford to break.

Dinner is a masterclass in endurance. A game of mental chess where she moves closer, and I pretend not to notice. My fists stay balled in my lap under the table, knuckles raw from the nights I spend pounding away at the bag in the gym, trying to sweat her out of my system. I sit there staring at my plate, laser-focused on not looking at her, even though every molecule of me is hyper-aware of the fact that if I turn my head even slightly, I'll be treated to a front-row seat to temptation.

My house—the last place I could retreat, the one slice of my world I could control—has been overrun. My sanctuary of glass, steel, and order? Gone.

Now when I step out of my room, I'm greeted by a blinding assault of sunlight. Every fucking blind thrown open like we're welcoming in the Renaissance. Who does that? Vampires avoid the sun for a reason. I used to thrive in shadows. Now I live in a Zen coach's wet dream.

She's invaded.

There are decorative tins on the kitchen counters. *Tins*. Like we live in a cottage where we forage for herbs. The couch? Once a beautifully minimalistic piece of art—now drowning in a colony of throw pillows multiplying like they're on a fertility treatment. Ironic, considering my wife isn't.

And then there are the flowers. Fresh, bright, offensive flowers. Sitting on my counter like a smug reminder of how fragile everything is. A daily, wilting metaphor for wasted effort—life cut short for beauty that won't last.

But the crown jewel? The clock.

The fucking clock.

It's obscenely large and ticking loud enough to drill into my skull. Every second, a reminder that time is marching on and I'm stuck here in this curated version of hell.

What kind of person needs a clock that big? What's she tracking—phases of the moon? My slow descent into madness? If it doubled as a mirror, at least I could check to see if I looked as exhausted as I feel. But no, it's strategically placed so that all I see is time—taunting me.

Tick. Tick. Tick.

Counting down to when I finally snap—or when she packs up her floral arrangements and throw pillows and leave me in peace. Whichever comes first.

But if she thinks I'm going to give her what she wants—emotion, connection, something real—she's more delusional than I gave her credit for.

She may have stolen my house, but she's not getting anything else.

At least my office remains untouched. A fortress of solitude, still blessedly free from her honeysuckle-scented tyranny. Small mercies, considering the rest of this house looks like Martha Stewart and Joanna Gaines had a decorating war—and both won.

Avoiding her should be easy. Used to be. Back before we were nothing but a signature on paper and a mutual understanding to stay the hell out of each other's way. Before I put my hands on her. Before I lost every ounce of control on that dining room table like some desperate man who didn't know better. *I should've known better.*

But apparently, my dick didn't get that memo. No, it stands at attention every time she walks into a room, like she's the commander-in-chief of my downfall.

I used to manage this shit. Used to schedule sex the way I schedule board meetings—efficient, controlled, forgettable. Now? I'm jerking off in the shower like a teenage boy with a hidden stash of Playboys. Which, for the record, I never did as a teenager because I wasn't that pitiful. But here I am. Thirty-seven and I can't take a five-minute shower without turning it into a full-blown session, complete with self-loathing and questions like, "When did you become this guy?"

And the worst part? She's not even trying. This isn't some calculated seduction designed to screw with my head. No. She just exists. And her mere existence is ruining my life.

Okay, maybe that's extreme.

Or maybe this entire situation is extreme.

Ignoring her texts is easy enough—simple, mechanical. Pretend I'm too busy, which isn't even a lie. But avoiding her in my house? That takes strategy. Precision. Like a tactical operation where the enemy is a five-foot-something woman with soft curves and tits I want in my mouth. *Fuck, no I don't. But I do.*

She probably thinks I don't care where she goes or what she does. And she'd be right—I don't. At least, that's what I tell myself. But the truth? I know *exactly* when she comes and goes. Security system pings every time she leaves. Every time she returns. I don't need her to check in or tell me where she is. I have technology for that. Cameras. Notifications. Maybe a little tracking app on her phone—not that she knows about that.

Effortless surveillance.

Just how I like my relationships—distant, efficient, and requiring zero emotional labor. And yet... she keeps stealing from me. *My* time. *My* peace. *My* sanity.

Tonight, though? Cooking night at Mama's. Normally, I wouldn't give a damn, but tonight? Tonight, I'm grateful. It means my petty thief won't be home, hovering in the kitchen, cooking meals that taste too damn good for how much I want to hate them. Meals she serves with that smile—half sunshine, half rebellion—that makes me want to punch or better yet, fuck her through the drywall.

So, I stretch out on the sofa, reclaiming what little territory I have left, ignoring the offensively large, fake potted plant she installed in the corner like a warning shot across my bow. Apparently, it's supposed to "add warmth" to the room. Right.

If warmth feels like suffocation.

What used to be a temple to simplicity—sharp lines, dark leather, glass and steel—now looks like a HomeGoods catalog exploded. Throw pillows breeding like rabbits on the couch. Soft blankets draped over every available surface, as if I'm going to wake up one day and decide I need to be cozy. And candles. So many fucking candles. Ones that smell like "Autumn's Whisper" or "Harvest Dreams"—which I'm assuming is code for "this house is no longer yours."

I pop open a beer, lean back, and pull up the game on TV. And because I'm feeling especially spiteful? I order takeout. Greasy, artery-clogging, fry smell that will linger for days kind of takeout.

Because if I'm going to live in a Pinterest nightmare, I'm going to at least eat like a man.

Her voice drifts through my head. An uninvited ghost. *"Why order delivery when I can cook?"* Like I'd just suggested eating roadkill.

Because I want to. *Because* I don't feel like washing her twelve-piece cookware set afterward. *Because* sometimes, a man just wants to sit on his couch, eat something that could kill him, and not negotiate over kale versus spinach or what garnish would "really make the flavors pop."

But sure, let's pretend for a second that this is normal.

That she's not taking over my house, my mind, and every inch of my willpower with her soft smiles and bright eyes.

Let her think she's winning.

I take a long pull from my beer and stare at the screen, willing the noise to drown out the fact that the second she walks back through that door, my body will betray me all over again.

Because the truth is, she's already stolen more than I'll ever admit.

And thieves?

They give nothing back.

Not that peace exists anymore, anyway.

Between my wife's incessant humming like she's starring in a cooking show, the unrelenting sunshine punching through every open blind, and the hacker at work treating my system like it's his personal playground, I'm a live wire just waiting for something to ignite.

And this hacker? He's not just poking around like some amateur on a Red Bull binge. No, this guy is living in my system. Feet up, shoes on the coffee table, probably helping himself to my virtual whiskey. Either he's a savant-level genius, or he's smarter than me. Neither option does much for my ego—or the growing rage that simmers just below my carefully polished surface.

Sixteen hours a day I've been at this. *Sixteen hours* of chasing a ghost I can't pin down, while everything else in my life spirals into anarchy I didn't allow.

Wednesday nights used to be for *therapy*. Now? They're for takeout and whatever booze is closest to hand. My fists ache from clenching—whether from stress, frustration, or the far less dignified reason: the endless, pathetic routine of jerking off in the shower like I'm sixteen just to relieve my morning erection.

And not the casual, roll over and forget it variety. No, this is the hostile takeover kind, courtesy of my wife—the woman currently infiltrating every inch of my life, my house, and the parts of my brain I used to keep untouched.

If I didn't know exactly how she looks bent over my dining table, I might still stand a chance at sanity. But I do. I know too well. And every time I close my eyes, that image is there, carved into my skull like a brand I can't scrape off.

I'm halfway through my third beer, pretending to watch a game I haven't followed for years—because what is the point of leisure when everything in your life is on fire—when there's a knock on the door.

I groan. Because only two kinds of people knock on my door: my DoorDash delivery, which the app tells me is still trapped in the clutches of some poor, underpaid soul circling the block—and my brothers.

And Marco? He doesn't knock. He waltzes right in armed with some smirk and a six-pack of opinions nobody asked for.

Honestly, I'm surprised he hasn't handed out my door code to Dom and Alex just for fun.

I don't check the cameras—I don't need to. When I swing open the door, sure enough, there they are.

Alex, standing there like a smug bastard holding a bottle of scotch as though it's a peace offering, and Dom, looking like he got mugged by parenthood. His tie's loose, his shirt rumpled, and his hair? Jesus. His hair looks like a cautionary tale.

"The girls are teething," Dom grits out, like that's supposed to explain why he looks like death's less attractive cousin.

Ah. Right. The joys of parenting. Not only do children rob you of sleep, but they also sprout tiny, razor-sharp daggers in their mouths to finish the job. Nothing like watching a grown man get broken by something that weighs less than a bowling ball.

I grunt—because why bother with words? They'd come in whether I invited them or not, so why waste the effort pretending I care? I step aside. Letting them in like this isn't yet another reminder of how nothing in my life belongs to me anymore.

"Who's winning?" Alex drops onto my leather couch, sprawling out like he's reclaiming lost territory.

"No clue." I grab three glasses from the cabinet—because God forbid we drink straight from the bottle—and settle back onto the couch, ignoring the way Alex takes up more space than any human being should.

I pour the scotch—*my* scotch now—and hand each of them a glass. Alex swirls the amber liquid like we're at some upscale tasting event and not in my living room where they've crashed what was supposed to be my quiet night of isolation.

"So, how's married life?" Alex asks, too casually, like he isn't dying to watch me squirm.

It's like being bitch-slapped by karma and then forced to stand in a spotlight while everyone watches. Every. Single. Day.

"Fine." I down half my glass in one swallow, welcoming the burn as it slides down and coils in my gut. It's the only warmth I've felt in days—well, outside of my wife's body, but thinking about that leads down a road I'm not taking tonight.

"We figured we'd keep you company since the girls are at cooking night," Alex adds, like they're doing me a favor.

Right. Because I'm just so desperate for company these days.

I glance at the bottle, weighing how much of it I'd need to drink before their voices faded into background noise. Probably all of it. Maybe twice.

"Don't let me stop you." My voice is dry, letting them settle in while silently praying they leave before I run out of alcohol or patience—whichever hits empty first.

Cooking night. The Bennetti women's sacred ritual of drinking wine like it's a competitive sport and exchanging gossip. Allegedly about cooking, but let's not kid ourselves—what they really serve up is unsolicited advice sprinkled with a heavy dose of judgment.

I can already hear Mama in my head, clear as glass and twice as cutting: *"Rico, she's your wife, not a phone you forget to charge until it's at 1% and begging for attention."*

Dom makes himself right at home, throwing his feet up on the coffee table—the new one. The one Allie bought because apparently my original glass and steel masterpiece was "cold and uninviting." Now I'm the proud owner of a reclaimed wood monstrosity. Maybe I can reclaim my sanity next. Wonder if HomeGoods has that in stock—aisle five, next to the "Live, Laugh, Love" signs.

"You enjoying the honeymoon phase?" Dom smirking like he's waiting for me to admit I've been broken.

"Does it look like I am?"

Of course, that earns me the look. The *we-know-you're-screwed-and-we're-here-for-it* look they exchange like I'm not sitting right here, watching them mentally high-five. If only they knew my manic-pixie wife is slowly eroding my existence, one decorative pillow and scented candle at a time.

Dom grins, eyes glinting with the smugness only a married man with twins and Stockholm syndrome can muster. "How do you expect to knock her up if you're not knocking her every chance you get?"

I blink at him, wondering if marriage really kills brain cells, or if Dom was always this stupid and I've only now noticed because he's taken to dispensing advice like some bootleg Tony Robbins.

"We will when she's ovulating." The words drop like anvils,. Because if I say them flat enough, maybe my body will stop revolting.

Two sets of eyebrows shoot up in disbelief.

Dom looks like I just slapped him with a brick. "You're seriously waiting for her ovulation window?"

"I'm efficient." I take a slow sip of scotch, savoring the way it burns. Beer doesn't cut it when you're trapped in the emotional equivalent of a hostage situation, also known as marital bliss.

Alex shakes his head, knocking back his drink like he's the one being tortured. "I figured you put that clause in the contract because you didn't know better. Thought once you had *sex*, you'd realize you could have it every day—hell, *multiple times* a day—and toss that rule right out the window."

"Well, you guessed wrong."

Dom leans forward. "Did you at least consummate?" Like he's asking whether I remembered to pay my taxes, not whether I've had sex with my wife.

I nod. One slow, deliberate jerk of my head.

"And it was...bad?" Alex prods, waiting for some story of catastrophic failure.

My jaw tightens. "It was fine."

Fine. Right. Like calling a Bugatti "a decent car." Like saying Mount Everest is a "mild incline." No, it wasn't fine. It was mind-blowing. The kind of sex that rewires your synapses and makes you question why anyone ever bothers doing anything else. It was so good that now, I can't walk past my dining room table without getting half-hard and debating whether I should just eat my meals standing up for the rest of my life.

But I'm not about to admit that to these two idiots.

"Fine?" Dom echoes, incredulous. "You enjoy sex with your wife and you've only done it once?"

I nod again, fighting the part of me that wants to throw back the rest of my drink and pour another.

Because yes, I want to do it again. Hell, I want to do nothing but that. But letting her see that? Letting her know she's gotten under my skin—into my bloodstream? Not an option.

"At least tell me you went a few rounds that night," Alex says, almost pleading, like he needs to believe I'm not as broken as I feel.

I don't answer.

"Jesus," Dom mutters, rubbing a hand down his face. "I don't know how you're surviving. After the first time I slept with Sienna, I couldn't stop. I'd sneak out of meetings just to get laid. I barely worked. Honestly, I'm surprised I didn't get fired."

Probably why you became a dad before you were ready, I think, glancing down at my phone as if salvation might be one tap away.

DoorDash is still crawling across town like my driver is powered by existential dread. Fantastic.

But then my eye catches something worse.

The calendar app.

A little red dot glaring at me like a smug bastard.

Thirteenth.

Ovulation day.

Of course, she didn't say a word. Because she's a menace—a beautiful, maddening thief of my peace and every shred of control I've worked so hard to maintain.

She'll drop that bomb on me tomorrow over dinner. Probably in that soft, casual tone, like we're discussing the weather. *Pass the salt, Rico. Also, I'm ready to get knocked up.*

I toss back the rest of my scotch, the burn doing nothing to erase the visual of her saying those words with that sweet smile and those eyes that already own me more than I'll admit.

Allie

"So, how's my Rico in bed?"

Nonna sips her wine like she's asking if I want breadsticks—not casually launching a missile into my sex life.

Wine halfway to my lips, I blink at her. Surely, I misheard? Nope. Sienna throws me a thumbs-up from across the kitchen like she's glad *she's* not in the hot seat. Traitor.

Honestly, Nonna's filter died in the '60s, and she's been partying on its grave ever since. First week I met her? Asked if Rico "knew what to do with all that," waving at me like I'm a buffet. Second week? Asked if I was "keeping it tight." Now? She wants *performance stats* like I'm about to leave a Yelp review.

If she asks for measurements, I'm dead. Just face-planting into this cheese board.

What would I even say at this moment? *Well, Nonna, it was one position, two life-ruining orgasms, with a side of* an identity *crisis?*

Because when Rico finally touched me—really *touched* me—like I was his to claim and ruin? Game over. The man kissed like it was life or death, and I was *so* ready to die happy. And then, of course, he ghosted the second reality returned.

But sure, let's unpack that at Sunday dinner.

Meanwhile, I'm over here ovulating like a fertility goddess with no worshiper. And if Rico can rewrite the marriage rules—coming home late, dodging me—so can I by not telling him that I'm ovulating. Hey, the contract never said that I was required to tell him when I was. See Rico? Two can play that game.

"Nonna, don't scare her off," Violet croons, prowling closer like she smells blood.

She settles on the counter, grinning. "Sooo... did Rico talk? Or did you have to hit reset between rounds?"

I paste on my "I'm fine, thanks for asking" society smile, but Violet? She's not buying it for a second.

If this keeps up, I'm moving to New Zealand and starting a farm. Goats don't ask about your sex.

Nonna leans in, tapping her nails like she *knows* I'll break. "Well?"

"He talked." My voice comes out a little strangled—because why am I discussing dirty talk with his grandmother?

Violet lights up. "Wait, *talked*? Like a word? A sentence? Woman, I need details!"

I sigh. "A few sentences."

The room goes *dead* silent. Even Mama, mid-sauce-stir, freezes.

"A few sentences," Nonna repeats, practically glowing.

Violet leans in, eyes gleaming. "But was he *Rico* about it?"

I chew my lip. *Yeah, he was Rico. And for a second, he wasn't.* For a second, he was *mine*.

"And... how often are you two working on a baby?" Mama asks.

I blink. "Uh... just once."

Mama gasps and if the woman wore pearls, she'd clutch to those bad boys for dear life. "*Once?*"

"Only when I'm ovulating," I mutter, draining my wine and wishing for something stronger.

Silence.

If awkward had a mascot, I'd be on the T-shirts.

Nonna's jaw drops. Violet's eyes widen, like she's watching a car crash she can't look away from. Sienna is definitely trying not to laugh and failing.

Mama crosses herself, muttering prayers.

Nonna grabs my wrist with a grip that could crush diamonds. "Listen, *bambina*. Men like Rico? Think they can control everything. But you—" she taps her temple, then gestures lower (and sweet hell, I am *not* following her hand movement), "this is where *you* win."

Oh God. Somebody pass more wine—scratch that, make it tequila.

I blink at Nonna, stunned into actual silence — which, for me, is like a solar eclipse: rare, unexpected, and slightly terrifying.

Sienna, ever the backstabbing backup singer, chimes in like she's warming up for a duet. "She's not wrong. Dom used to be a total binder-carrying control freak. I once threatened a sex strike and watched that man toss his color-coded planner out the window like it was on fire."

I squint at her. "Why... *why* did he even have a planner?"

Sienna shrugs, all innocent. "Very long story. We've all moved past it." Mama nods in agreement from the corner.

"So you're saying I should..." I glance up, like maybe God will open a skylight and beam me out of this conversation. "Appeal to his... *lower brain*?"

Nonna *beams*. "*Esatto*! Use what God gave you and make my little Rico forget all that big brain of his."

I choke on my wine, coughing into my sleeve. "Your *little* Rico?"

Nonna nods, completely unbothered that she's now responsible for permanently scarring my soul.

Violet snorts beside me, clearly living for this moment. And now my brain, being the traitor it is, immediately wonders if Nonna means Rico-the-man or Rico-the... other thing that is far from little. *Not even close.*

God, I need a drink. Oh wait — I'm already holding one.

I gulp half my glass, mentally adding *pre-drinking* to my future cooking night survival plans.

"So just... seduce him, huh? Simple." I force a smile, though inside I'm vibrating like an over-wound toy. Sure, let me just seduce a man who looks at me like I'm an IRS audit he can't avoid. How do you flirt with a guy who treats you like gluten and he's the poster child for Celiac Awareness?

I mutter under my breath, "Yeah, won't work. Rico doesn't even find me attractive."

Nonna *scoffs*, full on dramatics. "Oh, *dolce bambina*." She tuts, wagging her finger at me like she's scolding a puppy. "If my little Rico didn't find you attractive, you'd have gotten a polite peck and a handshake at that altar — not a kiss that would make a nun blush."

Nonna leans in, that knowing smile on her face — the kind that makes you feel warm and also like you're about to get hit with wisdom you didn't ask for. "We've paraded models, heiresses, women who could buy and sell this family twice over. You know what he did? Nothing. But *you*? I've caught him watching you. Touching you. *Wanting* you."

A lump forms in my throat, thick and immovable, like I swallowed a brick and now it's just... there, refusing to budge.

Because there's *one* person Rico's definitely touched more than me — his *therapist*. You know, the woman he swore he stopped seeing when we got married. But knowing Rico, I bet he's already found a loophole for that, too. Like he finds loopholes for everything.

The thought hits my stomach like a wrecking ball—cue Miley Cyrus—and suddenly my wine isn't so comforting anymore.

"She looks like she's gonna puke," Sienna says, and honestly, fair.

Before I can speak, Violet's rubbing my back like I'm a toddler with a tummy ache. "We need water over here!"

A glass magically appears in my hand — no idea who handed it to me — but I down it like I'm stranded in a desert.

Violet narrows her eyes. "You don't look so good."

"Because I'm *not*," I croak, my voice wobbling like I'm seconds from crying.

Yeah, Rico kissed me like I was his last breath. Touched me like he owned every inch of my skin. But let's be real — he never had to kiss a woman he was *forced* to marry. He touched *her* because he *wanted* to. No contracts or obligations.

Me? I'm just a job on his never-ending to-do list, somewhere between *fix server issue* and *avoid wife at all costs*.

Sienna pushes her chair back, already halfway to the door. "I'll grab Vinnie."

"And I'm getting you cleaned up before you face-plant," Violet says, yanking me up. Tiny but terrifying — like a fairy godmother with an attitude problem.

She drags me down the hall, past the Bennetti Family Hall of Fame — all those smiling photos like they're *so* perfect. Babies, weddings, family dinners where nobody looks like they're two seconds from a breakdown.

But it's one picture that stops me cold.

Rico — *maybe* thirteen — already nailing that world-famous Rico Scowl™, arms crossed, jaw set, eyes hard. Like even back then, he knew life was gonna take a swing at him and he was ready to hit back first.

Decades of walls. *Decades* of locked doors. And I'm supposed to believe a little flirting and some mind-blowing sex is gonna bulldoze all that?

Yeah. And while I'm at it, I'll teach a cat to sit, stay, and pay taxes.

Violet glances over, softening. "You're thinking too much."

"Story of my life."

But what I *don't* say?

Is that no matter how hard I push, no matter how many times I throw open those doors—Rico's still locked inside.

By the time Violet hauls me into the bathroom, I'm already coming apart at the seams, one tug away from a full-blown emotional wardrobe malfunction. She plants me against the marble counter and yanks open a drawer, fishing out a washcloth.

She douses it in ice-cold water, wrings it out, then slaps it on my face. "Look, Rico's a pain in the ass, but he's not impossible," she says, voice soft but firm. Her eyes, though? Yeah, they're loaded with *just* enough pity to make me want to crawl into the sink and turn on the garbage disposal.

I snort and lean into the coolness because my body is currently working overtime to have a full breakdown. "You're wrong," I mutter, swiping at my damp cheeks. "Everyone keeps acting like Rico's some misunderstood prince. But let's not forget—he *had* her."

Violet freezes, mid-dab, jaw tightening.

"I can't compete with choice," I whisper, throat tight. "She was his *choice*. Me? I'm just the obligation he signed up for because Papa shoved a contract in his face."

Violet tosses the cloth onto the counter and grips my face in her hands, forcing my gaze to hers. "Allie, listen to me. *She* was never a choice. She was a transaction. A way to scratch an itch. You—" she gives my face a little shake—"you are *not* a transaction."

Her words hit and I flinch, because guess what? That's *exactly* how I feel.

"And yeah," Violet continues, "he's been a giant jackass since you said 'I do'—" I snort despite myself. "That's putting it mildly."

"—but if you think for a *second* that man doesn't want you? You're blind. I've *seen* the way he looks at you when you're not watching."

My brow lifts. "You mean like I'm an unsolved math problem that's ruining his life?"

"No. Like a man trying not to devour something he *knows* he shouldn't touch."

I blink, trying to picture that—and *failing*—while Violet stands there like she just dropped the mic on my emotional crisis.

She pats my cheek like I'm five. I glare.

"Men are pigs. We know this," she adds. "But Rico? He went to her because he couldn't deal with himself. Not because he *wanted* her. She was married, Allie. *MARRIED*. It wasn't a relationship—it was an *appointment*. Like picking up dry cleaning."

My stomach flips. "Married?" I croak, because of course, *that's* where my brain gets stuck.

Violet rolls her eyes. "Yes, *married*. And if there *had* been anything more, Dom and Alex would've buried him under the patio. You think he signs a marriage contract if he's happy paying for... *services*? Please."

I chew my lip, my throat burning. "But he *touched* her," I whisper. "What if that's the only relationship he wants? One without feelings."

Violet lets out a long sigh, like she wants to strangle me and hug me all at once. "You *really* believe that? If all he wanted was easy, he wouldn't have married you. He would've stayed on his therapy loop, nice and numb. But he didn't. He married you."

I open my mouth to argue, but Violet steamrolls right over it. "You know what I think? I think he fought to keep those sessions in the contract because he's terrified to let anyone close enough to see the mess inside. He wasn't pushing *you* away. He was building walls because if you got in, you might see too much. And that scares the hell out of him."

"Yeah, well, if he wanted me so badly, maybe he should've chosen *me* instead of his loopholes," I snap, heat rising in my cheeks.

Violet's hair swishes as she shakes her head. "No, Allie. He's scared. He doesn't know how to want something real. And you? You're *real*. He can't control you, and that terrifies him more than anything."

I swallow, throat thick, and my chest squeezing tight.

Violet softens, stepping closer. "And I know about the shirt thing."

I freeze. "What?"

She nods. "Dom and Marco mentioned it. Didn't say why, but whatever it is? *It's big*. You want answers? You need to stop pretending you don't care and *ask* for them."

A choked laugh bubbles out of me, part sob, part *oh-my-God-this-is-my-life*.

Sienna calls from the kitchen. "You *can* talk to him, you know. Just expect to get judged by those psycho-pretty eyes."

Violet snorts. "Yeah, he listens. He just hoards words like they're Bitcoins. But he's processing. Everything. Trust me, Dom and Alex poke him for a reason."

I groan, rubbing my temples. "So Nonna's whole 'seduce him' plan is supposed to work on *that*?"

"Honey, even Rico Bennetti thinks with his dick first. And unlike his brain, *that* part isn't encrypted."

I blink, covering my mouth as a laugh bursts out of me.

"You wanna break through the fortress? Start where the walls are weakest."

"So seduce him," I mutter, shaking my head, but *definitely* considering it — even if it's ridiculous.

Violet shrugs, grinning. "Unless you've got a better plan."

I huff out a breath, cheeks aching from smiling for the first time today. "God help me, I might actually do it."

"Now that's the Allie I like to see."

Allie

IT'S JUST AFTER TEN when I walk into the house. I assume Rico's either still at the office or barricaded in his little coding cave, probably muttering sweet nothings to his six-monitor setup. It's why I don't bother looking for him. The man stashes himself away for a reason and I'm not about to go begging for attention.

The house is dark—shades drawn tight, blinds shut like Fort Knox. I left them open this morning *on purpose*, and the vampire-in-residence clearly couldn't handle the sunlight. Sure, I'm poking the bear, but I refuse to live in perpetual gloom. My life's dark enough without my home mimicking a crypt.

Besides, the sunshine is my only proof that my husband isn't one garlic clove away from bursting into flames.

I forget to close the blinds at night. *Forget*, as in, intentionally leave them gaping like a stage curtain, begging for a reaction. I'd trade my left kidney for the smallest flicker of emotion from Rico. A sigh, a grunt, maybe even one of those soul-draining glares that shouldn't be, and yet they are, very attractive. Can you blame me? A girl's gotta push a few buttons to make sure her husband isn't as emotionally advanced as a rock collection.

Nonna, Mama, and Violet's words churn in my head, drowning in the three—okay, fine, *four*—glasses of wine I downed after dinner. Liquid courage, they call it. I call it the only way I'm brave enough to do something incredibly stupid: confront my husband and tell him I'm adjusting the terms of our agreement. You know, the legally binding contract we negotiated like opposing world leaders, complete with glaring, pen-clicking, and Rico looking at me like I was an underperforming lab rat.

Dare I poke the beast? Demand a revision like I'm updating terms and conditions? My brain replays our original negotiation. I slipped in requests, one by one, like sneaking vegetables into a toddler's mac and cheese. He agreed begrudgingly, each nod tighter than the set of his jaw. A win? *Technically*. But the man looked at me the entire time like he was debating whether it was worth the paperwork to have me assassinated.

Tossing my purse and keys onto the entryway table, I murmur a quick goodnight to Vinnie as he heads down the basement stairs.

There's no point in seeking out Rico. If he's home, he doesn't want to be found, and I've officially retired from the search party. I get it, some things can't be rushed, like building Rome. They placed at least one stone daily while building Rome. Meanwhile, every stone I set with this man gets kicked over and hurled into the Hudson.

Slowly trudging up the stairs, I curse Rico under my breath. *My floor. My room. My entire domain.* The nursery's up here too, which means when I pop out these supposed heirs—because God forbid we stop at one—I'll be the one on night duty. Diaper changes? Me. Midnight feedings? Also me. Bleary-eyed at two in the morning while my darling husband slumbers away in his soundproof man cave like a king oblivious to the kingdom burning around him.

Honestly, the man could sleep through a nuclear detonation at his desk. A crying baby doesn't stand a chance of penetrating those walls. And to think, people call me the *lucky* one.

I'm almost giddy I didn't tell him I was ovulating. Should I feel bad about that? Probably. Do I? Not even a little.

Sure, my body's basically been stuck on smolder mode for days. Hell, at this point, he could breathe near me and I'd go poof. But do I want the orgasm he could undoubtedly deliver? Desperately. Do I want the regret-filled stare he'd slap on afterward like a partic-ipation trophy? Not so much.

Pathetic doesn't even cover it. I'm one flirt away from snapping at the bait like a starving trout, fully aware the hook will gut me, but too desperate to care.

I push into my room; the darkness swallowing me whole as I sigh and kick the door shut behind me. Clothes? Gone. Jeans peeled off and flung into a pile that would give Rico hives. Shirt? Tossed. Not even trying for the laundry basket. He doesn't come in here, anyway. It's not like I'm trying to piss him off. I'm just tired—*emotionally, mentally, physically*. Cooking nights drain the life out of me, and I'm running on fumes.

What else do I even have to do?

My days are a rinse-and-repeat cycle of cleaning, grocery shopping, meal planning, and cooking. Sometimes Violet and Sienna rescue me with coffee dates or lunch outings, but Violet's drowning in deadlines for her next book, and Sienna has her hands full with twin girls and a husband who looks at her like she cured cancer.

Jealousy? Oh, it's there. A big, ugly, green monster doing backflips in my chest every time I watch Violet and Sienna get wrapped up in hugs, kisses, and whispered sweet nothings from their husbands. I don't need worship. I'd settle for acknowledgment. A nod. *A hey, nice job not burning the house down today* would suffice.

But no. My husband, the High Lord of Indifference, prefers silence. Everything about him screams order and control. He's basically interior-designed his home to match his personality: sleek, cold, and emotionally nonexistent.

Well, until I got my hands on it. Still, the house is more barren than I like, and no matter what decorative piece I add, it doesn't feel like a home. With nothing but time on my hands, cleanings become my full-time job. It seems I'm in the 1950s and taking on the role of the housewife well.

My laundry's always done, not that Rico would notice. He refuses to let me near his clothes. Locks his bedroom door like I'm some master thief plotting to steal his underwear. It's laughable, really. Like I'd willingly walk into his space, the forbidden Sanctum of Solitude, just to unfold his perfectly starched shirts. Okay, yes, I'd do that, but not steal his underwear. Just so we are clear.

But the locked doors? They hit differently. They're not just doors—they're *reminders*. Of Papa's house. Of the life I clawed my way out of. And now I'm back to being the girl standing in a home that isn't hers, shut out of rooms she's supposedly entitled to. The house might have my touch now—flowers, throw pillows, candles—but it's not mine.

I'm not a wife. I'm a roommate with kitchen privileges and a shared womb. That's all Rico wants from me. His heir factory. A walking, talking incubator with a side of home-cooked meals.

The worst part? I *signed* up for it. Willingly.

Still jobless, aimless, and apparently husbandless—at least in the emotional availability department. Tomorrow's plan? Get up at an ungodly hour, hopefully catch Rico during his habitual crack-of-dawn escape, and ambush him into our agreed upon morning talk with a side of *"so, I was thinking about our agreement..."* Because nothing screams marital bliss like holding your husband hostage for conversation before sunrise.

Of course, that would require enough caffeine to resuscitate a corpse and the ability to navigate a looming wine hangover. But hey, I thrive under pressure. Or at least, I used to. Lately, I'm more whimpering under mild inconvenience than thriving.

But the real plan? Get my husband to think with his *other* brain. The one that doesn't operate like a NASA control center running diagnostics 24/7. Just pure, primal caveman instincts. Basically, *Little Rico*—I still can't decide if that phrase should make me laugh or seek trauma therapists.

Not tonight, though. Even with liquid courage still buzzing faintly in my veins, I didn't have enough chutzpah to pick that fight. Since when did I become such a chicken? My younger self would be horrified at what I've become.

In the bathroom, I scrub off my makeup—the one perk of my current existence: no need for the industrial-strength cleanser required to melt off the daily armor I used to wear.

Dressed in silk shorts and a matching cami—because if my life was falling apart, I'd at least look good doing it—I padded back into my room, only to screech like a horror movie extra at the shadow lounging on my bed.

My back slammed into the wall with a thud, and I winced, hand fumbling until it found the light switch. The room flooded with harsh yellow light, revealing none other than my adoring husband, casually stretched across my mattress.

Gray T-shirt. Black sweats. Phone in hand, thumb lazily tapping the screen like he was coding the downfall of civilization. Maybe he had an app for that.

"Rico!" I smoothed down my cami, pushing off the wall. "What the hell are you doing in my room?"

My room. If we were playing the separate spaces game, I was claiming this *entire* floor. Hell, I might get petty enough to slap a "No Boys Allowed" sign on the door.

He didn't bother answering. Instead, he tossed the phone onto the bed, rose with the grace of a predator—and stalked toward me.

Amber eyes dragged over every inch of my body, starting at my bare legs, pausing at the hem of my shorts, and crawling upward until they landed squarely on my chest. My nipples, the traitorous bastards, stood at full attention, practically waving hello.

Rico's gaze sharpened, his mouth curving into the slightest smirk. Not a full smile, because God forbid he actually enjoys life, but enough to tell me he'd noticed exactly how much my body appreciated his proximity.

For the record? It enjoyed it a lot.

"What's today?" Rico's voice is low and miles away from sensual. Instead, it's more cross-examining than anything. His fists clench and unclench. He's irritated.

Ah, *anger*. An *emotion*. Actual, *human emotion*. Progress.

"Wednesday?" I answer, brows lifting in question.

"And?"

I blink. Swallow. Probably not subtly. He's close enough that I catch the faint trace of cedar and something darker—and I want to rub against it like a cat while I purr. My body hums in agreement.

Crossing my arms, I channel every ounce of stubbornness I inherited from a long line of equally bullheaded Sicilians. "Care to elaborate, or are we playing cryptic caveman tonight?"

Big mistake. My eyes meet his. Because while his face stays locked in its signature resting dictator expression, those amber eyes tell a different story. Hunger and frustration, like he can't decide if he wants to devour me or throttle me and I'm fine with both because it would be amazing.

He grabs his phone from the bed, flipping the screen toward me, finger jabbing at the date. The thirteenth. A red dot sits under the number, like it knows something I don't. Tomorrow has a dot too. *And* the day after that.

"What am I supposed to be looking at? You planning a polka dot-themed party?" I sidestep him, only to yelp when his hand snaps out and grabs my throat, pinning me back to the wall. God, it's so hot. *Yes*, my panties are wet. And *yup*, I've officially set back feminism by a few decades.

In a blink, my front hits the wall, his hand releasing me almost like the contact shocked him. Before I can pivot and start swinging, his arms cage me in, one on either side of my head.

Then he leans in, breath warm against my earlobe, each word a direct line to my ovaries. "I'm not playing games, Allie. We had a deal."

My body? It used to have a spine in there I think.

I shove backward, back slamming into his chest. Solid, unyielding muscle. And, oh *hello*, impressive erection. *Focus, you spineless idiot.*

His arm snakes around my waist, pulling me flush against him. He hates touching, avoids it like it's poisonous. *Yet here we are.*

So, like the mature adult I am, I wiggle my ass against his *very* noticeable problem.

He groans. A sound so raw it should be bottled and sold as an aphrodisiac.

The grip disappears like I've burned him, and he stumbles back.

My nipples, those disloyal little accessories, stand at full salute, perfectly outlined by my silk camisole. Look, I didn't design the top. I just wore it. Not my fault if the fabric does more disclosing than covering.

I stroll past him, casual and calm. I'm not calm at all inside. Pulling back the covers of my bed, I take my time, debating what I'll do next.

Clearly, he's thinking with the wrong head.

And if I'm going to win this round?

Now's the time to strike.

"You're ovulating." Rico stands there, phone in hand.

I don't look at him. I don't want to know how he knows. And I definitely don't want to acknowledge the traitorous tingle low in my belly at what that means. For God's sake, woman. Pull it together. The man is literally arranging sex like it's an appointment.

I snatch back the covers and focusing on getting ready for bed. "So?"

His jaw ticks so hard I'm amazed a molar doesn't shoot across the room. "You're required to tell me."

"Oh, my sweet, delusional husband. There are plenty of things *you're required* to do, but you've mastered the art of selective obligation. And for the record, I'm not required to *tell* you. The contract says we have sex *when* I'm ovulating, *not* that I have to send you a 'Come Breed Me' calendar invite."

His nostrils flare. "You are now." He waves his phone like it's the holy grail of reproductive rights, the red dots glaring at me from the screen.

I blink, unimpressed. "Cute. Did you set that reminder before or after you fucked me on the table and then blew me off for a week?"

He steps closer, shoulders squaring like he's preparing for battle. "Allie." I would say the low rumble of his voice scares me, because it should, but I'm turned on.

"Rico," I mock, pulling the pin from my hair. Dark waves tumble down my back, and I don't miss the way his eyes track every single strand, like gravity suddenly shifted and my hair is the sun. My stomach somersaults.

I smile, slow and calculated. "Yes, Rico. *I'm ovulating.*"

The growl that rumbles from his throat is pure predatory. Not creepy stalker vibes, but the possessiveness romance novels promise—the *I'm-go-ing-to-ruin-you-and-you'll-love-every-second* kind. Oh god will I love it.

He places his phone on the dresser with deliberate calm, like a man about to commit a crime and ensuring no witnesses. One step. Two. Then his hand fists in my hair, yanking just hard enough to sting but not enough to hurt. Tears prick my eyes while my body sings hallelujah like I've just found religion.

"Bend over," he orders, voice like gravel.

Jesus. Why is that hot? It shouldn't be hot. It's caveman-level offensive, like being told to fetch a bone. Only, my body went straight to *Yes, sir.*

I tap a finger to my lips, feigning deep thought. "No."

His eyes darken, flaring wide. "No?"

I shake my head, dragging my finger down the center of his chest, slow and deliberate. He doesn't move. Doesn't swat me away like last time. *Baby steps.*

"Allie. We have a deal."

"And you've been dodging that deal since day one," I snap, stepping into his space, and yes, rubbing my tight nipples against him. I have no shame. "The notes instead of conversation. The grunts at dinner. You've treated our contract like a suggestion. So guess what? I'm just following your lead, *sweetheart.*"

His grip tightens in my hair, tilting my head back. His other hand fists at his side, flexing like he's restraining the urge to touch me more than he already is.

Do it. Touch me Rico. Not sure if I'm begging internally or pushing him at this point.

"Turn around. You have three seconds before I make this all about me and you get nothing."

I shove him back with both hands. He doesn't budge, but the shock in his eyes? Worth it.

"I'm *not* your therapist," I bite out. His face twists, eyes wide with something remarkably close to vulnerability. "I won't play your little wind-up doll. Bend over, get it done, barely touch me, and then leave like I'm a task on your to-do list. You know what I realized today? *You* refuse to let me touch you. *You* strip me bare, but keep yourself fully clothed. *You* talk dirty, but hold me at arm's length. And why? Because you spent years handing yourself over to *someone else,* didn't you?"

"Did you say the same filthy things to *her*? Did she get to touch you? Kiss you? What exactly did you pay for, Rico? Because right now, you're treating me with less respect than the woman you hired by the hour, and I'm not standing for it. I'm your wife, *not* your whore."

The word *whore* hits like a grenade. He cringes as he drops his hand from my hair, and takes two slow, deliberate steps back, chest rising and falling like he's restraining the urge to smash something.

He's going to leave. I can see it in the way his gaze flicks toward the door. Typical. Run before the conversation gets messy.

But I'm not done.

Nonna's advice echoes in my head—push until he can't think straight, then make your move.

So, I smile. Sweet. Defiant.

"Go ahead, Rico," I purr, climbing into bed like I'm perfectly unaffected, pulling the covers up and fluffing my pillow with exaggerated nonchalance. "Walk away. But just know if you do? You're not touching me again until the terms change. New deal. *My rules. My way.*"

His eyes narrow.

Checkmate, husband. Your move.

Rico

I'M POSITIVE MY WIFE is trying to kill me.

Not the quick, painless kind of death either. No, Allie's going for the slow, torturous route. Death by denial. One cock-hardening, pride-shredding, sanity-crumbling moment at a time.

Sure, I've skirted around our agreement. I did the bare minimum—just enough to tick the boxes without offering more than legally required. Like a man paying his taxes, begrudgingly and without fanfare. But now, she's tossing my loopholes back at me with the finesse of a lawyer fresh out of fucks to give.

And my cock? Fully on her side. A traitor standing at attention, pulsing against my sweats, and making it very clear who's really losing this battle.

"Congratulations," I bite out, voice rough enough to sand wood. "You found a loophole. But you're ovulating. We have to have sex tonight."

Never, in all my meticulously planned life, did I think I'd stand in front of a woman, calendar app in hand, dictating her biological duty like some deranged HR manager enforcing company policy.

She smiles, slow and sinful. The kind of smile that makes men sign away kingdoms and commit war crimes and I'd like to think I'm better than them, but a deep dark little voice from inside me says "Bro, you're not."

"We are supposed to have sex," she purrs, standing up from the bed, strolling closer, hips swaying and my mental breakdown swaying with them. "But I'm *not* taking ovulation tests anymore."

"What?"

"I'm done," she says, like it's the simplest thing in the world. "No more peeing on sticks. No more obsessing over dots on a calendar. If you want a baby, you're welcome to have sex every night." She pauses, tongue flicking out to wet her bottom lip, which is basically porn at this point. "But I'm not scheduling it like some corporate deadline. If you want a wife who plays by contract terms, go find someone else."

I hear her words, but they don't hurt. No, that's because all I can focus on is how her nipples pebble through that flimsy satin camisole begging for my mouth.

"We agreed," I growl, jaw tightening until I taste the metallic tang of my blood.

"You broke the terms first. I'm just leveling the playing field."

I stare at her. Papa gave her six months. If she refuses sex, she can hold out, file for divorce, and walk away without a backward glance. I could replace her.

Okay, no, I couldn't. I'm not exactly drowning in offers, but she doesn't need to know that.

"Plenty of fish in the sea." I instantly regret how pathetic it sounds, especially since I'm practically begging to get my dick wet at this point.

And that's when she *laughs*. Full-bodied, head-thrown-back laughter that makes her tits bounce and her hair cascade like liquid silk. Her throat stretches, bare and vulnerable, and all I can think about is sinking my teeth into that soft skin until she forgets how to speak in complete sentences.

"Then go fishing, honey."

She pats my chest—pats—like I'm an unruly dog, then turns and saunters toward the bed, leaving me standing there, hard, furious, and dangerously close to throwing her over my shoulder.

I don't chase women. I don't argue. I certainly don't negotiate with terrorists.

But this woman?

She just stole my last ounce of control. And I'm not sure whether I want to strangle her or fuck her until we both forget our names.

Actually, I want both.

I step forward, close enough to inhale the faint trace of honeysuckle clinging to her skin but not close enough to lose the upper hand. Assuming I still have it. Even though I know I don't.

"The chance of you getting pregnant while ovulating is thirty-three percent." My voice is flat, clinical, the way it always is when I'm trying to convince myself I'm a man of logic, not impulse. "In reality, it's closer to twenty, twenty-five percent. Which is fucking pathetic, considering it's supposed to be prime fertility mode. You'd think biology would offer better odds for survival."

"No. More. Tests." So, she's not wavering then?

And then, like the universe itself is conspiring to dismantle every ounce of restraint I have left, her fingers trail down her silky pajama shorts, hooking the waistband and sliding them down inch by torturous inch.

No underwear.

My brain resembles the dreaded blue-screen of Windows 95 in a storm. Not that it was functioning at peak capacity to begin with these days, thanks to her standing there like the fucking embodiment of temptation.

She peels off her top next, revealing smooth, golden skin and peaked nipples that my mouth will definitely be on. Faint bruises bloom along her hips—the ones I left there. Proof that, for one night, I forgot to be rational. Forgot to hold back...and *loved* it.

Allie flips her hair over her shoulder, like she knows exactly how much power she holds in that single motion. Then she climbs onto the bed, slow and deliberate, propping herself on her elbows and stretching out like a feast laid before a starving man.

"Say it, Rico," she purrs. "Agree to my new terms, and you can have this."

And just like that, the thief strikes again—stealing my oxygen, my pulse, my ability to think past the ache in my cock or the thunder in my chest.

Control? Gone. Logic? Obliterated. Not entirely sure I could tell you my full name right now.

I should walk away. Should remind her that biology doesn't give a damn about stubborn wives and their refusal to follow rules. But my feet don't move. My mouth doesn't form the words.

Instead, I stand there, watching my wife offer herself up like the prize she damn well knows she is, and realize...

I've lost.

Allie

I BITE DOWN A smile. Rico's fists clench and unclench as he steps closer, gaze locked on my body, *not* my face. Fine, we will work on that one.

"Once a week," he grinds out.

Negotiating. Cute.

I tilt my head, feigning consideration while lazily trailing a finger down my bare stomach slowly past my navel, swirling it around once, twice, then trailing lower, dipping as his eyes follow and my single index finger dips just one inch above where my body is humming for friction. "Wow, one whole time a week? What a generous offer. Should I also pencil in my annual orgasm while we're at it?"

His tongue flicks out, wetting his bottom lip, eyes shamelessly zeroed in on my breasts like they're the promised land. Good to know he appreciates the girls, because they're currently standing at attention for him and the dull ache in them is making sitting still very, *very* hard.

"Twice," he counters, though his voice is tighter, and no confidence.

I push up on my elbows, spreading my legs just enough to give him a front-row view. His eyes snap to the show, sharp and dangerous, as if I've just waved a red flag in front of a very pissed-off bull.

"No set days. No calendar reminders. It happens when *you* need a release, or when *I* do*." I pause, giving him an innocent smile. "And...that's *daily* for me."

His jaw ticks, but he doesn't step back. Doesn't run like he usually does when I push too far. Instead, he does the unthinkable.

He shoves down his sweats.

My mouth is so dry my tongue sticks to the roof of my mouth.

Thick, velvety, and already standing at full attention like it's on a mission, he grips himself, thumb running over the tip as he closes his eyes. The "I'm too smart for this shit" part of his brain is obviously losing to the one currently leading the charge south of the border.

"Tell you what, hubby," I purr, sliding off the bed and onto my knees, watching his cock jerk in his hand as my hot breath dances across it. "I'll give you the night to think about it."

Before he can process my words, I wrap my hand around him—warm, smooth, and so damn thick I almost forget my bravado. *Almost.* How did that thing fit the first time? No wonder I ached and sitting required leaning the day after.

"That looks like it's gonna hurt if you don't...relieve it." I lean in, running my tongue along the side, slow and deliberate. He hisses, but doesn't pull away. So I continue, purely for negotiation, of course.

For the record, I have *no* intention of finishing this. One, because I'm not feeling charitable right now. Two, because I have zero experience, and that beast deserves a warning label. I'll save that particular experiment for when I'm not trying to win a contract dispute and also pack a little more confidence for the trip.

"Good luck with that," I chirp, patting his thigh and I move to climb off the bed, smugness practically radiating off me, when—

His arm snaps around my waist, yanking me back like I'm nothing more than a rag doll.

"No schedule," he grits out, eyes wild, chest heaving.

I arch a brow, curling my fingers around him again and giving a firm tug that has his entire body jerking. "Say it, Rico."

His gaze drops between us, then back to me, pupils blown wide, like it's just now dawning on him that someone has the audacity to manhandle him. And that he likes it.

For a split second, I wonder if his "*therapist*" ever got this side of him. The unhinged, desperate side. Then I shove the thought down, because dwelling on that would ruin my very excellent evening.

His eyes flutter closed. "Say what?"

"Oh, you know what." I murmur, stroking again, feeling every twitch and throb in my palm. My body's already humming, slick heat pooling low as I watch his last ounce of control wave "later" and bounce.

With a guttural growl, Rico lunges.

One hand clamps around my throat, pressing me back onto the bed, while his mouth descends on my collarbone, trailing heat and teeth down to my breast. His lips latch onto my nipple, already tender from the last time he lost his mind, and the sharp pleasure sends my back arching off the mattress.

Yeah, there are worse side effects.

His other hand shoves his sweats off entirely, but his shirt stays on, and once again, I'm fully naked while he's still half-dressed like some brooding, hot version of a lazy stripper. How very Rico—always half-in, half-out, even when he's thrust deep into an argument...or me.

His strong thighs nudge my legs apart, and I gasp when the thick, blunt tip of him presses right at my entrance.

"Take off your clothes," I whisper, not bothering to hide the challenge in my voice.

His eyes flick up, dark and unyielding. "No."

Then, without warning—because apparently, foreplay is for people *not* married to emotionally suffocated assholes—he thrusts into me in one brutal, toe-curling stroke.

A gasp rips from my throat, hands flying to his biceps, fingers digging in like I'm trying to anchor myself to reality. His hand tightens around my neck—just enough to remind me who's running this show.

Or, at least, who *thinks* he is. Honestly? The jury's still out because every time Rico gets inside me, I'm convinced *I'm* the one holding all the cards. Or maybe we're both fooling ourselves. It's fuzzy. Like the inside of my head right now.

I grin up at him, smug and breathless, because look at that—*second* time breaking his own rule. So much for "only from behind."

He pulls out and slams back in, hard and fast, like he's trying to fuck every coherent thought out of my head—and judging by the way my toes curl and my nails rake down his arms, he's succeeding. No teasing. No build-up. Just raw, punishing need, and hell if I don't love it.

The headboard smacks the wall in a steady rhythm. Loud enough, I make a mental note to buy a padded one—because apparently, I didn't just marry a tech god, I married a jackhammer.

His hand slides from my throat to my hip, fingers biting into my skin like he's trying to leave a permanent mark. Good. Let him. I want *proof* of this. Of him. Of how good he can make me feel when he stops pretending he doesn't want me.

"Greedy little pussy," he growls, voice raw, like it's scraped from somewhere deep in his chest. "Takes every inch of my cock like she was fucking made for me."

God, he talks like that and somehow I feel more powerful, not less. Like I pulled those filthy words out of him with nothing more than my body and a tease.

His lips hover over mine, so close I can feel his breath, and for one stupid second, I think he might actually kiss me again. My heart stutters, hope rearing its head like a fool.

But instead, he drives in deeper—hard enough that stars explode behind my eyelids.

"I'm gonna ruin this pussy," he bites out, every word punctuated by another ruthless thrust. "All. Fucking. Night."

Oh God.

"You wanna be fucked whenever I want?" he rasps, voice like gravel and sin. "Fine. You're getting it. All night, *wife.*"

Wife.

And it's *that* word—said like a dirty promise—that sends me careening over the edge. No warning, no chance to brace. Just a full-body explosion that has me clawing at his back, my scream breaking free like I'm coming apart at the seams.

He doesn't stop. Doesn't slow down. He watches me, eyes dark and wild, his face all male satisfaction.

"Yeah," he mutters, voice rough and full of triumph. "That's what I thought."

Cocky bastard.

But hell if he didn't earn it.

Rico

HER ORGASM RIPS THROUGH her like a live wire, and fuck if I don't feel every pulse, every desperate squeeze, trying to milk me dry. Heat licks up my spine, curling low, threatening to drag me under with her. I'm two seconds from coming, which is exactly why I pull out and flip her over—because if I finish looking into those wrecked, glassy eyes, I'll lose more than just control.

She hits the mattress with a gasp, and I press her face down on the mattress, the duvet muffling her moans, burying myself to the hilt in one brutal thrust. Her moan fractures something in my chest, but I shove it down and focus on the rhythm—hard, fast, punishing. Sweat slicks between us as my shirt rides up, the muscles of my stomach grinding against her damp skin.

I can't face her. Not when she's soft and undone, looking at me like I'm more than a mistake she regrets.

Not when I *almost* kissed her as she came—like a fucking idiot desperate to taste the sound of his name on her lips.

No. This isn't about the connection. This is about fucking her until she's nothing but another scratch I've itched, and preferably, a woman carrying my child after this.

At least, that *was* the plan.

But when she tightens around me—again—another orgasm gliding through her, I nearly lose my footing. Her body milks me like she was made to ruin me, and fuck me if I don't hold back begging her to do just that.

I haul her up, her back flush to my chest, and drive into her harder, faster, each thrust raw and messy. No rhythm, no thought—just pure need. Her head drops back against my shoulder, her body pliant, wrecked, her skin dewed with sweat and glowing.

And when I sink my teeth into her shoulder—hard enough to leave a mark, soft enough not to break her—she *moans*. Loud. Shameless. Like she wants the entire world to know who's fucking her like this.

That sound? That's what sends me over the edge.

I thrust once, twice, then I'm gone, coming so hard it feels like my body's being torn inside out. My hand finds her throat—just holding. Because I *need* something to keep me grounded while everything else explodes. My other arm locks tight around her waist, anchoring her to me as my hips stutter, releasing every drop.

And when it's over, when I should collapse, rolling off, pretending this never happened?

I'm still fucking hard.

My cock twitches inside her, aching for more, and I breathe through my teeth, cursing her under my breath.

What the fuck is this?

Normally, I'm done after I come. But with her, it's like my body never got the memo.

Instead, I'm still buried deep, already thinking about flipping her back over and starting all over again.

Not helpful. Not when the whole point was to fuck her out of my system—*not* get addicted.

So why am I still holding her? Worse—why the fuck do words come out of my mouth next?

"You want my secret?" I mutter against her ear, my voice rough, ragged, as my hips slow but don't stop because her wet, silky heat is heaven.

Her head tilts, strands of hair sticking to her damp cheek. "Your what?"

I tighten my grip on her throat—just to make her feel the pulse pounding beneath my thumb. The only proof I'm still alive because I wouldn't be surprised if I keeled over from a heart attack just now.

"My secret," I repeat, lowering my mouth to the shell of her ear. "I fucking hate how good this feels."

And that's the truth. Because if this keeps up, she'll steal more than my breath and sanity. She'll steal the parts of me I buried years ago—the ones that remember how to feel anything but numb.

And I can't let that happen.

Not for her. Not for anyone.

"My secret," I mutter, dragging my teeth along the slope of her neck, where her pulse hammers like a drum. Soft, velvety skin—silk stretched over sin. Everything about this woman feels designed to fuck with my self-control.

Just like on the dining room table, when I told her she was my first kiss. A confession I'd buried so deep, not even my brothers could've excavated it. Yet I handed it to her like an idiot, gifting someone the weapon to slit his throat.

Her body stiffens. She turns her head, lips close enough that I can feel her breath feathering across my mouth, warm and sweet. Like she's daring me to close the gap. I don't. Because I know what I have to do. *Remind her.*

But the fact that I want to taste that mouth again? That's the *real* problem. Must be the endorphins. Or dopamine. Whatever chemical cocktail an orgasm spikes in your bloodstream. I'll research it later and figure out how to counteract the shit. Because this gnawing urge to keep her under me, around me, mine—that's dangerous.

Then she moves, hips tilting in slow circles, and I feel it: the slick heat welcoming me back inside, her moans vibrating against my jaw like she knows exactly what she's doing. My cock throbs, thickening further with every roll of her hips, and my already thin thread snaps.

I can't tell her a secret. I can't fuck her again either, even though I promised I'd ruin her all night. If I do, I'll fall asleep here, wrapped around her, and something else will slip. Something *real*. Something I can't afford to give.

So, I do what I'm best at when things are out of my control and I get pissy like a toddler throwing a tantrum—self-sabotage.

"My therapist never complained when I took her from behind."

The second the words leave my mouth, her entire body locks up like I just dumped a bucket of ice water on her. I could almost laugh at how predictably effective it is. Pissing her off is the only way to break the spell. And technically, it's *not* a lie. My escort wasn't paid to complain. But, comparing her and Allie is not a fair comparison. None of which Allie gets from me was ever, and I mean ever, offered to an escort. Right down to the arm I have banded around her waist or her completely naked body stiff against mine. Or kissing her. Or fucking saying a word to the woman.

But the look she gives me. Those doe eyes, wide and wounded, like I just kicked a puppy and spat on its grave.

"You asshole. How dare you," she hisses, scrambling off the bed. She snatches her clothes off the floor, the white silk tangling in her fingers as she jabs an accusatory finger at me. "Get the hell out of my room, Rico."

Her voice shakes, but not with anger. Hurt bleeds through every syllable, and for some godforsaken reason, it makes my chest tighten. Not a fan of that new sensation.

"If you ever—and I mean *ever*—mention your escorts while we're in bed, or... or anywhere, really, I swear to God—" She cuts herself off, shaking her head like words aren't enough to capture her fury. "Just get out."

"Allie..." I start, throat dry, brain scrambling for something to defuse the bomb I just dropped other than saying "sorry," because I don't do that. What the hell am I supposed to say? Sorry for comparing you to a woman I paid to leave after fifteen minutes? No, because that would mean admitting she means *more* than that. And she doesn't need to know that. *She can't.*

I only wanted to sever the connection, not slice her open and watch her bleed.

"Go back to your room. To your *floor*." The emphasis is a slap to the face.

I don't argue. I don't apologize. I just grab my sweats, yank them up, and stalk out of her room without another glance. Victory, right? I don't have to spoon her or accidentally kiss her again. Mission accomplished.

So why the fuck does my chest still feel like someone shoved a fist through my ribcage and started squeezing?

By the time I hit the first floor, my head's pounding. I bypass my room entirely, heading straight for my office and powering up my computer. If I'm dying, I might as well know what the cause of death is.

Chest tightness. Shortness of breath. Radiating discomfort. Google throws "heart attack" at me like it's trying to win a prize for the most dramatic diagnosis, but it might be accurate.

But there's a little voice in my head whispering something worse. *Guilt you dumbass.*

Bullshit. I don't feel guilt. I don't feel anything. This has to be a cardiac issue. Maybe I should schedule an appointment.

Doubt there's a cure for being an asshole husband, though. Which, judging by the shattered look on Allie's face, I've just confirmed I am.

Rico

I'VE BEEN MARRIED FOR *three* weeks. Twenty-one *days*. Five hundred and four *hours*. But who's counting?

Since my sweet little wife altered the terms of our contract, I've gladly given her what she wants. Every single night. Okay, *fine*—I want it too, but that's beside the point.

She didn't speak to me for three days after that escort comment. Not a word. Radio silence—unless you count the moments where we tore each other's clothes off like there was a damn stopwatch running.

Angry fucking, plain and simple. Hours of it. Two, sometimes three. Not a single word spoken. Just teeth, nails, and skin.

Pretty sure we left permanent dents in the drywall after that time I had her pinned against the hallway, too impatient to do anything but shove her skirt up and take what we both wanted.

And no, I haven't mentioned the escort again. Even I know there's a line. I might be an asshole, but I have a conscience. It's just... highly selective about when it clocks in.

Unfortunately, despite extensive research—including medical journals, psychology articles, and one very disturbing Reddit thread—I've found nothing to explain why I'm still craving her as much now as I was the first time. If regular access was supposed to cure the craving, I've been grossly misinformed.

Yesterday, I had to physically stop myself from leaving the office before six just to rush home and bend her over the dining room table before she could set it for our weeknight meal.

For the record, I've never given a damn about appetizers. Not the literal kind, and certainly not the filthy euphemism. But now? Now, I want the whole fucking seven-course meal, garnished with desperation and a side of *please, God, more* screaming from her mouth.

Thankfully, I've kept my distance outside of our nightly encounters and the forced-proximity dinners that redefine torture. Forget waterboarding. Just make me sit across from my wife while she chatters about her day, looking soft and flushed from the kitchen heat, while I pretend I'm not wondering how long it would take to clear the table and make her scream my name.

I still clung to the idea she'd stop texting. Nope.

Every morning: *Have a great day, Rico!*

Every afternoon: *How's your day going?*

Every evening: *Dinner's at seven.*

Every. Fucking. Day.

And every time, I read the message and do nothing. Not even a thumbs-up emoji, which is the universal sign for *I'm ignoring you but pretending I'm not.*

I'm not sure how much longer I can let this horrifyingly one-sided conversation thread grow before she realizes my silence is the loudest answer she's going to get.

Though, to be fair, I *am* reading them. Which means she sees that I've read them. Which technically means I'm actively ignoring her, not passively. That counts for something, right?

Apparently not.

Thanks to this damn marriage—or, more accurately, that I said *I do* while fully sober—my brothers have decided I'm fair game for social interaction, too.

We used to coexist at work like well-dressed shadows. Quick hellos. Silent meetings. Maybe a nod in the hallway. Words were only spoken if someone died, and even then I just nodded and acted like I gave a shit who Larry from accounting was.

Now? Now, they stop to chat. *Chat.*

"How's married life, Rico?"

"Has Allie redecorated yet?"

"Will you be at Sunday dinner and actually ride together this time?"

And because the universe has a twisted sense of humor, they've turned my living room into a chapter of the Unwilling Married Bastards Club. Every Wednesday, while the women are at cooking night—read: drinking wine and plotting how to tighten the leash on their husbands—Alex and Dom show up with a bottle of scotch and smug expressions.

Want even worse? Oh, I have it. I'm now on the Google calendar for *every* company meeting.

Every. Single. One.

My calendar pings twice a day like a digital middle finger, reminding me I've been roped into every brainstorm, project review, and corporate pep talk. I'm seeing emailed invites in my nightmares.

Which is probably why sleep has become a luxury. That, and the fact I occasionally forget myself and fuck my wife in her bed—rookie mistake.

It took me a week—seven excruciating, sleep-deprived, sandpaper-eyed days—to realize that if I didn't have sex with her in bed, I wasn't obligated to sleep next to her. A true life hack. Never did I think my success would be cracking the code of marital survival.

And yet, here I am, now enduring a game of how far my patience can stretch while sitting in another fucking meeting.

Evander Harrington sits across from me, looking every bit the golden boy Manhattan heir he was born to be. Blond hair slicked back, navy three-piece suit tailored solely for him and those signature Harrington eyes. Harrington Enterprises owns half the luxury hotels in the country and pays us an obscene amount to keep their cybersecurity airtight. Only now my little hacker friend has gotten bored with poking around our system and knocked on the Harringtons' digital front door, just to prove they could. Wiped the logs clean, left without so much as a fingerprint. Ghost-level shit. I hate being impressed.

To my left, Silas and Cruz Locke sit like twin Abercrombie mannequins—perfectly tailored suits, California tans, and that sun-bleached hair that screams bro trip to Maui. It's almost offensive how out of place they look against the cold, glass-and-steel backdrop of our Manhattan headquarters. They're here under the guise of "monitoring progress," but Cruz—*who the fuck names their kid that?*—came to "help." As if his Stanford degree and bleached white smile can out-code me.

And then there's Jaxon Wolfe, our family's overpaid legal guard dog, lounging at the head of the table. Someone, somewhere, nicknamed him the *Big Bad Wolfe*, which would be ridiculous if he didn't lean into it with every perfectly arched brow and $4,000 suit. I don't fault him for the nickname—idiots will idolize anyone with sharp teeth and a sharper mind. I do fault him for billing me in six-minute increments while delivering lectures on "corporate liability" like I didn't build half the systems he's trying to protect on paper while I'm the one doing the actual code.

"This hacker's slick," Evander says, tapping his Montblanc pen against a leather notebook. "I combed through the logs, flagged anomalies, even ran a deep forensic sweep. Came up empty." Admitting defeat stings, especially when you're supposed to be the Harrington prodigy.

He's decent enough, though. Not like his older brother, Griffin, who wears his arrogance like a crown. That man is certifiable—ruthless, brilliant, and allergic to human connection. Kindred spirit. Only difference? He surrendered to matrimony, and now he's been reduced to a damp kitten instead of the roaring tiger Manhattan once feared. The Monster turned house cat.

What the hell is it about powerful men in this city getting neutered the second they slip a ring on someone's finger? Is there an epidemic where men hand over their balls for regular access to what's between their wives' legs? Because I'm related to two victims already, and I'll be damned if I'm the next man down.

I glance at the clock, calculating how long I'll have to sit here nodding like a bobblehead while mentally running brute-force sequences. Every wasted minute is a minute I'm not at home, taking out my frustration on my wife. I'm aware of the contradiction, my cock is not. Sex with her is like stress relief in human form—hot, soft, and perfectly responsive, like squeezing one of those therapeutic stress balls. Except mine moans and glares at me afterward.

"I rechecked the firewall's redundancies," Evander continues. "If this hacker's in, they're deep. No breadcrumbs, no active pings. Either they're a ghost, *or* they're smarter than us."

My lips twitch, but I smother the smile. Smarter than *us*. Maybe smarter than *you*, Harrington. Not me.

"I'll find them," I mutter, half to myself. Half challenge.

Silas Locke leans back, fingers steepled like he's posing for Forbes' "Top CEOs Under Forty" cover shoot — which he was in, and something tells me it plays a vital role in his oversized ego. "Do we need to bring in an external team?"

The urge to laugh almost chokes me. External team? Sure, let's call in the JV squad while the varsity team sits courtside.

"I don't need backup." I don't do collaboration, especially not with men named Cruz and Silas who look more interested in catching the next wave than sitting in a Manhattan high-rise.

My laptop hums quietly in front of me, the screen glowing with activity logs for the Harrington account. Cruz Locke hovers behind me like a gnat — irritating, persistent, and one breath away from getting swatted. This, right here, is my sanctuary. Lines of code. Except now my peace is contaminated by sun-kissed West Coast arrogance and a room full of corporate chest-thumpers pretending they understand cybersecurity.

Evander is across the table, deep in conversation with Alex, Dom, the Locke bros, and Jaxon— because apparently Jaxon represents both us and the Harringtons. Conflict of interest? Please. This city runs on conflicts of interest, caffeine, and generational wealth. Jaxon's an all-purpose fixer, which is a polite way of saying he bends the law until it begs for mercy and somehow never gets caught.

Meanwhile, I'm here chasing shadows.

No phishing attacks. That would've been too pedestrian for my hacker friend. No brute-force login attempts, either. Of course not. Amateurs kick down doors. Professionals pick locks.

I scan deeper, eye twitching. If they exploited a vulnerability, it means *I* left one open. I don't leave doors unlocked. I don't make mistakes. Except, apparently, for saying *I do* and signing up for my wife's nightly "needs."

All software patches are up-to-date, every security measure triple-checked, because I oversee biweekly updates on every client system. My systems are airtight.

Except for the fact some genius just strutted through my firewall like it had a welcome mat.

Finally, I see it. A directory change that shouldn't exist. Malicious code slipped in under the guise of — *fuck me* — a patch update. My patch update. They piggybacked on my security measure to inject their backdoor access. That's not just hacking. That's art. Twisted, malicious art painted with my brush.

"He used our patch." I gesture to the logs glaring back at me, every corrupted line a middle finger from my anonymous adversary. Evander leans over my shoulder, those signature Harrington blue eyes narrowing as he scans. The Harringtons all look like modern-day Targaryens — platinum hair, eerie blue eyes. Unfortunately, no dragons. Just absurd amounts of wealth and superiority complexes.

"Well, that's impressive," Cruz chimes in, running a hand through his artfully disheveled hair. It's the tousled look that probably requires a personal stylist and $100 pomade. "But they'd have to know you update patches twice a week."

My jaw clenches hard enough to trigger a migraine. There are only a few ways they could figure that out. Monitoring update patterns is the most likely.

Flipping the laptop back toward me, I isolate the compromised systems. It's pointless, really. The bastard's long gone. Didn't steal data. Didn't plant ransomware. Just waltzed in, poked around, and left breadcrumbs to show me where I screwed up.

Petty. Brilliant. Asshole.

"How long to quarantine and repair?" Evander asks, his perfectly waxed eyebrow arching. Of course he waxes. No man's arches are that precise without professional intervention.

"Give me a day." I don't look up. If I work through the night, I can have it done by morning. But then it hits me. *Dinner.*

I groan. Loudly, apparently, because the room goes silent.

"What?" Dom, the nosy brother he is, asks. He's kicked back in his chair, arms crossed, watching me like I'm a live feed of his favorite reality show. I hate him.

"Nothing." I disconnect from another compromised system, ignoring their collective curiosity.

Cruz, thankfully, has backed off, so he doesn't see how deep this breach really went. Harrington's databases are lit up like a Christmas tree and our merger dude bros over there don't need to see that oopsie.

"I'll need until morning..." I pause, because the next words physically pain me. "Dinner. Seven o'clock. Wife."

There it is. My balls, officially on display and ripe for the taking.

Alex and Dom exchange shit-eating grins, and I briefly contemplate introducing their faces to the conference table. Swallowing bile would be less nauseating than enduring their looks.

Evander leans forward, blue eyes sparkling more than the obscene amount of fairy dust sprinkled at my niece's birthday. "Heard you got married. Thought it was a joke."

I glare at him. "You were at the wedding."

"My point."

"It's arranged." In our world, that's not unusual. Hell, his brother married for hotel acquisitions, so he gets it. Why didn't I get a hotel chain as my consolation?

"But you leave work to make it home for dinner?" Evander's grin widens, and whatever thin sliver of respect I had for him slides straight into the ninth circle of hell.

"We have an agreement."

"That you actually follow?" Dom's eyebrow is loaded with implication. Sienna, his big-mouthed wife, clearly blabbed. Which means my wife is running her mouth to my sisters, who funnel every word straight to their husbands like gossip-fueled carrier pigeons.

I make a mental note to remind Allie that sharing private details with the Bennetti women is like broadcasting on prime-time television. This family doesn't just meddle; they mobilize. Feed them a crumb, and they'll build an empire of interference.

After I isolate the compromised systems, the tension in my chest loosens. *Barely*. It's like duct-taping a cracked dam—functional, but ugly as hell and bound to fail if I don't reinforce it.

I glance at Dom, who's watching me like a lion eyeing a limping gazelle. "Yes, we follow the contract." Bold-faced, unapologetic lies.

"I heard there were...alterations." His voice drips with amusement, and my molars grind. I'd pay good money to feel my knuckles make alterations to his face right now.

I flex my fingers, noting the lack of bruises. When was the last time I hit something that wasn't my wife's G-spot?

Marco's been waiting for me at the gym, and I've been skipping out like a whipped husband who traded boxing gloves for oven mitts. I mentally scroll through my calendar for a free day to spar before this marital vortex sucks me into the abyss entirely.

"Minor changes. Nothing more."

Dom seems to not care we have an audience, because that mouth of his keeps moving. "*You*. Rico Bennetti. The man who treats protocol like scripture altered a written contract?" His glee is nauseating, and I suppress the urge to gag.

"You realize," Jaxon drawls from his corner, not even pretending to hide his entertainment, "that a verbal agreement makes up an official amendment? Enforceable, if challenged."

Of course, I know that. I researched every loophole, every shred of legal jargon that could undo the damage of my temporary lapse in judgment. How the hell do I tell my wife we're reverting to the original terms after I've indulged myself, night after night, trying to screw her out of my system? More importantly, what do I do when I have zero interest in changing it back?

My phone pings on the table by my laptop. I know exactly *who* it is, but I check anyway. Because apparently, I've developed a masochistic need to see her name light up my screen. I used to go hours without peeking at my phone—hell, I kept it on silent. Now? I'm practically Pavlov's dog, salivating at every notification.

> Allie: Dinner's going to be delicious tonight! Been working on this recipe for weeks. See you at seven. Can you grab a bottle of Merlot on your way home?

I stare at the text, dissecting every word like its enemy code. Too many issues to count.

First, *the dinner comment*. As if she didn't perfect cooking for me the moment she realized food was my weakness. The woman's been running a one-woman psychological warfare campaign, using butter and garlic weapons.

Second, *the wine*. She's been home all day and could've bought it herself. This isn't about convenience; it's about pushing me to do things. Small, seemingly innocuous tasks designed to weave me deeper into the fabric of domesticity. Death by a thousand errands.

"Is that...?" Alex's voice cuts in, but I tune him out, suspecting he's droning about the Evander meeting. He and Cruz will talk damage control, PR spin with Jaxon, and how to ensure our other clients—especially one's like the Harringtons, who probably use hundred-dollar bills as tissues—never hear a whisper of this breach.

But then Dom chuckles. "I think it is. How long until he notices?"

My head snaps up. They're all staring at me. Even Jaxon, who usually operates on a strict diet of indifference, looks mildly entertained. The man could squeeze blood from a rock if it meant winning a case, and apparently, my personal life now qualifies as premium entertainment.

Shoving my laptop shut, I meet Dom's gaze, voice flat. "Speak."

Leaning back in my chair, I cross my arms over my light gray sweater, the soft cashmere doing nothing to buffer the irritation prickling under my skin. Jeans. Clean shoes. No tie. Because unlike my brothers, the Locke clones, and Evander fucking Harrington—all decked out in custom-tailored suits—I have no intention of pretending I give a damn about appearances.

The Harringtons roam the same circles as my family. Same overpriced schools, same insufferable country clubs, same endless galas designed to inflate egos and shrink bank accounts. *None* of it shaped us into better men. It just taught us to smile through bullshit and throw money at problems until they disappeared. I, however, was the outlier. Kicked out of every institution by week two, usually for punching the first asshole who breathed wrong in my direction. Papa eventually stopped donating to keep me enrolled, realizing the investment had worse returns than crypto.

My phone buzzes, and I glance down. Another text from my wife. Chipper and borderline deranged in its enthusiasm.

> **Allie:** Dinner's going to be amazing. Been perfecting the sauce all week. Can't wait for you to try it! Don't forget the Merlot!

The sauce. The one she's been obsessing over for apparent months, experimenting with ingredients ranging from cinnamon to anchovies to—*help me*—chocolate. Like an episode of *Chopped* on crack.

My subconscious has the audacity to store these details despite my best efforts to tune her out during dinner. Mental clutter. Useless information. Like knowing the square footage of every Bennetti-owned building in Manhattan or the exact number of security cameras covering the Harrington flagship hotel. No practical benefit to my job, just noise rattling around in my head.

"You're smiling." Dom's words make my eyes snap away from my phone.

I can't go into the breakdown of how ridiculous that statement is, but one thing I can emphasize is *I. Don't. Smile.*

But I am, according to the reflection in my phone's now black screen. Fuck me. What has this woman done to me?

Only one solution to this nightmare. It's time to remind my wife of the asshole she married. Be late to dinner, piss her off, and enjoy the sight of her all flushed and furious—her most fuckable look. Not that I'd ever admit it. Yeah, that'll do the trick.

I glance back at my screen. "I'll fix the code tonight," I mutter more to myself than the room. I'll barricade myself in my office at home, ignore her, and—*most* importantly—not have sex with her. One night without her wrapped around me like a human sedative. I can do it.

My eye twitches at the thought, but I ignore it. So do my balls, which are already filing a formal complaint.

Last week, when she got her period, I nearly told her I didn't care, and we'd do it, anyway. That's how far gone I am—contemplating sex with zero reproductive benefit.

"Perfect." Evander stands. "I'll update my brother."

That's when it hits me.

"Evander," I say. Everyone stops. Even Jaxon, who typically gives zero shits unless someone mentions billable hours, peeks up. Yeah, I get it. I don't voluntarily engage in conversation. *Desperate times.*

Evander turns, brows lifting. "Yeah?"

"Via Napoli. Who owns it?"

Confusion flickers in his eyes before they narrow into focus. "Griffin. Why?"

Of all the Harringtons. This will certainly cost me.

"I need to buy it."

Silence. Then Alex drops his pen, the metallic clank echoing as it rolls off the marble table and hits the floor. His jaw practically unhinges. If this were a cartoon, his tongue would unfurl onto the table like a red carpet.

"You want to buy a restaurant?" Alex's voice rises, hesitant. "You don't *even* eat in restaurants."

I shrug, ignoring the fact he's not wrong. "My wife wants to run one. She's a talented chef. Could be the executive chef."

Even Evander stares at me like I've sprouted a third head. That wouldn't surprise me. Allie's already stolen my peace, my sanity, and apparently, my grip on reality. Her making me sprout an unwelcomed appendage isn't far off.

"Why not just ask Griffin to hire her?" Alex suggests, ever the pragmatic one. This from the man who bought his wife's publishing company to fast-track her promotion and didn't tell her. Dom's no better—he purchased an entire art gallery for his wife, like it was a coffee table on clearance.

"I *want* to own it. Give her full control."

And, more *importantly*, keep her busy. Long hours, constant stress, and peak dinner service right when I'd normally be subjected to her doe-eyed dinner invitations and incessant text updates. She'll crawl home exhausted, leaving minimal opportunity for our genitals to collide in yet another round of mind-blowing, sanity-stealing sex.

It's a flawless strategy. Buy her a restaurant, reclaim my autonomy, and finally sit my dick down for a long, strict conversation about who's really in charge.

Evander chuckles, shaking his head. "You realize Griffin will charge you over market value just to prove a point, right? He's generous like that."

"I don't care. Talk to him. Tell him I want to buy it. Today."

Evander blinks. "Today? As in...now?"

"Preferably within the hour."

He pulls out his phone, fingers flying across the screen. "I'll see what he says. Will you be ready to place an offer?"

I nod. "Whatever he wants, I'll pay."

Jaxon leans in, tugging my sleeve like an annoying toddler. I glare, and leans back, letting me embrace my crazy. "Whatever he wants?"

"Write the damn check. It's worth every penny."

A few hundred thousand or over a million? Pocket change. If it buys me peace, distance, and the chance to get my shit together, it might be the best investment I've ever made.

Rico

I SHOULD'VE KNOWN. THE second I walked out of the conference room, my brothers trailed after me, straight into my office—which, for the record, is *still* not large enough to accommodate two adults, let alone three. But here we are. Them in my office, again, a place they never frequented until I joined the married club.

"You're buying her a restaurant?" Alex asks, not even waiting for the door to shut behind him.

I sink into my chair, ignoring him as I pull up the isolated files I flagged during the meeting. Time to dig through code and pray I find some little breadcrumb our hacker might've left behind. A "fuck you" message, a signature, anything that proves they're human and not some sentient AI sent to torment me.

Nothing. Nada. Just a sneaky fucker slipping through my defenses, ghost-level stealth. I might admire the skill—if they weren't the second reason my head feels primed for a demolition crew. The first? Long dark hair, hazel eyes, and hips that sway with a sinful precision straight out of the devil's playbook.

I've seen ballerinas with less poise than this hacker. Same energy, too—graceful, disciplined, and smug as hell.

"Earth to Rico." Alex snaps his fingers in front of my face.

"What?"

Both of them stand there, arms crossed, matching suits. *Men in Black* should've recruited these two.

"She needs a job," I mutter, eyes glued to my screen as I isolate the corrupted databases.

"You could've gotten her a job," Alex fires back. "Paid off an owner to bump their head chef and slide her in. Hell, Marco has restaurants. He owes you."

True...

"She wants to own one. And that restaurant is her favorite."

Fuck. *How* do I know that? *Why* do I remember that? And, more importantly, *why* did I just tell my brothers?

"Her favorite," Dom repeats slowly, savoring the words. His hand drags along his jaw, and the bastard's already smiling. "So, instead of just getting her a job, you're buying her favorite restaurant."

"It'll keep her from texting me all damn day with updates, checking on my day, and now, apparently, sending me on errands to pick up wine that *'pairs perfectly with dinner.'* Why does dinner need to be an event?"

Silence. Just two pairs of eyes blinking at me.

"You're buying a restaurant...for a *break*?" Dom asks.

"And you just said more in that single outburst than you have all day," Alex adds, grinning like he's uncovered the key to fixing my emotional incompetence. He would be wrong.

"Or week, really," Dom chimes in.

My wife has officially stolen my ability to stay quiet. Thoughts that should stay locked in the prison of my mind keep slipping out, verbal jailbreaks happening in real-time, for the sole amusement of my idiot brothers.

I yank my phone from the desk, groaning. "I need to go."

They don't move. Still standing there, arms crossed, staring at me as if the third head I grew just started reciting poetry about emotions.

"Stop channeling Mama and your wives." I point at both of them, fully aware my phone is one bad squeeze from turning to dust. "She's bored. She needs a distraction. Then she'll leave me alone. You got Sienna a gallery," I jab a finger at Dom. "And you," I turn on Alex, "bought Violet God-knows-what."

Fuck. Did it again. Explaining myself. Justifying decisions I shouldn't have to justify.

My former self would have been horrified. Now? He's rolling in his grave after my wife took his life while the zombie version of me buys my wife luxury real estate to avoid awkward dinner conversations.

They say marriage changes people. For the better, allegedly. Bullshit. There's nothing good about these changes. The fact I'm not clenching my fists out of frustration worries me. That was my coping mechanism. My stress relief. Now, my wife has stolen that, too—along with my peace, my sleep, and my ability to think about anything that *doesn't* involve her.

Give it a few more weeks, and I'll end up the same as my brothers. Dom and Alex folded in less than seven days. I'd love to believe I've got more self-control than the two of them combined. I can hold out. I just need more distance between myself and the curvy woman currently redecorating my house and rewriting our contract.

Because she's getting through. That's why she keeps texting, keeps talking, keeps reaching for me in her sleep—her hand landing on my thigh the other night, warm, soft, and far too intimate. I didn't move. Blamed it on exhaustion. Told myself I physically couldn't lift a muscle.

It wasn't.

My wife has found *my* weakness, and it's located inconveniently between my legs, controlling every decision I make.

Which is exactly why I'm buying this restaurant and enforcing a new plan: spend as little time with her as possible.

She thinks she's winning. That she's cracking the armor. That's why she keeps pushing—texting, cooking, touching. The other night, she *"accidentally"* fell asleep on my chest. Bullshit. That was a tactical maneuver, not unconscious affection. I'm married to a woman running a long con, and somehow I'm halfway to signing over the deed to my soul—oh wait, you need one first to relinquish it, right?

No. I need to get ahead of her. Remove her from my immediate environment. Only then will I get my peace back.

Because here's the thing about burglars: if you don't stop them, they take everything.

Allie

THREE WEEKS. THAT'S HOW long I've been married to Rico Bennetti, and this marks our third official appearance as a married couple at Sunday family dinner. The novelty wore off five minutes into the first experience.

Sure, I won the battle of the ludicrous ovulation clause—no more peeing on sticks just to wait for the glow of ovulation. But in true Rico fashion, he retaliated by ditching our once-a-week date nights. Fair, I suppose. I scribbled out one requirement off the contract; he passed over another. He even came home late for dinner last night. I know he's testing my defenses and trying to irritate me.

Not that I'm really complaining. Hard to gripe when your broody husband gives you multiple orgasms every night.

He still eats dinner with me. Leaves his Post-It notes and speaks to me as seldom as possible—*unless* we're having sex. Then, suddenly, the man's a poet. Dirty words whispered in my ear, each one lighting me up inside and me whimpering for more.

Which brings me to today's Post-It, also known as my daily neon sign of passive-aggressive passion, sitting on the counter.

Rico: *I never went to school to learn what I do. Self-taught. Not bragging.*

I blinked at it for a solid minute this morning. Not because the handwriting was, as always, immaculate, but because this one *actually* said something.

Not a government conspiracy theory against kale. Not a hot take about why kittens are the spawn of Satan. Not some useless fact such as "Sharks existed before trees." (Yes, he actually wrote that once, and no, I did not let it go.)

This? This was real. A glimpse behind the iron fortress of Rico Bennetti.

And I hate I don't know how to respond.

Maybe that was his goal. To throw me off my game. To silence the bratty brief responses I leave every day. He probably figured if he tossed me something personal, I'd move on.

Cute. He must've forgotten who he married.

Balance is the foundation of our marriage. I executed the ovulation tests. He murdered date nights. He leaves passive-aggressive Post-Its instead of speaking like a normal human, and I write back because, unlike him, I don't believe in the silent treatment. I know why he does it. Post-Its don't invite conversation. He gets to lob his little fact grenade, and I get to reply after he's safely out of range. No talking. No eye contact. Just sarcasm on paper.

And yet, here I am, pen poised, brain suspended.

The worst part? The man's home.

For three weeks, Rico's been gone every morning before I wake up. *Every single one.* I roll over, sheets cold, body sore, and house unoccupied. He returns like clockwork for dinner, screws me senseless, and ghosts the bed before sunrise like it's his side hustle.

But this morning, I stumbled out of his room, half-asleep and craving coffee, only to freeze in the hallway outside his office.

The unmistakable click of a keyboard.

His door was closed. Locked, probably. But the man himself? Home. Not at work.

Seven days a week, he drags himself to the office, likely to avoid sharing oxygen with me. And yet, today, he was here.

I spent the day pretending not to care. Cleaned the already immaculate house. Did laundry. Rearranged the spice cabinet alphabetically, then by color because apparently, I'm now the woman who gets emotionally wrecked by Post-It notes and copes with paprika.

He didn't appear until three, stretching with the slow, predatory ease of a six-foot-three jungle cat shaking off hibernation. I stood at the kitchen island, piping the last swirl of ricotta into the cannoli I planned to bring to dinner, and when I glanced up—there he was.

Watching me.

I smiled. He glared.

Then, without a word, he pivoted and stalked off to his room, probably to shower and mentally prepare for another thrilling evening of pretending not to hear me talk.

God, I married the human equivalent of a grumpy house cat. Only affectionate when it suits him. Prime reasons I abhor cats.

I pull the Post-It from my pocket, staring at it once more. It means nothing, right? It's just another one of Rico's cryptic little love notes. (And by "*love*," I mean the bare minimum effort required to acknowledge my existence.)

I haven't responded yet, mostly because he hasn't left his cave all day. Not once. If he's not working, he's hiding, and I've stopped trying to figure out which is which. But screw it. I grab the pen from the drawer—the one he's stuffed with enough Post-Its to suggest this "communication" system isn't temporary.

Allie: I took culinary classes, but only to learn proper French techniques. Not bragging either.

I slap the note next to the coffeepot because caffeine is the only reason Rico functions, and I know he'll see it.

Sighing, I wrap the tray of cannolis I'm contributing to Sunday dinner. My eyes flick back to the note, then to the hallway.

Every Sunday, we arrive at his parents' house like awkward prom dates who forgot to coordinate.

Separate cars. He drives his two-seater death trap; I hitch a ride with Vinnie. We leave at the same time, pull up within seconds of each other, and pretend it's totally normal. *Nothing about this is normal.*

No one mentions it, but the raised eyebrows from his mom are louder than a foghorn. Like I don't already know how ridiculous it is. We live together, yet can't handle being in a confined space together for a forty-minute drive?

The soft rap of knuckles against the garage door pulls me from my thoughts. Vinnie steps inside, mouth open to say something, but he stops short, eyes flicking past me. I follow his gaze and—*holy hell.*

Rico.

Damp hair. Black jeans. White T-shirt. Oh, *and* my wet panties.

Why the hell does a basic outfit appear as if sin personally stitched it together just to ruin me?

It's infuriating. He's wealthier than half the city, yet he dresses as if he's about to fix a leaky faucet, then pose for a GQ feature immediately after. I wouldn't be surprised if his wedding tux was the first—and only—time he's worn a suit.

Not that I'm unfamiliar with his wardrobe. I snooped. The man is a walking enigma, and I'm only human. I found exactly three suits. That's it. Meanwhile, my dad's closet rivaled a Brooks Brothers flagship, and Vinnie treats his Armani rotation like a gym uniform.

Violet once mentioned he shows up to board meetings in jeans and a Henley, and no one dares to criticize. His robotic, passive-aggressive dismissal is probably why they know better.

"We can ride together."

His voice snaps me back to reality. He doesn't look up as he fastens his watch, treating the idea of sharing a confined space with his wife with the same enthusiasm as asking if I want extra cheese on my pizza.

I blink. "Together? As in... *your car?*"

The last time we were in a car together was on our wedding night. No one needs to tell me how messed up that is. I'm achingly aware.

Rico caps his sparkling — *that's right, I won that one* — bottle of water with surgical precision and levels me with a look.

Nodding once, he pulls his keys from his pocket.

Vinnie glances between us, brows knitted.

"Should we all go in the sedan?" I gesture to Vinnie. You know, the man who routinely chauffeurs me around. Honestly, I can't recall a time he didn't drive me. "Save gas. Help the environment. World peace and all that."

Rico shakes his head, pocketing his keys. "He's riding with Antonio."

Vinnie and I exchange looks, equally baffled.

"I guess I'll see you there, then..." Vinnie mutters, already pulling out his phone. Probably to text Antonio or draft an SOS. Both seem appropriate.

I, however, remain rooted to the spot, staring at my husband—the man who's dodged anything remotely mirroring quality time for three solid weeks.

Without another word, he snags the tray of cannolis off the counter and heads toward the garage. Am I the only one noticing he flipped the script on our entire dysfunctional routine?

Vinnie's smiles and mouths, Good luck, *bambolina*.

Rico

WHY THE HELL DID I offer to let her ride with me?

I blame Mama. And Papa. And the two oxygen wasters I'm genetically obligated to call my brothers. All chirping the same bullshit about "spending more time with my wife," as if giving an hour or more every night tangled doesn't count.

But when I saw her standing there in those fuck-me skinny jeans—painted on and custom-tailored by Satan himself—and that loose, short-sleeved blouse, the neckline dipping just enough to tease rounded cleavage; I snapped. My jaw clenched, my brain gave up on reciting rational thoughts, and before I could strangle the words, they clawed their way out: *We can ride together.*

Fucking idiot.

I should've swallowed broken glass instead. Would've been less painful than the heart-pounding regret that followed. Too late, though. Damage done.

To her credit, the look on Allie's face was amusing. Eyes wide, mouth parting as if I'd just suggested we adopt a golden retriever and name it after her favorite Disney prince. For once, the woman who treats silence as a mortal sin actually had no words.

Didn't even say a word when I opened the door for her, let her slide into the passenger seat, and passed her the tray of cannolis I was dying to eat—or, preferably, lick off her navel. Instead, she just sat there, stiff as a mannequin, observing me.

The silence was smothering. Not the comfortable, blessed kind I thrive in, but the-*might-drive-us-into-oncoming-traffic-just-to-break-this* kind. And since I had to operate a motor vehicle without crashing us into a lamppost, I focused on the road. On the weather. On *anything* but her.

Fall was creeping in. Thank fuck. The sticky hellscape known as summer in New York is akin to being slow-roasted in a garbage-scented sauna. Humidity. Heat. Random downpours that don't clean the streets just turn the stench into something worse. It's as if the city is marinating itself in its own filth.

But fall? Crisp air. Fewer bodies obstructing sidewalks. A socially acceptable excuse to stay inside and avoid humanity. Only now do I realize staying inside means I will be around the woman next to me a lot more. *Shit.*

And then I made the mistake of *looking* at my wife.

Dark hair, loose over her shoulders, curled and effortless. Glossy enough to tempt my hand into wrapping around the strands and testing how tightly they'd coil in my fist. It's fast — for the record.

Deep dark hair that could make a raven jealous. *Brown like the color of overpriced espresso minus the caffeine rush that would actually make it useful. Molten like silky brown melted dark chocolate. Like smooth, satiny, brown hair that wraps around my fingers* perfectly, *angling her back as I fuck...nope.*

Apparently, my wife's invasion isn't limited to my personal space anymore. No, Allie's now breached my thoughts—the *one* sanctuary I had left. My mental fortress, fortified with sarcasm, coding jargon, and the soothing hum of self-imposed isolation, now has her name spray-painted across the walls.

What's next? My manhood? Pretty sure that went out the door the moment I muttered *I do.*

The silence between us festers, thick and suffocating. I flick on the stereo, letting low-fi beats fill the void. Instrumental. No vocals. Just a smooth, rhythmic sound designed for people who enjoy the illusion of peace without the inconvenience of human interaction. My kind of music.

Allie glances at me, brows tweaked in curiosity, probably wondering if my taste in music is as broken as my social skills. I ignore her. Easier to stare out the window, counting down the seconds until we reach my parents' house and I can offload both her and my spiraling thoughts into someone else.

By the time we hit Greenwich, my stomach's knotted tougher than a triple-sailor hitch. I park, cut the engine, and get out without a word. One door, two doors, and I'm hauling the cannoli tray out of her lap before she can blink. It's not chivalry. It's logistics. She's slow, and I hate wasted time.

"I can carry it."

"I've got it." The words leave my mouth without getting the green light, and my hand—betrayal of all betrayals—shoots out to clasp hers. Fingers lacing together like we're some picture-perfect couple who hold hands because of feelings, not because I do not know what the fuck else to do with myself.

Her gaze drops to our intertwined fingers. She doesn't pull away. I don't let go. We're both too headstrong to blink first.

The estate manager doesn't even bother answering the door. He knows better. Small talk would've required me to engage with another human being, and I'd rather sandpaper my tongue.

"Rico! Allie!" Mama's voice chirps from the sitting room—sunny and nauseating, the human equivalent of a motivational poster about tolerance. She rushes over, eyes zeroing in on our joined hands.

I don't let go. In fact, I squeeze harder. Not out of affection. It's reflex—automatic, the same way you flip someone off when they cut you off in traffic.

Mama plucks the tray from my hand, practically frothing. "Oh, Nonna's going to love these. Better stash a few for yourself before she hoards them."

"No worries," Allie chirps, her voice syrupy sweet. "I made an extra tray at home." She flicks a glance my way, those green-and-gold eyes gleaming with something dangerous.

Maybe she'll use those extra cannolis to seduce, distract, or punish me. I don't particularly care, as long as her plan ends with her naked and me licking pastry cream off places the FDA didn't approve.

We step into the main living room, and I instantly regret everything. Showing up first means facing my family without the buffer more bodies would serve. I thrive in crowded rooms because, ironically; they make me unseen. Arrive late, shake hands, nod through small talk, disappear. That's the playbook.

Papa appears out of nowhere. I'm sure the scent of fresh cannolis and impending grandchildren has summoned him. His eyes flick between me and Allie, lingering on our hands before he plants both palms on her shoulders. If he could X-ray her uterus with sheer willpower, he would, and if he could, hopefully he could tell me I've succeeded so I can go back to my orderly life.

"Any news for us?" he asks, hopeful as a gambler betting his last chip.

Subtlety? Never heard of it. The Bennetti family operates on brute force—over sharing, emotional terrorism, and enough unsolicited advice to drive the most patient saint into a psychotic break.

"Allie made cannolis." I drop her hand and head straight for the liquor on the kitchen counter. Tumbler. Bourbon. Full pour. No ice. Because watering down good alcohol is what idiots do. I'm already married—that's enough bad decision-making for one lifetime.

Glass in hand, I grab a bottle of white wine, pour a generous glass, and walk it over to Allie. Her eyes narrow.

"What?"

She stares at the glass, then at me, head tilted in that way that makes her curls bounce. And I'm hard. Great. Nothing like attending family dinner with a semi.

"I didn't think you knew what I drank."

I didn't. But I noticed she only ever finishes the fruity, frilly bullshit wine, that tastes like someone melted down a gummy bear and called it vintage. Without answering, I shove the glass into her hand and retreat from the scene of the crime.

Because that's what this is. A fucking crime against my sanity.

Hope. That's what she thinks this is. A glass of wine and a handhold, and suddenly we're on the path to happily ever after. That word alone should make bile rise. It usually does, along with every other phrase that implies commitment, vulnerability, and the willingness to share personal space. But for her? The reaction flips. My insides warm, my chest tightens, and some traitorous part of me thaws.

My brothers aren't here yet, probably drowning in diaper duty and snack negotiations, so I do the next best thing and stalk toward Marco, who's lounging in an armchair. One leg draped over the other, drink in hand, eyes scanning the room for only hell knows what.

He clocks me instantly. "Ah, how's married life, cousin?"

The question follows me everywhere. Do they expect my answer to change every few hours? Is there a pool going?

Torture. But not the marriage itself. No, that's the real mind fuck. I don't hate the marriage. I hate I don't hate it.

I don't bother answering. I grunt, sip my bourbon, and scan the room. Loud considering only half the family is here so far, and full of bouncing babies and people who actually enjoy human interaction. It's hell. My version of purgatory. And then I see *her.*

Allie. Cornered by Eddie.

Eddie. The stand-in groom for my wedding rehearsal. The rehearsal for *my* wedding. I should feel nothing. Jealousy requires emotional investment, and I'm not invested. She's a contract, not a conquest. But irritation simmers under my skin, anyway.

Eddie, with his lazy smile and IQ rivaling a ballpoint pen, leans in, saying something that makes her laugh. The sound slices through the noise of the room, sharp and personal. I don't like it. I don't like him. And I definitely don't like the fact that my wife—*my wife*—is smiling at someone else like *that.*

Without a thought—because overthinking is how I usually avoid stupid decisions—I cross the room. Slide in behind Allie. Wrap an arm around her waist, and pull her flush against me. She stiffens, spine straight as a ruler, but she doesn't tear away.

Eddie's eyes flick to my hand on her hip, then back to my face. He forces a grin, but I see the hesitation. He might be dumb, but he's not suicidal.

"Don't let me interrupt," I say, voice all barbed wire. I feel the shiver run down Allie's spine, and my cock strains painfully against my jeans. Reason number 438 why denim beats slacks: better concealment. Not perfect, but better.

Eddie clears his throat, eyes darting between us. "We were just talking about Allie getting a job. I was telling her about the businesses your papa has. I'm sure he could get her something."

I go still. His words clang in my head with alarm bells going off. My cousin, suggesting ways my wife could spend more time around him? Hard pass. I promised her freedom, not *this* kind of freedom. The kind that ends with me breaking Eddie's nose. *Again.*

My grip tightens on her waist, just enough to remind her—and everyone else—exactly *who* she belongs to. As if they need a reminder. "I have other ideas."

Eddie blinks. Processing. *Not* his strong suit.

I don't elaborate. Just slide my hand lower, skimming the curve of Allie's hip as I steer her away. His gaze drops to my hand—right where I want it—and his jaw ticks. He can look all he wants. I get to touch it all I want.

Because, yeah. Her tits are superb. They're in my hands, my mouth, every damn night. Doesn't mean Eddie—or anyone else—gets to enjoy the view.

"What ideas?" Allie peels my arm off her waist with two fingers. Fair. It's not as if I've ever offered her anything resembling affection. I've perfected the art of touching her like it's an inconvenience, unless I'm deep inside her.

Even if it's *not*. It hasn't been for weeks. And that realization ranks high on the list of problems I'm actively avoiding.

Shrugging off the irritation clawing at my insides—because God forbid, I admit her rejection stings—I sip my drink; the bourbon burning less than my pride. "You'll see. Finalizing some details."

Her eyes narrow, lips curving into a smile that precedes either an ingenious argument or an epic tantrum. "It's a genuine job, right, Rico? Not some barefoot-and-pregnant fantasy where I'm chained to the sink, raising five kids and hand-washing your silk boxers."

The worst part? That vision doesn't sound half as horrifying as it should. Allie, barefoot and glowing, a baby on her hip, another tugging at her jeans. My pristine house turned into a war zone of toys, sticky handprints, and a loud, messy house.

Jesus. I need an exorcism.

"You'll see," I repeat, draining the last of my bourbon and turning on my heel before she can peel back any more layers I'm not ready to explain.

Marco watches me approach, his scotch swirling lazily in one hand while he lounges like the smug bastard he is. Sunday dinners always follow the same rhythm: I avoid my wife while she laughs with Violet, Sienna, and my cousins. Nonna corners her to conduct yet another inquisition about our progress toward filling the nursery. And me? I spend the entire evening pretending I'm above the fray, when in reality, I'm suffocating in it.

"I see you've finally developed some of those feelings you swear don't exist," Marco drawls, tipping his head back to study the ceiling.

"What?" I snap, *too* sharp, *too* fast.

He grins, slow and wicked, and nods toward Allie. She's across the room, head thrown back in laughter, dark hair cascading down her back in lustrous waves. She looks...*happy*. Someone without a care in the world.

She's never laughed like *that* around me. Not once. And I *hate* it. Irrationally, unapologetically hate that someone else gets it.

"Then why," Marco continues, sipping his drink with all the leisure of a man thoroughly delighted, "are you clenching your fists like you're about to redecorate Nonna's living room with Eddie's face?"

I glance down. Sure enough, I've balled my hand so tight that the skin around my knuckles looks ready to split. Raw and calloused. A testament to too many hours spent punching my frustrations into a boxing bag instead of saying them out loud, or at the very least connecting them with another person's face.

Marco's smile morphs from amused to downright predatory.

"Just making sure she's not uncomfortable."

The lie tastes bitter, but it's the finest I've got.

He laughs, low and knowing, then stands, draining the rest of his scotch before slapping a hand on my shoulder. "I believe that's referred to as *giving a shit*," he says, leaning in until I can practically taste the peat and oak on his breath. "And that," he adds, jabbing a finger between my brows, "is called *jealousy*."

I swat his hand away. It's not jealousy. It's diligence. Self-preservation. Making sure my wife doesn't get too comfortable here—because comfort breeds expectations, and expectations lead to disappointment.

And I don't do disappointment. Not for her. Not for anyone.

But if Marco sees it, the rest of my family will too. Worse, Allie might. And that's the last thing I need—her mistaking this...whatever the hell it is...for progress.

With me, there is no evolution. No change. Just a contract, a clock ticking down, and a wife who's already stolen too much.

Time to put some distance between us before she assumes I'm more invested.

Allie

WHY DO I TEXT my husband?

It's a multi-layered, deeply complex, borderline masochistic endeavor at this point. I tell myself it's for the greater good—a public service announcement for his cold, unfeeling heart. A daily reminder that, *surprise!* He's still married. That he's no longer a lone wolf roaming the concrete jungle of Manhattan, growling at anyone who dares to notice his existence.

But after message number ninety-three gets the same treatment as message one—read, ignored, ghosted into the void—I question my sanity. Why do I keep doing this? Do I expect him to suddenly develop thumbs capable of typing out a single response? A word? Hell, I'd even take a period. Just a little "." so I know he's capable of interacting with another human being outside of grunting and orgasm-adjacent dirty talk.

I'd love to say I'm above this, that I have some grand reason for my perseverance. That I'm trying to gently lure him out of his cold, calculated world. But let's be real—I *also* do it to annoy him. A little retribution hurt no one, right? I mean, if I have to deal with his emotionally constipated ass every night, he can deal with a few good morning texts and *How's your day going?* messages.

It's called baby steps, people.

And yet... there's this thing I can't shake. This flicker of something unhealthy that blooms in my chest when he walks through the door at night. Hope? Maybe just moderate insanity. It's subtle, but it's there—the way his eyes land on me, warm and assessing, rather than the dead-inside indifference I used to get. He still doesn't talk much, but when he looks at me, I feel as though I *exist*. Maybe I'm not just some contractual obligation or a walking uterus.

Progress? Possibly. Or I'm just that desperate for human interaction that I'm mistaking his resting I-want-to-fuck-you face for affection.

I still haven't caught him in the mornings, though. The man is a ninja. I set my alarm for four a.m., thinking I had him beat. Nope. Gone by 3:45. I'd bet money he's sneaking out through an underground tunnel.

He still leaves a note for me every day. Always some random fact or opinion—half of which could moonlight as unhinged Reddit conspiracy theories. He still shows up for dinner, still eats in silence, still nods and shrugs as if his vocal cords signed a non-disclosure agreement.

But he's there.

And then there's the other version of Rico. The one who only wakes up when he's buried inside me. That man speaks. Touches. Worships. He praises my body, vows to wreck it, and dear God, I devour every word—starved and desperate, and he's the only thing left on the menu.

Turns out, I appreciate dirty talk. Who knew? Not me. But apparently, I am very much not vanilla.

Not that I get too much time to dwell on it, because my husband—ever the mastermind—thinks he's slick. That by keeping sex anywhere *but* the bedroom, he can keep his distance. That if he fucks me over the dining table or the bathroom sink or the kitchen island (I will never see breakfast the same way again), he won't have to sleep next to me.

I let him *think* he's winning.

Because at least once a week, I leave dinner and go straight to my room. And without fail, he seeks me out. And guess what? If he wants to have sex in my room, *he has to stay*.

Does he sleep? No. He lies there, stiff as a board, his body rigid. *But he's there*, and that's enough—for now.

Because I don't want to be a means to an end. A vessel. A contractual obligation.

I know he wants me. That he finds me attractive *now*.

But that's as far as it goes.

And maybe... that's as far as it ever will.

This morning, while staring down at yet another oddly specific, utterly pointless fact from my husband, I wondered—who exactly is getting played here?

Rico: *I have a talent for burning toast, no matter the toaster, setting, or level of supervision. It's a gift.*

At first, these notes used to fuel my inner sass monster with ease. I had quippy, borderline genius-level comebacks locked and loaded. Now? My witty retorts take longer to plan, which is not ideal when my entire identity thrives on quick comebacks and dry humor.

I know why. I just don't want to admit why.

And before I could even form a single coherent thought—let alone a smartass reply—a large, rough hand snatched the note right out of my grip. The other? Wrapped tight around my waist, yanking me back against a wall of solid muscle.

What followed wasn't so much a conversation as a *caveman-sees-woman, caveman-takes-woman* situation. His mouth latched onto my neck, teeth grazing the sensitive spot that always makes my knees buckle, while my sundress was shoved up around my hips. My panties? Yanked down in one smooth, practiced move that told me he'd thought about this—*a lot*.

And then—God help me—he was inside me, thick and hard and filling me in one brutal thrust that knocked the breath right out of my lungs. No warning. No soft touches. Just the raw, desperate way he took me is enough to make my thighs clench thinking about it.

No one spoke—no words were necessary. Because apparently, my body is always on standby for him. And maybe I should be mad about that. Maybe I *should* demand more than this hot, frantic claiming. But when he's buried so deep, hitting that spot that makes me see stars? Yeah, good luck getting an argument out of me.

And then it was over. He pulled out, adjusted his clothes as if he hadn't just wrecked me against the kitchen counter, grabbed his bag, and walked out the door without a single glance back.

Our first—and apparently only—interaction before noon.

It's fine. I'm fine. Everything's totally fine.

I'm absolutely *not* fine.

Tonight, I had a different plan. A test. A tiny, ridiculous, *I need to prove a point to myself* kind of test.

I made *Spaghetti Aglio e Olio*—simple, light, and strategic. New York summers are a humid nightmare, and a heavy meal on a hot day isn't exactly appetizing. *But* I left the sundress on. The same one from this morning. *A reminder.*

And the best part of my test? The wine request.

See, I know my husband reads my texts. He just refuses to respond. So, I've started inserting minor tasks into them. Pick up a bottle of Merlot on your way home. The best part? I already have three bottles chilling in the wine fridge. I don't need him to buy it—I just need to see if he will. And guess what? Every single time, he *does*.

He might not *reply*, but he *listens*. Baby steps.

"Dinner will be ready in maybe two minutes," I call over my shoulder when I hear him come in. Like with the texts, I just keep talking. Even if he doesn't reply, even if he doesn't acknowledge me. Because one day, maybe, he will.

I turn around, wiping my hands on my apron, only to find him—right behind me, standing too close, staring too intently.

I yelp. Loudly.

"Jesus, Rico." I press a hand to my chest, my heart hammering. "Are you—uh—hungry?"

His gaze stays locked on me. Unreadable.

"No."

Okay... that's not weird at all.

I know his game. Sometimes, he just sits there, pushing food around on his plate and throwing a silent tantrum. He never had to eat with me—just sit with me. A loophole he clearly enjoys exploiting.

Fine. Be a weirdo.

"Well, I guess I'll eat. You listen." I move to untie my apron, but his hand darts out, catching my wrist with surprising gentleness.

"No."

My brows furrow. "No what, Rico?"

Here's the thing—I've been testing a theory. If I push at his one-word answers, sometimes—*sometimes*—he breaks.

So I wait.

He exhales, gaze dropping to where his fingers still wrap around my wrist—clearly he just realized he's touching me. I can see the inner debate playing out in his mind.

Finally, his eyes flick up to mine.

"No dinner tonight."

I blink. "You're fasting now? Should I be worried? Are you joining a cult?" Yes, I am a brat.

Nothing. Not even an eye twitch.

"Okay," I continue, hands on my hips. "I'll bite. Why are we skipping dinner? And please tell me it's not some intermittent fasting, alpha-male, 'I only eat raw liver' nonsense, because I really—"

"I'm taking you somewhere."

I freeze.

Somewhere.

Like... out?

Like together? In public? Where people see us and where he might have to acknowledge my existence outside of a contract and sex?

I narrow my eyes. "Define 'somewhere.'"

A pause. A beat. Then—he smirks.

Not a full one, just a ghost, just enough to make my stomach flip. And then, just as quickly, he walks past me, leaving me standing there, jaw unhinged, brain trying to process whatever alternate reality I just stepped into.

What the hell just happened?

And more importantly...

What exactly does my husband have planned?

Allie

HE'S NEVER DONE THIS before. Is he trying to change the terms now? Is this some new power move? A silent 'checkmate, wife' to counter my brilliant maneuver of removing the ovulation clause?

Look, I knew tweaking the sex terms was a risk. I wasn't just skirting the language—I was straight-up rewriting it. But dinner? *Dinner* was Switzerland. *Dinner* was the one thing we had that didn't involve me bent over a piece of furniture. Not that I minded that part, but still...*dinner*.

And now he wants to cancel it?

My mother always said the best way to a man's heart was through his stomach. Which is hilarious, considering she never cooked a meal in her life, thanks to Maria. Also ironic, considering my parents' respected each other in the way coworkers do when forced to share a cubicle for twenty-five years, but love? Attraction? Passion?

Yeah, no. If they made eye contact for too long, one of them would find an excuse to leave the room. It was all very *please GTFO* vibes, and I have yet to recover from witnessing it firsthand.

Still, whether my mother's advice was legitimate, I had a strategy. Two-pronged.

One: Feed him.

Two: Fuck him.

It was simple, really. Food and sex—basic human needs, right? And while sex could just be sex, it still built intimacy. Partnership. And sometimes—if I was lucky—full sentences.

Not that I was trying to fall for him. I'm not *that* girl. But if I had to play dirty to break through to my husband, then fine. I'd make him food. I'd sleep with him. I'd casually flash him thigh and leave him wanting and craving all I could.

Except now, he's canceling dinner, and my stomach twists.

I cross my arms, standing straighter to remind myself I *do*, in fact, have a spine and I *will* use it. "Rico, we have an agreement about dinners."

"I'm aware." He walks past me into the kitchen, his eyes scanning the pot of pasta like he's considering flipping it straight into the trash.

"It's ready now. You're home. Let's just eat." My voice is calm, reasonable.

"No."

I stare at him. That's it. I'm one more one-word answer away from launching a physical assault directly at his balls. See how fast he can pop out a baby while icing his gonads.

The problem is, I enjoy his balls. I have a very complicated, very intimate relationship with them. I cannot confirm, nor deny, that I popped them into my mouth last week just to see the expression of what I swear was his version of pure "awe" on his face.

And that, dear reader, is something I learned at family cooking nights.

Not how to cook, obviously. No, that part was useless. But Violet—god bless my scandalous, zero-filter, probably-going-to-be-arrested-for-public-indecency sister-in-law—had a five-page spread in one of her romance books specifically about how to take a man in your mouth. *Five pages.*

Some of which made me tilt my head, turn the book sideways, and genuinely wonder how the hell...

Yeah. It was a *lot.*

And now here I am, armed with knowledge I should not have, dealing with a husband who won't eat dinner but will rail me against a doorframe at 6 a.m. and then disappear.

I love Rico's family. Truly. I love the two sisters I never had. But there's only so much time I can spend with them before the existential crisis sets in.

Both are blissfully married. As in, the kind of married where their husbands worship the ground they walk on—so much so that if city regulations allowed it, I'm convinced these men would commission the streets to be plated in gold just so their wives' feet wouldn't touch common pavement.

And then there's me.

With my luck, Rico would just stamp "WALK HERE" into wet concrete outside the house and call it a day, as if I'd somehow get lost on the way to the mailbox.

And it wouldn't be the first time he treated me as if I were a toddler lost in IKEA. The day he showed me how to use the dishwasher? Just a sharp finger jab and a clipped, "Press this." Charming.

I'm getting antsy with all this free time. Sure, I help Sienna at the gallery sometimes, and I visit Violet, where I juggle her lawlessness goblins—aka her children—while she works on her latest manuscript. But it's all just a cycle of filler content. A mind-numbing loop where I exist on the periphery of everyone else's beautiful, well-structured, joy-filled lives.

Because the one person I actually want to spend time with? The one person I want to have a conversation with? Doesn't talk to me. At least, not outside of our very active sex life.

I told myself this was the price of my freedom. That this loveless, arranged marriage was a bargain. I got what I wanted—I was free from my past life. But what exactly did I gain? No job. No purpose. Just the same empty day on repeat.

Except for the mind-blowing orgasms.

So, I guess there's that.

"Get your shoes."

I blink, looking up from the kitchen counter, where I've been aggressively rearranging silverware because it's arrange them or stab him with them at this point.

"Meet me in the car in five."

Then, he turns to go.

Something inside me snaps. Without thinking, I reach out and grab his arm.

His whole body stiffens, muscles locked up, and for a split second, I swear I see something flicker in his eyes. It's not anger. No annoyance. Something *else*.

But just as fast as it appears, it's gone.

He yanks in a deep breath, flexes his fingers open and closed, then shakes them out.

"Five minutes," he repeats before retreating through the mudroom and into the garage.

I stare after him, confused, my pulse doing this annoying thing where it stutters. Then I exhale, annoyed with myself.

I cover the pasta, blow out the stupid candles I light at dinner every night—because apparently, I'm a pathetic romantic trying to boost the ambiance to my husband's dinner routine—and head toward the garage.

Even the candles seem disappointed in me, weeping melted wax as if they understand their efforts were in vain.

I step into the garage, stopping short.

That's *not* his car.

My gaze snaps between the sleek, all-black Tesla sedan sitting in the garage and Rico, who's standing beside the open passenger door with the tolerance of a valet.

"You bought a car? Is this why you didn't want to eat dinner?"

Rico follows my gaze, then looks back at me, unimpressed. "What? No." He jerks his chin toward the open door. "Get in."

Right. Super informative. So glad we cleared that up.

Still, I slide into the seat, inhaling the glorious scent of new car leather. "Well, it's nice."

Rico grunts.

Love our chats. Always so lively.

But my heart does this thing where it skips because I know—*I know*—I told him his Porsche was absurd before we got married. And now, he suddenly has a sedan? One that seats five?

Coincidence? Maybe.

I let myself hold on to that tiny spark of hope. Even if it's foolish. Even if it's pitiful.

Because right now, it's all I've got.

"So..." I glance over at him. "If you didn't drag me out here to show off your new ride, what exactly are we doing instead of eating the dinner I made?"

That's when I feel it.

The impact of his gaze.

My entire body shudders. His eyes are hooded, dark, the amber depths dragging up my body, mentally peeling off my dress with agonizing slowness.

Holy hell.

He doesn't talk much, but when he looks at me that way? My entire body turns into a human-sized fire hazard.

"You'll see."

Oh, for the love of—

Resigning myself to the fact that dragging information out of this man is as easy as negotiating with a spoon. "Fine. But what about Vinnie?"

Rico pulls out of the garage smoothly, not even glancing over.

"Don't need a driver."

"Yes, but he's not *your* driver. He's *my* bodyguard."

Rico's jaw flexes. "You don't need a bodyguard when you're with me."

Debatable.

Instead of arguing—because I've learned that's a game you never win with Rico—I lean back in my seat and let him drive.

I glance at the dashboard clock. 7:12 PM. Prime Manhattan traffic hour. Which means either we're about to spend the next twenty minutes sitting in a vehicular nightmare, or my husband has a secret tunnel system I don't know about. Knowing him, probably the latter.

It's weird how my life has changed.

Vinnie still technically works for me, but he's got a lot more freedom now. He gets nights off. But does that stop him from stalking—I mean, *monitoring*—me like the overprotective human Labrador he is? Absolutely not. I guarantee that somewhere, in the shadows, he's lurking. Probably sipping an espresso and watching through a sniper-grade lens just to make sure no one looks at me wrong.

Twelve years of being my oversized shadow. Hard habit to break.

And then there's *my family*.

They *still* haven't spoken to me.

Marco warned me that one of the hardest prices for leaving the Cosa Nostra was being shunned. I figured surely they'd come around. Eventually, they'd see I was happy and that I still loved them. But to them? I was a traitor.

I stopped calling. Stopped texting. And when Rico replaced my phone, I didn't bother saving their numbers. No point in keeping ghosts in my contacts list.

The car slows, pulling up to a valet station in front of The Grand Harrington.

For a fleeting moment, my heart catapults straight into my throat.

Did he...book us a suite? For a romantic evening?

Woman, you are married to Rico Bennetti. Read that question back to yourself.

Then I snort. Out loud. Loud enough for Rico to turn and look at me just as the valet opens my door, one brow quirked like I've lost my damn mind.

I mean...

The fact that I even entertained the idea that my husband planned a romantic night means I've officially gone insane. Forget checking into the hotel—I need to check myself into Bellevue.

Rico rounds the car, handing his keys to the valet with a nod before—and here's the part that really shocks me—grabbing my hand.

Willingly.

No flinch. No grimace. No look of sheer agony, as if touching me is the equivalent of sticking his hand into a blender.

Progress.

I look down at our hands. His is big, warm, and firm, wrapping around mine as if we've done this a thousand times. Which we *haven't*.

Still, I'd be lying if I said my heart didn't do a little skip.

I *will not* read into it.

Not at all.

We don't walk into the main entrance of the hotel. Instead, Rico steers me down the sidewalk toward Via Napoli, a high-end Italian restaurant nestled into the side of The Grand Harrington.

The doorman opens the entrance for us, and the maître d' straightens the moment he sees us.

"Mr. Bennetti. Mrs. Bennetti."

I almost snort again. Apparently, I've developed some kind of pig-like reaction to unfamiliar situations because I will never get used to being called *that*.

The maître d' fumbles with the menus, clearly intimidated by the sheer menace that is Rico's resting murder face. He doesn't even hand us one. Instead, he immediately gestures for us to follow, weaving us through the maze of full tables, clinking glasses, and quiet conversations before leading us toward the private dining suites in the back.

Via Napoli isn't just a premier Italian restaurant—it's *the premier* restaurant. This place has guest chefs flown in from around the world, a waitlist so long you have to sacrifice your firstborn to get a table, and private dining rooms so exclusive they make the CIA's secured files look accessible.

Most people have to book those suites months in advance. Some patrons pay a monthly fee just to guarantee a private table.

And then there are the Bennettis, who walk in and make entire dining rooms appear out of thin air.

I glance at Rico.

His face is unreadable.

When we reach the double cream-and-gold doors, Rico pushes them open without a word. Inside, two men are already seated. One I recognize instantly—Jaxon, the attorney who once sat across from me and had the absolute pleasure of discussing my sex life in contractual terms. A true career highlight for him, I'm sure.

The other man looks familiar, but I can't place him.

Blond hair styled in that I totally didn't try, but also definitely did kind of way. Tall, broad, sitting with the posture of a man who definitely irons his socks. His suit is tailored so precisely it might as well be a second skin, and when he looks at me, his ice-blue eyes are completely unreadable. Great. A blond version of Rico. Just what the world needed—more emotionally unreadable men with too much money.

"Mrs. Bennetti." Jaxon stands and reaches for my hand, but the second our palms connect, he stops, clears his throat, and pulls back with a chuckle.

I don't get it. Until I glance behind me.

Rico is staring at our hands, clearly debating whether committing homicide in a fine dining establishment is worth the cleanup.

Is he... *jealous?*

No, that would require him to give a crap. Clearly, this is just part of his no touching what's mine philosophy. News flash, husband of mine—you don't own me, and I will shake hands with whoever I damn well please.

In fact, I should hold on to Jaxon's hand a little longer, just for fun. But before I can properly antagonize my broody husband, Rico pulls out a chair for me. I sit, half-expecting him to plop down as far away as possible, maybe even across the table, where he can ignore my existence more efficiently.

Nope. He sits directly next to me.

I turn to look at him, but his focus is locked on Jaxon.

Jaxon straightens the papers in a neat pile before him. "Right, well, Mrs. Bennetti, we're here to discuss your wedding present from your husband."

I freeze. Every muscle, nerve, and possibly a few internal organs go into full system shutdown.

Wedding present?

Wait. Was I supposed to get him something? Because if so, I definitely failed. What was I going to gift the man who has everything except a personality? A book on how to communicate using more than one-word answers? A hug? A soul?

The mystery blond man slides a folder across the table to Rico and stands, buttoning his suit with a smirk that could probably buy him out of a murder charge.

"All there. Signed, and the wire transfer was received."

Then he turns to me, extends a hand, and the moment I slide mine into his, he kisses the top of my knuckles.

I glance at Rico, and then the mystery man gives a cartoon villain rivaling laugh.

"Yup," he says, still grinning, "your brothers were right."

And then he just... leaves. No name, no last words, just wiggles his fingers at Rico and waltzes out.

I lower my hand to the table, but Rico immediately snatches it, grabbing a napkin, and wiping it off.

Jaxon, to his credit, only barely suppresses his laughter behind a fist.

"Who was that?" I ask, still staring at my husband as he basically sanitizes my hand. If he had bleach I wouldn't be surprised to find my hand soaking in a bucket of it right now.

"Griffin Harrington," Jaxon supplies.

Griffin Harrington.

Now I place him. The name is synonymous with power, wealth, and manicured levels of arrogance. His family practically owns half of Manhattan, their name attached to everything from high-end real estate to the kind of luxury hotels where the carpets are definitely softer than my sheets.

Jaxon nods toward the folder. "Your husband mentioned this was your favorite—"

Rico cuts him a look so sharp Jaxon immediately clears his throat, changes course, and adopts a more professional tone.

"What I meant to say," Jaxon corrects smoothly, "is that your husband bought a restaurant for you. Griffin just finished signing over the property to Rico, who has now drawn up papers in your name. As of today, you are the official owner."

"Owner? I know nothing about running a restaurant."

Jaxon shrugs. "But you enjoy cooking, right?"

I nod.

"And you were in culinary school."

I nod again, throat suddenly dry.

"Well, you'll be taking over as executive chef. We'll vet a manager to handle the administrative side, so you can focus on what you love—menu creation, kitchen operations, making this place yours."

I glance at Rico, who still hasn't looked at me. He's scanning the papers in front of him, completely unbothered.

He bought *me* a restaurant.

My *favorite* restaurant.

First, the car. Now this.

I rant and ramble at dinner all the time, but I never thought he was listening. Clearly, he was.

But looking at his face? There's no joy. No excitement.

He might as well have accidentally bought me a cat with his demeanor. And this restaurant—it wasn't cheap. It had to have cost seven figures, minimum.

"But...I didn't finish my culinary classes."

Jaxon waves a hand. "We've secured someone to help with the transition. The previous executive chef, Monroe, didn't take kindly to new ownership. He's leaving in a week. But the sous chef, Kai Weston? Prodigy. Self-taught. He's been here longer than Monroe and is more than happy to help his new boss learn the ropes."

Jaxon stands. "How about I introduce you to the staff? You can start tomorrow with Kai."

My *own* restaurant.

The words swirl in my head, tasting sweeter than anything I've ever cooked. I can almost see it—*my* kitchen, *my* name on the door, customers lining up just for a bite of something I created. Tables filled with people who *chose* to be there. Not because of a name attached to my family. Because of *me*.

My fingers trace over the sleek tablecloth in front of us, as the vision builds in my mind—my menu, my signature dishes, my future.

My throat tightens, but in a good way. Maybe, for once, I'm not just some obligation to Rico. Maybe this is him seeing me.

I turn to Rico, warmth spreading through my chest, a tiny ember finally flickering to life. "Thank you," I say, voice softer than I meant it to be. A little breathless.

And for a second—*just a second*—he looks up from his stack of papers. Amber eyes meeting mine, sharp and unreadable, but *there*.

But then he speaks.

"No need. Don't read into it, Pearlina. You needed a job. Something to do."

The ember turns to ash before he's even finished the sentence.

I swallow hard, nodding as if that didn't just slice right through me, though my chest feels too tight to breathe properly. My fingers curl against the table to keep from shaking, nails digging into my palm and maybe if I press hard enough, I'll feel something other than this hollow ache.

Of course, that's all it is.

Not a dream. *Not* a gift.

Just something to get me out of his hair.

I force a smile, but it doesn't reach my eyes. "Right. Something to do."

It's amazing how quickly I can be reminded of exactly who I married in just a few words.

Rico

"You bought her a restaurant instead of just asking Griffin to give her a job as head chef?"

Marco leans back in his chair, twirling his glass of whiskey and waiting for a punchline that isn't coming.

I don't respond. Mostly because I refuse to validate his tone, but also because I'm currently occupying the worst office space known to man.

Of all places to summon me, he picked this. The strip club. *His* strip club.

Which means I'm now subjected to two of my least favorite activities:

Being in public.

Being in an office smaller than a broom closet while my cousin watches me for sport.

I sit, unimpressed, as music blares through the walls, men hoot as if it's the first set of tits they've ever seen, and a stripper dressed in approximately three square inches of material giggles at some poor bastard who's about to blow his rent money.

Marco, meanwhile, savors his drink, no doubt reveling in my discomfort. Only problem? I refuse to give him the satisfaction.

Not a flinch. Not a twitch. Not a single fuck given.

Even though, *yes*, I am two seconds away from yelling at the noise embracing my inner 80-year-old man on his front porch telling kids to get off his damn lawn.

Allie is at the restaurant. *Her* restaurant.

It's her third day there, working closely with Kai Weston, the tattooed culinary prodigy who gladly took her under his wing.

I didn't appreciate that word. *Gladly.*

The first time I walked into the kitchen and saw the guy—mid-twenties, too many tattoos, piercing green eyes, that smile that makes women coo and flutter their lashes—I had to physically unclench my fist.

I don't have violent impulses that peak to the point they may become reality. My threshold for bullshit is higher than most (now). But the moment I saw his pretty-boy face, my brain flicked through all scenarios where my knuckles could introduce themselves to his jaw. Thoroughly.

I didn't enjoy the reaction. Didn't understand it.

I do now.

I wanted to punch him because I wanted to punch him. No deeper meaning. No over-analysis. Just a sudden and overwhelming desire to rearrange his face and, in the process, my own rapidly spiraling thoughts.

Besides, I got what I wanted out of this, right?

Peace. Quiet. Nights alone.

My phone no longer pings all day.

No good morning texts beyond a quick *Don't know how late I'll be, don't wait up.*

No dinner updates. No annoying brief texts that used to buzz before I could fully process my day.

It's perfect.

Except it's not.

She doesn't leave the restaurant until ten, sometimes eleven.

Not because I care. That would be... concerning.

And now, instead of me coming home to her sitting at the dining table with some half-hearted attempt to engage, she goes straight upstairs. Shower. Bed. Nothing.

And I should be relieved.

I should be fucking celebrating.

Instead, I did something pathetic last night.

I walked up to the second floor at one in the morning, thinking maybe she was waiting for me.

She wasn't.

She was asleep. Eyes closed. Breathing soft and steady.

And I stood there, just watching.

Not because I miss her. *I don't miss her.*

I miss the sex.

I miss her naked body beneath me, her legs wrapped around my waist, the way she—

No. Nope. No. Absolutely not.

I miss convenience. Routine.

That's it.

So what's the problem?

I got exactly what I wanted—my wife out of my daily existence and a one-way ticket to peace. We're operating on opposite schedules, her bedroom might as well be in another time zone, and she's too busy running her restaurant to pester me with her usual texts.

And yet.

Not even a thank you fuck for buying the place.

I don't ask for much. A little gratitude in the form of legs wrapped around my waist or her mouth around my...yeah...shouldn't be a tall order. But *no*. I handed her the literal keys to her dream, and she rewarded me by disappearing. Okay, so my delivery of said keys might be part of the reason there was no thank you blowjob, but still.

The real problem? I'm *not* done with her.

I should have washed her out of my system before giving her a reason to never be around me. The distance is making it worse. I should be free, and instead, I'm counting down the seconds to my next hit.

Marco clears his throat, dragging me out of the mental spiral I refuse to acknowledge.

I sip my drink, hating how it burns down my throat, but appreciating the fact that if I feel it, I am still alive. *Barely.* "She needed a job. I needed space."

A lie so bold it should be printed on billboards.

I glance at my phone. A text from my wife at ten this morning.

> **Allie: Don't wait up. It will be a late night until I get used to things around here.**

I ignored it. Nothing new there.

Only this time, *ignoring* it *annoyed* me.

No. The *text* annoyed me.

No. I annoyed *myself* by *feeling* anything at all.

It's simple, really. I need to get laid. That's it. Biological necessity. Once I scratch the itch, all this bullshit in my head will straighten itself out.

Except I had a perfectly willing, absolutely addictive option. And now she's gone.

Allie was glowing when she found out she owned the restaurant. She looked at me with so much damn joy that I wanted to personally kick myself in the balls.

So, naturally, I did what any self-respecting asshole would do—I dismissed it. Made sure she knew this wasn't a romantic gesture. No hidden agenda. No deeper meaning. Just a convenient solution to my problem.

Her face fell so fast, and that itself should have felt as though I finally won.

It didn't.

But it's better this way.

Hope is a dangerous thing. It makes her assume there's more. That I actually give a shit. That I want something from her beyond the contract we signed.

And that is where she's wrong.

Right?

Marco leans forward, refilling my glass, some of the whiskey sloshing onto his desk. "I'm gonna call bullshit on that one."

He doesn't elaborate. He doesn't need to. The bastard knows me too well.

I eye the drink, swirling it in my hand, and glance around his office. "Are you ever going to refurnish this shithole?"

Everything is metal. Rusted, dusty, scratched-up and grating on me. The sound of the chairs scraping against the concrete floor makes my teeth ache.

And I know why Marco chose concrete. It's easier to bleach.

I also know why my body reacts to it.

The scrape of metal against concrete is *too* familiar. It tugs at things in my head I keep locked up, buried deep, suffocating under years of strategic denial.

Marco watches me, swirling his drink in a way that suggests he enjoys poking at my demons just to see what they do.

I mutter under my breath, "Stop it."

"Can't help myself." His grin is lazy and infuriating.

Marcello shifts in the corner, ready to intervene if I decide to launch myself across the desk and deck Marco in the jaw.

To piss Marco off just as much, I pivot.

"Marcello," I say, turning to him. "How's Max?"

Marco's smirk drops so fast I'd pay to see it on instant replay.

Marcello lights up. "Good, sir." He clears his throat, eyes darting between us. "We're doing fine."

Marco mutters something dark under his breath, shooting me a look that says, *Congratulations, you've successfully ruined my mood.*

Good. Because mine was already fucked.

"Okay, want to play this game?" Marco leans forward on his desk. "Nice Tesla."

I don't react. Can't a man be environmentally conscious? The car purchase means *nothing*.

"Time for a change," I reply, taking a sip of my whiskey. As if I don't buy new cars every few years. Since when did upgrading my vehicle become breaking news?

"Funny thing. I stopped by the restaurant the other day to see Allie. She was in the back with Kai Weston, going over the specials for the week. They seem... close."

I barely blink. Clearly, my cousin forgets I lack the energy or patience for jealousy. Possessiveness? Equally useless. My brothers have a caveman-esque obsession with their wives, practically growling at anyone who so much as breathes in their direction. Me? I have better things to do than swing a metaphorical club at every idiot with functioning eyeballs.

She's hot. *Of course* men are going to look.

And if they get too close, she can handle herself. I'm more than confident Allie could gouge out an eye—or hell, *steal it* if she really wanted.

"He's showing her the restaurant. She takes over next week." Marco's good at needling, but I'm better at not giving a shit.

"Does showing her the restaurant require him to stand that close? His hand was on her lower back when they leaned over the menu. So close. Almost intimate. And those late nights... I assume your wife doesn't come home at a decent hour anymore. But hey, you got your space, right?"

I stare at him, unimpressed.

"Kai's a good-looking guy, too. Young. Successful. Up-and-comer in the culinary world. Shares similar passions as Allie." His voice is all faux innocence, but he's watching me closely, waiting for a tell. "They'll make a great team."

I know where he's going with this, but for the record? I'd have to care about my wife for it to matter.

And I don't.

Right?

I know everything about Kai Weston—his age, culinary background, fourth-grade spelling bee results if we want to get specific. As if I'd drop 1.3 million dollars on a business without thoroughly vetting every single employee.

"Your point?"

"Just observations. He's single too, right?"

Subtlety was never one of his strengths.

And because the universe hates me, my phone pings with a message from Allie, right on cue.

> Allie: We are staying after the dinner rush. I probably won't be home until midnight, but Vinnie is here.

I grit my teeth.

Fourth night in a row.

Could I wait up for her? Yes. Will I? Absolutely fucking not.

I'm not that desperate for sex. Even if my body disagrees, and my mood has gone to shit because I apparently require daily physical contact now.

No. A few days without her will fix this. Reset the system. Get me back to once-a-week territory.

Whether I spent seven figures on peace and a biological reset is beside the point.

My fingers hover over the keyboard. She already knows I read the message. She doesn't expect a response. She never does anymore.

And yet...

The itch to say something crawls beneath my skin.

Before I let myself become the idiot Marco is waiting for, I slide my phone into my pocket and push my glass toward my grinning cousin.

"Fill it to the top."

"Sure. Might take the sting of jealousy away."

I pick up the glass, exhale through my nose, and take a slow sip before muttering, "Go to hell."

"Brother, in case you missed the memo, I am the devil, and we are in hell. Welcome to the underworld."

Allie

THE KITCHEN AT VIA Napoli is a dream. Every time I find something new—some obscure imported spice, a perfectly balanced chef's knife, or the industrial pasta maker that basically sings to my soul—every day is Christmas morning here.

Chef Monroe, the former executive chef (and certified drama queen), spent a ridiculous amount of money designing himself a lavish office. Leather chairs, an espresso machine, a freaking wine fridge. All for what? To sit there twirling a pen while the rest of the staff ran around resembling caffeinated squirrels?

I haven't had a single second to even think about sitting down. Between learning everyone's names, memorizing the menu, going over ordering procedures, and getting a crash course in how not to tank a Michelin-star restaurant, my office is officially the kitchen itself—where it *should* be.

It's been five days since my husband dropped the restaurant in my lap, and I still can't fully process it. Every night, I drag myself through the doors after midnight, smelling of garlic, tomato, and enough onions to make even my reflection cry. I shower, rub my aching feet, slather on my favorite lavender lotion, hoping to resurrect my soul, and then collapse into bed, half expecting to wake up and find out this was all some very elaborate fever dream.

By the time I roll out of bed, it's later than I prefer, but considering my body now operates on a restaurant schedule, I have no choice. My mornings are a blur of starting a load of laundry, inhaling coffee, and scrolling through my iPad to review recipes, specials, and menu additions. Vinnie has me at the restaurant by eleven, where the prep cooks are already buzzing around clearly with more caffeine in their veins than myself. I want to be the first one there, but the pastry chef comes in at three a.m., which—while impressive—is something I will never experience when I'm barely scraping past midnight coming home.

The prep team hands off to the line cooks, and before I know it, we're knee deep in dinner service, plates flying, pans sizzling, and my heart racing. The final seating is at ten, but customers linger, which means I do too. I refuse to leave until every dish is washed, every station wiped down, and every front-of-house staffer has clocked out. *If they're here, I'm here.* That's the rule.

Kai has been a lifesaver. He runs the kitchen with an ease that makes me jealous. While I'm juggling cooking, crafting new dishes, and making sure our servers don't accidentally murder the line cooks, he's effortlessly handling the backend operations. Jaxon's hire—the restaurant manager—handles the accounting, marketing, and all the HR nonsense, but I still have to oversee ordering, quality control, and, you know, actually make food people want to eat.

The first two days? Absolute hell. My brain felt scrambled, fried, and served with a side of *WTF am I doing?* I knew how professional kitchens worked, but nothing prepares you for being thrown straight into the fire. No line cook initiation. No working my way up the ranks. Just—*boom*—executive chef.

By day three, though? I had everyone's names down, started planning menus ahead instead of scrambling last minute, and—miracle of miracles—I figured out the ordering system without accidentally requesting fifty pounds of truffle oil. Now, if I could just figure out how to get through an entire shift without wanting to pass out in the walk-in freezer, I'd be golden.

Every morning, my brain wakes up at nine, and every muscle in my body immediately stages a protest, begging for me to wait until ten. Apparently, running a restaurant is a full-body workout. Who needs a gym when you can lift fifty-pound bags of flour, dodge rogue flames, and sprint to the walk-in freezer every fifteen minutes?

By the time I drag myself out of bed, His Royal Emotional Void is long gone. I didn't expect to wake up and find him reading the Times at the breakfast table, waiting to discuss current events with his wife.

I used to text him in the mornings, telling him to have a great day, as if I was some chipper little wife trying to crack the ice fortress he calls a personality. But eventually, I realized I was basically texting into the abyss. If I wanted to waste my energy, I'd go scream into a void for fun.

It's not that I *don't* want to text him. I *want* to. Desperately. But this marriage can't be a one-woman show where I do all the work, texting and talking while he just reads my messages like a silent overlord. If he wants to hear from me, he can put in the effort. Not holding my breath on that one, though.

Still, I can't help but send him quick updates—what time I'll be home, how late I'm staying at the restaurant. And yeah, maybe some tiny, idiotic part of me hopes he'll be waiting up for me when I get back. Not that I'd ever give him the satisfaction of knowing that. But so far, I've been dead wrong. Rico, the man who had the libido of a Greek god before I started working, suddenly has no interest in nighttime activities. Which means I definitely misread that entire situation. *Again.*

So, note to self: Rico's signals are not signals—they're just random electrical currents in a void of nothingness.

My phone pings beside me while I'm scrolling through my iPad at the dining table. I look up, smiling as I take in the space. The house is finally fully furnished, including decor that I handpicked with the sole purpose of making my husband's skin crawl. The kitchen—*his* kitchen, because let's be honest, he's barely acknowledged my existence in this house—is gorgeous, opening into a spacious dining area. The farmhouse table I chose fits perfectly, complete with white-washed wood panels and plenty of seating... in case we ever host people.

That thought makes me snort into my coffee. Rico hosting a dinner party? Might as well expect him to start handcrafting scented candles and journaling about his feelings.

I set my mug down and pick up my phone, instantly smiling when I see the message.

> **Kai: Want to ride in together? We don't live far from each other, and it's on the way. I don't mind.**

Kai's been the definition of accommodating. A total lifesaver. The exact opposite of Chef Monroe, who has spent the past five days barking orders and sporting nasty sneers. The man loathes my existence, and honestly? I'm this close to telling him he can finish out his last week from home... or wherever demons like him dwell. Kai has trained me on everything I need to know, which has only solidified my suspicion that Monroe was phoning it in long before I took over.

I quickly type out a reply.

> **Allie: I appreciate the offer, but my driver will take me there.**

> **Kai: The perks of being a Bennetti, I suppose.**

I stifle a laugh. If only he knew.

I'm still getting used to people calling me *Chef Bennetti*. I'd always pictured Chef De Luca, but my last name is legally changed now, thanks to Jaxon Wolfe and whatever airtight contract Rico had drawn up. I guess that's his version of commitment. Not romance, not affection—just a legally binding name change. What a dreamboat.

Vinnie has been just as punctual as ever, waiting in the driveway by ten every morning to drive me to work. The restaurant is across town, but I'd much rather live in this quieter neighborhood than be downtown in the constant symphony of honking and human misery that starts at sunrise.

Rico, in his usual confusing-as-hell way, swapped out Vinnie's Lexus for an SUV, which Vinnie awkwardly mentioned was because we'd "need the extra room, *eventually*." Right. Kids. The same reason Rico replaced his two-seater Porsche with a more family-friendly sedan—something that, for about two minutes, made my heart stupidly leap. Until I talked to Violet and found out he always swaps out his cars every few years already and was due.

So much for that theory.

With a sigh, I type out another message.

> Allie: Yup, sure is. See you there soon.

> Kai: I'll bring coffee. Your usual apple fritter too?

My smile grows. Every morning since my first day, Kai has brought me a cinnamon latte and an apple fritter. My husband doesn't know my favorite coffee order, let alone my apple-flavored weakness.

But sure. This marriage is totally normal.

"Why the smile?"

The smooth, sinful voice of my husband has me nearly flinging my phone into my coffee. I don't know what's more alarming—the fact that he's still here or that he's actually acknowledging my facial expressions. Most people ask why someone is frowning, *not* why they're daring to experience joy. But then again, most husbands don't treat their wives as though they're carriers of an exotic disease either.

I look up—and sweet baby Jesus, Mary, and all the saints.

Rico stands there, a full-on catalog ad for "Husband You Can't Touch But Desperately Want To." Sweatpants slung low on his hips, a T-shirt clinging to every inch of his chest and abs hand-delivered by the gods of torture. And sweat—there's *so much sweat*, dripping down his neck, soaking his dark hair, pushing it back in a way that makes me want to run my fingers through it knowing exactly how silky it is.

My thighs clench—*betrayal, party of one*—and every ounce of my willpower goes into not visibly squirming like a woman starved. And, let's be honest, that's exactly what I am.

I press my lips together, refusing to bite them, because I am strong. I am independent. I am not about to drool over my emotionally stunted husband just because he's sin wrapped in a sweat-drenched T-shirt.

But when he wipes his face with a towel, slowly, and tosses it over his shoulder, my lady bits weep.

Meanwhile, as my ovaries meltdown, he moves to the fridge to grab the green swamp sludge he drinks religiously after every workout.

I watch—*purely for science*—as his biceps flex when he opens the bottle and veins standing out along his forearms. The lid clicks, and then he tilts his head back, throat working as he downs the monstrosity in one long gulp, Adam's apple bobbing like a hypnotic pendulum.

Great. Now my thighs are at it again, and I'm two seconds away from crossing my legs so tightly I cut off circulation.

I tear my eyes away, catching the clock—*9:07 a.m.* He's *never* here this late. Usually, he's gone before the sun even thinks about rising, avoiding me at all costs.

"What are you doing home?" I blurt, my voice sharper than I intended, but my body and mind are fighting for control over my hormones. I can only do so much.

He glances at me over the rim of his bottle, wiping his mouth with the back of his hand—because why wouldn't he give me another image to sear into my brain? His gaze holds mine, cool and unreadable, but those amber eyes...

I shift in my seat, suddenly way too aware of every part of my body and how close he is. My coffee cup feels too small, my fingers too tight around it. Maybe if I squeeze hard enough, it'll distract me from the walking fantasy sitting in my kitchen.

I drop my eyes to my iPad, scrolling through nothing just to look busy, pretending I'm unaffected. Which is a *bold-faced lie*, because with the way my body is buzzing inside, I must have swallowed a beehive.

He takes a seat across from me, casual as can be, unaware he's responsible for every filthy thought I've had since the last night we were together.

"You didn't answer the question," Rico states in his usual monotone, his voice annoyingly deep and distracting.

I barely keep myself from flinching. He never sits with me unless it's required. Even that hasn't been happening since I've been at the restaurant late and not home for dinners.

"What question?" I ask, playing dumb as I flick through my notes.

"You were smiling."

I glance up, narrowing my eyes. "I know you avoid facial expressions like they're contagious, but is it a crime to smile?"

Yeah, I'm going for the jugular today. No more dancing around this ridiculous, silent, tension-laced dynamic we have going on. Nonna told me I needed to get creative if I wanted to break through to my husband. So, I'm improvising.

"Who texted you?"

My phone lights up on the table, another message popping up on the screen. I don't even hesitate. "Kai."

I go back to scrolling.

A heavy, palpable silence settles over the table. My senses scream that he's still looking at me, so I peek up. Yup.

Gosh, I wish this man came with a handbook. Something that translated those eyes of his that they say so much more than his actual words while his feelings are in "do not disturb" mode.

His gaze sharpens, and even though his expression remains neutral, something in the air shifts. My traitorous body registers it before my brain does—my stomach tightens, my thighs press together (*again*), and my eyes flick to the other end of the table.

Yeah, that part of the table.

The very same table that has been thoroughly broken in despite barely being a month old. A plank of wood that has seen far too much action for a piece of furniture meant for dining.

Rico's eyes follow mine, and his jaw ticks. Wonder if he has the same thoughts when he looks at it...

"Why is he texting you?"

I blink at him, then glance down at my phone before looking back up, just to make sure I heard him right. "Because he's my sous chef? We have to communicate?"

"At work. Not at home."

Oh, this is fun.

"You sound jealous."

"No."

Right. Because jealousy requires an emotion, and my husband isn't human enough for that.

"He was asking if I needed a ride, but I told him I was fine," I add, observing him, waiting for... *something*.

I get nothing.

Rico is silent as he drinks the rest of his protein shake, his throat moving with each swallow. The tension in the air thickens, pressing against my skin, and I swear I can taste it—bitter and lingering, turning my moment of inappropriate lust into full-blown annoyance.

If he wants space, I'll give him space.

I push back from the table, take my coffee mug to the sink, and rinse it out, mentally prepping myself for the day ahead.

But before I can turn around, I slam into something solid, warm, and sweaty.

"Shit, Rico!" I yelp, my hands smacking against his chest, which is still damp. Oh, how I'd love to peel it off him, see the abs that I only glimpse through wet shirts in person.

Touch them. Explore them. Okay, also lick them. Before I can even recover, he presses me back against the counter, arms caging me in.

"I don't like it."

I blink up at him, still a little frazzled. "Like what?"

"Stop being cute."

Oh, this fucking man.

"So you think I'm cute?"

"I don't think you're cute."

Wow, that was unnecessarily fast.

"Gee, thanks. Every wife's dream is to hear from her husband that he doesn't find her attractive."

I try to duck under his arm, but he shifts, blocking me again. His hand snaps up, fingers curling under my chin, tilting my head up so I have to look at him.

"Did I say that?"

"You just said you don't think I'm cute, Rico. How else am I supposed to interpret that?"

"Cute and attractive are different words."

Oh, we're doing this today?

"So you find me attractive but not cute?"

"Didn't say that either."

I exhale sharply. "Rico, I have things to do. I need to get ready for work. Why are you even home, anyway? We both know you prefer to avoid me, so why the surprise reveal?"

That jaw of his? Yeah, it clenches so hard I think I just heard his molars cry for help. No response. He'd rather suffer internal bleeding from biting his tongue than actually answer a question.

"Yeah, that's what I thought." I shove at his chest again, determined to escape.

Only, I don't. Because instead of letting me go, he does the exact opposite. His arm snaps around my waist, yanking me closer.

"Rico—"

His mouth crashes into mine—hungry, ravenous—and suddenly I'm drowning. Heat. Tongue. Teeth. My head spins as he devours every breath, every coherent thought, inhaling me as if he's been suffocating without.

His fingers slide from my chin to my hair, threading through the braid I didn't bother taking out this morning, tugging just enough to make my toes curl. He tilts my head back, angling me exactly where he wants—because of course he takes control, and I let him. Gladly.

A whimper slips out before I can trap it, and the second he hears it, his grip tightens, the kiss turning rougher, deeper, urgent. Possessive.

I don't realize we're moving until my back hits the cool marble of the kitchen island, a shock that only sharpens the edge of everything. My legs part on instinct when he lifts me onto the surface, stepping between them with the confidence of someone who knows damn well he belongs there.

And when he drags me closer, until there's no space left between us and I feel *all* of him pressing hard and thick against me, I can't control the moan that comes out of me. Those sweatpants don't hide a thing—and right now? I'm not sure I want them to.

My hands, traitorous as ever, fist in the front of his T-shirt, pulling him impossibly closer. Fingers find their way into his damp hair, scraping against his scalp, and the low growl he lets out vibrates through both our bodies.

"I have needs," he grits out against my lips, his breath ragged, voice wrecked as if he's fighting himself and me all at once.

And then he's kissing me again, more demanding than before.

But even as my pulse races and my body arches into his, that one word echoes in my head, splashing cold water all over my fire.

Needs.

Not *want.* Not *desire.* Not *you drive me crazy and I can't stay away from you.*

Nope. Just a body in reach to scratch an itch.

Despite the grip he still has on my hair, I pull back, breaking the kiss, shoving lightly at his chest.

"So, this is all about you getting off?" My voice is breathy, but I still pack in as much judgment as humanly possible.

Rico doesn't let me go. His fingers grip my waist, his amber eyes darkening as they roam over my body—lingering on my silk shorts and camisole.

"No."

The single word sends an unexpected thrill down my spine.

I should push him away. I should tell him to go get himself off with his own hand. But the way he's looking at me? He wants to devour me.

Yeah. My traitorous body is not on the same page as my petty-ass mind.

"So you stayed home to screw me? That's why you didn't slip out early to avoid me. Just figured you'd drop in for a quickie and then disappear for another few days until you need it again?"

Without a word, he releases my hair and shoves me down against the island, his hands gripping my shorts and yanking them down my legs in one fluid motion.

I let out a small gasp as the cool stone kisses my bare thighs.

"I have to get ready for work, Rico."

I say this, but do nothing to stop him.

Because my body, that traitorous little witch, wants this. Wants him. And it's been five very, *very*, *very* long days without an orgasm, and let me tell you, I have learned things about myself in these past five days. Mainly? That I am not the woman who can just go without.

A flicker of something passes through his eyes, and for a moment, I think he might actually respond, but instead, he grips my thighs, spreading them apart as he settles in between them.

"I am home..." He pauses, jaw working as if forming words scrapes against his instincts. "Because I needed my breakfast."

That's all the warning I get before his head dips between my legs.

Rico

I WANT TO FUCK my wife, but for some inexplicable reason, her questioning how I see her is the thing bothering me. Not the fact that I haven't touched her in five days, or that my balls are one unfulfilled orgasm away from filing for emancipation. Not even the fact that I can't get through a single work meeting without images of her thighs—bare, spread, open—haunting me like a damn specter. No, it's the way she asked.

As if my opinion mattered.

It shouldn't.

It doesn't.

Except I'm here, between the legs that have become my personal brand of psychological warfare, proving her wrong in the only way I know how. My tongue flattens as I drag it through her slick center, and her protests? Gone. Now, she's gasping, her fingers twisting into my hair, hips trying to grind against my mouth as she chases more.

I chuckle, catching myself and hoping she didn't hear it. Of all the times for a laugh to snake out, it's when it can vibrate against her thighs?

I take her clit into my mouth and suck, savoring the way she cries out my name. I could make a religion out of this—worshipping her, consuming her, letting her break apart under my mouth, my hands, my body. But that would imply a level of devotion I'm not willing to admit to, so instead, I pin her hips to the island, slip a finger into her tight, dripping heat, and watch her fall apart.

She's so fucking perfect.

Silky, hot, and wet—soaking before I even touched her. A fact that soothes the primal, possessive part of me I refuse to acknowledge exists. I add a second finger, then a third, and she moans, her walls clamping down so tight around my fingers that my cock throbs painfully in my pants.

I need a release.

Badly.

It's made my entire fucking week intolerable, but instead of getting myself off, I'm here, torturing myself, listening to her gasp and plead because—for whatever reason—I need her to know that she's wrong without telling her.

That I see her. That I think about her more than I should. That this isn't just about my body demanding hers, but something else.

Something dangerous.

"Rico... please...oh God."

I press a slow, deliberate kiss to her thigh before biting down hard enough to make her yelp—half pleasure, half pain. "No God here baby, but I am."

Her fingers in my hair tighten, nails digging into my scalp, and fuck, if that isn't the best kind of pain. I crave it. The sting. The way she marks me. Because when I step out of the shower and see those crescent-shaped bruises on my skin, I enjoy knowing she was there. That she needed me enough to leave an imprint.

She moans louder, her pleas growing desperate, and that does it. That breaks me.

I curl my fingers, hitting the exact spot I know will send her over the edge, and when she comes, I don't stop. I don't pull away until I've wrung every tremor from her body, licking and tasting until I'm completely, unapologetically, drunk on her.

Then I stand, wipe my mouth, and let my eyes meet hers.

Wide.

Blown.

Vulnerable.

That's what undoes me—not her body or her moans, but *that* look.

I grip her wrist, tugging her until she's flush against me, my cock so fucking hard it's a miracle I'm still standing. I could have her right now, take her on this counter, bend her over, claim what's already mine.

But I don't.

Instead, I kiss her.

And fuck if it doesn't feel like a victory.

She steals another piece of me every time I touch her, and instead of stopping, I let her.

I should walk away, regain control, remind her who's really in charge here.

But then her hands skim the waistband of my sweats and tug them down.

"You want me to fuck you?" My voice is hoarse, strained.

I need her to say yes, but I refuse to beg. Okay, maybe I'm willing to beg.

Because if she doesn't, it's going to be me and my palm in the shower—again—cursing her name as I come apart picturing this.

She shakes her head, sliding off the counter, and any trace of that sweet, doe-eyed innocence evaporates. In its place? A woman with dark, wicked eyes. Her tongue flicks out, slow and deliberate, wetting those swollen lips, and when she drops to her knees, my head grows dizzy, considering all my blood has migrated to my cock and refuses to circulate anywhere else.

When her fingers wrap around my length, stroking me with just enough pressure to make my spine lock up, I consider that maybe this is how I go. Not in a blaze of gunfire, not from some long-overdue retribution, but from the ruthless way my wife licks the bead of pre-cum from my tip before dragging her tongue down the underside of my shaft.

Fuck.

This woman is about to ruin me. And I think I might want her to.

She moves with a patience that borders on torture, licking, teasing, until my jaw clenches so tight it might snap. And when she drags her tongue up again, swirling it around the head before taking me into her mouth?

Yeah. I might actually fucking die this time.

I've never had my cock sucked before. Never gave a shit about it. Now, I'm questioning every decision I've ever made, because this? This is a revelation.

My fingers tangle in her hair, gripping, and when her mouth slides lower, taking me in deeper, I don't just feel it—I fucking ascend. My hips jerk instinctively as the head of my cock brushes the back of her throat, and she gags. A delicious, sinful sound that has me white-knuckling my control.

One. More. Inch.

Just one more and I might explode right here.

"Fuck..." The growl rumbles from deep in my chest, my head rolling back along with my ability to function as a rational human being. My entire body is coiled, tight, and when she sucks harder, her teeth barely scraping my length, I hiss.

I glance down, and the smirk she's wearing around my cock is obscene.

My thief strikes again, this time stealing my breath, my restraint, my fucking soul.

She moans, low and eager, the vibrations shooting up my spine, and I lose the last frayed thread of control. My hips move, slowly at first, pushing deeper, my grip in her hair tightening as I ease myself into the hot, wet silk of her mouth.

"Do you want me to fuck that pretty little mouth of yours?" I rasp, glad that I didn't say *please let me,* since it was on the tip of my tongue.

She blinks up at me, her lashes thick, with tears pricking at the corners of her eyes. My thumb grazes over one, plucking it up as I suck the salty goodness from it.

And then she nods.

I groan, dragging my lower lip between my teeth as I hold her in place, thrusting in deeper, testing her limits, and fuck, she takes it. No hesitation, no pulling away—just pure, unapologetic submission. Her nails biting into my thighs as she urges me on.

My cock throbs. My balls tighten. I'm about two seconds away from coming right there. The sensation is too much; the vision is an overload.

"I'm gonna come in your mouth," I warn, my voice a raw, wrecked growl. "And you're going to take every drop."

Her moan of approval is enough to end me.

Heat rushes down my spine, my thrusts growing erratic, desperate, wild, and when she gags again, eyes watering, my control shatters. I grip the back of her neck, holding her in place as I bury myself deep, my cock throbbing as I empty down her throat.

And to my complete and utter fucking delight, she swallows.

I brace against the counter, trying to regain some semblance of reality, because I swear, my soul just left my body. Floated the fuck away into the ether. No one will miss it. Hell, I was sure it wasn't there, anyway.

I expect her to pull back, to wipe her mouth, maybe even throw a self-satisfied smile my way. Instead, she licks, cleaning up the last of me before pulling away, her tongue darting out to catch the moisture at the corner of her lips.

Holy. Fucking. Shit.

I grip her wrist, hard, yanking her to her feet, my hands framing her face as I crash my mouth against hers. I don't care that I can taste myself on her tongue, don't care that her lips are still swollen from taking me so fucking deep.

I just need her.

I suck and nip at her mouth, branding her, making sure that when she walks into that restaurant today, there's no doubt who she belongs to.

Who she fucking wrecks.

I pull back, dragging my teeth over her lower lip before dropping my gaze to her body. Her nipples are straining against that silk camisole, her messy hair framing her still-flushed face.

I should let her go. Should put space between us, remind her what this marriage really is.

But I don't.

Instead, I lean in, my mouth at her ear, and murmur, "Want to know a secret?"

She nods, still breathless.

"I've never had my cock sucked before."

I savor the way her eyes widen, the subtle hitch in her breath. Then, without another word, I turn and walk away hating that, yet-a-fucking-gain, I tossed out something no one knows to this woman.

Allie

MY INNER THIGHS CLENCH every time I think about Rico going down on me in the kitchen. Not *this* kitchen, obviously—this is a professional establishment, and I'm fairly certain health inspectors frown upon that sort of thing.

And then there's the *other* part—the way he came apart the second I took him in my mouth, a controlled demolition of the most emotionally iced-over man on the planet.

But what's been gnawing at me all morning—besides the memory of his hands gripping my hair—is the fact that of all the contract terms he's ignored, there's one he hasn't even tried to weasel his way out of.

The secrets.

He waits until post-orgasm to share them, as if that somehow makes it less of a thing, but he shares them. First, he told me I was his first kiss. Then, this morning, after I swallowed every drop of his releases, he coolly dropped that he'd never had a woman go down on him before. And considering my expertise in that department came strictly from books (and one very detailed family discussion that I will never recover from), I'm suddenly feeling pretty damn good about myself.

I *haven't* shared a secret. And he *hasn't* asked.

And if there's one thing I'm realizing about my mysterious, emotionally walled-off husband, it's that he's full of contradictions. Layers I hadn't expected.

I assumed he was experienced. He's cold, he's distant, he's the epitome of a man who seems to have done it all and been unimpressed. And yet... I was his *first* kiss. His *first* blow job. His *first* relationship.

Ever.

And suddenly, so much about him makes sense. The avoidance. The control. That every time I try to talk to him, he looks more eager to be locked in a room full of screaming toddlers than deal with the conversation. He doesn't know *how* to do this, and neither do I. We're two people navigating our firsts from opposite ends of the emotional spectrum.

Are we moving toward each other? Or just coexisting in the same house until one of us figures out how to walk away?

"Chef?"

Kai's voice snaps me out of my downward spiral, and I blink, realizing I've been standing here, spacing out, while my sous chef waits for me to return to planet Earth. Probably not an impressive look for someone about to launch a new restaurant concept.

"Sorry, what?"

Kai points to the materials spread across the worktable in the kitchen's corner. "The debut? You know, that thing happening in three days where you show the city that Via Napoli isn't just coasting on its name anymore?"

Oh. Right. That.

In seventy-two hours, I'm unveiling *my* new menu, *my* new concept, *my* new everything to Manhattan's most insufferable food critics and socialites, and if they don't leave raving about it, I'll probably have to pack my knives and fake my death.

No pressure.

The Bennetti name ensured a sell-out night. No one in this city turns down an opportunity to say they rubbed elbows with one of Manhattan's most powerful families, even if it's just to see the wife of the quiet one debut her restaurant experiment.

I just hope they come for the food and not because they're expecting some kind of exclusive access to the family's influence.

I've invited everyone—Marco, Violet, Sienna, and yes, *even* Rico, though his response was a grunt at best, a text read but not answered at worst.

Kai taps the menu in front of me. "Do you want to go with the usual five-course for the debut tasting?"

A *prix fixe-style* menu—where the dishes are curated by the chef and served in a specific order, building flavors deliberately—was one of my biggest changes to Via Napoli. It's an experience, *not* just a meal. No chaotic ordering, no plates that don't complement each other. Each dish complements the last, the wine pairings carefully selected to enhance the flavors.

Sort of like... an orgasm. But for your mouth.

I look at the menu laid out in front of me, the courses meticulously planned, each dish designed to build anticipation before leading to the grand finale.

Yeah. It's oral foreplay.

Yup, now I'm back to thinking about my husband and how he still hasn't RSVP'd.

I tap my pen against the menu drafts spread across the table, my teeth sinking into my bottom lip as I weigh my options. One menu is a *"safe"* five-course, foolproof, almost unimaginable to mess up unless someone spontaneously forgets how to use a stove.

The other? A riskier, more baroque option that could either cement my reputation as a culinary genius or lead to a Yelp massacre if the execution isn't perfect.

Decisions, decisions. Do I play it safe and be a coward? Or do I gamble with my career like I'm in Vegas on a three-day bender? Which, for the record, I've never experienced.

"What do you think?" I finally look up at Kai, who's watching me with those obnoxiously disarming eyes of his.

He's attractive. Objectively, unreasonably, ridiculously attractive. And if I were single—hell, even if I had met him a year ago—I would have definitely batted my lashes and tried to flirt my way into his good graces. But I'm *not* single. I'm married.

Happily? Debatable. But legally? One hundred percent.

My wedding and engagement rings, which I used to wear proudly, are now on a chain around my neck because the health department frowns upon wearing jewelry while cooking. It's safer, sure. But it also means my marital status isn't flashing in neon lights on my left hand anymore.

Kai leans against the counter, arms crossed. "Is your husband coming? I still haven't met him."

Oh, we're asking loaded questions today? Great.

I ignore him and focus back on my menus because I can't even answer that. Rico hasn't responded to my text, which I knew he wouldn't, but the petty part of me that still believes in miracles had hoped. All I got was the standard read receipt—cold, dismissive, and somehow still the most communicative thing he's done all week.

Taking a deep breath, I skim both options again. The safe menu would be the smarter choice, but then what? I play it safe for the rest of my career? No. This is *my* debut. This is my name attached to the restaurant now. I either go big, or I go home and cry into a bowl of store-bought pasta.

"Knock, knock!"

A singsong voice interrupts my culinary existential crisis, and both Kai and I turn toward the kitchen entrance to see Sienna standing there, looking as effortlessly stunning as ever. She's pushing the twins in their double stroller, the two little angels wiggling and cooing like a Gerber commercial.

Sienna is the picture of a glowy, happy, put-together mom. Long golden waves cascading down her back, flawless skin, minimal makeup, and the mellow confidence that makes me question if I'll ever look that way when I have children.

She's also nothing like the women I used to surround myself with—botoxed, designer-draped, and perpetually bored while their nannies did all the actual parenting. Sienna? She's *real*. And she makes motherhood look... I don't know. Nice.

"Hey, gorgeous ladies," I coo, bending down to tickle the tiny little feet poking out from their rompers. The girls kick happily, their cheeks chubby and pink, their wisps of dark hair tied into teeny-tiny bows that could probably make a grown man cry from sheer cuteness.

Sienna clears her throat dramatically. "Oh. Hi Allie. Nice of you to acknowledge me, too."

"Sorry, you can't compete. They have chubby cheeks and the intoxicating baby smell that tricks people into wanting kids."

Sienna smirks, but her attention flicks behind me, where Kai is still leaning against the table, watching us.

"Oh!" I wave a hand between them. "Sienna, this is Kai, my sous chef. Kai, this is Sienna, my sister—" I pause before the words *in-law* can slip out, because I've learned the hard way that in this family, there's no such thing as *in-law*. "My sister, Sienna."

Kai's gaze flicks between us, clearly assessing how we share DNA. "Nice to meet you." His smile is pleasant, comfortable. A complete opposite of my husband's, which I've seen a grand total of nada.

And for some reason, that comparison makes guilt twist in my stomach.

It's not that I want to compare them—it just *happens*. Kai is friendly, expressive, and easy to talk to. Rico is... *not*. And every time I catch myself noticing the difference, I feel as if I'm betraying my husband, even though he's done absolutely nothing to warrant my loyalty.

"Are you okay?" Sienna tilts her head at me.

Shit. I've been staring at the floor, lost in thought.

"Yeah! Totally. What brings you by?"

"I thought I'd see if you wanted to grab coffee across the street. The girls do better getting out and having fresh air before their nap, and I have the day off." She smiles at Kai awkwardly, which makes me wonder—does she think something is going on between us?

God, I hope not.

Yes, Kai *is* attractive. And yes, my husband treats me as if I'm an obligation. But I'd *never* cheat. Ever. I may not have the marriage I imagined, but I at least have my integrity.

"Sure," I say, shaking off my thoughts. "Give me one minute."

I turn back to Kai. "We're doing the more elaborate menu."

He grins, taking my chef's coat as I shrug it off. "Great choice, Chef."

Sienna watches the exchange with raised brows, and I suddenly feel the need to over-explain. "It's totally professional. We're just coworkers."

Kai deadpans. "*You're* making it weird."

I groan. "I am making it weird, aren't I?"

Sienna bites back a smirk. "A little."

"Right, let's go," I mutter, grabbing my purse.

We step out of the kitchen into the main dining area, where Vinnie sits in a booth, drinking coffee and reading *The Art of War*. He's an odd duck, that one. Reads the most mysterious choices out there—for example, the one time I caught him reading one of Violet's novels. Yeah, he wouldn't look me in the eye for a full twenty-four hours after that one.

He peers up as I approach. "We're going across the street to the café."

Without a word, he nods, stands, and falls into step behind us, seamlessly merging with Elias, who's already waiting by the door.

"How come you and Dom share Elias? Doesn't he need a bodyguard too?" I ask, watching as Elias follows behind us.

"When Dom's at the office, there's no need. No one's getting past security. So Elias sticks with me when I go out. We make it work. No point in having an extra body lurking around." She glances down at the twins, adjusting one of their bows. "Maybe we'll reevaluate when the girls get older, but honestly, we're so far removed from that side of the family, I don't think we even need to worry about it."

Must be nice not having to worry about it.

Me? I could move to a remote island, learn how to spear fish, and live off coconuts, and I'd still have to look over my shoulder. The Cosa Nostra doesn't just withdraw from your life. And while my parents might not be speaking to me, it doesn't mean I'm free. It just means I'm an easier target. Which also means any kids I have will be targets too.

I walked away from that life, only to find myself still shackled to it; the more I try to run, the more I realize how short the leash is.

For now, I'll ignore that fact.

We step into the café across from the restaurant, the scent of espresso and fresh pastries filling the air. It's packed, the lunch rush just about to hit, but the hostess doesn't even pretend to look around for an open table. Nope. We get seated instantly, which I assume is the Bennetti name at work.

I should probably start flexing the last name myself, but I haven't settled into it yet. It still feels assigned—temporary, almost—more sticker slapped on my forehead at a conference than something I truly own: *Hello, my name is: Wife of Rico Bennetti.*

Vinnie and Elias take seats at the bar, ordering coffee as if they've both survived one too many war zones and trust is a currency they ran out of years ago.

Sienna parks the stroller, making sure the girls are positioned with their little sippy cups of juice front and center. Once she's satisfied with the setup, her blue eyes swing to me, locked and loaded with the intensity of a tactical laser sight.

"So... Kai *seems* nice."

"There's nothing going on between us," I say immediately, because I know exactly where this is headed.

"Oh, I didn't think that. Besides, the marks on your neck are so visible that NASA is tracking them from space."

I groan, hand flying up to my neck. "What?! Where?"

Sienna reaches into her bag, pulls out a compact mirror, and hands it over. I flip it open and sure enough, there they are—several little red and purplish nips dotting my skin like a connect-the-dots puzzle.

"Oh my God, can you see them with my chef's coat on?" I ask, flipping the mirror from side to side to assess the destruction.

She nods. "Sadly, my concealer isn't your shade, or I'd offer it. But, uh, those bad boys aren't going anywhere."

I groan, digging through my bag in desperation, but of course, I don't have makeup on me. Because why would I? I work in a kitchen. The closest thing I have to a beauty routine is washing marinara sauce off my arms before I go home.

"I'll have to stop at the drugstore before work," I mutter, snapping the compact shut. "No one takes a chef seriously when she's walking around with hickeys like a teenager after prom."

"That might explain why Kai kept looking at you weirdly all morning."

My stomach drops. "Oh, my God. No wonder he kept acting off."

"I don't think that's the reason."

"I told you, *nothing* is going on."

"Nothing going on and him checking you out isn't the same thing."

She's enjoying this way too much.

She pulls out little snack cups for the twins—puffy crackers that smell like bananas.

"So," she goes on casually, popping a cracker into one of the twin's mouths. "How are things with Rico?"

I gesture ferociously at my neck. "Clearly, no problems there."

She chuckles. "So I take it you were able to get rid of the ovulation-only agreement?"

"It's wide open."

Yet there's no victory in my voice. No success.

"You don't sound thrilled."

Before I can answer, the server arrives, fawning over the babies, physically restraining herself from scooping them up. Understandable. These girls could single-handedly solve world peace with their cuteness.

Once she takes our orders, I let out a slow breath.

"We haven't, you know... since he bought the restaurant," I admit. "It almost feels like he bought it just to keep me busy. Seems he wanted to shove me into a kitchen so I'd stay out of his way."

I don't mention that he said that outright the night he gave it to me. No reason to say it out loud when it's already on repeat in my head.

I glance at the twins. Twins run in the Bennetti family. My odds of having a single baby are basically *zero*.

And what if I end up raising them alone? Not physically alone—Rico would never let that happen—but *emotionally* alone?

It's already obvious he wants our lives to be separate. He bought me the restaurant. He put me in a bedroom on another floor. The nursery is with me, *not* with him. He's setting up a life where I have my space, and he has his.

It doesn't take a genius to do the math.

"Well, you did *something* if you have those marks."

"He, uh... did something in the kitchen this morning. And I... returned the favor."

Her eyes light up as she leans in. Nothing is off-limits in this family, and I'll never be used to it. Back home, I had to pretend I barely knew what an orgasm was.

"But no sex?"

I flush. "No?"

Her smile grows. "Interesting."

"How so?"

"Well, your husband originally only wanted to sleep with you when you were *ovulating*. Then, he suddenly agreed to whenever. But instead of actually having sex, he just... enjoyed himself and left it at that?"

"Uh... yeah?"

"Sounds to me like your husband just wanted to make sure everyone—especially your attractive little sous chef—knew exactly who you belong to."

I scoff. "That's ridiculous."

"Is it? Rico doesn't let anyone in. But he marked you up, even though that doesn't exactly get you pregnant." She waggles her eyebrows.

"Jealousy would require feelings. Rico doesn't have those."

Sienna just hums, sipping her water as if she knows something I don't.

And now, I hate that I'm thinking about it too.

Rico

THE PUNCHING BAG IN my home gym has taken a beating the last few days—literally. My knuckles are raw, my hands are bruised, and yet the tension in my body still hasn't depleted. The fleeting relief from my last encounter with my wife barely lasted an hour before the itch came back.

A new and highly inconvenient addiction.

Between my newfound inability to go five minutes without thinking about her thighs wrapped around my head and the infuriating cyber ghost currently toying with my security systems at work, I need to hit something. *Hard.* Preferably a face. And since legally I can't do that in board meetings, I came here.

I usually stop by Marco's underground sparring gym once a week, a little recreational violence to keep myself balanced. But since my marriage, I haven't had time for extracurricular activities. Combine that with the fact that my balls are so blue they could be mistaken for Smurf testicles, and I'm two seconds away from throwing a grown-man tantrum.

I push through the doors of the gym, greeted immediately by Mindi—the receptionist, part-time massage therapist, and full-time walking sexual harassment lawsuit.

"Well, well, look who finally graced us with his presence."

Her voice is as IQ crumbling as the spelling of her name.

Mindi is the woman who dawdles. *A lot.* She's got a wardrobe that consists only of crop tops and leggings that leave nothing to the imagination, and based on the way she's popping that obnoxious pink bubblegum, she has no intention of making this a hasty chat.

I nod, giving her the bare minimum acknowledgment as I go on walking.

"Where have you been, Rico?" she sulks, twisting a strand of bleached-blonde hair around her finger.

"Married."

"What?" She practically chokes on her gum, her eyes widening as if I just told her I took a vow of celibacy and joined a monastery. *Sort of accurate with my marriage at this point.*

I don't bother slowing my stride, moving through the double doors that lead to the main gym. Behind me, I hear the rapid click of her heels against the concrete floor as Bubblegum Barbie chases after me.

"You got married?"

Her tone is pure betrayal, which is impressive considering I've exchanged all of three words with this woman in the past four years. I stop walking just long enough to turn and hold up my left hand, wiggling my fingers so she can get a good look at the platinum band on my ring finger.

"Go away."

The pout drops instantly, and I keep walking, leaving her behind.

The gym is already full, the air thick with sweat and testosterone. A few men nod in my direction, some eyeing Mindi, but I barely register them before a familiar voice cuts through the noise.

"Rico! You here to get your ass kicked?"

I turn toward the ring to see my cousin, Marco, grinning like the deranged sociopath he is, sweat dripping from his brow, and his latest opponent slumped in the corner nursing a bloody nose.

"Perhaps."

Marco wipes his face with the back of his glove, smearing a little blood across his cheek. "You're looking tense. Marriage not keeping you relaxed?"

Blue balls will do that to a man.

But, I don't respond. Instead, I toss my gym bag to the floor, pull out my gloves, and start taping up my hands.

Marco leans on the ropes. "You've been MIA. I take it wedded bliss is keeping you busy?"

I scowl up at him. "Painfully."

Marco barks out a laugh. "I knew I picked a good one."

I climb into the ring and swing without warning, slamming my fist into his ribs with a delightful thwack.

Marco lets out a grunt, followed by another damn chuckle.

"You fight dirty," he shakes out his shoulders, unfazed.

"And yet you still get in the ring with me."

He shifts into position, ready to return the favor.

"Watch the kidneys this time," he warns. "Last time I pissed blood for a week."

"Then learn to block."

I move fast, aiming for his ribs again, but the next thing I know, my face explodes with white-hot pain, a punch slamming into the side of my head so hard it rattles my skull.

Everything goes silent for half a second—then my ears ring.

And now my mood officially plummets into *fuck everything* territory.

Marco drops his hands, frowning. "Since when do you not block your face?"

Since I started fucking a woman who plunders everything—including my ability to see a punch coming a-fucking-pparently.

I don't answer. I just swing again, landing an uppercut that sends his head popping back. The familiar metallic tang of blood coats my tongue, and when Marco grins through his mouth guard—red staining his teeth—I feel slightly better. Good. We can both bleed today.

"Trouble in paradise, cousin?" The smug little shit pouts.

I hate him.

I drive another punch, but he deflects it, thrusting me back. "Oh...wife not letting you have a taste in between contractually obligated days?"

I scowl. "Who the fuck talks like that?"

Marco shrugs, getting back into stance. "You're the one who turned sex into a ne-gotiation like you were drafting a fucking merger agreement. No offense, but if I had a hot-as-hell woman like Allie in my bed every night, I'd be taking advantage. Especially with those hips." He bites his bottom lip and lets out a low groan. "Tell me they're as good to grab as they—"

Before that nitwit can finish a sentence that might force me to commit a felony, I jab him right in the jaw.

"Shit!" Marco tumbles back, spitting blood onto the mat before he roars with laughter. Because of course he does. My cousin is a certifiable psychopath who probably gets hard at the idea of getting his ass kicked.

"Sooooo, you aren't getting any, I take it?"

"I'm not talking about my sex life with you."

"You should. Clearly, you need the *therapy*."

That motherfucker.

I swing again, securing a punch to his ribs this time, but he barely grunts. Even when I go for another shot, he just absorbs it, laughing.

"You know, for a guy who pretends he doesn't give a shit about his wife, you're really leaning into those *touch her and you die* vibes Vi keeps writing about in her books. So, what's got you all bent out of shape? That your wife is attractive and every man in this gym would trade places with you in a second, or—"

The fact that this psycho has read Violet's books already concerns me. But what's worse? The bastard knows every romance trope.

And so do I.

Marco thinks I'm jealous.

I'm not.

Okay, maybe I'm seeing red, but that's just my general disposition. It has nothing to do with some moron making eyes at my wife.

She's mine.

...Fuck, I don't appreciate where my thoughts are going.

Stick to the facts, Rico. You have blue balls and it's making you temporarily insane. That's all.

"She said she's not tracking ovulation anymore. We can have sex whenever."

Marco blinks. Then blinks again. His mouth opens, closes.

"Sooooo. Why is that a problem? Oh, but she's not putting out, huh? Cock-blocking?"

I swing. He dodges. I despise that he's good at this.

"I bought her that restaurant. She's *never* even home to put out."

There. *I said it.*

My plan is fucking me over.

Sure, I wanted her out of my way. I wanted to avoid those dinners where she talked endlessly and I had to pretend to give a shit. But what's the point of having a wife if she's never there? She forced monogamy. Worse? Even if she hadn't, the thought of touching another woman makes me physically sick. And I don't enjoy that.

I don't appreciate that she's rewired my brain. That I can't even find another woman attractive. That even thinking about going back to my old "*therapy*" appointments makes my stomach churn.

Let's add that to the growing list of things she's stolen from me. The list is perilously long.

Not that I was ever the type to stare at women. *Or care.* But it would've been nice to have the option, just in case I ever wanted to summon it one day.

Marco watches me, his face caught between amusement and sheer disbelief.

"You realize that's not a *real* problem, right?"

I scowl.

"Oh, but you're not just sexually frustrated. You *miss* her."

I throw a punch just as he lands a brutal uppercut to my jaw. My vision goes blank for a second as my body meets the mat.

Next thing I know, Marco is kneeling beside me, shoving me onto my back with a grin that rivals The Joker. "You're a smart man, cousin, but right now? You're a dumbass. The solution is right in front of you." He slaps my chest. "Go Carpe diem that shit."

Allie

I SPENT AN HOUR with Sienna, nimbly dodging all Rico-related topics. Instead, we talked about my upcoming restaurant showcase, her art, and the adorable chaos of teething twins. All subjects that didn't make my eye twitch or my chest tighten.

Since marrying into the family, I've gotten closer to Sienna, not because I don't want to get to know Violet—I do—but because the reigning Queen of Romance is currently locked away in her writing cave, churning out another novel that will set panties (and *probably* Kindles) on fire. The woman writes smut for a living, and judging by how often she and Alex disappear together, she takes her research *seriously*.

Honestly, the idea of getting paid to live in a world where love always wins, orgasms are life-altering, and broody men miraculously figure out their feelings before completely ruining their relationships sounds...intriguing. No real-life ghosting, no cold shoulders, no wondering if your husband bought you a restaurant just to get rid of you.

But alas, my reality is *not* a romance novel.

Because I spent that extra time with Sienna, I ended up staying later at the restaurant, not leaving until almost midnight. Vinnie looked just as dead on his feet as I felt, and all I wanted was a hot shower, a glass of wine, and my favorite book. I'd placed one of Violet's latest releases on my nightstand—signed, because autographed copies comes as a marital perk. My plan was to dive into it and live vicariously through her heroine, preferably one whose husband actually *talks* to her.

"I'll see you tomorrow, Vin," I call over my shoulder as he heads toward his basement unit and I walk through the garage into the house. I don't check to see if light creeps out from under Rico's office door or if his bedroom door is closed. I also didn't text him when I was leaving, and—surprise, surprise—he didn't text me either.

He really found the perfect way to keep me occupied.

The sheer exhaustion of my job, combined with my thoughts tormenting me at every turn, has left me too drained to try anymore.

And that's *exactly* what he wanted.

Besides, even if there was a light under that office door, I know what that means—he's dealing with the *hacker* problem (as Sienna called it, air quotes and all). Apparently, it's causing pressure between him and his brothers, and they think he's dragging his feet on fixing it, hoping to tank the merger. I had to hear that from Sienna—*not* my husband.

Because why talk to your wife when you can talk to anyone else?

So, yeah. I *don't* go looking for him. And if this is the peace he wanted, he's got it.

But if he expects to make an heir, he'll have to come meet me.

I haven't given up, but I also refuse to do all the effort. Despite Sienna's theory that my husband is jealous, she doesn't see the way he shuts down around me. She doesn't know how he reads and ignores *every* message I send. How he's straight-up told me I mean *nothing* to him.

I don't want them to think of him as a monster.

Some things are better left between a couple. Even if I'm dying to talk to someone about it.

My legs scream at me as I take the stairs two at a time, my body officially clocking out for the night. I don't bother flipping on the lights when I get to my room, just grab a pair of pajama pants and an oversized T-shirt. I'll ditch the pants once I crawl into bed since I always end up kicking them off anyway, but walking around this house exposed doesn't sit right with me.

Despite the fact that I was *very* uncovered on our kitchen counter this morning.

Maybe it's because Rico doesn't make me feel as though this is *my* home—no matter how much furniture I've added, no matter how many cozy little touches I've tried to bring in. It's still *his* house. And I'm his contracted roommate.

That's my reality. And one I need to accept before I fall off the deep end and start hoping for more.

Example one: thinking he was jealous.

Sienna wants me to believe that. But I can't.

Sure, it would be nice to think my husband gave a shit. That he wanted me. But that's not what this marriage is to him.

I needed an escape. He needed a wife.

We're bound for *different* reasons, but stuck in the *same* fate.

Where this goes from here is up to both of us.

But I will not be the one dragging him to the finish line, only to end up shattered when he refuses to meet me halfway.

I refuse.

My shower is quick because my grand plan for the night is simple: settle in, read a chapter or two of Violet's latest book, and pass out. No overthinking. No obsessing over my husband. Just me, a book, and a small glass of white wine.

I tiptoe downstairs, grab a bottle from the wine fridge in the kitchen island, pour myself the perfect (okay, large as hell) glass, then head back up, humming to myself. But the moment I set my wine down and reach for my lavender lotion, I pause.

It's not there.

Weird.

I check the floor, under my bed, the en suite bathroom, even peek behind the nightstand, because where the hell is it?

And then I notice something else.

My book.

Gone.

Now, the lotion? That could've fallen. I could have knocked it over in my pre-coffee morning haze. But the book? I explicitly put it on my nightstand before I left this morning. There is *zero* chance I misplaced it.

I drop to my knees, wildly searching under the bed, hands fumbling over the plush rug.

And that's when a voice that should not be there sends my soul straight out of my body.

"Looking for something?"

I yelp, whirling so fast I nearly land on my ass.

Rico stands in the doorway, arms folded, leaning against the frame, exuding the confidence of some arrogant asshole of a Greek statue. And—because my sleep deprivation is clearly making me hallucinate—I swear there's a gleam of enjoyment in his eyes.

"Did you take my book and lotion?" I accuse, still kneeling, hands on my hips.

He brushes a hand over his jaw, and god help me, that simple action sets my entire body on fire. It's infuriating. Why does my body have *zero* survival instincts?

"Didn't take. Moved."

I blink at him. Then at the empty nightstand. Then back at him.

I open my mouth, prepared to go full *Karen at a customer service desk*, but before I can let loose, Rico closes the distance between us in two steps and hooks a single finger under the chain around my neck, tugging it out from under my oversized sleep shirt. My engagement ring and wedding band dangle between us.

His gaze flicks from the rings back to my empty finger.

I snatch the chain from him, pulling it back and debating if I should slap him with it. "I didn't have time to put them back on," I mutter, unclasping it and sliding the rings off before securing it around my neck again. With a sigh, I slide my wedding band and my engagement ring back onto my finger.

Even after just a few weeks, a faint tan line has formed where they belong.

As if I needed more of a reminder.

As if the marks Rico left on my skin weren't enough to let the entire world know someone claimed me.

"Why are they off?" His voice is mild, but his jaw ticks, and something flashes in his eyes.

Is he mad?

I cross my arms. "Because I cook for a living, Rico. Ever heard of food safety? Can't exactly have a diamond falling into someone's pasta."

He stares, his expression indecipherable.

"I have to take them off in the kitchen," I continue, adjusting the chain and tucking it back under my shirt. "I *usually* put them back on before I leave work, but I forgot. I don't know why this is suddenly a crime." I wiggle my fingers in his face. "See? They're back where they belong. Crisis averted."

His silence stretches between us, playing the role of an awkward horror movie jump scare, until *finally*, he speaks.

"Forgot," he repeats, voice low, jaw tightening even more.

Okay, Mr. Pissy Pants, join the damn club.

I huff, throwing up my hands. "Where did you *move* my book and lotion to?"

He doesn't answer. Instead, he casually picks up my wineglass and, clearly intending to test me, walks toward the door.

"My room."

I blink. Then blink again.

Wait.

"You what?" I sputter, marching after him and stealing my glass back. "Your room? Why?"

Rico keeps walking, not even allowing me a peek. "You're moving there."

I stop dead on the threshold, staring at his retreating form. He might as well have declared we're moving to Mars.

"Excuse me? Since when?"

He pauses in the hallway, looking at me as if I'm being unreasonable for questioning why he's suddenly gone full deranged Sims player by rearranging our living arrangements.

"You'll be in my room until you're pregnant. Then you can move back."

"I—You—What?" I splutter.

Pregnant? Until *I'm pregnant*? So, I'm some seasonal tenant?

I look around my room, the one I decorated without even seeing it first because Rico, in all his broody control freak glory, insisted we have separate rooms.

I'm on my floor, for crying out loud.

Hell, I'm one missed signature away from being in an entirely different ZIP code.

And now, suddenly, I'm supposed to pack up and move to the dragon's lair?

And let's not ignore the fact that this logic makes no damn sense.

Rico stalks toward me, all predator eyes as he closes in on his prey. Annoying, arrogant, sexy-as-hell predator, but predator nonetheless.

"Because you get home late. Last I checked, no sex, no baby. You in my bed means we *will*. No matter what time."

I gape at him. *Actually gape.* "So you're moving me to your room just to make sure I'm conveniently available for your nightly baby-making agenda?"

"Glad you get it."

"Oh, I get it." I cross my arms, doing my best toddler on the verge of throwing a massive fit routine, planted feet and all. "I also reject it."

"No?"

"*No.* You don't get to move me on your whim." My voice climbs, and my hands flail because what even is this conversation? "What happens when I have my period, Rico? Do I then get exiled back to my room because I'm temporarily useless to your *plan*?"

I expect a flinch. A grimace. Hell, maybe even a blush. *Something.*

"You'll still sleep downstairs. *Until* you're pregnant."

"But you hate sharing a bed! You lie there counting down the seconds until I leave!"

"I'll manage."

"Oh, screw you, Rico!" I snatch my wine glass back from him. "You want a baby? You know where to *find* me."

With that, I spin on my heel and storm into my bedroom, slamming the door with a theatrical flair. My wine sloshes over the rim, pooling onto the nightstand. *Perfect.*

Before I can even grab a towel, the door bursts open, and I'm airborne.

"What the actual—*Rico!*"

He throws me over his shoulder.

"I gave you the option to walk." He hauls me down the hallway, through the kitchen, and toward his bedroom.

I beat my fists against his back. Kick my legs. Scream colorful threats about his future as a eunuch.

He doesn't care.

The bastard tightens his grip around my thighs, effortlessly carrying me through the house.

It's infuriating.

It's degrading.

And I'm turned on.

What kind of pathetic gremlin enjoys being manhandled like a 140-pound sack of flour?

Me. Apparently, me.

He doesn't stop until we're in his room, where he effortlessly tosses me onto the massive king-sized bed. The mattress bounces beneath me, and I sit there, wide-eyed, absolutely dumbfounded.

For the first time in my entire life, I have no words.

Then my eyes land on the nightstand.

My book and my lavender lotion are sitting neatly on top.

Oh. Hell. No.

"Are you insane?" My voice is a high-pitched squeal of disbelief.

Rico shrugs as if he just moved a throw pillow and *not* his wife. "Likely."

Then he strolls into the bathroom and slams the door shut, and seconds later, I hear the shower turn on.

"I can just grab my shit and leave, you know!" I holler after him.

Water sloshes. He's in the shower now, and his voice carries over the stream, completely unbothered.

"I will carry you back."

"Asshole," I mutter under my breath, stomping over to *my* side of *his* bed and flipping on my new lamp out of spite. Fine. If he wants me here, I'll make sure I'm comfortable.

I plop down dramatically and crack open my book, pretending to read while my heart pounds in my chest.

Then the shower turns off.

And suddenly, reading is impossible.

Because now I can hear him moving around in the bathroom.

And now I know that in approximately thirty seconds, he's going to walk out dripping in steam, the embodiment of a scented candle ad coming to life.

Don't look, Allie. Be strong.

The bathroom door swings open.

I look.

And regret everything.

Rico walks out, steam swirling behind him, his dark hair wet and slicked back, small droplets still clinging to his jaw. He's in sweatpants and a cotton shirt, and I hate myself for finding it attractive.

Focus, Allie. He's an asshole. A manipulative, emotionally stunted, bed-rearranging asshole.

"I'm reading," I blurt, jabbing a finger at my book, hoping he doesn't notice that I haven't actually turned a page.

He doesn't say a word—shocking—but walks right to my side of the bed.

And suddenly, my stomach is full of butterflies. Not those sweet kinds, but the kind ready to fist fight their way to a grand exit.

He infuriates me. He confuses me. He makes me feel worthless one second, and then the next, he just exists within five feet of me and my body practically screams *I'm yours, sir.*

I hate him.

And I really hate that I don't.

I do my absolute best to ignore him, which is a Herculean effort, considering he exists in my general vicinity. But when I see him casually pluck my lotion off the nightstand, followed by my book from my hands—only to toss it onto the table—my restraint goes up in flames.

"Hey!"

Does he acknowledge me? Nope. That would require effort. Instead, he flips the lotion cap open, squeezes a generous amount into his palm, and—without so much as a warning—yanks the covers back and frowns at my pajama pants.

"What are those?"

I blink. "Pajamas. You wear sweats." I gesture dramatically to Exhibit A—aka his own pants—and instantly regret it, because now I can see Exhibit A in entirely too much detail.

My mouth goes dry.

There is a perfect outline of his erection.

The instinct to suck my lower lip into my mouth is strong, but I fight it. Sort of. Okay, not well at all. *Fine, I fail.*

His gaze flicks to my pants again, and he mutters something opaque before climbing onto the bed and straddling me.

"What are you doing?"

He doesn't answer. Instead, he snatches my wrist and starts rubbing lotion into my arm. His hands are methodical, and—unfortunately—strong enough to make me whimper in pleasure like an unhinged lunatic.

He moves to my other arm, massaging the lotion into my skin before casually reaching for the bottle again. And that is when I realize my mistake.

Rico doesn't apply lotion.

Rico plans.

And my pajama pants are apparently his next target.

I open my mouth to protest, but the bastard yanks them down before I can so much as inhale, pulling me down the bed with him. I gasp, the cold air nipping at my legs, goosebumps instantly prickling my skin.

"Rico!"

Nothing. His entire focus is on my legs.

He rubs more lotion between his hands, then—without hesitation—presses his fingers into my sore calves, rubbing slow, deep circles into the muscle.

It's not sexual.

I mean, I *am* turned on, obviously. Tragically so. But he is not performing some grand seduction. His hands don't linger in places they shouldn't. He's simply massaging as if this is normal and rubbing lotion into my skin is some nightly husbandly duty he's always done when I get home from work.

And that's what makes it worse.

Because it feels good.

So good that a groan slips out before I can stop it.

Damn traitorous calves.

How the hell does he even know where I'm sore? Did he Google it? Did someone snitch?

By the time he's finished, I am a wreck. Not in a sexy, just-ravaged kind of way. More of a what-the-hell-just-happened-and-why-am-I-tingly kind of way.

Rico sets the lotion back on the nightstand, flicks off the light, and just... sits there. In the dark.

For a full minute, the only sound in the room is my breathing.

Then, finally, his voice breaks the silence.

"You *owe* me."

"I owe you? If you think I owe you sex just because I'm in your bed like some whore, you're—"

"You are *not* a whore."

His voice raises, barely, but it was enough to notice.

I blink up at him, surprised. "You moved me into *your* room so you could ensure a convenient pregnancy schedule, Rico. I don't exactly feel as if I'm an honored guest here."

"You owe me a secret."

I pause. "Wait... what?"

"I've given several. You, none."

So he noticed.

I chew on my lower lip. "Can I think about it?"

"No."

God, he's insufferable.

My mind scrambles. What can I tell him? What's safe to share? Why does this feel monumental when it's really just exchanging random facts?

Then, it comes to me.

"You weren't my first kiss."

The words spill out before I can reconsider.

"*But*," I add quickly, "I've only been kissed once before you." If you can even call what happened a kiss.

Silence.

He doesn't move. Doesn't breathe. His entire body freezes.

"Rico?" I whisper.

Nothing.

I can feel his breath on my skin, warm and steady, but he stays perfectly still.

Maybe that wasn't the right secret to share.

Or maybe... maybe he cares more than he lets on.

Rico

I DON'T ENJOY THIS secret game.

It unsettles me. Makes my stomach twist and my thoughts spiral into places they shouldn't go. Every little secret I've given up so far has slipped past my lips when I'm buried inside this woman, like some kind of twisted confession booth where she plays priest and executioner.

As I've said—she steals shit.

And if we were keeping track, and of course I fucking am, she's stolen:

My oxygen.

My biological responses.

My time.

My secrets.

Yet this time, she drops the bomb instead of extracting one.

I wasn't her first kiss.

It shouldn't matter. It doesn't matter. I didn't expect to marry some chaste, untouched bride, wearing a white dress and a halo, untouched by the grubby paws of Manhattan's most mediocre men. And yet—there's a flicker of something hot and violent twisting in my gut at the thought of some other bastard's mouth on hers.

Before I can stop myself, the words slip out. "How many?"

I didn't mean to ask. I didn't need to know. I moved her into my room to speed up the process of impregnation, not to get the full documentary of her tragically short dating history.

I blame the lavender.

Apparently, it relaxes people. At least, that's what I read when I researched why the hell my wife slathers herself in it every night in some kind of sacrificial ritual. According to Google, lavender has calming properties—good for stress, muscle relaxation, and apparently ruining my life because now I know entirely too much about it.

I could have been working on the actual problem that has been plaguing my company for weeks. But, instead? I was deep-diving into the world of women's nighttime skincare rituals because my wife has, *yet again*, stolen my time.

She tilts her head. "How many what?"

"Men."

Her eyebrows lift. "Why?"

I don't answer. Because I don't know *why*. But suddenly, I *need to know* how many men have seen my wife naked. How many men touched her before I did? How many men had the privilege of knowing how she tastes, how she sounds when she moans, how she—

One. It better be one.

She exhales slowly. "One."

Well, at least I can name what I'm feeling now. *Relief*, with a generous side of *shame*.

Shame because, apparently, I'm pathetic enough to care about my wife's past when mine isn't exactly saintly.

Hypocritical? Absolutely. But self-awareness is key, and I'm nothing if not painfully aware that I'm the pot calling the kettle scandalous.

"Same one that kissed you?"

"Yes."

I'm done with this conversation.

Unwilling to waste another second, I grip her legs and yank her down the bed, enjoying the little screech she lets out. A sound I should not enjoy as much as I do.

Lips I cannot fucking touch again.

Because she steals kisses. That's for damn sure.

Okay—maybe this morning was a lapse in judgment. But when a man has been suffering from perpetual blue balls, he is not liable for his actions.

Tonight, I have no intention of repeating that mistake.

I flip her onto her stomach, waiting for a protest. Nothing.

Even as I slide her panties off. Nothing.

I narrow my eyes. "So you're just going to take it?"

Yes, I'm actively inviting my wife to fight me on this.

Because, for reasons I don't care to unpack, I *enjoy* that sharp tongue of hers—even if it costs me an extra five to ten minutes. That she's just *letting* me move her in and strip her down without so much as a snarky remark? *Concerning.*

Apparently, I need this woman to argue with me. Preferably about everything. Because, as it turns out, I find it unreasonably arousing.

She pushes up on her elbows, looking back at me, and I hate how excited I get. She looks pissed off. "Do I have a choice?" Her voice is soft. "You moved me in here for one reason."

Several, actually.

But I'm not about to tell her that.

And all of them? Self-serving.

Her comment grates.

"You *have* a choice."

I say the words as if I believe them. As if I didn't move her into my room purely for efficiency—to ensure that even if she stumbled in at two in the morning, I could wake up, roll her over, and conduct my regularly scheduled impregnation attempts. I'm a man on a mission, right?

But her assuming she doesn't have a choice? That pisses me off.

"What if I said no?"

The words sound real enough. The way her ass presses back against my hard cock? Not so much.

She's testing me. Pushing me. And although my control is hanging on by a thread, I don't bother pointing out the obvious. That she's rubbing against me hoping to spark a fire.

Instead, I yank her panties the rest of the way off, toss them onto the floor where they belong, and shove my sweats down with one hand. Then I press my body over hers, weight barely there, supporting myself on my forearms as I cage her in.

"Say no." My voice is low, vibrating against her back. "And I'll go to sleep."

Not that it'll do much for my cause, which is knocking her up, getting her out of my bed, and—preferably—no longer having to deal with the way she steals everything, including my sanity.

She moans.

Fucking moans.

And my cock practically gains an extra inch in pure appreciation for the sound.

Great. Add that to the list.

My secrets? *Stolen.*

My ability to think straight? *Gone.*

My dick's autonomy? *Completely hijacked.*

I slide a hand down her side, fingers tracing the dip of her waist before I grip her hip and tug her up, positioning her exactly how I want her.

No response.

Oh, so that's the game we're playing?

She's trying to kill me. That's the only explanation.

Logical, really. If she's already stolen everything else, why not go for my actual life?

I grit my teeth. "Allie—"

"Fuck me, Rico."

Well...shit.

Who am I to tell my wife no?

Allie

I'M AT WAR.

A battle between my rational brain and my absolutely traitorous, husband-obsessed vagina.

Seriously, there's no gracious way to say it. The thing between my legs has gone completely rogue. It doesn't care that Rico is an infuriating control freak. It doesn't care that I want to punch him square in his chiseled, broody face. Nope. It only cares about one thing—getting another orgasm (or, let's be honest, *several*) before I take my swing.

It's been two days since dear husband decided to forcibly relocate me to his room, and if he insists on having me in his sacred little man cave, then he's going to get the *full experience* of living with a wife.

Which means?

I am waging a slow, calculated, aesthetic takeover.

When he left for work on Day One, there was a Post-it Note on his pillow with his "Thing of the Day." The bastard.

So I retaliated.

It started the morning after my unapproved relocation. While my coffee brewed, I hiked my happy ass upstairs, grabbed *every* single item of clothing I own, and moved it straight into *our* closet.

Let's talk about this closet. It's the size of a boutique, complete with built-in drawers, a center island, and lighting and the poor thing is sobbing at how empty the glorious space is — it's a crime that Pinterest lovers would faint to see. The man's *entire* wardrobe occupies maybe a quarter of it, if that. A few bespoke suits, some fitted dress shirts, polos, and exactly three variations of the same black T-shirt. His drawers? Denim. His shoes? Sneakers—except for the two lonely pairs of designer loafers I'm positive he breaks out for only special occasions.

Don't worry, I quickly fixed the imbalance.

Every single one of my dresses, skirts, handbags, and heels now graces the racks, claiming their rightful space. And just to add a sprinkle of *petty seasoning*, they're all clothes Rico *bought* when he handed me a black Amex after our wedding and said, *Use it.*

Oh, I used it, baby.

His once minimalistic, neutral-toned, limited palette wardrobe? Banished to the far corner of its own kingdom.

Welcome to *married life*, sweetheart.

When I got home that night, Rico was standing in the closet, arms crossed, exuding enough brooding energy to fuel a Hulu series. The closet—now fifty percent high fashion and seventy-five percent mine—was his personal nightmare, and it took a lot of self-will to not smile.

So, I did what any dutiful wife would do.

I wiggled my fingers in a cheerful *hello*, breezed past him with my toiletries, and waltzed straight into the bathroom, ignoring the fact I had just committed high-level spousal warfare.

Two minutes later?

I was pinned.

Apparently, my bold display of defiance hit a nerve, because Rico tossed me onto the bed and proceeded to ruin me in the most delicious way possible.

Three times.

By the end of the night, we were sweaty, panting, and sprawled out more exhausted than if we'd just finished an aggressive CrossFit session.

So, obviously...

I had to test the theory again.

Enter Day Two.

First order of business: operation bathroom invasion.

I gathered every single toiletry from my en suite—makeup, skincare, hair products, my entire collection of shower gels, and even my bath salts—and moved them all into his bathroom.

But I didn't stop there.

I strategically left out my curling iron on the counter, because before I arrived, his bathroom looked unused. Everything tucked away. Counters bare.

Well, not anymore.

Now, my very necessary products are everywhere.

Next? Home decor.

I draped my light teal fluffy blanket over his depressingly dark bedding because contrast. I even roped Vinnie into helping me move my favorite reading chair from my room into his.

Rico's eyebrows will twitch when he sees it. Vinnie's eyebrows never recovered from seeing it happen.

I'm not stopping there.

I lined my nightstand with books from Violet, set up my alarm clock, and even—*gasp*—casually tossed a few of my clothes on the floor instead of in the hamper.

Because if we're playing house, then we're *really playing house.*

Tonight, when Rico walks through that door and sees his once sterile sanctuary now bursting with me?

He's going to lose his damn mind.

And I'm going to love every second.

Even if my thighs clench at the thought of his reaction, I'm fully committed to this plan. And let's be real—if his reaction involves a lot of sex, is this a punishment for me or him? Hard to say.

I pluck this morning's Post-it from his pillow, more than aware that dear husband left at the crack of dawn. I mean, five in the morning? What kind of sadist willingly wakes up when it's still basically night?

But the real shocker? He didn't toss and turn all night. No staring at the ceiling. No silent suffering. He was *out* cold. Maybe all the "activity" helped. Or maybe the sheer exhaustion of putting up with my antics finally caught up to him. Either way, he looked obnoxiously peaceful when I got up at 3 AM to relieve my bladder.

And of course, in his perfect, borderline *psychopath-who-probably-alphabetizes-his-socks* handwriting, he left his daily share on the pillow. I'm wondering if these are breadcrumbs. Follow them enough and they lead me to the secret vault where all of Rico's personality hides.

Rico: I need a fan on when I sleep, which is why there is a ceiling fan in this room and not in yours.

I blink at the note. Then again.

That's why he made this the master bedroom? The fan?

For months, I thought he stayed down here because he wanted to be as far away from me as possible. To strategically remove himself from the general area where a husband and wife might have to—*gasp*—interact. But no. It's the fan.

Honestly, I wouldn't put it past him to have simply installed one in my room and then moved upstairs instead. Which means this revelation is either a weird, unexpected insight into his preferences or just another way to mess with my head.

For all I know, he Googled, random useless facts to share with your wife just to mess with her.

Regardless, I have returned the favor by leaving my own Post-it note responses. But unlike him, I don't put them on his pillow. No, that would be too easy. Instead, I leave mine on the one thing I know he touches first thing every morning—the coffee pot.

Allie: I've decided I no longer like my coffee with cream and sugar. Instead, it's just a splash of half-and-half.

If he's going to keep things random, why can't I?

This is war, after all.

Allie

"OPENING NIGHT! ARE YOU excited?"

Sienna's voice pierces through my eardrums and I physically flinch, pulling the phone away before my eardrum files for assault.

Vinnie glances at me in the rearview mirror, clearly amused. I just smile and nod, because what else can I do? We're on our way to the restaurant, and I need to focus.

Instead of opening at our usual five in the evening, we're holding off service until seven, only for those who booked reservations for the debut celebration. Tonight isn't just about introducing me as head chef—it's about launching the *new direction* of Via Napoli.

Changing the way a restaurant operates is risky. It's akin to telling a die-hard coffee addict they can only have decaf from now on—people panic. Some don't survive the transition. But, I have a vision.

Chef Monroe had a system—one that worked for years. Guests booked months in advance to enjoy his à la carte menu, expecting the same flawless execution every time. Now, I'm flipping the script.

Via Napoli will no longer be just a restaurant—*it'll be an experience.*

Gone are the days of leisurely ordering from a menu. Instead, we'll serve a tasting menu—an ever-changing, carefully curated five-course meal that keeps guests on their toes. No repeats. No spoilers. You book a reservation; you get whatever I decide you're eating that night.

Risky? Hell yes.

Worth it? Jury's still in deliberations and taking their sweet ass time about it too.

The restaurant will open at six, allowing us to seat everyone, get drinks and the first course out, and then from seven to ten, it's game on. A three-hour culinary adventure.

Will people love it? I sure as hell hope so. Will some of the food critics, a.k.a. blogger gremlins who couldn't fry an egg if their life depended on it, hate it purely for the drama? Absolutely.

"I am. But I also want to puke."

I finally respond when I'm sure I can hear properly again.

Sienna, a walking bottle of sunshine with a high SPF rating, gasps.

"Oh my god, are you pregnant?"

The squeak. The *actual* squeak in her voice.

I swear, in this family, nausea equals pregnancy. Stomach bug? Pregnant. Ate bad sushi? Pregnant. Drank one too many espresso shots and now you're vibrating at a frequency only dogs can hear? Definitely pregnant.

I, however, am not pregnant. Nope. Not even a little.

Aunt Flo arrived with the enthusiasm of a vengeful ex that first week at the restaurant—which, conveniently, also doubled as the reason I didn't end up crawling into my husband's bed, desperate and ready to lure him in with siren-level seduction.

Did I tell Rico?

Nope.

Interesting how the second I stopped seeking him out, he moved me to his room.

Nonna might've been onto something—apparently, my husband operates on exactly one brain, and it's not the one responsible for logic and reasoning.

Not that I was exploiting it. I was too busy juggling a new job, mood swings, and cramps that made me want to commit crimes.

But he didn't know that.

"You'll do fine! Dom and I got a sitter, and we'll be there. Is Rico excited?"

"Is Rico ever excited?"

"Okay, fair point. But hey, Vi's emerged from her writing cave, and she's coming with Alex, which means cameras everywhere, since the paparazzi track her like she has an AirTag glued to her behind. Rosa, bless her soul, is watching all the kids—ours and theirs. I offered to hire a babysitter, but Dom has scared away every qualified childcare provider on the East Coast. So, we'll see you at seven?"

"I mean, I'm headed there now, but yes, I'll see you both then."

When I hang up, my stomach twists, and not in a good way. Not the *had too much coffee and my intestines are staging a revolt* way, but the *might throw up in my lap from nerves* way.

I didn't eat breakfast, which is probably mistake number one, and the two cups of coffee sloshing around in my stomach aren't helping. But, if I'm being honest, my anxiety has nothing to do with the debut itself.

I left a note for Rico on the coffee pot this morning, a simple reminder about tonight. Despite our newfound game of coexisting in the same room—where taunting each other seems to be the primary love language—I also sent him a text. *A real one.*

I told him I hoped he'd come.

That it would mean a lot.

And in doing so, I basically flayed myself open and handed him a knife. Because the brutal truth is, despite my best efforts, I think I'm falling in love with my husband.

A man who barely looks at me unless he wants sex. A man who speaks to me in five-word sentences, max. A man who has made it painfully clear that we are nothing more than a contractual obligation.

And yet, here I am, *hoping*.

I won't be heartbroken if tonight goes poorly. But if my husband doesn't show up for my debut?

I might be.

He's made no promises. He's done nothing to suggest he wants to be here. So why am I sitting in this car, pathetically hoping that—for once—he will?

"You doing okay?"

Vinnie's watching me in the rearview mirror, fingers drumming against the steering wheel.

"Just nervous."

"Don't be."

Easy for him to say.

"I've watched you work your ass off for two weeks. The staff loves you. Trust me, when I sit in the corner, they forget I exist. You'd be surprised what I overhear."

"You? Invisible? Vinnie, you're a six-foot-something wall of muscle who wears all black and looms in the corner. No one forgets you exist."

He shrugs. "Still. They're happy with the changes. That means you should be too."

I nod, gnawing on my lower lip before realizing—shit, I cannot show up with a chewed-up lip for photos. I force myself to stop.

"What are you really stressed about?"

Vinnie masterfully maneuvers the monster SUV between two cars, effectively blocking three lanes of traffic in the only acceptable method of merging Manhattan-style—pure, unadulterated aggression.

"The debut. What else?"

Lie. Big, fat, ugly lie.

Okay, sure, I'm a little nervous about the debut. Specifically, about the food bloggers, whose sole purpose in life is to nitpick every spice choice and splash of presentation on your plates. I mean, if you want a job where you can rip apart every microscopic detail of someone's life work and act superior while doing it, become a food critic.

But that's not what's tying my stomach in knots.

"I think you're nervous he won't come."

Vinnie doesn't even look at me when he says it. He just casually drops that truth bomb while ignoring the cab driver, who is now leaning halfway out his window, screaming a rather colorful array of curses at us.

"So what if he doesn't come? He never said he would."

And there it is. The deflation. The tiny bubble of hope popping when reality pokes it with a needle.

Hope. That bitch. She gets me every time.

I know Rico doesn't care. I know he values his computer keyboard more than me. And yet, there's still this tiny, ridiculous part of me that wants to believe he might surprise me.

Vinnie clears his throat, glancing at the cabbie, who is now rolling up beside us, still cursing at full volume. Without hesitation, Vinnie rolls down his tinted window, slides down his sunglasses, and stares.

The cabbie takes one look at him, goes dead silent, and slowly slinks back into his seat, facing forward.

To me, Vinnie is just a human-sized teddy bear who carries a gun. But I'm not stupid. He was trained as a Cosa Nostra bodyguard, and fun fact, he was supposed to go to the Bennettis—aside from the Bratva—bodyguards for the Bennetti family are quite talented. Had he not changed places with his brother, I might never have had such a reliable person next to me for most of my life. He can be all warm smiles and bear hugs to me, but to everyone else? He's a terrifying motherfucker.

"If he doesn't come, I can break a bone or two."

Vinnie's jaw clenches, and he's serious about it too.

"No broken bones. My marriage is already hanging by a shredded thread. I don't need it completely incinerated."

But as I stare out the window, watching the city blur past, I say something I don't even believe.

"He'll come."

And even as the words leave my lips, I know I'm lying to myself.

Rico

"RICO, LET IT GO, dude."

Dom is standing at the entrance of my office again, arms crossed and all judgy — as if he wasn't the same workaholic who used to survive on two hours of sleep and spite before he domesticated himself.

I don't even bother looking up this time. "No."

"You can work on it tomorrow."

"I could. Or I could not let some basement-dwelling hacker breach my systems while you sip wine at my wife's restaurant."

That earns me a sharp exhale—Dom's version of flipping me off—but he doesn't leave. Just lingers.

If we were actually identical, that whole twin telepathy nonsense would tell him to sit his ass down and help me solve his merger crisis. But no, instead, he's here doing his obnoxious fairy hovering routine.

I've been staring at this screen since four in the morning.

I should be exhausted—the kind of exhaustion that turns your brain to cement and makes your body move with all the grace of a rusted-out engine. I should be clawing for caffeine and begging someone to hook an IV drip of espresso straight into my veins, but that would require talking and begging—two things I don't do.

But no.

I blame my wife.

Apparently, she steals my energy now too, because after fucking her into the mattress last night, I passed out. Dead. Slept straight through the night as if I'm some well-adjusted human being.

Unacceptable.

Worse? I forgot she was even there.

Then I woke up—somewhere between midnight and dawn—and there she was. Sprawled across my bed. Her braid half undone, lips parted, hogging my space.

A space thief, and I didn't *not* enjoy it. Can't say I'm enjoying this alternate side of me.

That should've been in the contract. I should've asked Marco before signing my life away if she was a closet clepto—because so far, the list keeps growing.

She even moved her crap into my closet. My perfectly organized, highly efficient closet. And now? It looks as if a boutique threw up in it. Clothes everywhere. Colors where colors shouldn't be. Shoes taking up valuable real estate.

And the bathroom?

Kill me now.

Her shit is *everywhere*. Skincare, makeup, a curling iron. I don't even know what half the bottles do, but I know I knocked one over this morning, and it leaked some kind of shimmering liquid that glittered. *Glittered.* I had to wash my hands three times to get it off.

And yet, instead of telling her to haul her ass back upstairs where she belongs, I don't.

Instead, I keep hoping she'll finally tell me she's pregnant so I can kick her out of my bed and reclaim my sanity.

This isn't how this was supposed to go.

I *should not* be enjoying this.

I *should not* be watching her mouth while she talks just because I know how it looks.

I *should not* be thinking about the way she smells—honeysuckle and vanilla and fucking sin—when she's not even in the room.

And yet, here I am.

What is wrong with me?

Besides, there's something far more irritating than my wife right now—a feat I didn't think possible.

The hacker.

The faceless, self-important little shit who's screwed with our systems and introduces themselves as Blue.

Blue.

What kind of pretentious jackass chooses a color as their alias? If you're going to go that route, at least put some effort into it. Something ominous. Blood Red. Phantom Black. Rusted Soul Brown. Hell, even Decaying Corpse Green would show a little creativity. But no. Just Blue—as if they're trying to be cryptic, cool and failing spectacularly or he has a dark fantasy involving a Smurf. Either way, he's a pain in my ass, regardless of his name.

Alex and Dom have been stuck fielding panicked calls from the board—ancient old geezers who wouldn't know a firewall from a fire hazard—while I've been working ungodly hours with my skeleton crew, hunting down every backdoor this Smurf-lover boy keeps leaving open.

The rate I've been clenching and unclenching my fists hasn't gone unnoticed. I'm positive that at some point, I'll wake up to find them permanently balled up.

I can't tell if it's the hacker pissing me off or if it's something deeper.

Something I've buried.

Something my wife has taken a sledgehammer to, breaking down walls I spent years fortifying.

Not. Good.

Dom still stands there, as if my ignoring him wasn't hint enough.

"You have Allie's restaurant thing tonight. You'll be there, *right*?"

Fuck.

The restaurant.

She's only texted me about it a dozen times. Left a note on the coffee pot. Brought it up in person. And yet, I still pushed it to the back of my mind, because unlike my wife, I actually respect the terms of our agreement—which technically states she's not allowed to discuss work with me. Not that she gives a shit.

I exhale through my nose. "I'll be there."

I may be an asshole, but even I know that missing my wife's grand debut as a chef is a low I'm not willing to sink to.

Dom tilts his head. "Sienna and I are going straight from the office. I could have Elias grab your suit and bring it here so you can ride with us."

I freeze mid-keystroke and stare at him.

Dom.

The brother who has never once in his life offered me a ride. Or to have his driver rummage through my closet.

All violations. *All* unacceptable. *All* major red flags.

Hard. Fucking. Pass.

"I'm fine."

Besides, I rushed to the office the second I got an alert that Smurf Dick had attempted another breach. So, I need to get home, shower, and change into one of three suits I own—because unlike the brother standing before me, I don't have a personal stylist or a closet that resembles a high-end men's boutique.

Dom's wardrobe is disturbing.

Custom suits. Three dozen of them. Organized by color, season, and thread count.

Thread count.

I'll be throwing on whatever suit is closest to the door, probably missing a tie, and hoping for the best.

At least Allie won't care.

"Rico..."

I keep my eyes on the screen, fingers tapping impatiently on the keyboard as if the rhythmic clicking will somehow signal my disinterest in whatever urgent family matter Dom is here to lecture me about. But when his looming presence doesn't dissipate, I exhale sharply and—against my better judgment—look up.

"You *can't* miss this."

"I'm aware." My voice is edged with an irritation that should send him running. It doesn't. If anything, Dom looks encouraged. Clearly, he enjoys being a massive inconvenience in my day.

Without another word, I tug my headphones over my ears. If I'm lucky, he'll take the hint and—

Knock. Knock.

The asshole actually knocks on my doorframe.

"You aren't dragging this hacker situation out to..." He trails off, choosing his words carefully, and I have a feeling I won't appreciate what comes out next.

I arch a brow, waiting for him to grow a spine, and spit it out.

"...delay or possibly even ruin the merger?"

I blink at him. Seriously?

Do I hate the merger? With every fiber of my very being. I'd rather go through a full-body wax (and that includes the undercarriage of my balls) than watch our family business get diluted by the corporate douchebaggery of the Locke brothers. But would I sabotage the company I've dedicated my entire life to?

Not even on my worst day.

"You're more than welcome to step in. Maybe have Cruz or Kaden or... whatever the fuck their names are, take over."

"You really don't know their names?"

"Why would I?" I type out another line of code. "I have no intentions of speaking to them. Ever."

Dom pinches the bridge of his nose. "Look, I had to ask. It's a convenient excuse to avoid your wife. And it gets you out of a merger we all know you hate."

"I'm not a selfish prick."

I don't need to look up to know he's rolling his eyes so hard he probably just gave himself a concussion.

"...I'm not *that much* of a selfish prick," I amend.

"Better." Dom taps his phone against his mouth—an action so repulsive I nearly gag. The number of germs on a phone's surface? Seventeen thousand bacteria per square inch. Yeah. I googled it. Yeah. I nearly dry-heaved when I read it. Therefore, I keep industrial-strength sanitizing wipes in my pocket.

"If you must work, have someone else do it. There are other competent people here. You don't have to do everything yourself."

"But I am the only one with the skills for this."

"Locke's people are good. You'd know that if you, well... met them."

Sure. Let me just schedule a meet-and-greet with my new colleagues right after I host a farewell party for the last shred of my freedom.

Before I can tell Dom exactly where he can shove his helpful little suggestion, my phone pings.

And then another ping.

And another.

One from Mama. One from Papa. One from Allie.

I stare at my screen, unimpressed.

> Mama: Do not miss Allie's restaurant opening. You are a husband now. You have to show up and support your wife.

> Papa: You will be there tonight, right? Your Mama has threatened me in Spanish and Italian if you don't. We all know what that means, and I will be the victim since you will run away faster than she can catch you.

> Allie: I know you will read this, and not respond, but if you could please come tonight, it would mean the world to me.

My jaw tightens.

I tap on Allie's message, scroll up to the very first text she ever sent me, and open the info tab.

194 messages.

Not a single one ever replied to. Every single one read.

We've been married for five weeks and two days.

I'm not counting.

But apparently, my wife has had my number for fifty-three days and has sent an average of *3.6 texts per day*, still expecting a response.

And I never noticed...

Not until she slowed down her texting frequency.

I scroll back down, my thumb hesitating over the keyboard.

Then, before I can think too hard about it, I type.

> Rico: I will be there.

I hit send.

Flip my phone to silent and turn it face down.

And then I get back to work.

My brothers think I'm dragging my feet with Smurf Man, but eradicating a hacker who actually knows what they're doing takes *time*. If they understood even half of what I do, they'd know that. But they don't. They assume I press a few keys, mutter some dark magic, and voilà—problem solved.

Idiots.

This isn't some cut-rate movie where the hacker taps a keyboard three times and announces *I'm in*. No, it's a war. A patient, calculated game of outmaneuvering someone who, unfortunately, is *almost* as good as me. *Almost*.

And that's what I live for. The rush. The challenge. The electric thrill that hums in my veins when I finally take them down, when I watch them scramble, knowing I've outplayed them. That's when I feel *alive*. It's all here—staring at a screen, locked in a battle only I can win.

This is my passion. My addiction. The one thing I excel at, the one thing that makes sense. And I'll be damned if I let my brothers piss all over it with their baseless accusations. I'm not taking my time. I'm playing the long game. And when I strike?

It's game over.

Allie

"Allie, this is unbelievable."

Mama's hand wraps around my arm, tugging me down to her level at the table before she presses a kiss to my cheek. Her eyes are gleaming, her smile radiant, and her entire presence beams with pride. It should make me feel warm. Happy even.

But the only warmth I feel is the heat simmering under my skin from rage.

Not at her. Not at the restaurant. Not even at the food bloggers sitting in the corner with their notepads, whispering what I can only hope will be positive reviews that go live before midnight.

No. I reserve my rage exclusively for one person.

Rico.

The one person who has never shown an interest in this marriage outside of its sole purpose (read: pregnancy) said he would come, and yet he's not here. So, why am I disappointed? Shocked even?

The doors opened at seven, reservations filled every table, and the night has moved seamlessly. The wine pairings are on point, each course is rolling out specifically when it should, and the restaurant is filled with murmurs of praise. It's exactly the opening every chef dreams of.

The Bennetti family has taken over the entire back half of the restaurant on the dais that sits just below the private dining rooms. A sea of dark suits, perfectly styled hair, and the undeniable presence of power. Everyone is here.

Cousins. Siblings. Nonna. Mama. Papa.

The only person notably missing—three courses in?

My husband.

I force a smile, but my entire body is wobbling under the weight of it.

"Thank you, Mama," I manage, squeezing her arm.

Papa watches me closely, his affectionate brown eyes filled with something too familiar and definitely not something I need tonight of all nights. Pity.

I know that look well. I saw it in the weeks leading up to my wedding. I saw it *on my wedding day* when I stood at the altar with a man who showed up with all the enthusiasm of a tax audit. And I see it now, in the middle of what should be *my night*.

"I need to get back to the kitchen, but I'll come out again after dessert, okay?" I kiss Nonna's cheek, but before I can step away, her hand clasps around mine, holding me in place.

It's a simple touch. Just a small squeeze.

But it's enough to make my carefully contained emotions threaten to spill over.

I nod quickly, pulling away before the dam cracks and I become *that girl*—the one who cries in front of a full dining room on the most important night of her career.

The moment I slip through the double doors of the kitchen, I let out a long breath, but my body is still humming with tension.

Smiling at the patrons.

Thanking them for their compliments.

Acknowledging how much they love the new concept.

I nod. I smile. I thank them.

Over and over.

All the while feeling as though my face is cracking into a million tiny pieces and my heart has already demolished itself.

The food is exceptional. Every course was flawlessly prepared. The team is streaming along, and yet every bite I take from the line turns to ash in my mouth.

Kai finally took over tasting, throwing me a glance every five seconds but wisely keeping his mouth shut. He made the mistake of asking if I was okay once, then quickly realized I was a woman on a warpath and he was in a place loaded with nothing but very sharp objects.

When I eventually find a minute to breathe, I duck into the small alcove where we store the pottery, pressing myself against the cool wall and wiping away the one persistent tear that dares to escape.

You will not cry over him.

You will not cry over a man who made it abundantly clear what this is.

I pull my phone from my pocket, checking the time—8:42 PM—and then, against my better judgment, I check for a text. A missed call. *Something.*

Nothing.

My stomach clenches as another tear betrays me, sliding down my cheek.

I wipe it away fast.

I should have known better.

I *know* better.

But that naïve flicker of hope? That ridiculous belief that maybe, just maybe, I matter to him in some capacity? It refuses to disappear.

Did he do this on purpose? Did he ignore my messages all day just to toy with me? To punish me for taking over his closet? For pushing his buttons?

Would he really be that cruel?

A throat clears, and my head snaps up.

Kai.

His arms are crossed, and his expression is unreadable as he stands in front of the alcove, watching me.

I shove my phone into my pocket and straighten, forcing every ounce of emotion from my face.

"Yes?"

Kai holds up both hands, like he's warding off an *actual* beast. "I know you said not to ask, but..." He pauses, eyes softening. "Is there *anything* I can do?"

"Yes. You can focus on making sure the Secondo is ready to go out." My words are clipped as I adjust the chain around my neck—a chain that suddenly feels heavier than ever.

Kai hesitates, then glances over his shoulder at the kitchen, where the line is still running efficiently.

"Allie..." His voice is quiet as he takes a slight step forward, placing a hand on my shoulder. "I know you're upset he's not here, and it's okay to be upset."

"It's fine. I told you. Our relationship isn't like that."

"So, you're crying because... what? You snorted an onion?"

"Maybe I did." Hell, I wish I had an onion right now. At least then, I'd have a justifiable reason for the tears burning the backs of my eyes.

Kai doesn't buy it.

And instead of pressing, his hand tightens on my shoulder before he pulls me into his chest, wrapping both arms around me.

It's warm. Solid. Safe.

I don't even care that my face is currently buried in his chef's coat, probably smearing mascara and the remnants of my dignity all over the lavish fabric.

"Maybe he's running late," he offers.

I snort. *Loudly.* "Yeah. Maybe he's giving a TED Talk on how to emotionally scar your wife in five easy steps.

Kai chuckles, pulling back just enough to examine my face. He reaches into his apron and pulls out a tissue, handing it over.

"Here. For the lingering goth look you're sporting."

I take it, ignoring that comment, and start dabbing at my eyes.

"Thanks."

I follow Kai back into the kitchen just as the Secondo is being plated. The saucier catches sight of me and visibly stiffens, her eyes darting to Kai like he's her emotional support human. I may have... over-corrected her plating on the Antipasto. Okay, I *definitely* did. First, the sauce was too far to the left. Then, too far to the right. Then, well, just *wrong*.

I was emotional. Sue me.

But right now, I'm all smiles—cool, collected, and totally not a kitchen dictator on the verge of a breakdown. "Looks perfect," I say, flashing what I hope is an encouraging grin.

She offers a smile in return, though it resembles someone narrowly escaping an encounter with a mountain lion more than someone receiving a compliment. Progress.

One of the biggest changes I made to the restaurant was ditching the godforsaken white chef's coats. Chef Monroe had insisted on tradition. I, however, did not need my team walking around looking like a crime scene by course three — we deal in marinara for hell's sake. Instead, I switched the crew to a deep red—practical, elegant, and way better at hiding every splatter of sauce, grease, and sanity-draining moments. Their names and stations are embroidered in gold, tying into the restaurant's aesthetic. My coat? Black. Because I like to look the part of the kitchen overlord. Kai, meanwhile, wears the deep red but with black accents on his rolled sleeves, setting him apart on the line.

We make our way toward the back of the kitchen, and he holds out a shot of tequila.

I narrow my eyes. "Why do we have tequila in an *Italian* restaurant?"

"Because it solves the world's problems?" He downs his in one go, not even cringing.

I follow suit, the burn searing down my throat, instantly heating my already very warm body. Between the tequila and the suffocating tension pressing against my ribs, I'm teetering between relaxed and ready to throw myself into the nearest walk-in freezer.

Kai takes one look at my expression and pours another.

I wiggle my empty shot glass with dramatic flair. "Make it a double. Apparently, my husband has mistaken my very public, very important debut for an event he definitely does not need to attend."

Kai doesn't even hesitate. "I'll make it a triple."

Rico

THERE'S A LOUD CRASH—SHARP, jarring, muffled slightly by my noise-canceling head-phones. Then hands—multiple—grip my arms, shoving me upright. They yanked my headphones off, and instantly, the blissful white noise replaced by a disorganized chorus of Italian curses.

I blink, slowly peeling my eyes open, and what greets me is nothing short of a horror scene.

Mama stands over my desk, fury transmitting off her petite frame. Nonna is right next to her, clutching her rosary and likely praying for my soul. And just when I think this fever dream can't get worse, my gaze shifts past them to find my entire family crammed into my office.

Cousins. Siblings. My father. Even my sisters, who I'm fairly certain only show up when they can capitalize on my suffering.

"What the hell? Who died?" My voice is like sandpaper scraping against my throat.

Did I fall asleep?

Between spending my nights wearing my wife out—because apparently, my solution to every problem is to make sure she's too exhausted to start any more shit—and waking up at the asscrack of dawn to stay one step ahead of Smurfie, I haven't exactly been resting.

Smurfie. That keyboard-toting little shit.

I'm out here battling an IT gremlin who probably lives in his mother's basement, existing solely on Mountain Dew and Takis.

"You will soon," Mama bites out, her accent thick with bitterness as she turns to my father. "You talk to him before I break his face."

She storms out, my cousins trailing behind her while she curses threats in all three of her languages. Not going to lie, my balls have wormed their way up into my stomach quivering at the idea.

I squint at my screen. Every blink might as well drag a Brillo pad over my corneas. My screens are too bright. My office lights? Too sharp. Even my existence is too much effort right now.

"What time is it?" I reach for my phone, ignoring the shrill ringing in my skull. No clocks on my monitors—perfect. I check my notifications, and... Jesus.

Dozens of missed calls.

Sixty-two unread messages.

And not a single one from my wife.

That's when I see it. The time.

11:29 pm.

"Rico," my father starts, his voice eerily calm, which is oddly more unsettling than Mama's fury. "You worked? You stayed at *work*?"

He says it as if I haven't spent my entire life doing *exactly* this.

"I fell asleep waiting on my checks. Why is everyone acting like I just—"

Then it hits me.

Shit.

I fumble with my phone, scrolling through my texts.

Nothing from Allie.

Not a single message.

Just the one sent by me at noon. Twelve hours ago.

> Rico: I will be there.

I scour a hand over my face. "I fell asleep."

I'm not sure who I'm talking to—the room full of judgmental relatives or the cruel, merciless God above—but it's the truth. I fell asleep.

"No, you fucked up," a voice snaps, and my head jerks up just in time to see Sienna standing there, arms folded, blue eyes blazing.

Oh, shit.

Little Miss Sunshine and Rainbows just swore at me. The woman who says *sugar snaps* instead of *shit*. The woman who refuses to utter the word fuck and instead will say *fudge noodles*.

The entire room falls silent. Even my siblings, who thrive on my downfall, look concerned.

"I believe what my wife is trying to say," Dom interjects, placing a hand on her shoulder like he's handling a wild animal and I am hoping someone is armed with a tranquilizer dart just in case, "is that you didn't show up to Allie's debut."

Then he looks around. "Can you all give us a minute?"

Sienna doesn't move.

"I'm not done with him," her voice a low growl.

Dom leans down, murmurs something in her ear, and she huffs, shooting me one last death glare before storming out.

And just when I think I can breathe, I turn and find another set of murderous eyes trained on me.

Violet.

She just *tsks*—a simple, condescending little sound that somehow hurts worse. Then she walks out.

I sit there, staring at the door, feeling the weight of my stupidity smother me.

I didn't just fuck up.

I really fucked up.

Alex and Dom step into the office, followed by Marco, who closes the door with the comic finality of a mob hit. The space is compact, but now it feels like a coffin, one I'm being sealed into with three judgmental pricks looming over me.

Marco, who doesn't go anywhere unless it involves violence or high-end liquor, is the first to make eye contact. "You went?" If there's one person I expected to dodge an event with a carefully crafted excuse, it was him.

"Of course." His tone is dry, unimpressed. "That woman's cooking—your *wife's fucking cooking*—is amazing. I ate her food all the time when she crashed at my apartment. So, where the fuck were *you*?"

Considering they just found me unconscious at my desk, I feel no need to state the undeniable. But Dom and Alex? They're staring at me as if I ran over their metaphorical dog.

"I fell asleep."

I should call her. I *have* to call her. *Even though I have literally never called my wife before.* Not once. That realization alone makes me feel like an even bigger asshole than I already knew I was.

Wait.

"Where is Allie?" Because she's not the type to sulk in a corner. No, my wife would kick down my office door, give me a lecture laced with profanity, and then—knowing her—leave a post-it note somewhere in my office reminding me exactly how and why I'm the worst.

Marco is clearly enjoying this too much. "We told her to go out and celebrate."

I exhale, but he's not done.

"With her team..." He pauses. "And *Kai*."

The muscle in my jaw ticks. I hate that guy. I really, really do.

Not entirely sure if I mean Marco or Kai at this point. They both qualify.

Ignoring my cousin's smug little sneer, I tap the call button on Allie's contact, hating the fact that this is my first time calling my wife. I always assumed the first time would be something mundane, like *Hey, grab milk* or *I locked myself out*. Not I'm a bastard, and I fell asleep instead of showing up for your big night.

The phone rings.

And rings.

And rings.

Then goes to voicemail.

A cheerful voicemail. A voice I rarely hear from my wife, one that's light, taunting—one that sure as fuck isn't meant for me.

Hey, you've reached me! I'm busy right now, but leave a message, and I'll call you back!

I lower my phone, staring at it, then look up at the three men waiting for me to confess the obvious.

"I fucked up."

Marco snorts. "Oh, did you? I was just wondering."

"Ya think?" Dom deadpans.

This next part is going to physically pain me, but I have *no* choice.

"What should I do?"

Alex doesn't hesitate. "Go home."

I frown. "Go home?"

"Yeah. Go home, be ready to grovel and beg when she gets back."

Beg? Beg?

Absolutely *not*.

Why can't I just go to her now? Preferably drag her away from Kai while I'm at it? I grind my molars together, and Alex, knowing exactly where my mind is going, cuts me off before I can even suggest it.

"She's out." He glances at his phone. "Vinnie is with her. He already checked in with Antonio. She's laughing, having a good time. You've done enough harm. The last thing you need to do is crash her night and make it worse."

I don't like this. Not one bit. But my brother is right. If I show up, if I storm in and demand to talk to her, I'll look even more like an asshole than I already do.

Marco shakes his head, scoffing. "If you were gonna fuck up this bad, you should've done it early on, man. Set expectations real low. Now? Now, you've gotta make an effort."

The last thing I need is to turn into my brothers—men who willingly handed over their balls to their wives, gift-wrapped and all. I'm not begging. I'm not groveling.

I'll apologize, sure. It *was* a mistake. I intended to leave work, go home, change, and go to the restaurant. I fell asleep. Partially her fault, really. If she wasn't keeping me up at night with all the sex—

Yeah. That wouldn't go over well. Probably best to keep that to myself.

"Fine." I push back from my desk. "I'll go home."

Allie

WE LEFT THE KITCHEN with the team promising to come in early and clean up. A miracle, really, considering half of them were already six shots deep and talking about getting matching tattoos by the end of the night.

It was a night to celebrate, and I refused to be the gloomy wet blanket that ruined the vibe, even though all I wanted to do was go home, ugly cry into a pillow, and let my good friends Ben and Jerry emotionally support me through the five stages of grief.

Instead, I let the team drag me out to a dive bar that no doubt violated multiple health codes, sat in a questionably sticky chair, and nursed a single glass of wine while my fingers compulsively tugged at the chain around my neck. My rings were still on it. Not because of some dramatic, *screw you* statement to Rico. I just... didn't have the energy. The energy to be mad. To yank the rings off the chain. To scream. Nothing.

I was tired. Tired from the day, from the stress, from the defeat.

And I was so over feeling this way. Getting my hopes up only for them to crash and burn spectacularly.

This was *my* night. *My* achievement. *My* success. Rico hadn't shown up—so what? The contract never said he had to support me, just that we had to be a couple in public.

Still, I'd wasted too much emotional energy stewing, and now I was running on fumes.

"You should go home. You look like shit." Kai grinned at me over the rim of his drink.

"Wow. Thank you. Really. That was the boost of confidence I needed."

"I just felt someone should point it out." He glanced down at his phone and frowned. "Besides, it's late, and we all have work tomorrow. Unless you want to give us the day off?" His brows waggled.

"Not a chance."

I stood, groaning and feeling three times my age. It wasn't even that the day was longer than usual, but I felt as though I'd physically been put through an Olympic-level endurance test. Vinnie stood near the entrance, his hulking form practically blocking out the bar's dim lighting. Cassie had picked the place, which meant it was a true dive—rickety chairs, mismatched tables, and a collection of rusted metal decor. The only benefit was that booze at dive bars was more affordable. The fancier the decor, the higher the price tag on the same damn drink.

Vinnie's eyes met mine, and I gave him a small nod. He returned it without a word. We'd been together long enough that words were optional. The man could practically read my mind, which was good, because mine was...complicated right now.

"See you tomorrow, boss!" Someone yelled, and the rest of the drunken crew echoed their goodbyes, one of them sloshing their beer over the table in an overzealous salute.

"You all better show up. Hungover or not." I waved as Kai followed me out, Vinnie a few steps behind us.

"You gonna say anything to him when you get home?" Kai asked, hands in his pockets.

"Why bother?"

"Because he's *your* husband."

I stopped walking and turned to stare at him, deadpan. Kai knew it was an arranged marriage. There was no point pretending otherwise. We don't have an NDA about it. I could stand on the rooftop and announce to all of Manhattan that I was contractually obligated to be the mute Bennetti brother's wife, and no one would care. Hell, half the world didn't even know he existed because he refused to show up to public events.

Like this one.

Nope. Not going down that road again.

"You and I both know that him being my husband is a legal term and *nothing* more."

Kai stopped me, hands firm on my shoulders as he turned me to face him. Thank God I'd only had one glass of wine. If I was as hammered as my kitchen staff, I'd be hurling all over his stupidly polished boots right now.

"It means something to *you*. Don't be a pushover. Besides, you're basically a mafia princess. Why not go kick his ass?"

I jabbed a thumb toward Vinnie. "That's his job."

"Okay, then go yell at him. Be the nagging wife."

I rolled my eyes. "Yeah, I think I already do that well enough."

Kai pulled me in for a quick hug, pushing a kiss to my forehead like an overprotective big brother. "Okay, you do you. I'll see you tomorrow. But remember, don't come in until noon. I'll cover for you."

"Thanks." I smiled up at him. His usually neat blonde hair was a tousled mess, and I hated that even at his most exhausted, he still looked completely handsome. Pulling away, I gave him a small wave as he turned back toward the bar, only to find Vinnie standing by the car, eyebrow raised like he was about to start some real shit.

"Yes?" I sighed, already climbing into the backseat.

"You wanna talk about it?"

"Do I look like I wanna talk about it?"

He shrugged, shutting the door behind me. "Do you want me to kick his ass?"

I considered it for a long moment. "I'm thinking about it."

"Well, think quickly. We're only ten minutes from home."

I snorted. Home. *Right.* More like the world's fanciest prison.

Allie

VINNIE PULLED INTO THE garage, and I sat there, staring at the dashboard like it was about to give me life-altering advice. It didn't. Not even with a little alcohol in my veins to push that along.

With a sigh, I forced myself out of the car. Half of me wanted to march straight to Dom and Sienna's, but the thought of dealing with teething babies at this hour? Hard pass. I needed sleep, not the soundtrack of newborns wailing like they'd just been evicted from the womb.

Instead, I settled on a plan. *A real plan.* I was sleeping in my damn room tonight. And I was *staying* there.

Except... I groaned, rubbing my temples. That meant moving all of my stuff back upstairs. Again. It had taken an effort to move my things into Rico's closet, my toiletries into his bathroom, my entire existence into his space—purely out of spite. And now, I was about to drag it all back like a prisoner of war waving a white flag.

And somehow, that felt worse.

Muttering under my breath, I stepped inside, shutting the door with a little too much force. The house was dark. Not a single light. Not even the low, traitorous glow from under his home office door. If he was in there, I might have actually lost it. Would've stormed in, ripped those ridiculous monitors out of the wall, and yeeted them into oblivion.

But no. No office glow. No Rico.

I stomped toward the bedroom hallway, tossing my shoes off at the bottom of the stairs. Only when I hit the fourth step did reality smack me upside the head.

All. My. Stuff.

It was still in his room. My clothes. My toiletries.

With the grace of a sleep-deprived zombie, I turned around, shuffled back through the kitchen, past the living room, and down the hall toward Rico's room. I pushed open the door, ready to grab my essentials and flee—only to freeze in my tracks.

A sliver of golden light spilled out from beneath the bathroom door.

That motherfucker.

Apparently, my exhaustion had lied to me because suddenly, energy surged back into my body like I'd been hooked up to an IV of pure violence.

He didn't call. Didn't text. Didn't show up to my debut.

But oh, he had time to come home, kick back, and take a shower?

Over. My. Dead. Body.

Or *his.*

Sicilian. Daughter of a mob boss. Raised to know at least six ways to kill a man without getting blood on my shoes. If Rico thought I didn't know exactly where to stab to make it hurt, he had another thing coming.

I launched across the room, yanking the bathroom door open so hard it nearly came off the hinges. Steam billowed around me, heavy and humid, like a personal fog machine created solely to mock me.

And then, through the mist, I saw him.

Standing there.

Dripping.

Shirtless.

Towel slung low on his hips.

I'd love to say that I stayed laser-focused on my righteous fury. That I didn't immediately zero in on the taut, olive skin stretched over perfectly sculpted muscles. That my eyes didn't betray me by drinking in every inch of his broad chest and the flames inked into his back, licking up his shoulders like they belonged there.

But that would be a lie.

And I'm a lot of things—dramatic, stubborn, a sore loser—but I'm *not* a liar.

I tried. Tried to look past all of it. Tried to remember that I was here to erupt, not have an out-of-body experience over my husband's absurdly perfect body.

And then he turned.

My anger flickered, fizzling out like a dying match.

Scars.

Dozens of them.

Some faint and white, some jagged and stretched, all twisting over his ribs, his chest, curling around his back like a story carved into his skin. Old. Worn. Fused with him like they'd grown alongside his body.

My stomach knotted.

Rico just stood there, silent as ever, his unreadable gaze locked onto mine.

The furious monologue in my head—the one that had pages of colorful insults ready to fly—screeched to a halt.

Instead, I stood there, unmoving, cataloging every inch of destruction scribbled across his body.

Then I blinked, swallowed hard, and looked him in the eye.

"You didn't show."

Rico sighs. Tossing the towel onto the countertop like this conversation is just another chore on his to-do list.

"Nothing? You're not going to say anything?" My voice climbs an octave. "You didn't show, even though you said you would. You didn't call."

"I called."

I blink. "When?"

"After I realized I missed it."

Oh, he's going to die tonight.

I didn't get a call, but that might be because Kai forced me to turn off my phone after he caught me checking it every five minutes.

I take a slow, deep breath—because I read somewhere that's what rational, composed people do before they commit murder—and let it out through my nose. "After you missed it?" My voice wobbles between incredulous and homicidal. "After? *After!?*"

Before I know it, I'm marching across the room, ignoring the fact that Rico is currently fresh out of the shower and standing there like a walking, talking Michelangelo sculpture.

And what do I do?

I slap his ridiculous, perfectly defined pec.

"Why. Did. You. Miss. It?"

His hand scrubs over his jaw, then drags through his wet hair, slicking it back, and my stomach flutters.

Oh, for fuck's sake. *No. Nope. Not happening.* I refuse to let my ovaries betray me like this. This man is an emotionally stunted, self-absorbed asshole—and yet, somehow, I'm still two seconds away from fanning myself like a Southern belle in a heatwave.

"I fell asleep."

I lunge. No hesitation. No second-guessing. I go for his face, prepared to leave a handprint so deep it'll be his new birthmark.

Only, the bastard catches my wrist.

"I'm going to kill you," I seethe.

And then...

He *smiles*.

Not a smirk. Not one of those half-assed, barely there things that men do when they think they're smarter than you. No. A *real* smile.

And that's the *real* problem.

Because I—Allie Bennetti, woman with an actual backbone—likes it.

Oh, and worse? It's the most devastating smile I've ever seen in my entire life.

What is wrong with me?

"You fell asleep?" I manage, voice slightly strangled.

The smile disappears, and thank God for that, because my nipples were about three seconds away from clawing their way through my bra.

His grip on my wrist tightens—firm but not rough—as he tugs me in. My body collides with his, warm and hard and utterly unfair, and I forget how to breathe for a second.

"I'm sorry."

I squint. "How hard was that for you to say?"

He smirks.

I groan. "Stop *that*."

"Stop *what*?"

"Don't smile."

His jaw clenches, his face shifting back into that usual stoic, unreadable expression—the Rico I'm used to. The one I pretend doesn't make me weak in the knees.

"I'm sorry, Allie."

I tilt my head. "Not sorry enough."

He exhales slowly, like he's *actually* putting effort into this. "I'm very sorry."

"When's the last time you apologized to a human?" Why use *human*? Because he would count the time he hit a key too hard on his precious keyboard or scowled at his monitor. No, I want to know the last time he was sorry to an *actual* person. One with a heart beat and lungs.

"A few years. Don't make a habit of it."

"Oh, so I'm someone special to you, then?" I snap, driving the point home that I mean *nothing* to this man outside of me and what my uterus is offering.

His lips part, his voice dropping into something low and devastating as he murmurs, *"Very."*

We both stop breathing. That or the Earth stopped spinning. Both are likely since hell just froze over.

Then, suddenly—we crash.

A storm. A collision. A riot of need so sharp it feels like it might cut. His grip on my wrist loosens, only to slide into my hair, fisting my ponytail and yanking my head back just as his mouth crashes onto mine.

It's not a kiss. Not really. It's war. A brutal, no-holds-barred battle of lips and teeth and tongues, all hunger and frustration and pent-up *everything*.

His other hand drops, grabbing a handful of my ass, yanking me against him so hard it knocks the breath from my lungs. And—oh. Yeah, that towel? Useless. That Egyptian cotton might as well be made of tissue paper for all the good it's doing in hiding what's pressing against my stomach.

I moan into his mouth, nails digging into his bare chest, and that's it. He snaps.

Rico

I'D LIKE TO GO on record that I am, in fact, sorry.

Not for what I'm about to do to my wife. No, I have zero regrets about the plans I have for her body.

But for earlier? Yeah. I might actually be sorry for that. Which, for the record, is new territory for me.

I don't think this is going to miraculously fix whatever is currently boiling in that sharp, lethal mind of hers, like a pressure cooker set to explode.

Nor am I doing this, for the record, to distract her from murder.

No.

I'm fucking crazed.

The second her hand lands on my chest, the part of me that no one touches, no one sees. It's like a match dropped onto a lake of rocket fuel.

Her mouth—God, that smart-ass mouth—is still moving against mine when she moans, and that's it. Game over.

I tear at her clothes, no thought spared for buttons or seams. There's a rip. Another. A snap of elastic, and then she's bare—soft, warm, mine.

She doesn't hesitate. Doesn't shrink away. Doesn't so much as flinch when my scars are laid out before her.

No.

She slapped me.

Right on the chest, where the scars wind across my skin like a roadmap to every painful memory I don't talk about.

Marco always looked at them like they were some grotesque masterpiece. My parents avoided them like they were a stain on the family name. And me? I stopped thinking about them altogether.

Until now.

Until *her*.

And now, she's wrapped around me, her legs locked at my waist, her hands stealing another piece of me I didn't know I was offering.

I drop us onto the mattress, covering her body with mine, and the second her bare skin presses against my scars, my entire nervous system forgets its primary function.

Because this—this—shouldn't matter.

It's skin. Flesh. Nerve endings. Biology, *plain and simple.*

So why does the feel of her against me ignite something I don't know how to name? Why does her touch—her bare, fucking skin against my wreckage—send something real slithering up my spine?

A catalyst.

A live wire.

A big fucking problem.

I tear my mouth from hers, trailing hot, open-mouthed kisses along her throat, tasting her pulse, the faintest trace of wine on her skin—*her.*

I press into her just enough to feel the way her body molds against mine, the warmth of her skin fusing into mine like she belongs here, tangled up in my bed, in me.

And then my mouth brushes against the cool metal of her chain.

A metallic clink.

I freeze.

All logic, all rational thought, every shred of self-control I pride myself on? Gone.

My teeth clench as I lift the chain, dangling the rings between us, my irritation a tangible thing that coils low in my gut.

The rings she *should* be wearing.

The same rings I slid onto her finger when we sealed this whole arrangement with a signature and a contract.

"Yes?" Her voice drips with challenge, with amusement, with her. Like I just interrupted her primary plan to get me to snap and do something stupid.

Like I'm not already so far past that point, I can't recall where the line to good decisions begins.

"Why aren't these on?"

"Oh, are we really talking about rules and expectations right now?"

No. Absolutely not.

Not when my dick is this hard. Not when I'm two seconds away from forgetting why I'm even mad.

Still, I don't let it go.

I reach around her neck, unclasping the chain, yanking it free with an irritated flick of my fingers until the rings slip into my palm. Snatching her left hand, I slide each band back onto her finger, my grip firm, my movements deliberate.

"These stay *here.*"

"Says who?"

The grin is still there. Just enough light from the bathroom to catch the wicked glint in her eyes. She lives for this. The push and pull. The battle of wills. The war she's waging without ever declaring it.

I exhale sharply, shaking my head. "You know, I was going to apologize by licking every inch of your body—"

"Was?" She tilts her head, faux innocence dripping from her voice.

"Yeah." I lean in, my lips ghosting over her jaw, down the column of her throat, my fingers tightening on her hip. "Not feeling as sorry anymore."

I brace for the fight—expect her to shove me, to smirk up at me with that infuriating mouth and tell me to *earn* my way back between her thighs. Maybe she'll demand I grovel, make some smart-ass comment about how I should be on my knees. For the record, I'm so desperate, I would do it. She doesn't need to know that though.

But she doesn't.

She surges up instead, her hands skimming over my skin, her lips finding my chest—soft, teasing. And then she bites.

A sharp sting. A possessive fucking claim.

Heat licks up my spine, my breath locking in my throat as her tongue flicks over the mark, soothing it before her teeth drag again, slow and deliberate, over my skin. Not just biting. *Branding.*

She's not just beneath my skin—she's under it, woven into every part of me, leaving her fingerprints all over my soul.

Always fucking stealing.

And I let her. I *want* her to.

Because as long as she never stops, she can take whatever the hell she wants.

Allie

I BARELY GET OUT a breath, let alone the caustic, witty retort I had lined up—one that would have made angels weep and men fear for their lives—before Rico does what Rico does best: ruins me completely.

He shoves my thighs apart, thrusting inside me to the hilt like he's been waiting his entire damn life for this exact moment.

Holy mother of f—

The wind leaves my lungs, along with any and all coherent thought. My nails dig into his chest, my body arching, and when my teeth find his shoulder, he growls—a deep, primal sound that rumbles through him like thunder before a storm. His grip tightens on my ass, dragging me closer as he pushes even deeper, and we both moan.

"I'm still mad at you," I pant, because apparently, I don't let shit go even if I'm about to orgasm.

His hand tangles in my hair, jerking my head back. "Good," he grits out, slamming into me again. "I want an angry fuck."

Oh, well, lucky for him, I'm livid.

I nip at his ear, and he punishes me with a sharp thrust that has me gasping and gripping his biceps like they're the only things keeping me from flying straight into another realm.

"I would have eaten you out," he mutters darkly, his fingers bruising my hips as he pounds into me, deep, dragging strokes that make my entire body tremble. "But you decided to be a brat."

"And you're an asshole," I shoot back, breathless, because talking while having the soul fucked out of you is more challenging than one would think.

His response? A rough chuckle, one that makes my spine tingle, before he suddenly pushes up on his hands, changing the angle, his cock sliding in and out with long, brutal strokes that have my vision going fuzzy at the edges.

So, naturally, I do what any woman in my position would do: *I* take control.

I wrap my legs around him, shifting my weight, and with a sharp push, I flip him over onto his back.

"Oh, fuck," he hisses as I sink down onto him, taking him all.

My hands press into his chest, my nails scratching down his firm, sweat-dampened skin as I move, grinding against him, feeling him so deep inside me that my lungs protest.

"Jesus," he mutters, head falling back as he watches me ride him, his hands branding my hips like he's memorizing the feel of me, like he's not sure if this is real or some fever dream where I finally break him.

I lean forward, rolling my hips, enjoying the way his jaw clenches, his abs tightening beneath my fingers. "Want to know a secret?"

He lifts his head, eyes blazing as his grip tightens.

I pick up my pace, bouncing, riding him slow at first, then faster, leaning in just enough so every motion sends him hitting so deep, my bones vibrate.

"I've never ridden a man before," I whisper, just as his head snaps up, his hands flying to my neck, dragging me down to his mouth.

He kisses me roughly. Desperate. Possessive. His hips thrust up into me, his control snapping like a rope set on fire.

The orgasm that had been teasing me for the past five minutes detonates, my entire body shaking as the pleasure rolls through me in wave after wave, leaving me gasping into his mouth, clawing at his shoulders.

"There you go, baby," he rasps against my lips, his hands sliding over my body like he owns every inch. "Squeeze my cock."

I barely have time to recover before he's flipping me back onto the mattress, pressing me down, taking control again *because Rico always has to be in control.*

Not that I mind.

He drives into me harder, faster, one hand gripping my thigh, the other slipping between us to find my clit, rubbing the already oversensitive, swollen bundle of nerves until I'm shaking again, gasping for air, my head tipping back as he destroys me. I want to hate him for it. Considering I'm supposed to be outraged, but it's hard to hate a man that has you on the brink of something so delicious and rewarding and what you thought you'd never actually have in real life.

"Come around my cock again, Allie."

And fuck me if hearing my name like that isn't enough to send me spiraling into oblivion one more time, only this time it's so powerful I'm positive I'm screaming, and yet can't hear anything except my heart beat echoing off every inch of my skull.

I lose control of everything—my limbs, my lungs, my dignity—as the orgasm rips through me like a damn freight train, barreling down my spine and detonating at my core.

My fingers claw down his back, gripping his perfectly sculpted ass, pulling him in deeper, as if he isn't already nailing me to the mattress like it's his life's mission.

"Fuck, Allie," he groans, his voice gravelly and wrecked. His hips jerk, his cock thickening inside me before he slams in one last time, his body locking up as a shudder rolls through his muscles.

He doesn't pull out. Doesn't even attempt to move. Instead, his fingers wrap around mine, dragging them away from his skin, pressing them against the mattress by my head as his mouth slows, kissing me like we have all the time in the world.

And maybe we do.

Or maybe he's just biding his time, thinking about ways to make me forget that I still want to murder him. Mind-blowing orgasms, for the record, do not make me forget everything.

His body is still flush against mine, our skin slick with sweat, and I don't know how much time passes before he moves again, rolling his hips just enough to make my breath hitch and my stomach clench.

"I'm going to pull out," he murmurs, voice thick with lust. "And if you keep your mouth shut, I'll eat that pretty little pussy of yours, and then I'm going to fuck you until you tell me you can't take anymore." He pauses, his lips brushing over mine, teasing me, taunting me. "Because I'm sorry."

I blink up at him. "You can't apologize with your dick."

His smirk is lethal. "Watch me."

Allie

OF ALL THE THINGS I expected to walk into my restaurant and see tonight—an entire table of food bloggers secretly plotting my demise, Kai double-fisting espresso shots while simultaneously flirting with one of the line cooks—this wasn't on the bingo card.

My parents.

Sitting.

At a table.

In my restaurant.

I freeze mid-step, the stack of freshly printed menus in my hand teetering precariously as my brain decides it served its time and ships off for an overseas vacation. A reasonable person might assume this is a good thing, that maybe—just maybe—they're here to congratulate me. You know, normal parental things like *Wow, we're so proud of you!* or *Look at you, living your dream!*

But no.

Because my father looks like he'd rather be anywhere else. The DMV. Jury duty. A funeral. His own funeral.

My mother, ever the perfect Cosa Nostra wife, sits beside him, her expression unreadable, her posture rigid. And my father? He's already gripping the edge of the table, something he does when he's impatient or holding back irritation.

Great.

With a deep breath, I steel my spine and walk over. "Wow, didn't expect to see you two here. Are we celebrating a change of heart or just here to critique my menu?" I plaster on my best *I'm totally unaffected by your presence* smile and rest my hands on my hips.

My father's gaze lifts from the table, slow, the way a mafia boss looks at someone before he decides whether they live or die. I used to be on the "live" list, but after being ghosted and leaving the family, who knows anymore?

"Allie, you look well." If only his voice wasn't so impersonal when those words came out.

That's all I get? I could be missing a limb and he'd still say the same damn thing.

"Thanks, Papa. I'm happy with my life, so that helps."

Mom clears her throat, a prim, disapproving sound. "We wanted to see you."

Did you, though? Because this feels an awful lot like an obligation, like someone held a gun to their heads and forced them to pretend I still exist. Marco. I wonder if he forced them to come here. There are few my Papa would follow orders from, but if the Don *says*, you *do*.

"And why is that, exactly? You suddenly remembered you have a daughter? Thanks for coming to the wedding by the way."

My father's jaw tenses, his fingers tapping against the newly ironed linen covering the table. "We wanted to make sure you're happy."

"Uh-huh."

"We also wanted you to understand why we cannot see you," my mama adds, voice smooth and practiced, as if she's rehearsed it in front of a mirror. "Because of the family."

Right. *The family.*

Not our family. Their family.

The one I left. The one that decided I was nothing more than a prize to trade and when I refused, I was worthless.

"Oh, no, totally get it. You can't be seen with someone who leaves. It would be bad for business. God forbid someone sees you enjoying a meal with your own flesh and blood and assumes you've suddenly gone soft."

Mama flinches. Papa doesn't. He just exhales slowly, nodding like this is exactly the outcome he expected. Like he knew, deep down, I'd never come crawling back. "We *do* hope you're happy, Allie."

That's the closest thing I'll ever get to an apology. Or affection.

And damn, if that doesn't sting more than I care to admit.

What the hell was I expecting? Some grand, tear-filled reunion? Maybe *we love you no matter what* tossed in for good measure?

Stupid. So stupid.

I swallow against the lump in my throat, lift my chin, and force a nod. "Yeah. Me too."

Mama clears her throat. "The restaurant looks...well?" Her voice lingers, like she's offering a question rather than a statement.

"Yes. I had a reopening night. You were invited."

Her skin pales, guilt flickering across her face before she tamps it down. "Allie, you chose to leave. This is hard for both of us."

"Hard because I left? Or because you didn't get to tie yourself to the Romanos?"

Papa pushes back his chair, buttons his suit jacket and barely looks at me. "You left. You knew the consequences. Don't act like we did something wrong."

I tilt my head, studying the man who taught me everything about power, control, and how to hold my emotions hostage until they suffocate. "There's no rule that says you have to shun me."

"If we don't, it makes us look weak." His voice drops, his gaze shifting around the room like someone might overhear. "Do you understand what it would look like if the men who work for me thought I *let* you leave?"

Ah. There it is. The heart of it all. His reputation. His power. His over-inflated ego.

"Well, good thing you've handled that flawlessly, Papa," I say, flashing a sweet smile.

Then I turn on my heel and walk away, because if I stay a second longer, I'll say something I can't take back.

I head straight for the kitchen, grabbing a tray and pretending to check the order tickets, even though my vision is blurring. My stomach twists like I just ate bad sushi, like my body knew this was coming and still wasn't prepared.

Work. Family. It feels like I've lost both. After all, I might live my dream of owning my restaurant, but am I happy in every aspect of my life? Not really sure how to answer that question.

"Allie."

I startle, glancing up to see Vinnie leaning casually against the doorframe, arms crossed, his expression unreadable.

"You good?"

I huff out a laugh, except it's not really a laugh. More like a *ha-ha, isn't life just a cosmic joke* kind of exhale. "Fan-freaking-tastic. Family reunion of my dreams."

Vinnie tilts his head, watching me like I'm an unsolvable equation. Then he shrugs, pushing off the frame. "You know Rico made them come, right?"

"What?"

"Yeah. He called your father, made it clear they couldn't just ignore you. That if they were going to cut you out, they needed to own it to your face. No more pretending you didn't exist."

I stare at him, processing.

Rico did that? Rico?

The same man who barely speaks, who avoids emotional conversations like they're a virus, who treats our marriage like a business contract with occasional orgasms?

That Rico?

For some reason, my chest feels tight. Not in the *oh shit, I need a doctor* way, but in the *why does my cold-hearted husband actually have a soul* way. Why would he do that? Better yet, what the hell did he threaten my Papa with to get him to come here? Like I said, there are very few that Papa would bend to.

I cross my arms, trying to shake it off. "Well, good to know I'm now a charity case he felt the need to advocate for."

Vinnie smirks. "Or maybe he just wanted you to have closure."

Closure.

Allie

MY PERIOD IS LATE.

Not fashionably late, like showing up twenty minutes past the reservation time with an "Oops, traffic was terrible!" excuse. No, it's ominously late. The kind of late that makes horror movie violins screech in the background.

And I am *not* happy about it.

No. I am full-on, DEFCON-1-level terrified.

Three months of marriage is not long enough for this. Sure, Rico and I have sex. A lot. *Like, a lot a lot.* But that's just biology. There's no deep, meaningful connection outside of our contractual obligation to tolerate one another. At least, that's how he sees it.

Rico doesn't talk. He doesn't share. He is the epitome of mixed signals—one day, he pulls me into his orbit like I'm the missing puzzle piece to his existence, and the next, he's back to robot mode. And the second I get pregnant? Game over. His job will be done, the contract fulfilled, and I'll be gently (or not-so-gently) shoved back into my room. *Thanks for your service, Allie. Enjoy your lifetime membership to Single Motherhood.*

I ignored the tardiness of it at first. No symptoms. Nothing. Just stress, exhaustion, and that my body could just be screwing with me because, well, life. But then this morning, before heading to work, I grabbed a pregnancy test. Just a precaution. And then I called Kai and told him he was in charge tonight because if this test was positive, I was going to need a night off to fully process my impending doom.

There is no way I can go into work pretending I'm fine if that test tells me my uterus has decided to play host for the next nine months. One, because I'd have to cut back my hours to accommodate my new reality, and two, because any progress I've made with Rico will be erased faster than my last attempt at online shopping when I realized my credit card bill existed.

Time has flown by. Days have bled into weeks, then months, and somehow, here we are—*three months married*. It doesn't feel that long. Maybe because I've been too busy playing marital gymnastics—ducking his avoidance, sidestepping my own delusions, and trying (failing) to convince myself I don't care about him beyond what's necessary.

I know this marriage isn't real. It never will be. But the realization that one stupid little test could reset everything back to zero? Yeah, that makes me want to scream into a pillow.

No one knows. Not even Violet or Sienna. Because if I told them, they'd be excited. And I'd be sitting there, full of dread, reminding them I am nothing more than a womb in this scenario. And I'm not ready for that. Not now. Preferably never when the reality of it all sinks in.

So here I am, in Rico's bathroom—*our* bathroom, technically, because I moved my stuff in out of sheer spite and refused to move it back—staring at a pregnancy test like some cursed relic, afraid to even pick it up and look into the screen like it will doom me for good. Because, apparently, this tiny little stick holds an outrageous amount of power over my life.

The damn thing is just sitting there, mocking me.

I set the timer on my phone. Two minutes. The slowest, most excruciating two minutes of my life.

Two minutes to seal my fate. Or doom. Depending on your perspective.

I stare between the test and my phone like they're dueling executioners. And the worst part? I have no one to wait with. No one sitting beside me, holding my hand, cracking jokes to lighten the mood.

In a normal marriage, wouldn't the wife tell her husband she might be pregnant? Wouldn't they wait together? Their voices thick with emotion, their hands tangled as they stare down at the test like it holds the secret to the universe?

That's what I always imagined.

That's what I wanted.

But here I am, *alone* in a bathroom, gripping the counter like it's my last line of defense.

I hover my finger over my group chat with Sienna and Violet. *The Queens,* because obviously, the Bennetti brothers have their own little group chat, and Sienna declared ours infinitely superior.

I should tell them. I need to tell them.

I type out a message—because if anyone can talk me off the ledge, it's them—but before I can hit send, my phone timer blares in my face.

Time's up.

I take a breath, steadying myself.

One second.

Two.

Three.

I glance at the test.

Not pregnant.

Two words that a relieved sigh and a celebratory fist pump should follow, maybe even a shot of tequila. Instead, hot, stinging tears blur my vision, my stomach sinks like I just free-fell off a skyscraper, and my heart is doing this weird, fluttery thing that's definitely not excitement.

I should be relieved. Thrilled. Jumping for joy. Hello, I'm not a walking womb.

Instead, I feel like a failure.

We've been married for three months. Three months of daily—sometimes multiple times a day—activities that should have resulted in at least something by now. I mean, if teenagers in the backseat of a Honda Civic can get knocked up after one bad decision, how the hell am I still at zero?

This was different. This was hope. That stupid, deceitful emotion that always ends in disappointment. Had I not pathetically let myself believe—just for a second—that I might actually be pregnant, I wouldn't be sitting here feeling like someone just sucker-punched my uterus.

Am I sad it's negative?

I don't know. While I took the test, I wanted anything but "positive" to pop on the screen, but now that I know it's negative, I'm disappointed. If that's not an emotional whirlwind, I'm not sure what is.

All I know is that my hands are shaking as I grip the test, and before I can even process why this feels like the world's cruelest joke, I collapse onto the edge of the tub, curling in on myself as silent sobs turn into loud, gasping ones.

What if I can't get pregnant? What if I'm broken? Young and healthy doesn't mean a damn thing if my body has other plans.

And what then?

Rico married me for *one reason*. One. And if I can't give him that? He'll leave. He'll walk away without a backward glance because that's the logical thing to do, and Rico is nothing if not brutally logical.

He didn't ask me to marry him. He signed a contract. He made a deal. A transaction. And if the goods don't deliver?

I'm expendable.

A womb. That's all I am. And somehow, that realization cracks something inside me, sending more tears streaming down my face, because the reality is I'm nothing to him, and yet I know that I'm in love with him. Flaws and all. But knowing that an outcome of a test will derail our progress or seal us together forever hurts more. It hurts in every scenario. Whether I'm knocked up or turns out I can't be. Rico doesn't love me and never will. He won't have the same feelings. He won't feel hollow at the idea of shoving me out of his room. He doesn't feel a fucking thing because that's who he is.

The bathroom is silent except for my pathetic sniffles, and I think I have the freedom to wallow in my existential crisis for at least a few more minutes, but then—

The pregnancy test is plucked from my fingers.

I let out a scream so impressive, I'm sure the neighbors are considering calling 911.

Standing in front of me, in all his tall, brooding, emotionally unavailable glory, is Rico. Holding my test. *Reading my test.*

My first instinct is to snatch it back, but my limbs are apparently non-functional, so instead, I just sit there, looking up at him with wide, bloodshot eyes, waiting for him to say something.

He doesn't.

Instead, his dark eyes flick to the single line. The one that means not pregnant. His brows lift slightly, then his gaze shifts back to me. "What's this?"

I blink. "A pregnancy test."

His lips twitch. "I gathered that. Why are you taking it?"

I sniff, because I'm one sob away from needing a hydration IV. "I was late. I figured...maybe..." I wave my hand in the air like poof, baby magic, but then shake my head. "Doesn't matter. It's negative."

I push to my feet, reaching for the test because, hello, I can dispose of my own shattered dreams, thank you very much. But before I can grab it, Rico chucks it into the trash.

Then he does the last thing I expect.

He reaches out, wipes away a tear with his thumb.

My breath catches.

I've been married to this man for ninety-something days, and we have not once sat down and shared a meal together outside of the required weekly ones which are almost never now, and Sunday dinners. He barely talks to me unless it's during sex. And now he's standing here, looking at me like I'm some puzzle piece he's trying to fit into his meticulously crafted world.

"Why are you crying?"

Oh, good lord. Does he want the full list? Because I have a list. And if I start rattling off all the reasons I'm currently holding it together with emotional duct tape, he's going to need to clear his schedule for the next forty-eight hours.

So I opt for the one excuse I know will satisfy him without requiring too much emotional effort on his part.

"I failed. I'm not pregnant."

His brows pinch together, arms crossing over his bare chest, and great, now I'm distracted by the sheer injustice of the universe that a man like him gets to look like that while ruining my life. "You didn't fail."

"I didn't give you what you wanted. That's the *only reason* we're here." I don't even care if my voice is bitter. It's the truth, and if anyone can appreciate a hard, cold truth, it's him.

And that's when it happens.

Rico steps forward, his hands cupping my damp cheeks, and before I can figure out what the hell he's doing, his lips are on mine.

Not rough. Not possessive. Not a distraction tactic.

It's...soft. Deliberate. Unreal.

We've kissed plenty, but never like this. And for the first few seconds, I stand there, frozen, trying to figure out if this is some elaborate Inception-level dream.

But then his hands move, his grip tightens, and suddenly, soft turns into something else entirely. Something hotter. Hungrier. His fingers tug my shirt up, my hands move to his bare chest, and I swear I can feel his heartbeat hammering beneath my palm.

Which is ridiculous because Rico doesn't do that. His heart doesn't race at the idea of me.

Mine, on the other hand? Full-blown cha-cha.

His lips leave mine, trailing lower—over my jaw, my throat, my collarbone. Then he's on his knees, his mouth ghosting over my stomach as he grips my hips, kissing lower as he drags my pants down.

I gasp, fingers tangling in his thick hair. "Rico, obviously I'm not ovulating. I won't get pregnant if we have sex right now."

His lips curve against my hipbone as he looks up at me, dark eyes flashing.

"I know."

And then he wrecks me.

Rico

CRYING IS NOT SOMETHING I handle well. Nope. I avoid that shit like a biohazard outbreak in a poorly ventilated subway car. It should be a federal mandate that women can only cry in soundproof rooms, preferably in another country.

And yet, I don't run.

I should. I want to. I even consider it for a solid five seconds.

The sobs are loud—obnoxiously so. The acoustics in this house turn every sound into a full-blown symphony, and right now, I'm getting the Allie's Emotional Breakdown live concert, featuring heavy breathing, broken whimpers, and the occasional sniffle that sounds suspiciously like my worst nightmare.

Why the hell am I even home this early?

Because I noticed the SUV hadn't left for work on the security cameras. I normally don't care. Allie takes days off—rarely, like a solar eclipse—but it happens. Only today, instead of spending it with Violet or Sienna like she normally would, she ran a quick errand, came back home, and stayed there. That alone was enough to raise an eyebrow.

So I texted Vinnie, who, for the record, is fully aware that I use him as my Allie informant, and he confirmed she took the day off but refused to tell me why. Which, frankly, pissed me off. I could hack the NSA if I wanted to, but no, apparently, I have to play detective with my own damn wife.

Old me would've shrugged, gotten back to work, and let her do whatever she wanted—as long as it didn't involve me unless she was naked and moaning my name. That's how we function. It works.

Or *worked*.

Because instead of ignoring it, I shut down my computers, stood up, and walked out of my office.

I didn't even have an excuse when my brothers looked at me like I'd been body-snatched. Alex, ever the concerned older sibling, looked two seconds away from calling an ambulance.

"Everything okay?" Dom asked.

I just held up a hand and shook my head. No explanation, no discussion. Let them stew. I left before I started questioning why I was leaving in the first place.

And now here I am, standing in the doorway of the master bathroom like an idiot, watching my wife sob into her hands while clutching a pregnancy test.

Everything in me tells me to turn around. Escape. Retreat to my office, pretend I never saw this, and let her cry it out. But my feet stay planted. The same part of me that's been slowly eroding under her presence refuses to walk away.

So I step forward instead.

Her crying is relentless, echoing off the marble like a opera. It's uncomfortable. Too raw. Too messy.

At first, I assume she's crying because it's positive. And for a solid two seconds, I brace myself. My pulse spikes, the air leaves my lungs, and a slow, creeping dread snakes up my spine.

I don't want kids. Not now. Maybe never. That's a discussion I haven't had with myself because avoiding difficult conversations—especially with myself—is one of my best skills.

But then I pull the test from her fingers.

Negative.

I blink at it. Then at her.

She's crying because she thinks she failed me.

I almost laugh. The irony would be funny if it weren't so fucking sad.

She thinks this is the only thing keeping me here. That her sole purpose in this marriage is to pop out an heir, and if she can't, I'll cut my losses and walk.

Would I?

I don't know. I don't want to know. Because knowing means facing the fact that the idea of walking away doesn't sit right. That, despite my best efforts, she's burrowed herself into whatever abyss exists where normal people have emotions.

The problem is, I'm not *normal people*. I don't do the soft, affectionate husband thing. I don't care. Or at least, I didn't.

I should feel something about this test. Something big. Excitement. Disappointment. *Something.*

She looks so sad and defeated it would almost break my heart—if I had one that actually functioned. Instead, what's left inside my chest is some shriveled, useless organ that only kicks in when my wife cries, apparently.

When I pull her up to me and kiss her gently, my body responds before my brain can process the emotional landmine I just stepped on. It's instinctual, stripping her down to nothing, including the tiny lace thong designed by Satan himself to turn any rational man into an idiot.

Sex right now will result in absolutely *nothing*. I know that. She knows that. But I hate it more—deep, bone deep—that she believes it's the only thing I care about.

Okay. Yes. That's mostly my fault. Yes, I may have led her to believe that. Yes, I have reinforced the idea by not talking, not engaging, and making a habit of treating our post-sex interactions like escaping an audit. But that's not all I enjoy about her.

I enjoy her warmth—and not just the warmth of her naked body against me, even though that resides high on the list. Then, I run away like a coward because those urges make me feel *things*, and I'm not built for *things*. It's a classic fight-or-flight response, and for thirty-seven years, I've successfully chosen flight. Giving in would be like flaying my skin off and wearing my insides on the outside for public display—a truly horrific visual, and also not a good look for me.

Placing her on the bed, I keep kissing her. Her legs wrap around me, pulling me in like she's hellbent on stealing every ounce of my restraint. My cock is already nudging at her entrance, and fuck me, this woman went from crying her body weight in tears to being wet and ready for me. A miracle. A mystery. A fucking enigma. I'm not going to question it. I have needs. A very specific one right now.

Foreplay be damned. I need this.

I press in, sinking deep, and we both moan into each other's mouths. I pause, my hips circling gently, stretching her tight-as-hell pussy just enough so I don't lose my mind. Three months in, and she's still so damn tight I have to breathe through it, reminding myself that, no, my cock will not snap off from sheer pressure. I even researched it. Called a few professionals, just in case.

Our mouths don't break. I move—slow, deep strokes, her body gripping me like she was made for this. For me.

Her heels dig into the backs of my thighs, her nails claw at my shoulders, her lips—fuck, her lips—stay fused to mine like oxygen. And maybe she is my oxygen source, because every second our mouths aren't connected, I feel like I might stop breathing entirely.

I could go faster. I want to go faster. I could fuck her so hard the mattress dents. I could pin her down and ruin her in the way we both love. And I will. *Later.*

Right now? I need this slow, aching crawl toward insanity. I need to feel every gasp, every moan, every little shudder rolling through her body as I bury myself inside her, over and over again, the only thing tethering me to sanity.

"Come for me, baby." My voice is rough, wrecked, my control fraying as I shift my hips, angling to hit that spot that makes her fall apart.

She cries out, squeezing around me so tight I groan, thrusting deep, letting go as I spill inside her, feeling every shudder of her orgasm milk me dry.

How is it that every single time with her is better? Just when I think nothing can top the last time, she proves me wrong. Again. And again. And again.

Normally, this is the part where I'd roll off her. Distance myself. Pretend none of this meant anything. But instead, I stay exactly where I am, kissing her with slow, lazy, indulgent kisses as if I have any intention of stopping.

I don't.

I pull her with me as I roll to my back, keeping her draped over me, my arms wrapping around her waist like a cage. Her head rests against my chest, her fingers tracing circles over my skin, and I let them. I like them.

I should push her off. I should want to push her off. But I don't. And that is the real fucking problem.

Because the past few weeks, I've actually slept. With her on me. Stealing my space. A hand in my hair. A leg over my body. An arm draped across my chest like a toddler's security blanket.

And none of it bothers me.

What does?

That it *doesn't*.

Allie

IT's BEEN ALMOST A week since that night. The night Rico had sex with me, willingly, knowing full well it would not result in a baby. A shocking development, I know. But don't worry—I'm not about to get sucked into the black hole of delusion, also known as hope.

Sure, for a fleeting moment, I thought we had a connection. Something warm and real, like maybe my emotionally suffocated husband had cracked open just a little. He knew I was upset; he knew I couldn't get pregnant, and he made slow, torturously good love to me. And then? Poof. That euphoria? The kind that made me wake up all starry-eyed, literally sprawled across his chest like I belonged there?

Gone.

Like a mirage.

The second we untangled, his face turned cold, like someone had flipped a switch in his beautifully aggravating brain. He got up, showered, dressed, and left for work, moving through the motions with robotic precision, as if I hadn't just spent the entire night worshiping every scar, every taut muscle, every inch of him.

There was no connection. *No moment.* Just two people using sex to get through emotions neither of us had the courage to talk about. Well, I feel things. Rico? He doesn't do emotions. I'm starting to believe he was built in a lab.

And now? He's avoiding me.

Oh, not obviously. That would require effort. No, my brilliant husband has somehow found a way to keep me too busy during the week for our so-called date nights (which, let's be honest, barely existed in the first place). Even dinners together? Poof. Gone like his personality in a social setting. And, of course, my only day off is reserved for the one event neither of us can escape—family dinner at his parents' house.

But tonight? Tonight, I'm flipping the script.

I took the night off, and it just so happens that it's the grand opening of Sienna's latest art exhibit. And before Rico has the chance to worm his way out of it, he's going. He just doesn't know it yet.

I had his suit dry cleaned. I cleared my schedule. And since his brothers will send him home at a reasonable hour from the office—because even they know the man needs sunlight once in a while—he'll walk through that door, expecting peace and solitude, only to be ambushed.

Is this the best way to get my husband out of the house?

No.

Would giving him any notice guarantee an immediate and strategic escape?

Absolutely.

The thing about Rico is, he *needs* a shove. A gentle nudge won't cut it. He requires a push off a cliff to get him to do things. And I am happy to provide said shove.

At exactly five, I hear the garage door open. Right on schedule.

I'm already dressed. Red Valentino gown, all satin and form-fitting, because if I'm forcing my husband to socialize, I'm damn sure looking good while doing it. A pair of black Louboutins to match, a glass of wine in hand, and my wedding ring twirling between my fingers as I stare at it under the dim kitchen light.

Rico doesn't even know I took the day off. He'll come home, see me waiting, and boom—his anti-social plans for the night? Gone.

Ever since I got my job, I've kept my money separate from Rico's. He still deposits an allowance into my account, not that I use it. It was in the contract, back when I had no income. Now? The money just sits there, untouched, because if there's one thing I refuse to do, it's owe him anything or be owned by anyone.

Not that he notices.

The deposits are probably set up as an automatic transfer—just another financial transaction he never thinks twice about.

And let's be honest, it's not like I need the money. I live in a ridiculously gorgeous brownstone for free, drive a car I didn't buy (well, Vinnie drives it, but still), and my husband—who never once acts like a man dripping in wealth—paid two million dollars in cash to buy my restaurant.

Two million.

To keep me out of his hair.

He spent two million dollars for peace and quiet.

And he didn't even blink.

That realization alone? Not really sure how to categorize the feeling that trails it.

I stare down at my rings again. The engagement ring—a stunning, absurdly expensive diamond he *didn't* pick out for me. The wedding band—one I didn't buy myself. When I was planning our romantic (*ha*) wedding, I was told to only pick out Rico's ring. Mine? "Already taken care of," Mama had said, waving me off with a knowing smile.

I assume she and Nonna picked it out.

A sweet gesture, considering my husband likely wouldn't have bothered.

Because Rico's idea of romance?

Apparently, it begins and ends in the bedroom or whatever surface he can use as long as I'm bent over it.

It's been a measly week since Rico made love to me. And yes, I'm calling it that. Not just sex. Not just another sweaty, orgasm-fueled workout. It was different. Slower. More deliberate. Less about getting off and more about something else—something I've been too afraid to name because the second I do, my husband will promptly kill it with his bare hands.

And yet, here I am again, that pathetic flicker of hope still burning in my chest like a stubborn candle wick that just refuses to die.

The way he kissed me, held me, moved over me—it wasn't rushed or aggressive, wasn't born out of frustration or obligation. It was intentional. And the worst part? He knew there was no chance of me getting pregnant that night. I was already late, had already taken the test, and he still touched me like I mattered. Like he *wanted* to.

Which is why, as much as I hate myself for it, I leave my heart's door open just a crack. You know, just in case my husband wants to walk through it.

When Rico walks in through the mudroom, he stops. Really stops. His eyes rake over me from head to toe, slow and measured, like he's taking inventory of every inch of exposed skin before landing back on my face. And for once, I appreciate that his first reaction isn't *What the hell are you doing home?*

Baby steps.

After a long pause, he takes a few steps closer. "What's the occasion?"

I glance down at my wineglass, suddenly wondering if I should've had a lot more of it before attempting this little game. Hindsight is a real bitch.

"Well," I start, swirling the wine dramatically like some smug villain in a soap opera. "We're long overdue for a date night."

His lips part like he's about to argue, but I hold up my hand.

"No, don't even try it. We haven't gone on a *single* date, Rico. My only days off, we spend at your family's house—which, for the record, is not a date. So, I figured we could compromise."

His brow lifts as he gives my dress another once-over. "What kind of compromise?"

"You come with me to Sienna's gallery exhibit tonight, and in return, I'll let you take this off with your teeth." I gesture up and down my body, channeling my best Vanna White, presenting a brand-new car energy.

"No."

Just like that. No hesitation. No, let me think about it. Just No, as if I'd asked him to donate a kidney on the spot.

He moves past me toward the kitchen, but I reach out and grab his arm before he can make a full escape. He doesn't flinch at my touch anymore, which, let's be honest, is progress. And maybe, possibly, I've tested touching him while he's asleep—strictly for research purposes, of course—and he didn't even flinch then either.

So, yeah. Progress. Or pathetic optimism. Jury's still out.

"Rico. Please." I soften my tone, trying desperately not to sound whiny because I know he hates that. "Your family will be there, so technically, you're supporting the family. All you have to do is show up, sip your scotch, and look broody in the corner. I'll do all the talking. It's our first actual date, if you think about it."

He exhales through his nose, clearly unimpressed. "When I bought you the restaurant, that was our first date."

I gape at him. "We didn't even eat! You signed some papers, handed me a contract, and left. That's not a date, Rico."

"And this is?"

"No, but it's closer to one." I cross my arms over my dress, tapping my heel against the floor impatiently. "Unless you'd rather I demand a real date—fancy restaurant, expensive wine, a full four-hour affair." I pause, letting my next words land with maximum impact. "And if we go that route, this dress? Stays on after."

His scowl is instant. Intense. Like I've just suggested we spend the night scrapbooking instead. Which I might force him to do next if he refuses this date offer.

That expression used to scare me. Now? It's practically his default setting. I could frame it and label it *The Rico Special*.

"How long until we leave?" he grumbles.

My grin is pure, unfiltered victory. "Forty minutes. Vinnie's driving us, which I know you don't love, but hey—at least you can drown your sorrows in whiskey without worrying about getting behind the wheel."

He glares at me. I do not bat my lashes, because I know that doesn't work on him.

"Fine."

I wait until he turns down the hall before dropping the last bomb. "Oh, and I put out your suit. Freshly dry-cleaned."

He spins on his heel, the glare of all glares locked onto me.

"You have to dress up. Look at me." I wave my hand dramatically over my body, as if the siren-red dress I'm wearing isn't already impossible to miss.

Rico stands there, rocking back and forth in his sneakers, hands shoved into his denim pockets like a petulant child being forced into a school play. I'll never get over the fact that this man has so many zeroes to his name and yet still dresses like someone who hates money. Is it for comfort? An elaborate scheme to stay under the radar? Some philosophical rebellion against wealth?

But after a few seconds of silent brooding, he finally exhales. "Fine. You win."

I choose to ignore the fact that he says it through gritted teeth, or how he storms down the hallway and slams the bedroom door like an angsty teenager.

Because a win is a win.

Rico

IF SOMEONE WERE TO compile a list of all the things my wife has stolen from me, we'd need an Excel spreadsheet, multiple tabs, and a dedicated forensic accountant to keep up.

Tonight is just another tally on the ever-growing list.

She's stolen my time, considering I had every intention of coming home, eating one of the pre-prepped meals she obsessively stocks in the fridge like an overachieving housewife, and then losing myself in code.

Instead, I've been ambushed.

I should be at my desk right now, drowning in algorithms, keeping Smurf—or Blue or whatever the hell this hacker's name is—from worming into my system again. But no. I'm here. Being dressed up like a damn show pony.

I slam the bedroom door behind me, fully embracing my inner toddler, and groan when I see the three-piece suit neatly laid out on the bed.

Oh, for fuck's sake.

I know this woman. She did this to piss me off. She picked the vest on purpose. And the red tie? Cute. But not happening. I'll put on the jacket, the slacks, and that's where I draw the line. Ties are for men trying too hard, and vests are for people who think they're auditioning for a *Peaky Blinders* reboot.

And yes, both my brothers wear the full ensemble. And yes, I judge them for it.

Grumbling every curse word in existence, I head into the shower, taking my sweet, sweet time. If I have to suffer, so does she. Let her sit out there in that sinful dress, wondering if I'm going to make us late. Then again, knowing Allie, she probably built in extra time just for this exact scenario. She knows me too well, and I'm not a fan of that fact.

I should probably check the family text thread to see when this exhibit actually starts. But the *Bro Chat*—the unnecessary and entirely insufferable group Dom created for us—moves faster than Wall Street on a trading day. Scrolling through it would require actual effort, and frankly, I'm not in the mood.

Screw it. I shave, dragging the blade across my jaw with exaggerated slowness—not because I need to, but because I know it'll piss her off. A glorious side bonus.

But if I'm being honest, as much as I don't want to go, I owe her.

Even I can acknowledge that showing up for my sister while failing to show up for my wife was an ass-backward move. And maybe—*maybe*—this is a way to make up for it.

And if that means I get to rip that dress off of her later? Then fine. I'll suffer through one night of overpriced champagne and pretentious art-speak just to get her out of it. Because that dress? It's never seeing the light of day again. The number of men I will have to punch (preferably eye gauge) for looking at her tonight already makes my fists itch.

I glance at my watch. Right on the forty-minute mark. I've been ready for *fifteen*, lying on the bed, staring at the ceiling, contemplating all of my life choices that have led me to this exact moment.

When I step out of the room, Allie is leaning against the kitchen counter, nursing a glass of wine.

I pray it's her first one.

One fun fact I've learned about my wife? When she drinks, she gets sleepy. Sleepy means less sex for me.

I've crunched the numbers. It's a pattern.

Her hazel eyes widen the second she sees me, and for a moment, I'm enjoying the way she looks at me—like she might rip the suit off herself just to get to what's underneath.

Then she ruins it.

"Wow." She puts the glass down, sauntering toward me, and I tell myself—do not focus on how her hips move in that damn dress.

Do. Not. Focus.

Because if I notice it, every other red-blooded man at this event will too, and I have shit to do. Being bailed out of jail isn't part of the plan.

She stops in front of me, her hands smoothing down my suit, the warmth of her touch igniting something dangerous. My cock twitches, and I almost growl.

What the fuck is this woman's control over my body?

I've researched. Deeply. There are no answers.

Okay, the answers I did find? I didn't like.

I'm attracted to her. *No shit.*

I love her? *Not a chance in hell. And for the record, how does love make you want to bend a woman over every available surface?*

I have a sex addiction.

Or, more likely, she *gave* me one.

I suppose that's just another thing she's stolen from me.

My self-control.

If we were keeping score on how many things my wife had stolen from me, tonight would be another bold tally. Right up there with my peace of mind, my self-control, and the dignity I lost the day I let her move her crap into my room.

Now? She's stolen my evening.

And my ability to avoid social interaction.

I should be at home, eating whatever she stocked in the fridge and not standing in a three-piece suit like I've just been prepped for a GQ spread I never asked to be part of.

And yet, here I am.

"You look amazing, Rico." Her voice drips with something dangerously close to admiration, which I do not trust. Those hazel eyes, flecked with gold and green, scan me like she's mentally undressing me, fingers playing with the lapels of my jacket. Tempting. But if I let myself think about flipping her over my shoulder and letting her show me just how amazing I look, we won't be making it to this art exhibit soon. Which isn't the worst idea...

"The only time I saw you in a suit was at our wedding." She laughs. I can't tell if that's a good or bad thing. Probably bad. Most things are when they involve me.

"Though, to be completely honest," she continues, "I barely looked at you that day. I was too afraid."

I tilt my head. Afraid? Of me?

"Why?"

She cocks her head at me like I just asked why people breathe air.

"Rico, you wanted to be there about as much as you want to go to this gallery exhibit. Not only were there people there, but you were tying yourself—" She stops herself, lips pressing together.

Go on, say it. Say the part where I tied myself to a woman I didn't choose. That this was a deal, not a choice. Say it, so I can stop pretending I don't already know.

She doesn't.

Instead, she shakes her head. "Doesn't matter."

It should.

But I don't press. That would require effort.

She exhales and smooths down her dress—a movement I shouldn't be focusing on, but it's hard not to when the fabric hugs her like a second skin. "Anyway, we should get going. Vinnie's ready with the car."

"You both look nice."

Vinnie gives Allie one of those polite, borderline affectionate smiles he saves just for her. The second she slides into the backseat, that smile vanishes. Gone like it never existed.

Yeah, he hates me.

Not that I give a shit.

I could speculate on the why, but I don't need to. *I know.*

He's not exactly thrilled with how I've handled this whole marriage thing. Too bad for him. It's my marriage, not his. And as long as he's willing to do his job and throw himself in front of bullets or rogue psychopaths for my wife's safety, he can scowl at me all he wants.

Despite Manhattan's prime traffic hour, we make it to The Gallery a lot faster than I'd like.

And that's when I realize.

Vinnie pulled up to the entrance.

Right up to the red carpet.

The one with flashing cameras and reporters waiting like vultures.

I grip my fists—clench, hold, unclench, hold—trying to ignore the full-body panic setting in. I don't do press. I don't do crowds. Hell, I barely do people.

I don't exist publicly. That's Dom or Alex's world.

But now, standing here in a suit that feels too tight, next to a woman who commands attention with nothing but a glance, I feel like a target. Doesn't help my wife's dress is the color of a bulleye.

Vinnie hops out, circles to open the door, and I step out, buttoning my jacket. I hold out a hand for Allie because I'm not that much of a jackass, and cameras...

Her fingers slip into mine, soft but firm, and I hear the surprise in her voice when she whispers, "Thank you."

Like I'm incapable of basic human decency. Fair assumption, but still.

The flashes come fast.

Retinas? Officially fried.

Allie, on the other hand, thrives in this. She smiles, confident and effortless.

Meanwhile, I am mentally composing my obituary.

The peace is short-lived.

"Dominic!"

A woman with an impractically perfect blonde bob—probably synthetic, because real hair doesn't gleam like that—charges toward us, her designer heels clicking like gunshots against the pavement.

I keep walking.

Allie stops, tugging me with her.

Damn it.

"This is Enrico Bennetti," she corrects, her voice polite but firm. "Dominic is his twin."

The woman's painted-on brows lift in shock. "Oh. You're the *other* Bennetti."

Fucking wonderful.

I love being called the *other Bennetti.*

It's like being the consolation prize no one wanted.

Before I can snarl something sarcastic, she shifts her attention to Allie, scanning her from head to toe like she's an art piece under auction.

"And who are you?"

My jaw clenches so hard I hear my teeth creak.

"Alessandra Bennetti," my wife says smoothly, chin lifted. "Enrico's wife."

Alessandra Bennetti.

It's not new information. I know this. I signed a contract. I wear a ring. I share a bed with her.

But hearing it like that—her name, attached to mine, in public—somehow makes it more real than the fact that she's literally infiltrated every corner of my life.

"Oh, what a treat," the blonde continues. "I had no idea the youngest Bennetti was married."

Youngest.

Because, even though Dom and I are twins, somehow, I'm always the one they talk about like I'm the little brother following behind him like a lost puppy.

I'm a grown man. A grown man with an IQ that probably exceeds most of the people in this room, and definitely my fucking brothers. And yet, I know if I stay here a second longer, this woman will start talking to me like I'm twelve.

I lean down, murmur in Allie's ear, "Let's go."

And, to my relief, she lets me.

The second we step inside, I'm hit with a cacophony of noise and perfume so potent it should come with a warning label. The stench of overpriced floral musk and too much cologne mingles with the overwhelming hum of a hundred conversations overlapping like a poorly mixed track.

I'm not sure if I should be grateful for the constant drone—because at least it keeps me from spiraling into a get me the fuck out of here meltdown—or if I should start mentally drafting my will because this level of social interaction has to be lethal.

Allie, of course, is thriving.

"You made it!"

Violet materializes in front of us, wrapped in a deep purple gown that molds around her already noticeable baby bump, her face glowing in that infuriating way pregnant women do. And I feel my jaw lock.

That should be my wife.

Not wearing a damn siren red dress that makes every man within a ten-foot radius risk whiplash.

No. She should stand here with my kid inside her, making it painfully obvious to every suit-wearing, smug-smiling bastard in this room that she's claimed. That she's mine. That looking at her the way they are is not in their best interest if they want to keep their hands intact. Or eyes. Or limbs. I'm not picky really.

I clench my fists so hard my knuckles scream.

A server strolls by with a tray of champagne, and I snatch one off for Allie before asking for a scotch—neat. The drink that says *don't talk to me unless you want a death stare in return.*

"You look so beautiful." My wife's voice is a soft, affectionate coo as she reaches out to rub Violet's belly.

Violet, in turn, beams like an actual fucking saint. Her stomach is still small, but considering there's another set of twins brewing, it won't stay that way for long.

God help my brother and what's left of his sanity.

Triplets nearly ended him. Now he's headed on the path to five kids.

That man needs therapy. Ideally, a vasectomy.

And speaking of Alex, he's in full-blown territorial mode.

His arm wraps tightly around Violet, his entire body angled as if he's ready to take out any poor soul who dares breathe in her direction. Alex is possessive on a normal day. When Violet's pregnant? He's one step away from snapping at people like a feral wolf.

"You are too sweet," Violet says, sipping her sparkling water, before her attention shifts directly to my wife.

And then it happens.

Her hand pats Allie's—*very flat*—stomach.

"You'll be sporting one of these soon enough, right?" She winks at me.

I sure as shit am trying every day over here.

It's incredible, really. Dom and Alex sneeze in their wives' general direction and—*boom*—knocked up.

Meanwhile, I have a gorgeous, willing wife, plenty of...*effort* being put into the process, and still—nothing.

Maybe I should just stare at her womb and will it to take a baby. Or burn through all the absurd AI-generated fertility advice Google keeps shoving at me.

Because clearly, whatever I'm doing? Not working.

"Hey, you two."

Sienna glides over, looking ethereal in some floaty gown, Dom's arm locked around her. She barely gets free before wrapping my wife in a hug and patting my arm.

Patting.

My fucking arm.

A casual touch—something most people wouldn't care about.

Except, I hate being touched.

And my entire family knows this.

They never touch me.

They never try.

Except for her—the woman who not only ignores my personal space but actively defies it.

"Do you mind if I steal your wife for just a minute?" Sienna asks sweetly, making a minuscule gap between her thumb and index finger like this temporary abandonment won't result in my imminent demise.

Yes. Yes, I mind.

Very much.

In fact, I need her here in case I have to thrust her in front of some overly chatty stranger and use her as a human shield.

I am not above that.

Unfortunately, my wife and I do not share the same telepathic superpowers my brothers have with their wives. No, those men can have entire conversations without speaking. Allie and I? We're over here playing two separate games—her a romantic comedy, me a psychological thriller.

Worse, judging by the wicked smirk tugging at the corner of her lips, she knows *exactly* what she's doing.

And she's enjoying it.

"So, I see you were let out of the doghouse long enough to grace us with your presence?"

I turn to Violet, who is batting her lashes with a saccharine amusement that makes men question whether they're about to be complimented or verbally annihilated. I don't talk to her much—she's definitely closer to Dom than to me—but I respect her. She took my overbearing, control-freak of a brother and turn him into something that resembles a functional human being. She also gave me three incredible nephews and, more importantly, keeps my brother in check.

There's not a single flaw I can pin on her, except that she voluntarily married my older brother. But, hey, nobody's perfect.

"Funny." I pluck a scotch off a passing server's tray before they even have the chance to offer it. Hope it wasn't meant for someone important. I need the alcohol more than they do and the one that scurried off with my order is nowhere in sight.

Violet grins. "Has she forgiven you yet?"

Considering the way my wife moans my name every night like it's her new favorite prayer, I'd say yes.

I nod.

Violet tilts her head, her perfectly arched brows lifting. "Why *did* you miss it anyway?"

Alex—her personal human shield—presses a kiss to her forehead before I can answer. "I told you, babe. He fell asleep."

"I know that. I was there. But *how* do you fall asleep and miss your wife's event?"

I know I'm not like my brothers. I don't do grand romantic gestures. I don't bring flowers home or plan surprise dates. But even I recognize that falling asleep during a significant moment in my wife's career is something only a special brand of jackass pulls off.

Not that I did it on purpose.

If anyone's to blame, it's the low-budget vigilante hacker who has made it his life's mission to ruin mine.

Maybe *he* should be in the doghouse.

I shrug. "Didn't mean to. It happened. It's done. It's history."

Violet just stares.

"What?"

She blinks. "Do you realize this is the most you've ever spoken to me in your entire life?"

I don't miss Alex poorly disguising his laugh with a cough.

I open my mouth to refute her claim—because surely I've spoken to my sister-in-law more than this—but stop short.

Do I talk to her?

I must.

Right?

I do some rapid mental math, skimming through past interactions. Surely, I've racked up at least a few hours of conversation over the years.

I come up empty.

Shit.

"Doubtful," I say, my voice void of conviction.

"Truthful." Violet counters smoothly.

Allie is sassy, but Violet is the undisputed queen of sass. She doesn't hesitate. She doesn't blink. She just fires off verbal bullets and watches you reload while she preps another round.

Add pregnancy hormones into the mix?

Yeah. You don't fight that battle. You surrender.

"And your point?" I sigh, knowing full well I just made a critical error.

Violet's smirk turns into a smile, and I groan. Why the fuck did I ask?

I just invited more conversation. I opened the damn door and practically begged her to waltz through with an opinion I don't want to hear.

She takes a sip of her sparkling water, frowns at it like it's offended her, and sighs. "God, another pregnancy with no liquor. Anyway," she continues, setting down the glass, "all I'm saying is your wife might actually be a good little change in your life. Clearly, she's gotten you to open up more than you used to."

So, let's add yet another thing to the list of shit my wife has stolen from me:

My peace.

My time.

And now, my ability to remain an emotionally repressed asshole.

Honestly not sure what's left to take at this point.

Allie

Honestly? I was done with this exhibit two hours ago, but watching my husband suffer through social interaction is a rare treat. So, like any dutiful wife, I'm dragging this out for as long as humanly possible. Unfortunately, that also means I have to suffer through it, and there's only so much art I can stare at before I question my life choices.

I squint at the painting in front of me. Either I've had too much wine, or someone made a serious mistake between the artist's photo and the work displayed.

The artist—pictured in the little bio section—looks like he moonlights as a cage fighter or is fresh out of a maximum-security prison. His painting? A soft, pastel fever dream of pinks and yellows that appears to be...a unicorn.

Yep. I'm officially drunk.

A long, warm arm wraps around my waist, and I let out an embarrassingly undignified yelp as I'm pulled into a familiar wall of heat and scent—*his*.

Rico's head tilts slightly as he examines the painting, his brows pinching together.

"You see the unicorn, right?" I murmur, needing confirmation that I haven't hit the point of hallucinating mythical creatures.

Rico's frown deepens. He glances between the painting and the artist's photo. "I think so..."

His grip tightens around my waist, pulling me flush against him, but I fight the urge to smile. He thinks he's in control here. *Cute.*

"Done with the torture?" he murmurs, his voice rough and unfairly arousing.

I blink up at him, giving him my best *who, me?* face. "What torture? We are absorbing culture."

Total lie. I hit my culture limit an hour ago, right around the time I mistook an emergency exit sign for an abstract art piece.

His nose brushes up the column of my neck, his breath warm and teasing against my skin, sending a shiver down my spine. Goosebumps erupt over my arms like they're staging a coup.

"You know."

I inhale, tilting my head slightly. "Do I?"

His lips ghost just below my ear, pressing a wet, open-mouthed kiss there like a declaration of war.

"I'm owed."

I swallow hard. "Owed what? This is our weekly date, which—just so we're clear—we haven't done since getting married. If anyone is owed, it's me. Like, a lot of weekly dates."

His response? Another kiss. This one slower, more deliberate, just above my racing pulse.

"Let's. Go."

I barely hold in a whimper. "I still need to see the paintings."

Without another word, he snatches my champagne flute and his tumbler, hands them off to a passing server, then grabs my hand and drags me through the gallery. Our fingers lace together, warm and firm, and I don't even pretend to fight him.

We pass Alex and Violet on the way out. Violet looks five seconds from slipping into a pregnancy-induced coma, and when we catch sight of Sienna and Dom near the door, Dom simply raises a brow.

"Leaving so soon?" he drawls, his eyes locked on our hands together because despite us being married three months, this is still a rare sight.

I open my mouth to make up an excuse, but before I can get a single word out, Rico beats me to it.

"I have a wife to impregnate."

Well then.

Dom, completely unbothered, sips his drink. "You do that, then."

We step into the cool night air, and I take a deep breath, grateful that the press has mostly cleared out. A few stragglers remain, but none of them seem interested in us. I pull out my phone, firing off a text to Vinnie, letting him know we're ready to go.

As I lower my phone, my gaze drops to our hands—still entwined.

My right hand in his left.

His wedding band—one he's never taken off—glowing under the streetlights.

Just because he wears it doesn't mean he means it.

The drive home is quiet—so quiet you'd think we just buried a body together instead of attending an art exhibit.

Tension simmers in the air, thick with anticipation and, knowing Rico, a solid dose of silent animosity. I did, after all, make him endure hours of forced social interaction when I fully expected him to throw in the towel an hour in. But no. The stubborn jackass stayed the entire time. Maybe out of guilt for missing my event. Maybe because he actually wanted to be there.

Big *maybe* on that last one.

There's a difference between doing something because you want to make someone happy and doing it because you feel bad about screwing up. One is effort; the other is damage control. And I do not know which side of the line Rico's motives land on.

Not that he'd ever tell me.

The only time he actually opens up is in bed, and only because his mouth is too busy doing things other than ignoring me. Right now, in the car, I stay silent, waiting—*hoping*—for him to say something. I could poke the bear, force him to grunt a response, but honestly? I want *him* to try. I want *him* to be the one to break the silence for once. For us to exchange words in person rather than through passive-aggressive Post-It notes or mid-orgasm declarations.

But, as usual, I wait. And wait. And get nothing.

By the time we get home, lost in each other's bodies, tangled in sweat and exhaustion, I should feel euphoric, floating on some blissed-out, post-sex high. Instead, I feel like I just got checkmated in a game I didn't even know I was playing.

Because this entire marriage? It's a damn chess match.

And I'm the only one moving the pieces.

Rico pulls away—physically, emotionally, entirely. The second our bodies disconnect, the cord is severed, and he rolls back to his side of the bed. No lingering touches. No whispered words. *Just space.*

Sure, maybe he's not a cuddler. Fine. I can live without spooning. But would it kill him to give me something? Some kind of sign that I'm not just here for one reason only?

It took months to see him with his shirt off. And even then, it wasn't by choice—I walked in on him. That's the problem, isn't it? He doesn't trust me. He doesn't let me in. If I hadn't caught him, I never would've known his torso is littered with scars, just like I wouldn't know anything real about him if it weren't for the rare moments he let something slip.

Even then, the only time he really kisses me—the kind that turns my insides to lava and makes me think, just maybe, I mean more to him than he lets on—is when we have sex.

Every bit of warmth and closeness I felt the night he made love to me is gone.

Because I don't think he *wanted* to.

I think he felt like he *had* to.

Like some deeply buried part of him knew I needed it, so he gave it. Not because he wanted to. Not because he felt anything. Just obligation.

Obligation to be a decent husband. Obligation to show up to events. Obligation to leave his stupid Post-It notes.

And once I'm pregnant?

He won't even have that obligation anymore.

I'll be moved to my room, tucked away on another floor like an antique vase he doesn't want to break but also doesn't want to look at every day.

Because that's all I am, right?

A body. A vessel. A checkmark on his damn list.

Rico

FOUR MONTHS.

One hundred and twenty days of Alessandra Bennetti living under my roof, in my space, in my bed.

She works so much even my brothers would be horrified, and that's saying something considering Alex used to call a work-life balance a conspiracy theory. Her only day off is Sunday, which is devoured by mandatory family dinners, and even then, I don't get her alone. Occasionally, she surprises the hell out of me by taking a night off during the week. But lately? That's been rare.

What's also rare? My wife being pregnant.

Not that I'm keeping track or anything.

Okay, I am.

The odds are slim even when she's ovulating, but every month, she tells me she got her period, and I feel an unsettling mixture of relief and something else I don't have the bandwidth to analyze. I'm not ready for kids. Might never be. I've seen what parenting does to my brothers—Alex has been driven into some hyper-protective, borderline un-hinged version of himself, and Dom glows like some insufferable, doting husband out of a Hallmark special.

Not me.

I look at my nieces and nephews and all I see are therapy bills waiting to happen if I'm their father figure.

Besides, I have more immediate concerns—like the fact that my wife is slowly but surely stealing from me.

First, *my* time. Then, *my* privacy. *My* quiet at work. *My* bed. *My* ability to sleep through the night without waking up to an aching, pathetic, attention-starved erection because she slid into bed at some ungodly hour and my body decided that meant it was time to wake up and beg.

It's ridiculous. I don't chase. I've never craved. My sex life before this marriage was efficient.

Now?

Now I'm spending hours tangled up in my wife, rolling around in the sheets like some lovesick teenager, and even when I pull myself out of bed in the morning, I have to resist the temptation to wake her up and start all over again. The second she falls asleep, her limbs find me—an arm draped across my chest, a leg curling over mine, her face buried into my side like I'm some human-sized body pillow she claims she doesn't need.

I don't like being touched.

Yet, somehow, she's snatched that too.

I know she's pushing me. She wants me to open up. To talk. To go out in public. And I endure it because I need her to comply with one thing—*to get pregnant.*

Because once she is, this primal, feral, brain-dead need for her will stop. *Right?*

Right.

Which is why I'm here, in my brother's kitchen.

Every Friday night, Alex and Dom sit in this exact spot, drinking and discussing things, but I don't show up for their teen girl gab sessions. Every few weeks, poker night gets thrown into the mix, and I show up for that because it gives my brain something to focus on other than my wife and the war zone she's left behind in my head.

Not tonight, though.

Tonight, I need noise. Distraction.

Because my demons?

They've gone quiet.

She walked into their domain, kicked them the hell out, and set up permanent residence, claiming squatter's rights.

And the worst part?

I'm not even mad about that one. Those voices were getting old.

"So..."

Alex draws out the word as he slides a tumbler of scotch toward me, landing across the counter. Dom, next to him, stares at me like I just sprouted a second head. Which, honestly, fair. Me sitting here willingly? This is as rare as spotting a unicorn smoking a cigar while riding a bicycle.

"I need advice." Holy shit, that one hurt to say. I'm tempted to check myself for signs of a stroke.

Dom chokes on his drink. Alex freezes mid-sip, eyes narrowing like I just told him I'm planning to become a monk.

I get it. I've asked for their advice more times since marrying my wife than in my *entire* lifetime, and it's taking a toll on my self-respect. But facts are facts. These two idiots somehow impregnate their wives at alarming rates, and I—despite *extensive* effort—am coming up empty.

It's not for a lack of trying. My wife, bless her stubborn little soul, refuses IVF, refuses to track ovulation, refuses to do anything that might increase our odds of success. So I'm left with one solution: have as much sex as possible and hope my army of swimmers eventually breaches the walls.

Which brings me to my current predicament.

"How do you two knock up your wives so easily?"

Silence.

Alex blinks at me like I just asked him to explain quantum mechanics. Dom, who has been swirling his drink like he's some sophisticated intellectual rather than a man who impregnates women with the efficiency of a malfunctioning condom, quirks a brow.

"You're serious?" Alex asks.

"No, I came here to discuss my feelings," I deadpan.

They exchange a glance before turning back to me. "You know how babies are made, right?" Dom asks, and I want to punch him. "Like, you've covered that step?"

"Yes, Dom, I'm well aware of the mechanics."

He lifts his hands in surrender, though he doesn't bother hiding his amusement. "Just checking. Because, I mean, if you're still treating it like some clinical experiment instead of actually enjoying it—"

"Oh, I enjoy it," I cut him off, rolling my glass between my fingers. Maybe a little *too much*. Enough that the second Allie walks into the house, my body drafts battle plans for round one, two, and—if we're feeling ambitious—three.

I don't share that, though. No need to give them details they didn't ask for. *Wait, no.* That's not right. Details that are none of their fucking business. Even if they asked, why would I tell. Clearly, my head is no longer in the right place.

"The more you stress about it, the harder it is," Alex says, taking a sip. "Women's bodies are weird like that."

Dom snaps his fingers. "That's right. I read that in one of the baby books. Stress messes with their hormones. Good thing my wife is never stressed."

The absolute idiot winks at me.

"Same," Alex adds, as if his pregnant wife isn't currently wrangling a small army of children.

They both turn to me. "Is Allie stressed?"

How the fuck should I know?

We only talk when I'm buried inside her, and that conversation usually comprises her calling out my name while I try not to lose my damn mind over how amazing it feels. Outside the bedroom, we exchange minimal words. She *still* texts. I *still* ignore them. The last time I did text her, I apparently gave her too much hope, and when I didn't follow through, she got mad. Rightfully so. I apologized—with my tongue, my fingers, and my dick.

But now that they mention it...

She hasn't been poking at me as much.

Normally, she's scheming. Moving her shit into my bedroom out of spite. Decorating the house in ways that offend my eyeballs. Exposing me to the sun like I'm a vampire. Manipulating me into social events under the guise of "date night."

When did she stop?

I frown.

Shit.

That might actually be a problem.

"Did Papa give you a deadline for knocking her up?" Alex asks, swirling his drink like he's in a Bond movie.

"No. Why would he?"

"Then why are you acting like a man on death row waiting for the governor's call?" Dom gets up, walking into the living room to retrieve Cici, who is currently mid-squeal. The kid is permanently attached to his hip, her chubby little hands gripping his shirt like he's the only person she trusts in the world.

Dom, a former playboy with a revolving door of women, is now the human equivalent of a Build-A-Bear dad. Soft, compliant, wrapped around his daughter's tiny, sticky fingers. That girl is going to bleed him dry one day, and he's going to thank her for it.

"It's been *four* months," I say, rubbing the bridge of my nose. "Four months of her in my bed. Dragging me to gallery openings. Forcing me to engage in conversation on Sundays."

"We know," Dom says while bouncing Cici on his knee. "It's been nice seeing you act more human and less... well, *you*."

I shoot him a look that would have most men re-evaluating. Unfortunately, he's immune.

"I don't like it."

"You like nothing that requires human interaction," Alex points out, completely unfazed. "But you have a wife who tolerates you, and that's a miracle enough."

Yeah, because I gladly dish out multiple orgasms every night.

"I want my bed back. My space. My peace." Her constant pushing has my whole body tense, my patience stretched thin. Okay, it doesn't, and that pisses me off more.

"You're seriously kicking her out the second you knock her up?" Dom looks at me like I'm the devil reincarnated.

Is he actually shocked by this? Has he met me?

"I like my space," I remind him, because apparently, we need to review the fundamentals of who I am as a person.

"I almost hope she doesn't get knocked up," Alex mutters, leaning back against the counter.

I glare at him, as if he just tossed a curse into the universe, ensuring my wife's womb stays vacant. Like my soul. I *don't* miss the irony of realizing that. Regardless, if I see black cats and broken mirrors, I'm holding him personally responsible.

"What?" He shrugs, lifting his drink. "You're literally counting down the days until she's pregnant just so you can ship her back to her floor like she's a borrowed library book. I thought maybe, just maybe, months of sharing a room, acting more like a functioning human, meant you were changing." He sighs, dragging a hand down his face before knocking back the rest of his scotch. "Guess we were wrong."

I don't respond. Because fuck, that noise. Instead, I flip my phone over on the counter. It's just past ten, but that's not what I'm fixated on.

It's the text messages.

Or lack of them.

She didn't text me when she left today. Hasn't texted me at all about when she's coming home.

Opening our thread, I see the last text she sent was three days ago.

Three.

I remember reading it. I was deep in my coding—drowning in patches and releases, trying to rid myself of a pest with the most insufferably dull hacker handle known to man. I read it, like I always do. And, like always, I didn't respond.

But she hasn't texted me since.

My stomach tightens.

I've always been gloomy, but I've been especially aggravated for the past few days, and now I understand why. Since when does a woman not texting me, especially one I never text back, make me feel like my equilibrium is off?

There's only one logical solution.

Go home tonight. Tell her we're doing IVF. If we've been having sex almost daily for four months with no results, something's got to give.

This woman has stolen everything else.

She's not taking my mind, too.

Rico

THE MOMENT I REALIZED we had to do IVF, I felt a flicker of relief. There. Problem solved.

No thanks to the two idiots I'm cursed to call my brothers, who droned on about how I was a massive asshole for planning to knock up my wife only to boot her back to her own floor like she was an Airbnb guest whose stay had expired. Disappointment. Shame. *Blah, blah, blah.* I tuned them out somewhere between *you need to rethink this* and *I can't believe you're this emotionally stunted.* Honestly, it's like they just met me.

They were there when I moved her in. She had her own room. The only reason she shared mine now was because Marco, that dumbass, put the idea in my head. Seemed logical at the time—constant proximity meant constant access. The math checked out.

Only, it *wasn't* benefiting me.

I sat on the bed, arms crossed, scowling at the throw pillows.

I hate throw pillows.

They serve no purpose. Zero. Every night, I have to toss them onto the floor only to pick them up in the morning like a slave to home decor gods. Whoever invented them should be exiled from Earth. Straight to hell, where I assume they were conceived by a demon with a sick sense of humor.

And my wife, the woman who keeps inching her way into my personal space and—worse—my subconscious, had brought them into my room.

The same one who walked in three minutes past eleven.

Not unusual. She always comes home late. What was strange was her expression. Normally, she walks in radiating that post-work happiness, the high people get from doing what they love. Tonight? She looked broken. Actually, come to think of it, she looked like that yesterday. *And* the day before that.

Maybe that's why she stopped texting me.

Not that I noticed.

Or cared.

Except I had noticed.

She also *stopped* responding to my notes. The ones I left her out of habit. And the ones she always—*always*—left a sarcastic remark on before sticking them right back where I'd find them. When did she stop?

A week.

It's been a week.

I watch her move around the room, acting like I don't exist, like I'm a piece of furniture.

She thinks she's winning. Thinks she's worming her way into whatever organ exists in the empty cavity where my heart should be. She probably assumes I'm in love with her by now.

I'm not.

Not even close.

I just tolerate her shit because saying I don't love you and I don't care wouldn't exactly benefit me.

"Not tonight, Rico." Her voice is flat, exhausted, as she breezes past me into the closet.

I follow. Lean against the doorframe.

"We had an agreement."

Her fingers still over the dresser. She turns, eyes narrowed, and some long-dormant self-preservation instinct flares to life in my gut. Possibly my fight-or-flight reflex trying to warn me. Retreat, *you dumbass.*

I ignore it. Like I ignore every other feeling that doesn't serve me.

"None of that agreement said that after a long day, I have to have sex with you," she says, voice sharp.

"We agreed that when one of us needs it—"

"I *don't* need it," she cuts me off, turning back to her drawer, pulling out those silky pajamas she knows I hate. The ones she wears every night just to annoy me because she knows I'll waste precious minutes peeling them off her.

I watch her move, jaw tight.

Fine.

Maybe I enjoy taking them off.

It's like unwrapping a present.

Right now, I have a gut feeling I won't get the satisfaction of peeling those silk pajamas off her, and if she thinks she's sleeping in my bed like we're some blissfully married couple, she's severely miscalculated.

"Then I suppose you can sleep upstairs."

The words slip out before I can stop them, which is rare, considering my verbal output is usually as controlled as a nuclear launch code. And yet, here I am, spewing pointless bullshit like I'm trying to win an argument I didn't even know I was starting.

Why? Because looking at my wife's face—those eyes going wide, her lips pressing into a tight, thin as hell line—I'd say I just set off a chain reaction that leads straight to a fight. And what does a fight mean? Fifteen to twenty minutes of a back-and-forth verbal sparring match that could've been spent with her naked legs wrapped around me, making progress toward the entire reason I sought my brothers' advice in the first place.

Which, for the record, I will never live down.

Does this woman realize the depths I have sunk for her? The sheer humiliation of sitting through a heart-to-heart with Dom and Alex, listening to them lecture me on women and emotions like they were delivering some TED Talk I never asked for?

And yet, her reaction isn't what I expect.

"I suppose so."

Not the response I wanted.

And now I'm annoyed.

Annoyed in the way a toddler is when they reach for candy and their mom slaps their hand away. The way my nephews sulk when Violet tells them no, like it's the most offensive word in the English language.

"You need to take the tests."

She blinks. "Tests?"

"Ovulation tests."

Cue the dramatic eye roll. If she added a sigh and a head shake, I'd have had the full trifecta of female exasperation.

"No."

With that, she pushes past me into my bathroom, because apparently, room separation doesn't apply when it comes to using my space. She stands at the sink, pulling off the thin chain around her neck, setting it in some fancy little dish *she* put in my bathroom, next to an ungodly amount of feminine products, all designed to pluck, curl, scrub, or god knows what else.

Fine. I'll push further.

"Then we do IVF."

Now I'm just poking the bear. But this bear gets horny when she's mad, so really, I don't see the problem.

Her hand freezes over the faucet.

"You want to do IVF?"

I nod.

She turns off the water.

Her expression isn't anger—it's something worse. Something I don't have the time or energy to unpack.

"So that's all this still is?" Her hands wave between us like she's outlining some invisible thread. There's nothing there by the way.

"You just want me to get pregnant."

"That *was* the agreement."

"And we've made changes." Her voice wobbles marginally, and I don't like it. That... *sound*. The crack. Like something fragile snapping under pressure.

I ignore it.

"So moving me into your room was what? Just to make sure you got me pregnant? So I could be here, at your beck and call, so you could knock me up and then move on with your life?"

"Not sure why that surprises you."

It's direct. Honest. Cold. And for some reason, something in my brain, some deep, traitorous instinct warns me I should back the hell down. Maybe even reverse course before I say something I can't take back.

But then there's the other part of me.

The logical part.

The one that tells me I need to make this clear, once and for all. *She needs to stop pushing. Stop provoking. Stop trying to change me.*

I *won't* change.

She's my wife in the contractual sense.

Nothing more.

And it's better that reality sinks in now—before she gets any deeper into this delusion. Before she convinces herself she can steal something from me that she will never be able to take.

Because the truth is simple.

I'm too broken to give her what she wants.

That's just reality.

Allie

TODAY WAS A DAY.

Not the *Ugh, I need a drink and a bubble bath kind of day*. No, this was the send me to a deserted island where my only problem is coconut-related kind of day.

Two of my line cooks called in sick, which meant I spent most of the night running around the kitchen like a contestant on a cooking competition show—only instead of Gordon Ramsay yelling at me, it was my damn inner monologue screaming, *Why the hell do you still do this?*

Physically drained? Absolutely.

Mentally drained? A slow, two-week-long spiral into an existential crisis.

And now, as if life wanted to give me one final *screw you*, my husband—my emotionally nonexistent husband—is standing here proving that I mean absolutely *nothing* to him.

Rico, in all his grumpy, broody, emotionally repressed glory, has finally confirmed what I've been trying to deny.

That *he doesn't love me.*

That *he will never love me.*

That all those small moments I'd let myself believe were something—waking up wrapped around each other, the way he reached for me in his sleep, the way his body practically devoured me whenever I was near—meant absolutely nothing to him.

Like a fool, I thought I'd gotten through to him. I needed to believe that I was more than just a warm body he happened to share a bed with.

Turns out? I was wrong.

Painfully, stupidly, gut-wrenchingly wrong.

"I will not do IVF," I snap, arms crossed as I gawk up at him, because fuck that. I might not be getting love out of this sham of a marriage, but I refuse to be reduced to some science experiment just because my husband wants to speedrun the baby-making process.

"You will," he fires back, his tone clipped. "We got married so you could give me a child."

And there it is.

Not, we got married because I wanted to build a life with you.

Not, we got married because I saw something in you worth fighting for.

Nope.

Just a transactional brief sentence that makes me want to hurl something at his stupidly flawless face.

I step into his space, shoving him. "And that can take months! You, of all people, should know that. Last I checked, you Google the shit out of everything, so tell me, does your research mention it doesn't just happen overnight?"

His jaw twitches, his expression a perfect replica of a statue—completely unreadable. "It doesn't with IVF *either*."

He shrugs. Like we're discussing a grocery list.

"I will have my baby the traditional way."

"Our contract says otherwise."

He folds his arms across his chest, and I catch the slight clench in his jaw. He's grinding his teeth. Good. Let him be mad. I've *been* mad. And *sad*. And *confused* for weeks. Come join the party, hubby. Experience an emotion.

"We amended that contract," I point out, voice rising. "As you oh-so-kindly reminded me just minutes ago when you clearly wanted to have sex with me." I throw my arms out, nearly knocking over the useless decorative vase on the dresser I put there just to piss him off. "Is that all I am to you? Your personal stress relief on call every night so you can get off and hopefully get me pregnant?"

Something flickers in those amber eyes—something. A spark. A reaction.

Finally.

Then he opens his mouth and extinguishes it.

"You're a good fuck," his voice flat. "But that's it. A warm hole to use *until* you get pregnant. Which, clearly, you can't do."

I freeze.

The words land hard, direct, and with surgical precision.

For months, I've been starving for words from him. Craving conversation, looking for anything beyond the grunts and clipped responses he gives me when he's not currently inside me. And this?

This is what he shares?

"What about everything you say while we..." I trail off before I call it making love, because God, that would be pathetic. "What about all those secrets you share?"

His response is instant. Emotionless.

"Whatever gets you off."

And that knocks the air from my lungs.

Not the sex.

Not the coldness.

Not even the confirmation that I'm nothing more than a means to an end for him.

It's the casual indifference.

The realization that none of those moments meant *anything* to him. That *I don't mean anything* to him.

And yet, like the fool I am, I still ask.

"So you don't love me?"

Why am I doing this to myself?

Why am I begging for him to stab the knife deeper?

Because I *need* to hear it. I need him to pound the final nail into the coffin so I can bury whatever shred of hope I had left and move the hell on.

Rico stares at me. His jaw tensed. His Adam's apple bobs.

Then, finally—*finally*—he speaks.

"No." A slight tilt of his head. His tone was completely devoid of hesitation. "Why would I?"

And that is it.

The final blow.

The brutal confirmation that the last four months of me pushing—fighting, trying, hoping—were for *nothing*.

I nod, pushing past him, heading straight for my old room.

My room.

A room I haven't slept in for almost four months. A room that was empty—because I made it empty. Because I moved all my things into *his* room.

Half to piss him off.

Half to push him into something resembling a normal marriage.

Push.

That's all I've ever done.

Push him to share a room with me.

Push him to let me make our house a home.

Push him to go in public with me.

Push him to leave me those stupid, useless little notes.

Push. Push. Push.

And it never mattered.

Because he never pulled me back.
Not once.
And the worst part?
I love him.

Rico

It's been two days since I told Allie I didn't love her.

Forty-eight hours of avoiding the house like it was rigged with explosives and booby traps meant to force me into an emotional reckoning.

And yet, despite my impeccable avoidance tactics, her face haunts me. The moment still loops in my mind, like a cursed YouTube ad with no "skip" button. I see it in my monitors, in the reflection of my coffee mug, behind my eyelids when I attempt to blink like a normal human. The whole gutted expression, glassy eyes, lips parted in disbelief—I see it everywhere.

So now, I just don't close my eyes. Problem solved.

Immediately after she stormed out of my room, I did what any relationship-impaired man would do—I went to my gym and beat the shit out of my punching bag until my knuckles split and bled. Then, since I clearly possess the self-preservation instincts of a rock, I kept going, like a psycho reenacting a Rocky training montage but without the victorious ending or stellar soundtrack.

Then I showered. Then I went to work. And I haven't been home since.

Two days.

Forty-eight hours of downing ungodly amounts of caffeine and working myself into a stupor, all to avoid going home and facing the fact that, for the first time in my life, I might actually owe someone a genuine apology.

And not just any apology—the mother of all apologies. The kind you probably have to Google how to do because you lack the sentimental range to figure it out yourself.

I don't love her. I don't even know if I *can* love someone. But do I hate her? No. Do I see her as just a body to warm my bed? Absolutely not. Sure, she's all of those things—warm, tight, dangerously addictive—but that's not all she is. And yet, I basically told her she was nothing more than a human incubator and a decent way to pass the time before fatherhood. So yeah. I need to fix this.

The problem? I have no fucking clue how.

I've never apologized in my life. Not once. I don't even know what one sounds like. It makes me nauseous just thinking about it—like all the coffee I've been mainlining might make a sudden, dramatic exit. Have I eaten anything? I take a sip of what's left in my cup and grimace. Definitely not. Judging by the sludge consistency, this coffee predates the fall of Rome.

I rub my eyes and glance at my phone.

No texts.

Nothing.

For two days.

That's what finally has me gripping the phone tighter than necessary.

Allie, the woman who floods my phone with useless updates—about her day, what's for dinner, the tragic state of her favorite coffee shop running out of non-fat milk—has not texted me once in forty-eight hours.

And I don't like how that makes me feel.

I'm not even sure what I feel. It's not panic. Not sadness. Not even guilt. It's something worse. Something foreign. Something gnawing at my insides like a parasite I can't kill.

It's absence.

She's stopped *pushing*. Stopped *trying*. And now my body is not okay with this development.

So what do I do? I double down on being an idiot.

I decide to "fix" things the way I fix everything else in my life—by throwing logic at it. By solving the problem.

Which is why, in the middle of my self-imposed exile, I decide the best solution is to call and schedule an appointment.

With a therapist.

Allie has officially driven me to the point of needing to go backward.

That thieving woman has already stolen my time, my peace, my bed space, and now—now—she's taken my ability to even find joy in my own work.

I need control back.

I need to get back to myself.

Because *this*? Whatever we've been doing?

This is *not* working.

I don't like this.

This itching, nagging, foreign sensation clawing at the edges of my usually well-ordered mind. It's like an allergic reaction to human decency, and the only cure is avoidance.

I do not grovel. I do not bend my life around someone else's feelings. And I sure as hell do not apologize for being exactly who I've *always* been.

Yet, here I am, sitting at my desk, debating whether I should go home and grovel.

Disgusting.

If Allie wanted some emotionally accessible, communicative, bend-over-backwards husband, she should've made better choices. Like not agreeing to this marriage. Her mistake. *Not mine.*

And yet—here we are.

Instead of basking in my hard-earned victory after finally outmaneuvering that hacker prick and keeping him out of our systems for over 48 hours, I feel...*nothing.*

Not relief. Not satisfaction. Not the usual, well-earned smugness that comes with obliterating someone else's entire sense of self-worth via code.

No, instead, I have this.

This awareness—this irritating itch in my brain that refuses to be scratched—because my wife somehow stole my ability to enjoy my own fucking job. My job is the one thing I have. The one thing I've always felt comfortable in. If I felt any satisfaction in life, it came from the successes here. Today I should celebrate, which really is a mental pat on the back and I get to work, but I can't do that. Can't even tell Dom and Alex their headaches are over.

What the actual fuck.

This entire company merger—this billion-dollar acquisition that should be my priority—is being drowned out by the realization that I might have to go home and talk about my feelings.

And by talk, I mean apologize, which is possibly worse than being waterboarded.

To make it all worse? I already know that when this merger is finalized, the office will be overrun with California tech bros whose entire vocabulary comprises "dude," "vibes," and "let's circle back."

I'd rather jam my head into a wood chipper.

So, to summarize:

My company is being invaded by surfers in Patagonia vests.

I can't even enjoy humiliating a hacker.

And my wife, the actual bane of my existence, has somehow made me feel guilty.

I dislike guilt.

It's invasive. Suffocating. Makes your chest tighten. There's a reason I've avoided it my entire life—it's useless. And yet, here it is, wrapping around me like a noose.

Fuck that.

She's pushed too far.

She needs a reminder of *who* she married.

I am not soft. I do not bend. I do not break. And I sure as hell do not let a woman mold me into something I am not.

I had structure before her. Order. Routine. Life made sense.

Now? I live uncomfortably. Everything is out of place. Out of sync.

And if I can't even be happy at work, if my mind isn't a sanctuary anymore, then what do I have left?

Allie

I DIDN'T GO TO WORK today. Instead, I did something far more reckless. I cooked dinner.

For him.

Like some desperate housewife from a 1950s sitcom, I made a meal and planned an actual conversation with my emotionally stunted husband. Because clearly, I am the crazy one here.

It was stupid—delusional even—to think I could change someone who has spent decades perfecting his I don't give a shit personality. Rico never pretended to be anything but who he is. He never sold me a fairytale. I was the one who clung to that stupid, infuriating, all-consuming thing called hope.

Hope, for the record, is a menace. The serial killer of all joy.

I knew what I was walking into when I married him. I just refused to fully acknowledge it. I thought I could change it.

Fine. Lesson learned. I get it.

So, I recalibrate. Shift the focus. My restaurant will be my pride and joy. When we have kids, I'll throw myself into them, love them so fiercely they'll never question their worth. And unlike my husband, my children *will* love me back. Unconditionally.

That *will be* enough.

I won't have the picture-perfect marriage, but Rico will be a provider, and I know—*I know*—he'll love our kids. I've seen him with his nieces and nephews. He lights up. He feels something for them, even if he refuses to feel anything for me.

It's almost eight. I never texted him about dinner, but he always assumes I'm at the restaurant, which means he usually comes home before seven. So, where is he?

My fingers tap against the wooden dining table, the food in front of me long past cold, the wine in my glass untouched.

When I hear the garage door open, my stomach does an annoying little flutter that I immediately want to stab into submission. Two days of silence. Two days of not knowing where we stand. Two days of stewing in my head, trying to figure out how to talk to him without sounding like an unhinged lunatic.

And then there he is.

Rico stills in the kitchen's doorway, his eyes landing on me, his entire body pausing. The surprise on his face is almost comical. What? You think I died? Packed up and left? All were tempting options, and I'd lie if I said they didn't cross my mind.

"I... I made dinner," I start, suddenly feeling ridiculous for even attempting this. "Thought we could talk."

He steps into the kitchen, silent, opening the fridge, grabbing a water bottle, and chugging half of it—obviously avoiding looking at me.

"Were you at the sparring gym?" I ask, noting the slight mess of his hair, the exhaustion dragging at his eyes. That usual hunger he has for me when he sees me? Gone.

He shakes his head. No explanation. No further details.

"I can heat up the food," I offer, nodding toward the now-cold meal sitting pathetically on the table. I spent all day cooking—literally simmering marinara sauce, stewing over my thoughts, and now I get this?

"Not hungry."

And just like that, he walks right past me, straight down the hall.

I shoot out of my chair and chase after him. "Rico. We need to talk about the other night."

He stops, back still to me, and then sighs like I'm the most exhausting person he's ever met, then turns around slowly.

"Why?"

I blink. Why? WHY? Is he for real right now?

"Why do you *think*?" I bite out. "We need to discuss how to move forward."

"There's nothing to discuss." Icy. Detached. Worse than the man I married a few months ago.

The tone that ends conversations, not starts them.

I swallow, tugging at the hem of my shirt, steeling myself. "I moved my things back to my room," I tell him, my voice surprisingly steady. "I thought maybe we could talk about where we go from here."

He studies me, his face unreadable, and then—without any inflection, like he's announcing the weather—he says, "I was with my therapist this evening."

And then—he walks away.

Rico

ANGER. DISGUST. REMORSE.

Three fucking emotions.

In case we're keeping track, that's three more than I'm equipped to handle.

She did this to me.

Despite my meticulous efforts, my wife has done the unthinkable. She's infected me with feelings.

Worse? None of them are aimed at her. No, I'm the target. A one-man firing squad executing my sanity.

I'm angry at myself for being angry. And then I'm angry that I don't know how to process the first two layers of anger, which creates an endless cycle of bullshit I refuse to dissect.

Therefore, proving emotions are *useless*. You get caught in a loop, obsessing over the same feeling you felt in the first place, and suddenly, you're spiraling in a psychological blender without an off switch.

Still, doesn't change the fact that they're here.

Festering.

Clawing through me like they've been caged for too long and finally found a crack in my perfectly built walls.

I want to hit her with them. Not physically—despite my monstrous tendencies, I'm not that *kind* of piece of shit. No, I want to slam these feelings right into her, make her carry the unrelenting weight of them. I want her to suffocate under the same unbearable pressure, feel her own ribs crack under the strain of caring too much.

But she already does.

That's the problem.

Even after what I said—after I all but carved her open and left her bleeding on the floor—she still fucking loves me.

And that makes me disgusted with myself.

So, what do I do? I lash out. Because that's what monsters do. They don't reflect. They don't acknowledge. They don't fix. *They destroy.*

I took my time in the shower, scrubbing myself raw, as if I could scrape off the filth of my own existence. It didn't work. Neither did standing under the scalding spray until my skin felt like it was melting off. If I thought the look on her face two nights ago was bad—this one? This new one?

It's burned into my brain.

A permanent stain on whatever semblance of a soul I have left.

So I stalled.

I shaved with deliberate precision, dragging the blade over my skin like it was some kind of ritualistic punishment. Took my time drying off, dressing, straightening things that weren't out of place. Anything to delay what I knew I needed to do.

Go upstairs.

Tell her the *truth*.

Tell her that, yes, I saw *a therapist* today. But not *the therapist* I blatantly suggested I'd seen because I have the emotional capacity of a four-year-old and lashed out instead of dealing with these newly found feelings from hell.

No, my therapist doesn't even have tits. I went to see a nerdy, bug-eyed intellectual who wore a tweed jacket, crossed his legs like he was settling in for afternoon tea, and—just to top off the irony—took notes on an iPad which was the only thing that seemed to be from this decade.

The office was a time capsule from the seventies, like he decorated it with the explicit goal of making people more depressed. The entire thing reeked of self-righteous academia, and yet—I made another appointment.

Not weekly.

Three times a week.

Apparently, I'm more fucked up than I realized.

Turns out, trauma doesn't just go away when you shove it under the rug. No, it festers, rotting beneath the surface until it forces its way back up.

And guess what?

It's here.

It's in her eyes. In the way she looks at me like I'm someone worth saving.

It's in me, in the way I don't fucking know how to tell her I don't hate her.

In fact, I hate myself more than I ever have for making her believe I even dislike her.

I was so pissed that I actually stepped into a therapist's office today. So furious that I let her get inside my head, crack open things I've kept locked up for years.

And now?

Now I want to throw it in her face.

Tell her that because of her, my neatly organized, perfectly functional, emotionless life is a wreckage of shattered pieces.

And the worst part?

Now I have to pick them up. One by one.

When I'm in my sweats, I glance at the nightstand where a clock sits. A clock she bought just to piss me off.

At least this one doesn't tick.

It's been two hours. Two hours since I dropped the therapist bomb on her and walked away like the emotionally stunted asshole I am. Two hours since I realized—against my will—that I should probably go upstairs, tell her what I actually meant instead of what I insinuated, and smooth this over before it festers into something even worse.

I trudge up the stairs, an unfamiliar route considering I've had zero reasons to be up here since giving her the grand tour months ago. Her door is open, so I knock once before pushing it wider.

She's not in bed.

It's made, pristine, untouched. The bathroom door is wide open, the lights off. But the closet light is on. I step inside, expecting to find her fussing with something, maybe clutching a pillow to beat me over the head with the moment I walk in. A pointy heel to stab me with when I least expect it. All deserved.

She's not there.

Neither are half her clothes.

My stomach tightens. Not sickly way. More like an immediate *you fucked up* way. The kind that comes right before you realize you don't have control anymore.

I yank my phone out of my pocket and check the security feed.

Fifteen minutes ago.

Fifteen fucking minutes ago, the SUV pulled out of the garage.

Twenty minutes ago, she handed suitcases—*plural*—to Vinnie. Vinnie, who hugged her while she wiped tears from her eyes.

And then they drove off.

My chest constricts, my brain goes static, and for the first time in my entire life, I understand why people punch walls. I have punched walls, that's not foreign. But what is, is the understanding of *why*. The fucking feelings again.

I pull up her contact. Stare at the thread. The endless list of blue-bubbled texts from her. The silence from me. The texts I never answered.

She didn't even check where I was when I disappeared for two days.

That shouldn't bother me.

It does.

And that jab—childish and unnecessary—delivers the final shove.

I hit call.

Declined.

I hit call *again.*

Straight to voicemail.

Pulling up our text thread, I type my second-ever message to my wife in five months.

Yeah. Karma is a bitch, and she's currently sinking her claws into me with pure, unrelenting spite.

> Rico: I know you're pissed. We need to talk.

Read. No response.

My stomach churns.

Is this what it felt like for her? To see me read and ignore?

> Rico: I know you saw the message. Come home. We need to talk.

Read again.

No response.

Fuck. Me.

I don't send another. Instead, I think.

Where would she go?

If she went to either of my brothers' houses, they'd be here any minute to shove their uninvited opinions down my throat. I don't care. If she's at one of their places, I don't have to chase her through half of Manhattan. I can knock on the door, explain that there was a misunderstanding, acknowledge that I'm an asshole for saying it, and move on.

We can live in this house. Keep our separate spaces.

We can make it work.

Only when I get into my car and drive past both of my brothers' places, the SUV is nowhere in sight.

I call again.

Voicemail.

I grit my teeth, flex my hands on the steering wheel, and let out a slow, measured breath.

"We need to talk, Allie. I don't play these games."

Only I do, because here I am, calling and texting like a madman, as if I haven't been treating my phone like a glorified paperweight for months.

She could be anywhere. A hotel. Her parents'. My cousin's.

Or—

Kai's.

As if I didn't see the way he looks at her. The way he tracks her across the room.

My jaw clenches so tight it might crack.

And I can't ignore the hypocrisy.

I just insinuated I cheated on her, and yet here I am, jealous as fuck over a man who has never once laid a hand on her. A man I'm fully aware has spent the past five months watching her the way I do—only I have the right to.

Shit. Had the right...

The phone rings.

I glance at the screen, hands tightening around the wheel.

Marco.

Fan-fucking-tastic.

I push the button on the steering wheel, answering through the car's Bluetooth.

"What."

"Want to explain to me the call I just got from Vinnie?"

So she didn't snitch. Vinnie did.

I take a slow, measured breath. Even with all my training, I'd rather not take on that fight. Not because I don't think I could land a few hits, but because then his brother, Antonio, would step in. And Antonio? Antonio doesn't stop until you're unrecognizable. Hard pass.

"No clue."

A lie.

Not sure how much Vinnie told him, and I'm not about to serve myself up to the grand and powerful Marco for a lecture.

Also, since when did Marco give a shit? The man avoids family drama like it's contagious. He usually leaves the meddling to my parents, my brothers, and their nosy-as-hell wives.

"You fucking idiot."

His voice is a low growl, and I grip the steering wheel harder.

"Therapist, Rico? Your fucking *therapist*?" He scoffs, and I can practically hear him pacing. "I knew you had issues, but are you kidding me? Your hot-as-fuck wife wasn't enough?"

I don't respond.

"I knew you were an asshole," he continues, "but if I'd known you'd stoop this low, I never would have pushed her to marry you."

Click.

He hangs up before I can explain. Before I can tell him that yes, it was an actual therapist. Licensed and everything. That I actually sought someone who specializes in childhood trauma and emotional repression—because apparently, I need that shit.

But no. He doesn't want an explanation.

Because in his mind, I just admitted to seeing a therapist for cheating on my wife, and it's my fault. I did, in fact, tell my wife that — truth or not.

I let out a sharp breath.

Marco owns multiple houses. He rotates them randomly as a precaution. Only his bodyguard and Uncle Tony know where he actually is on any given day.

Which means asking Uncle Tony for a favor.

And I'd rather be disemboweled.

That man would relish making me grovel for information. Then he'd warn Marco, so he could skip town, leaving me empty-handed and in his debt. After all, this is the man that spawned the creature known as my cousin. He's got more nuts and bolts missing than a junkyard car.

No thanks.

Which means I have one other option.

I need to turn to my brothers. *Again.*

This is getting real old, real fast.

Rico

"So, what brings you in today, Enrico?"

Dr. Dingleberry—not his actual name, but it's the energy he radiates—crosses his legs, looking down at the massive intake form he made me fill out before I was allowed into his seventies-era relic of an office.

A leather chair that looks like it's swallowed a few patients whole. Wood paneling that screams "my career peaked in 1982." An actual rotary phone on his desk, which I can only assume is there for aesthetic purposes.

I don't sit.

I don't want to be here.

"I filled out the form."

He looks up at me, unimpressed. Beady onyx eyes, bird-like nose, a graying mustache that twitches like it has its own agenda. The man is pushing sixty and looks every bit of it—though, in his defense, if I had to sit and listen to people sob their way through their "woe-is-me" monologues all day, I'd age like curdled milk, too.

"I see that." He taps a finger on his iPad. "But therapy requires talking. Which, according to your responses, is something you struggle with."

"Not a struggle. Just a preference."

"To remain silent?"

I shrug. "Works for me."

He hums, tapping his stylus against the screen like he's about to diagnose me with something I already know I have, and from what I know there's no cure for it.

"To get anywhere in therapy—or life, for that matter—you'll have to use your words. Sitting in silence won't let me help you."

"Rico."

"I'm sorry?"

"I prefer to be called Rico." Especially since Enrico is only used when my Mama is ready to commit manslaughter—which she almost did over the phone two nights ago, flinging Spanish and Italian at me so fast my brain had trouble processing which language I was being verbally castrated in. As if I wasn't already aware of my colossal fuck-up.

As if I haven't spent the past two days chasing my wife down, only to realize she has vanished off the face of the earth.

She's not at my brothers' houses. Not at Marco's. Not at a hotel—not one under her name, anyway.

Which means she's somewhere I haven't considered.

Which means she's actually gone.

And that realization?

That gnawing, pit-in-my-stomach, my-world-is-off-its-axis feeling?

It's made me dangerous.

I've spent more time at the sparring gym in the past forty-eight hours than I have in my bed. Relishing the sound of bones crunching under my fists, using pain to drown out the fact that she left. That I pushed too hard. That the woman who *should've* never walked away finally *did*.

The split in my knuckles reopens as I clench my fists, a sharp sting breaking through my thoughts.

"Do you always do that?" Dingleberry nods toward my hands.

"Yes."

"And it helps?"

I flex my fingers. Watch as a bead of deep red blood wells and slips down my knuckle.

Red like the dress she wore to the gallery. Red like the lipstick she smeared on my neck on the ride home. Red like the flush that spreads down her neck when I whisper in her ear. Red like the warning signs I ignored telling me this woman would be my undoing and I wanted it.

"It keeps me from having an episode."

His thick, raccoon-rivaling eyebrows arch. "Episode?"

Jesus. He's really committed to this whole talking thing.

"When I get too angry, I need to hit something."

"I see." He doesn't even blink. "Is that why your knuckles are bruised?"

I nod. "A punching bag. Mostly."

His fingers move over the iPad, typing something, before looking back at me. "How often do you have these... urges?"

Every. Fucking. Day. Right now at least.

"Normally? Under control." I crack my neck, my pulse an aggravated thud in my temple. "Past few months? Every day."

"Every day." He repeats it slowly, like he's cataloging the exact moment I lost my sanity.

"Clenching my fists," I correct. "Not always a punching bag."

"And what happened a few months ago to make these urges worse?"

I snort. They're not urges. They're outlets. This guy's supposed to have a Ph.D.?

"I got married."

His mouth twitches. "Ah."

I know what he's thinking. I can see it in the way he taps his stylus against the screen, making mental calculations about my deep-rooted commitment issues.

"So, you're here to control those urges?"

I shake my head, scanning his bookshelf—filled with nothing but psychology textbooks and clinical journals. No photos. No personal touch. The walls are bare. No paintings. No distractions. Just a vacuum of emotion.

I should love this place.

I hate it.

Shit. When did I start liking décor?

"I *can* control them."

His beady eyes flick to my hands. "Clearly."

"That was this week."

He leans back, pulling off his glasses and twirling them between his fingers. "So, what made this week different?"

I grit my teeth, the image of her expression slicing through me like a rusted blade. The way her face crumpled when I told her I didn't love her. The way she didn't argue when I insinuated I cheated but deflated, and right there I should have taken it back because of that look? She'd given up. Defeat was all over her perfect face.

"I got into a fight with my wife."

"Marriages have fights." He waves a hand. "No couple sees eye-to-eye every day."

No shit, Sherlock.

"I'm aware."

"So, why did this fight bother you?"

It didn't.

It shouldn't.

I could lie. Keep this surface-level and fix the parts of me that are wrong. But instead, I hear myself say:

"I told her I didn't love her."

His expression stays neutral.

"And then I told her I cheated on her."

A sharp pain twists in my stomach. Apparently, this is a side effect when you feel shit. Physical pain and mental anguish. Why the fuck does anyone volunteer for this? The words are acid on my tongue, burning on the way out. I don't know why I admitted that. Maybe my subconscious has decided that if I'm going to do this whole therapy thing, I might as well light the entire house on fire.

"So, you cheated?"

"No."

"But you told her you did?"

I nod.

He cocks his head, clearly trying to determine if I'm insane or just a run-of-the-mill masochist. I'd appreciate a clarification myself. I'm genuinely curious at this point.

"And why would you tell your wife you cheated on her if you didn't?"

"To push her." I say it plainly. Like it's the most logical response in the world. "She knew I don't do feelings. She knew what our marriage was. But she pushed and took." I shake my head, anger flickering in my pulse. "I don't know why she loves me. No one should."

His silence stretches.

"And?"

"And I can't love her back."

He studies me for a long moment. "So, instead of explaining that, you told her you cheated?"

No, I said it because I wanted her to be angry like I was. To feel disgust looking at me just like I did looking in the mirror. To regret every marrying me. Unfortunately, I can't say I regret marrying her, which is part of the problem.

"I needed to make it clear."

He exhales through his nose, rubbing his jaw. Then, with a completely straight face, says, "Did it—just tossing this out there—occur to you that maybe you *do* love her, and that's exactly why you lashed out?"

I blink.

"What?"

He shrugs, casual as hell. "You're describing classic self-sabotage. Pushing someone away before they can reject you first."

I glare at him.

Because fuck, I'm really getting sick of people being right.

Allie

I GAVE MYSELF THREE days.

Three days to mourn what I shouldn't have to mourn. Because technically, you can't lose something you never really had, right? That's the saying. *Can't lose what was never yours.*

Well, whoever came up with that rubbish can shove it.

Because it feels like I lost *something*. And for three entire days, I wallowed. I ugly cried. I made dramatic declarations of independence to the walls of Kai's guest room. And I definitely sobbed into a pot of broth at work, which—not to brag—was a new low, even for me. Turns out, tears do not add the perfect amount of salt. They just make you feel pathetic while you dump an entire batch of soup down the drain.

Kai, being the only rational adult in my life at the moment, took one look at my blotchy, red, puffy mess of a face, sighed like a man carrying the weight of too much estrogen, and dragged me away from the kitchen line before I could contaminate another dish.

I'd crashed at his place because it was the safest, most uninvolved option. Violet and Sienna had both offered guest rooms and aggressively supportive hugs. Their husbands, in turn, had offered to kill mine, which, while stimulating, felt like a little much, even for me. Marco had offered one of his many apartments, but I refused to take advantage of him again. And my parents? Yeah, no. Going home would have felt like reverting, like undoing all the progress I'd made.

So, Kai's guest room it was. Annnnddddd his couch. Because apparently, even the comfort of a high-end mattress couldn't make me sleep right now. Instead, I spent my nights curled up on his sofa, reading Violet's books—the only thing I'd remembered to grab before I packed up and bailed like a wimp.

Priorities.

Now, standing in the kitchen, wiping the last of my tears off my face like a an operating adult, Kai gives me a look. The one that says I should go home, cry in private, and stop freaking out the line cooks.

"You need to take another day," he keeps his voice low. As if the entire kitchen doesn't already notice I'm an emotional train wreck. Not that it's hard to tell. Between the blotchy skin, the bags under my eyes, and that I'm currently sporting the pale, lifeless hue of an uncooked scallop, I'm not exactly radiating *put together* energy.

"I'm fine." I wave him off, ignoring the way a server sidesteps me like I might burst into tears at any second. "I've spent enough time on your couch."

"I'm well aware. Your body imprint has permanently embedded itself into the cushions."

"Okay, dramatic."

"Just take the night off," he insists, rubbing the back of his neck. "I've got dinner service. We're fine."

"You sure?"

"Considering you just cried into the last pot of bone broth, I think the prep team tomorrow will thank me for offering."

I groan, tilting my head back toward the ceiling. "That was one time—"

"*Twice.*"

"—and it won't happen again."

"Take. The. Night. Off." He slaps my purse into my hands and casually waves toward the entrance, where Vinnie is already waiting like the tyrannical, mafia-bodyguard-slash-big-brother I never asked for but I'm so grateful to have.

My eyes narrow. "Did you rat me out?"

Kai shrugs, completely indifferent. "Maybe."

"I hate you."

"Lies."

Before I can argue, he leans in, presses a quick peck to my cheek, and slaps my shoulder in a *you're-a-survivor-kid* sort of way. Then he's turning back to the staff while I march toward Vinnie, muttering under my breath about traitors.

Because obviously, my misery is a group project now.

I don't go back to Kai's, where I'd inevitably plant myself on the couch, cry into a romance novel, and single-handedly deplete his tissue supply—which, by the way, I've done twice. No, I need reinforcements. The kind that only comes from a mother's unsolicited wisdom and an endless supply of bone-crushing hugs.

So I go to my parents' house.

Not to stay—hell no, thank you very much. That would be like throwing myself into an emotional pressure cooker, where every communication is seasoned with guilt and a side of *when are you giving us grandbabies?* No, I just need to talk to my mama. Because even though we lost time, she's still my mother, and when the world feels like it's crumbling, she's the one I turn to. Even if she's possibly the worst person on the planet for marital advice.

Vinnie pulls up, and before the car even fully stops, Mama is already floating down the porch steps like some tiny, well-dressed, vengeful angel. She practically rips the car door open and yanks me into her arms, squeezing me tight.

"I'm so sorry, Allie."

Not *principessa*. Just Allie. And weirdly, I don't mind. Maybe that means they're finally letting go of the past, accepting my choices, even if those choices have led me to this moment—on the brink of divorce before I even had time to change my driver's license.

Mama keeps her arm tightly around me as we walk inside, where Papa stands waiting in the foyer. The smell of cigars clings to his suit, warm and woodsy, and when he pulls me in for a hug, it's the bear hug only a man who terrifies grown men can give.

He steps back, giving me a hard once-over. "Did you come to stay?"

I shake my head. "Just visiting."

His face stiffens, his jaw clenching. "I *will* kill him."

Mama swats him. "Don't be ridiculous."

"I am ridiculous? You heard what he did. He deserves to have his kneecaps broken—at the very *least*."

Mama rolls her eyes. "She loves him, you moron. Killing him won't do her any good."

"It would remove the sight of him."

"And send you to prison," I add, patting his arm. "While I appreciate the... offer... let him be, Papa."

Not that Rico deserves anyone coming to his defense, but the man has enough obstacles without my father coming after him like some Cosa Nostra version of Liam Neeson in *Taken*.

I hate everyone knows I'm pathetic enough to have fallen for a man who could never love me back. It's demeaning. But it's also why I came to Mama—because *she gets it*. She married a man who doesn't say I love you, but they've made it work. They have a mutual respect, an understanding. No cheating. No outside distractions. Which, in our world, is rare. Cosa Nostra men treat infidelity like a hobby—a side quest for their criminal enterprise.

But my parents have something that works for them. And if I was going to settle for a loveless marriage, that's all I wanted—*respect*. Which is exactly what Rico threw in my face waiting while I watched as he set it on fire. No wonder my mouth feels like ash.

"Come." Mama tugs me toward the study, leaving Papa and Vinnie to do God knows what. Probably brainstorm unique and inventive ways to maim Rico. Which, knowing Papa, means I should explicitly tell Vinnie to intervene before things escalate past the threat stage.

We settle into the study, Mama already pouring me a cup of ginger and honey tea like she's about to give some sage wisdom on me.

"So, are you going to file for divorce?"

Leave it to Mama to cut the small talk and go straight for the jugular.

I sigh, wrapping my hands around the warm mug. "I don't know, Mama. We're married."

"He cheated on you. I know you can't forgive that, even though we were raised to ignore such things."

I stare into my tea. "Papa never cheated on you."

Her lips twitch into a smirk. "That's because he didn't want to find himself with his balls cut off and stored in the freezer."

"That's... comforting."

She shrugs. "The point is, Rico didn't *respect* you. No one will judge you for leaving him." She pauses, then adds, "His parents expect it."

That flashes my attention up. "What?"

"I spoke to Cecilia this morning. She and Ricardo support it."

Oh. Great. So now my in-laws have officially written us off. I don't know what's worse—my mother openly planning Rico's demise or his parents acting like they just want to cut their losses.

Mama studies me, her expression softening. "You don't want to divorce him? Even after what he *did*?"

I exhale slowly, my chest throbbing.

I do. I should. But I can't admit it. *Not yet.*

I will accept a life with a husband who doesn't love me. But not a husband who shames me. Who discards me for a mistress—or worse, seeks them out to punish me. I might have been in love, but I'm not a nitwit.

The rest of the evening is filled with Mama's compassion—her voice, her tea, her reassurances that I will be okay. That I deserve more. And as much as I want to believe her, I don't leave feeling lighter.

If anything, I feel heavier.

Because deep down, I know what I have to do. I know what needs to happen next. And unfortunately, it involves Marco.

Allie

"So, you want to file for divorce?" Marco leans back in his chair, looking thoroughly unbothered, like I just told him I accidentally ran over his cat instead of dropping a bomb about ending my marriage. The bass from the club on the other side of the doors vibrates under my chair, a nice little soundtrack to my utter humiliation.

I nod, exhaling slowly. "I know the whole reason you let me out of the Cosa Nostra was because I married Rico, and I understand if that means I have to go back, but I'm asking—*begging*—please don't make me. I love my job. My restaurant. I don't want to go back."

Marco frowns, clearly unimpressed by my dramatics. "I'm not making you go back. I gave my word."

"But I'm divorcing him. That was the deal, right?"

He stands, resting his hands on the desk before glancing at Vinnie. "Give us a minute."

Vinnie pauses. Because while he is my bodyguard, he's also my big brother in everything but blood, and Marco is... well, *Marco*. Which means Vinnie is probably deciding whether he needs to warn him with words or just brute force.

Marco raises an eyebrow, like he dares Vinnie to confront him. Vinnie doesn't, but the slow, measured way he stands makes it clear he thought about it. Then, with a quick glance at me, he follows Marcello out; the door clicking shut behind them.

Marco exhales. "Do you know *why* I asked you to marry my cousin?"

I shake my head.

"I owe Rico a lot." He doesn't look at me as he wipes a hand over his jaw, staring at some invisible point past my shoulder. "Literally *my life*." Then his eyes snap back to mine, and for a second, it's unsettling because they look so much like Rico's—same intensity, same guarded darkness. "I'm assuming no one's told you what *actually* happened to him twenty-four years ago?"

"No. Just that something happened. And he doesn't talk about it."

Marco lets out a low laugh—cold, humorless, and a little deranged. "Yeah, *something* happened." He leans back in his chair, tapping his fingers against the desk. "And because you grew up in a family like mine, I think you can handle the truth. Well, most of it. Some of it, I'll leave for Rico... assuming he ever gets his head out of his ass and actually talks."

My stomach knots. That doesn't sound promising.

"Twenty-four years ago, some men came looking for me. They wanted the son of Tony Bennetti. You probably know why."

I do. Sadly. Because just like I was a valuable asset to my father, Marco was one of his. A bargaining chip, a target, a liability, depending on who you asked.

Marco waits for my nod, then continues. "Rico told them he was me. Took my place. Let them drag him off instead of me. He was gone for two days." His jaw tightens. "And let's just say Uncle Ricardo lost his mind."

I shift in my seat, fingers in front of me.

"I'm not sure if you know this, but Ricardo was the *original* Don. Didn't want the life anymore after he had kids. So, he handed it off to my father, who... well, thrived in that role. And by *thrived*, I mean he gave zero fucks about what it meant for my childhood." Marco lets out another humorless laugh. "It was peachy. Good times."

He stands and walks over to the bar cart in the corner, pouring himself a drink before glancing at me. "You drink whiskey?"

"Not really."

"Yeah, well. You will now." He slides a tumbler my way. "It helps numb the blow."

I pick it up, take a sip, and immediately regret it. What fresh hell is this liquid? It burns all the way down, igniting a fire in my chest like I just swallowed a Molotov cocktail.

"Good, right?"

I glare at him, coughing into my sleeve. "It tastes like death."

He takes his seat again, looking far too satisfied as he crosses his ankle over his knee and continues like he didn't just casually drop a trauma nuke on me.

"Once those assholes realized Rico was actually Ricardo's son, they panicked." His lip curls. "But it was too late. They'd already beaten the shit out of him. Cut him up. Left him in an alley somewhere to die."

My stomach twists vigorously.

"I'm *sure* you've seen the scars."

I nod. Yeah. I've seen them. The ones he kept hidden from me for weeks. The ones I traced with my fingers in the dark, wondering how he got them.

"My pops and Uncle Ricardo found him. And let's just say"—Marco's expression darkens—"they handled it. The men who took Rico? Got it worse. Much worse. And I got a front-row seat to the execution as punishment."

I blink. "Punishment?"

Marco swirls the whiskey in his glass. "For letting someone take my place. Someone who *isn't* family."

Silence hangs heavily between us.

I swallow, my throat raw from the whiskey and the pure horror of what I'm hearing.

Marco shrugs. "Before you ask—no, that's not why I'm like this. I was already screwed long before that. My father made sure of it. Not like my pops was known for his *sane* life choices. My mother is one of them. But, this just sealed the deal."

He takes another sip, watching me thoughtfully, waiting for something. Maybe for me to flinch. Or cry. Or freak out.

But I don't.

Because I get it.

I might not have known exactly what happened to Rico before now, but I always knew something broke him. And hearing it... yeah. I can see why.

But it doesn't change the fact that he broke me, too.

And there's *no fixing either of us.*

"Why are you telling me this?" I take another sip of the whiskey, and this time, it slides down smoother, leaving hints of honey and oak on my tongue. Maybe once it numbs all your internal organs, you taste flavors instead of pure fire.

Marco watches me over the rim of his glass, his expression indecipherable. "Because you deserve to know."

"Well, congrats." I hold up my glass in a mock toast. "Mission accomplished. I feel awful. I love him, and I always knew he went through something. But it changes nothing."

Marco shakes his head. "No, it doesn't. See, my cousin refused to get help. His parents spent three years dragging him to therapist after therapist, but he wouldn't talk. Not a single word. The first few years after it happened? He didn't speak at all. What little he says now?" He huffs out a dry laugh. "That's progress. If you can believe that shit."

My stomach twists. Rico barely talks. If this is progress, what the hell was he like *before*?

"They gave him a break, tried again when he was seventeen. He still refused. By eighteen, he was old enough to say fuck off, and they stopped pushing. That's when the whole family collectively called it the *incident* and pretend it never happened." Marco shakes his head like the entire concept is ludicrous—which, yeah, it is. "Meanwhile, Rico stayed angry. Violent. He used to have outbursts. *Bad ones.* Especially that first year. He'd break stuff, break people, break himself."

I wince.

Marco flicks a finger toward his nose, which has clearly been broken more than once. "Let's just say my cousin has honored me with a broken nose six times. Probably a seventh headed my way after he finds out I told you all this."

I exhale through my nose, my grip tightening on my glass. "So, what am I supposed to do with all of this? Fix him?"

"No." Marco's index finger tracks the rim of his tumbler. "He refuses to get help. Which is where you came in."

I take another sip. Substantial this time. And yup, still burns like liquid sin. But now it's pooling in my stomach, warm and buttery, spreading through my limbs until my whole body feels loose and heavy. Vinnie might have to carry me to the car.

"Look," Marco sighs. "When you came to me asking to leave the family, I looked into you. Watched you. You had a spine. You were secretly taking classes, rejecting your family's wishes, basically flipping off the entire Cosa Nostra without saying a word. Sassy, a little mouthy if I'm honest, but ideal for Rico. He needed a wife. And some meek little creature who rolled over and took whatever he dished out wouldn't work. No, he needed someone who would push him, stand up to him, force him out of that shell he's been hiding in for too long."

"Well," I swirl my glass, watching the amber liquid coat the sides. "I thought I did that." Memories hit me like a sledgehammer. The gallery opening he went to, the minuscule changes he made without admitting they were for me. "But clearly, I was delusional. Turns out, I was just putting meaning behind things that meant nothing."

"No, you got through to him. I saw him right before he moved you into his bedroom. For a man who doesn't feel, he sure was *feeling* a lot that night. I poked the bear—because let's be honest, I'm not sane." He grins, that special grin with all sorts of Jack Nickolson vibes before he goes straight to serial killer—the one that makes me wonder if he's two seconds away from pulling a knife out of thin air. "Problem is, Rico felt like the more he let you in, the less control he had. And that's when he lashed out."

"Yeah, I don't consider cheating 'lashing out'."

"I don't think he cheated on you."

I glare at him. "Guess we'll have to agree to disagree. Because I was there when he admitted it, and trust me, he was serious."

Marco just tilts his head. Like I'm adorable for thinking that. "He also called you a *thief*."

I freeze, glass halfway to my lips. "What?"

"You heard me."

I set my glass down, my pulse ticking in my throat. "I stole nothing."

Marco rolls his eyes. "*Metaphorically*, Allie. Though, from the one time I was at his house, there wasn't much to steal."

I squint at him. "And?"

"And I figured out what he meant."

I cross my arms. "Do share, *Sherlock*."

He leans forward. "You stole his control. You stole the quiet, comfortable, minimalist prison he called a home. You stole his ability to decide *when* and *where* things happened. And worst of all, you stole every single wall he put up so he wouldn't have to feel anything."

I stare at him, my throat narrowing.

"And that?" He points at me. "That scared the shit out of him."

I push out of my chair, smoothing my skirt—the first *real* skirt I've worn in weeks. Like, what is this? Some subconscious attempt to reclaim who I used to be? Yeah, I'll examine the darker meaning of that one later.

"Well," I say evenly, "I didn't steal *love*. Or *respect*. Or *honor*. The three things I demand in a marriage."

Marco nods. "As you should. Which is why you can stay out of the family. Though the Bennetti family? You know, the nosy, never-shut-the-fuck-up one? Yeah. No escaping them, so I can't help you there." He salutes me with his tumbler.

"Awesome."

"Also. Your papa may have asked me if he could marry you off to Carlo Romano once the divorce is final."

My stomach forcibly mutinies. "You better be joking."

He waggles his brows.

I grab my glass and drain the rest in one burning gulp. "You got a lawyer or what?"

"Yeah, yeah." Marco waves a dismissive hand. "He'll call you tonight."

I nod, gripping the chair. "Thank you, Marco."

I turn for the door, already gripping the handle, when his voice stops me.

"Allie?"

I glance back, expecting another satirical comment. But Marco's expression is unreadable.

"I really am sorry," he says, and this time, there's no teasing, no amusement, no Marco bullshit. "I wanted this to work. You and Rico? I hoped you'd finally made him... I don't know. *Happy*. He doesn't even realize he's miserable. But he is. And I thought—*I really thought*—you two would work. I wanted that for him. And for you. I hate you got hurt. Truly."

I am not about to cry in front of Marco Bennetti.

I swallow it down, nodding. "Yeah. Me too."

Rico

"YOU MOTHERFUCKER."

The door slams open like a scene from a low-budget action flick, Marco kicking it with unneeded force, sending it bouncing off the wall. As much as I'd love to point out that this is the most I've been called "asshole," "fucker," "prick," and "mother fucker" in my life, now isn't the time.

Dr. Dingleberry—not his real name, but let's be honest, it fits—practically levitates from his chair, clutching his chest like a geriatric on his third bypass. For fuck's sake, don't die, old man. You're actually *somewhat* useful. And considering I haven't fled the premises screaming, I'd say progress is being made. If he drops dead right now, I feel like that sets me back a few decades emotionally. Which is a fun thought I will unpack never.

"I'm calling the police!" Dingleberry screeches, scrambling toward his desk to grab—sweet Jesus—a landline. A corded phone. What is this, 1996? Should I expect him to whip out a fax machine and page his secretary while he's at it?

Before I can tell him to relax, Marco marches over like the unhinged lunatic he is and rips the phone cord straight out of the wall.

Dramatic. Even for him.

"You could call them," Marco muses, twirling the severed cord like he's deciding whether to strangle someone with it, "but it won't do you any good. Because, fun fact, they're all in my pocket. And I'm feeling real generous today, so I'd rather not make you disappear." He jerks his chin toward me, eyes burning with a hellfire kind of rage. "I'm here to kick his ass. You can watch. Maybe take some notes. He'll need coddling when I'm done."

Dingleberry nods. Fucking traitor. After all our hours of discussing my childhood trauma, he folds like a cheap suit at the first sign of *actual* violence.

Before I can even react, Marco storms across the room, and the next thing I know—boom. His fist connects.

I feel the break before I hear it.

The crunch of bone. The snap of cartilage. The sharp explosion of pain that shoots straight to my skull, radiating outward until my entire existence is just pure, unfiltered agony.

And then comes the blood.

Warm. Thick. Metallic.

It rushes down my face in a hot river, dripping onto my shirt.

"Mother fucker." I pinch my nose, voice muffled from the sheer carnage that is my face.

Marco, the sadistic prick, tosses a monogrammed handkerchief at me.

An *actual* fucking handkerchief. With his initials embroidered on it.

What. A. Pussy.

"What kind of man carries these?" I mumble, pressing the fabric to my nose while trying not to drown in my blood.

"A classy one." He dusts off his shirt, looking thoroughly pleased with himself. "So. This is therapy, huh?" His gaze flicks around the office, unimpressed. "I was expecting more... *moaning*. Maybe some scented candles. Where are the condoms?"

I don't dignify that with a response.

Instead, I glare at him through blurred vision, assessing the situation while wondering how much blood loss it takes before you actually pass out.

Marco tilts his head. "Tell me something."

I brace myself. Nothing good follows when Marco tilts his head.

"Is this where you were the week you told Allie you were in therapy?"

I exhale through my mouth because my fucking nose is out of commission, then nod. A small, insignificant nod. The kind that shouldn't be readable.

Marco reads it.

The grin that spreads across his face is the kind that gets men stabbed in alleyways.

"Well then," he drawls. "I stand by my statement. You are, in fact, a motherfucker."

"First," I mutter, adjusting the pressure on my probably shattered nose, "I don't fuck mothers, so your statement is illogical." Though, if I had impregnated my wife, I sure as hell would've still been fucking her until the day she popped out my kid. And probably after if she let me. But I sure fucked up that opportunity.

Marco scowls. "I didn't come here for your semantics, you dumbass."

"Then why are you here?" I shift in my seat, ignoring the way Dingleberry is silently watching this like it's a National Geographic special on feral male dominance. "If you knew I was *actually* in therapy, why the grand entrance? Why not, I don't know, wait?"

"Oh, sorry," Marco says. "Were you about to come?"

Dingleberry makes a noise that is—and I cannot stress this enough—*not* okay.

I roll my eyes, instantly regretting it when pain rockets through my skull.

"Jesus, Marco." I tilt my head back, trying to keep my nose from leaking all over my only clean shirt. "Did you really have to break my nose?"

"Yes." He leans against the desk, arms crossed like an asshole mafia overlord. "Because this is your own damn fault."

"How is any of this my fault?"

Marco's expression darkens. "Because, dumbass, you let the best thing that's ever happened to you walk away."

That hits me harder than his fist did.

But I don't let it show.

Instead, I exhale slowly, fingers tightening around the monogrammed handkerchief because, honestly, fuck Marco.

I narrow my eyes. *Or* they're swelling shut. Hard to tell at this point. Everything feels like it's been run through a meat grinder, and I wouldn't be shocked if my face has taken on the distinct shape of Marco's knuckles.

"Is there a reason you're here interrupting my *actual* therapy?" My voice comes out nasal, stuffed with blood-soaked cotton.

Marco crosses his arms, staring down at me like a disapproving principal about to deliver a suspension. "Yeah, because you told your wife you went to *therapy*"—he throws in aggressive air quotes, complete with a dramatic hand flourish—"and not this... well, therapy."

I grit my teeth. "I *was* in therapy."

"Not the kind where you're fucking another woman!" He roars, and I swear to God, if my nose wasn't already broken, I'd break it myself just to stop the throbbing that spikes at his volume.

Marco turns to Dr. Dingleberry, who looks about three seconds from pressing a panic button, and jabs a finger in his direction. "Did he tell you he made his wife think he cheated on her? That the last time he said he was in therapy, he was actually screwing someone else?" Then, with a grimace, Marco gives the doctor a once-over, his lips curling in visible distaste. "No offense, but I really, really hope you aren't what he used to see for therapy, because if so, I'm traumatized for life."

Fucking hell.

"Marco. Stop." I spit a mouthful of blood into his monogrammed handkerchief.

He holds up his hands. "I just want to make sure you're being honest." Then, to my actual therapist, he asks, "So? Did he tell you?"

"Yes," Dingleberry says, nodding cautiously like he's just realized he's sitting between two highly capricious chemical compounds.

Marco stops mid-rant. Blinks. "Oh." A beat passes. "Well, that makes this easier, then."

Before I can even hope that's the end, he reaches into his coat and pulls out a thick yellow envelope. The kind that should have been eradicated with the 90s but, much like my cousin's flair for dramatics, has refused to fucking die.

"Here." He slaps it against my chest, not giving a shit that my blood is actively dripping onto it. "Consider yourself *served*." Then, because he's a walking migraine, he sighs dramatically. "Gotta say I was hoping to interrupt something more *interesting*, though." He pouts. Actually pouts. "Oh well. At least my suspicion that you weren't a cheating asshole was correct. Still got it." He fist bumps the air like the fucking tool he is.

I stare at the envelope in my hands. The legal weight of it feels heavier than the actual contents.

"She wants a divorce?" My voice is hoarse, barely audible. I don't recognize it. Don't recognize the feeling curling in my chest either.

Marco bends forward, hands on his knees, like he's addressing a child and not a fully grown man currently bleeding into one of his designer accessories. "What did you expect, jackass?" His brows shoot up, his voice adopting that slow, mocking tone I hate. "You told her you didn't love her. You told her you cheated on her. Did you really think she was gonna meet you at home for dinner, maybe rub your shoulders and call it a day? No, dumbass. She packed her shit and got the fuck out. Away from you. Because the message you sent was crystal clear."

I swallow hard, but it doesn't go down right. Instead, it feels like I've swallowed glass.

I'd thought she'd come around. That I could explain that I said it to hurt her, *not* because it was true. That I didn't cheat, that I do—fuck, I can't even say it. Not out loud.

But I know. I know *now*.

I love her.

There. I admitted it. Even if it's just in my own fucking head, while my cousin, my therapist, and my bleeding, miserable existence all stare at me like I'm a lost cause.

It took three hundred dollars an hour, three times a week, for me to come to that conclusion. Nine hundred dollars just to admit what should have been fucking obvious.

And now?

Now, I'm sitting here, nose broken, soul bleeding, holding divorce papers from the woman I love.

She stole everything from me, including my fucking heart.

No. *Especially* my heart.

And I was too stupid to realize it before she walked away.

Marco straightens, dusting off his fucking coat like this has been a mild inconvenience for him. "Well, my job here is done." He gestures lazily between me and my therapist. "Glue that shit back together. I'm sick of his pity party."

The door swings shut behind him with a finality that makes my chest ache.

I stare down at the divorce papers.

And for the first time in my life, I feel something close to fear.

Because if I don't fix this—if I don't get her back—

I will never recover.

Allie

I SHOULD BE AT work, knee-deep in saucepans and barking orders at my line cooks like a culinary drill sergeant. Instead, Sienna practically abducted me from Via Napoli, dragging me out of the kitchen with all the subtlety of a wrecking ball.

"Sienna, I have to be at work. Wednesday nights are our busiest," I try, my voice filled with just the right amount of desperation to sell the lie.

"They're actually the slowest," Kai chimes in, *traitorously*, without even looking up from where he's meticulously dicing herbs.

I turn on him, narrowing my eyes. "And you love me being there, right? Keeping everything running smoothly?"

Kai sighs dramatically, glancing at Sienna. "Please, take her."

Sienna claps her hands, beaming. "Great! Settled then."

I glare at them both, muttering under my breath as I strip off my chef's coat and throw it at Kai, who catches it like I just handed him a pile of dirty laundry. I follow Sienna out of the kitchen, groaning the whole way.

Cooking night. With *his* family. On the same day my soon-to-be ex-husband got slapped with divorce papers at *his therapist's* office. I still can't believe that's where he was served. I'd hoped maybe, just maybe, he'd be using those extra therapy sessions for something productive—like, I don't know, untangling his emotional impairment. But no. Apparently, I drove him straight back into old habits. He's seeing his *"therapist"* multiple times a week now.

"I cook all day at work," I grumble as Sienna shoves me into Elias's car like a hostage. I nod at Elias, who just grins and opens the door. The moment I slide into the backseat, Sienna follows, practically pinning me in, as if she expects me to bolt. Which, fair. The thought crossed my mind.

Then I spot Violet sitting next to me, and all escape plans die a swift death.

Damn it. I should have clocked my surroundings before getting in. Rookie mistake.

"You've done nothing but work since you left Rico," Violet points out, leaning over and buckling me in like I'm a toddler.

I blink at her. "Did you just—"

"Just making sure you don't have a quick escape plan," she says sweetly, patting my boob.

I swat her hand away. "You do realize I can unbuckle myself and open this door, right?"

I try just that, yanking the handle. Nothing. I click, unlock. Then lock. Then unlock again.

The door doesn't budge.

Sienna grins. "Child locks."

I sigh and collapse back in my seat as Elias pulls away from the curb. A glance out the rear window confirms that Vinnie's trailing us in another car like the world's most overworked babysitter.

This is my life now. A prisoner in a child-locked car, heading toward an emotionally laden dinner with my *almost* ex-in-laws.

Fantastic.

I stare out the window, my chest tight. I should feel... something. Relief? Freedom? I got out. I did it. I escaped a life I never wanted, filed for divorce from a man who never loved me, and now I have a successful restaurant, amazing friends, and a future that belongs to me.

So why do I feel so meaningless?

"What if it's too awkward?" I break the silence, turning to Sienna. "I left Rico. Won't Mama and Nonna be mad at me?"

I don't mention the divorce. Do they know? Rico was served today. His parents must know by now. Do they even know he's back to *therapy*? And not just casually back—he's practically a frequent flyer. Three times a week. It's as if I pushed him straight into his therapist's arms, only on speed.

Congrats, Allie. You broke your husband so thoroughly, he's now in professional maintenance mode.

Violet frowns. "What? Why would they be mad at you? Allie, you did nothing wrong."

I scoff. "I left Rico."

She rolls her eyes so hard I swear she just saw last week. "Please. Rico did nothing to make that marriage work. He actively pushed you away. We all know you did everything—and I mean *everything*—to pull him out of that concrete bunker he calls a personality."

She's not wrong.

"No one blames you," she continues. "Why do you think Papa gave you his blessing after six months? He's not mad at you. Mama and Papa fully support you, Allie. They know you're getting divorced, even if you don't hit the six-month mark. They wouldn't expect you to stick around after..." She trails off, her cheeks flushing.

After, he cheated on me.

I look down, fingers twisting in my lap. Six months. We're still a month away from that marker. Whether or not they know I already filed, I'm not sure. But I only feel worse knowing they're so supportive.

Why do I feel guilty?

Is it because some sick, twisted part of me wonders if I'm to blame? I pushed and pushed, knowing he didn't like it, knowing he was at the brink. What if I drove him to therapy? What if I—

No. I shake my head. Don't be stupid. You could have nagged 24/7, and that still wouldn't justify him running into another woman's arms.

I set my jaw, blinking away the sting behind my eyes.

Violet and Sienna keep watching me, but for once, they say nothing.

I stay silent for the rest of the drive, but I feel Sienna and Violet's eyes on me the entire time, burning a hole through my emotional fortress. I pretend not to notice. Instead, I focus on the weight of my engagement ring and wedding band—still snug on my finger.

Every day at work, I slip them onto a chain around my neck, a habit so ingrained that I don't even think about it anymore. The second I leave the kitchen, they're back where they belong.

Only, where do they belong?

My fingers twitch over them, and out of the corner of my eye, I catch the look Sienna and Violet exchange. They don't say a word, and for that, I'm grateful. I'll take them off. *When I'm ready.* As if I'm clinging to some decades-long love story instead of a marriage that barely made it past the six-month mark and gave everyone involved a headache.

When we step inside the Bennetti Family House, my stomach nosedives.

The women are gathered in the kitchen, chatting and laughing—*until* they see me. The room quiets, but the smiles remain, only now they're paired with *that* look.

The same one I saw at the wedding.

The same one at my debut night.

The same one now.

Pity.

Mama pushes through the crowd, her violet-and-vanilla perfume wrapping around me before her arms do. I used to hate that scent—too floral, too much. But right now, it doesn't bother me. Right now, it almost—*almost*—makes the pain fade.

"Oh, *Tesoro*," she murmurs, squeezing me tight. "I'm so sorry. I had hoped it would work out, but Rico is..." She pulls back, shaking her head. "He's *Rico*. That's my fault. We let him stay this way. No one pushed him. Maybe if I had forced him earlier..."

I shake my head. "No. It's not your fault." Because the last thing I need is this woman taking responsibility for his choices. Though, after hearing Marco's version of events, I would love to hear hers. But I don't ask. I'm not *that brave.*

She pats my cheek, then tugs me toward the kitchen, planting me on a stool next to Nonna. A generous—*no*, absurd—glass of wine slides in front of me.

I stare at it. Is this one of those novelty glasses? The kind you buy as a joke for wine moms who pretend to only have "one glass" a night?

Nonna takes my hand, her warm, frail fingers rubbing gentle circles over my arm. "How are you, *dolcezza*?" she asks, her chocolate eyes soft with concern.

I glance up—and yep.

The entire Bennetti female population is watching me, gathered around the island like I'm the evening's entertainment.

Oh, good. This is exactly what I wanted.

I take a gulp of wine. A big, much-needed gulp and now I'm thankful the glass is more than generous.

"I'm fine," I say. "I'm staying at Kai's for now."

Mama tsks. "You could have stayed here."

Right. Because that wouldn't be weird. Imagine Sunday dinner. *Hey, ex-hubby-to-be! How's it hanging? Miss me? How's your therapist?*

"Or my house," Violet chimes in.

"Um, hello? Mine?" Sienna adds, as if this was some kind of bidding war.

"You both live down the street from—" I stop. I cannot say his name. Nope. Not happening. Instead, I settle on, "—*him*."

They exchange a look. "Oooooh."

Did they seriously not consider that?

Probably not.

"Have you spoken to him at all?" Gloria asks—right before Violet whacks her arm.

"I meant, how are things at work?" Gloria backtracks, throwing Violet a glare that doesn't even nick her composure.

I sigh, taking another sip of wine. Might as well rip the bandage off. I don't want to spend the night being fawned over only to blindside them later. These women have been nothing but welcoming, and divorcing Rico probably means I'm out of the family for good.

I owe them honesty.

I twist the wine glass stem between my fingers, watching the deep red liquid swirl. "I filed for divorce. He was served today."

Silence.

No gasps. No *oh my Gods*. No *how could yous?*

They knew.

"I don't blame you, *mia cara*," Mama says, pulling me into another hug while Nonna rubs my back. "We know what Rico said to you." She shakes her head. "That boy was never good with words."

I arch a brow, locking eyes with Violet. Because I definitely didn't tell them everything.

Violet shrugs. "Okay... so I *might* have mentioned how he told you he didn't love you." She waves her hands, way too dramatically for my taste. "Listen, these women are relentless. They're like bloodhounds. One whiff of something, and they will latch on. I had no choice."

Yeah, sure. No choice.

I shift my attention to Sienna, who suddenly looks very interested in her own hands.

"I might have told them about... the *other* thing."

My stomach drops. "What *other* thing?"

Sienna bites her lip, her usually sunshine-and-rainbows expression dimming. "How he, um... suggested you weren't doing your job... you know... getting pregnant?"

Oh.

I blink. Once. Twice. Then down the rest of my wine in one go because I cannot deal with this sober.

Valeria mutters something in Italian and spits right next to the cannolis. My stomach clenches as I make a mental note to eat nothing in her immediate vicinity again. Meanwhile, Nonna straight-up curses in English, which is so rare that half the women turn and stare at her like she just drop-kicked a priest. Normally, she saves her most colorful commentary for Italian, which only means one thing—Rico has pissed off even the sweet, doting Nonna.

Impressive.

Funny enough, I had completely buried that little gem of a memory. The one where he insisted on IVF so he wouldn't have to touch me. The one where he all but declared I wasn't doing my "*duty*" by providing him an heir, so he needed to "explore other options."

Yeah. Let's pile that into the trauma buffet.

Maybe that's why he was seeing his "*therapist*" three times a week. To knock her up. Maybe they struck some sort of deal—he knew I'd file for divorce, and she agreed to carry the next generation of emotionally stunted Bennetti children. It's hard to decide what's more humiliating: being cheated on or being completely replaced.

"You know, this was my muse for my next book," Violet announces, swiping her wine and sighing fiercely. "But it's getting real angsty."

We all turn to her.

I just blink.

"You were writing a story about...*us*?"

Her green eyes widen, as if this is brand new information to her, and not the wildest thing she's ever said to me. "Oh, did I not tell you? I mean, I told them." She thumbs toward the rest of the women at the island, all of whom nod along like this is a normal topic of discussion.

I glance at them. They knew? They were all in on this?

"It's grumpy-sunshine! You, *obviously*, are the sunshine."

Obviously.

"Anyway," she continues, swirling her wine, "when Mr. Grumpy refuses to pull his head out of his ass, it makes writing an HEA really difficult."

Alena sips from her glass, looking wholly uninterested. "Maybe we should focus on real people's problems."

"This is a *real* people problem!" Violet argues, motioning to me like I'm Exhibit A in a courtroom. "What's her happily ever after? She and Rico just...divorce? Gah." Then her eyebrows arch. "Unless she divorces him and finds someone who *actually* makes her happy. A chef. With gorgeous eyes. And fantastic arms."

Sienna cocks her head. "Aren't you married?"

Violet gives her an expression. "Are you blind?"

"No," Sienna sighs wistfully, eyes glazing over. "He's *hot*."

"Who?" I honestly shouldn't have.

"Kai, silly," she sing-songs.

I nearly choke on my wine.

"Excuse me?"

"You and Kai." She shrugs. "Why not date Kai?"

Oh. My. God. I just told these women that I'm divorcing their son-slash-cousin-slash-brother-in-law, and they're already trying to remarry me off.

Marco wasn't kidding when he said they were meddlers.

Allie

Two weeks later...

"Did he sign them yet?"

Violet slides a mug of coffee across the table and lowers herself into the chair with a dramatic sigh. Her bump is on full display, glowing and perfect. Meanwhile, I'm over here hoping caffeine will cancel out the sting of divorce limbo.

I take a sip and plaster on a smile that tastes as bitter as the coffee. "I wish. Then we could both move on and pretend this whole arranged-marriage-meets-emotional-silence experiment never happened."

Violet hums into her cup, eyebrows raised—she's not buying it.

"What?"

She tips her chin toward my phone.

And right on cue, it lights up. Rico.

"Still?"

"Yup." I flip the phone over so that if I don't see it, it doesn't exist. It works for five-year-olds, why not adults?

The first text message came the morning after Marco handed him the divorce papers. That was two weeks ago. And just for context, it was the second text Rico had ever sent me. *Second.* In nearly six months of being legally bound by holy matrimony.

> Rico: I have an irrational hatred for the color red. To the point I refuse to look at it. I'd rather set the room on fire than acknowledge it. Problem is, fire is red, so you can see the flaw there. There's this red lantern in my living room now. Small. Mocking me. I can't bring myself to throw it out, though.

I didn't respond. Not because I didn't want to ask why he suddenly was texting me now after acting like I was part of the wallpaper for months.

But because it didn't matter. That was the whole point of the divorce—cutting the cord, legally and emotionally. The marriage contract was never built on romance. Obligations? Sure. But affection? Not even in the fine print.

Then, a few hours later, another text buzzed through.

> Rico: Ask me why I won't throw it out.

I didn't.

I *couldn't*.

Violet eyes my overturned phone just as it vibrates again, skittering across the table.

"Still doing the silent treatment?" She asks.

I stare at her. "You mean the man who ignored me for months is *now* trying to start a conversation, and I'm not immediately throwing myself at the opportunity? Wow. How shocking."

"So, this is a tit-for-tat thing?"

"No. Also, who says that?"

"Me," she says unapologetically, sliding my phone toward her. "What's today's fact?"

I narrow my eyes as she taps the screen.

"What? I find them fascinating. Like getting a glimpse into some rare, cryptic novel. Besides, don't you want to know what goes on inside that head of his?"

"No."

She gasps dramatically. "Oh."

I regret everything.

I hold out for three full seconds before cracking. "What does it say?"

She holds up the phone, waving it. "Read it. I'm now regretting wanting insight into Rico's brain."

I snatch it.

> Rico: I memorized the periodic table when I was ten. Not for school. Just because I was bored and had a weird obsession with the elements. So yeah, I can recite all 118 of them in order, but will forget to buy toothpaste when it runs out.

Violet grips my wrist, making me look at her. "He's trying."

I scoff.

She tightens her hold. "No, really. I wouldn't say it if I didn't believe it."

"You just want my life to have a happily ever after."

"I mean, duh. But that's not why."

I glare. Hard. But she doesn't let go of my wrist or the topic.

"Okay, not the entire truth." Violet corrects herself, stirring her coffee like she didn't just poke a very raw, very exposed nerve. "But truly, I wouldn't nudge you if I didn't think Rico was being genuine."

I snort. "He's only trying because it's the easy out. Because if we get divorced, he knows he'll have to go out and find another woman who can tolerate him." I blow out a breath, flipping my phone face-down. "I'm the convenient option. The most logical choice. And Rico always picks the logical choice, even if he doesn't actually want me."

"You didn't exactly *choose* him either," Violet points out, waddling back from the counter with a bottle of Bailey's. She wiggles it at me before pouring a generous amount into my coffee with a shrug. "Live vicariously and all that. I can't drink. You need a drink—sip, sip, baby."

I take a sip and immediately scrunch my nose. Irish coffee was never my thing, but whatever.

Violet, unfazed, settles back into her seat. "So, if Rico told you he was in love with you—and actually meant it—it wouldn't matter?"

Nothing matters anymore. Not when it comes to my sham marriage.

I blink at her. "Vi, he cheated on me."

"Allegedly."

I shoot her a glare so sharp it could cut diamonds.

"It's not love, Violet. It's a strategy. He's hedging his bets. Throwing just enough 'daily fun facts' my way to keep me dangling while he works out whatever brooding nonsense is happening in that brain of his." I blow out a breath and flip my phone screen-down again, as if that's enough to block the next incoming text from my possibly sociopathic *almost*-ex.

She crosses her arms. "So you're telling me he's doing all this just for convenience?"

"Yes! That's what this entire marriage has been about! I was the convenient womb with a pulse. Now he's realizing finding a new woman who'll tolerate his communication skills—which are basically on par with a rock—won't be easy. So he's backtracking." I gesture wildly. "Sure, maybe he misses me on some deep, emotionally repressed level buried beneath the mountain of avoidance and those tragic sweatpants, but that's not love."

Violet raises a brow. "You do know I write about forced proximity all the time, right?"

"That's fiction," I huff.

"Exactly. Fiction where people fall in love after sharing space, beds, and body heat. Sound familiar?"

I groan. "Just because you share a bed doesn't mean it's love. Sometimes it's just... logistics. Forced proximity doesn't mean he chose me. We shared a bed. Things happened. You know. Things that lead to that." I say while waving at her stomach.

She grins. "You know I write *much* dirtier words for it, right? Want me to remind you? I've got a complete list, courtesy of Sienna's refusal to curse. Bumping biscuits. Submitting an application for the O-Face Club. Greasing the gears. And my personal favorite—playing hide the cannoli."

The laugh that bursts out of me is ugly. Somewhere between a cackle and a snort, and Violet fist-pumps the air like she just won something.

"I could use a game of hide the cannoli," I mutter.

"Well, last I checked, you are married, and he has a cannoli—"

"He's playing that game plenty with his *therapist*."

Violet scrunches her nose. "Ew. Please don't make me picture Rico 'playing' anything."

I sigh, dragging a hand down my face. "Marco literally served him at his therapist's office. Three times a week he goes there now, Vi. That's not an occasional drop-in energy—that's a punch card situation. Before we got married, he went *once*."

"Honestly? I don't think he's seeing *that* type of therapist three times a week. I don't even think he saw that type of therapist at all—despite what he said."

"Did you not just hear where he was served?"

"It's the way Marco said it, though." She fumbles for her phone, groaning dramatically as she leans to the side. "God, this belly. I miss putting on my shoes like a big girl."

"Focus, Vi. I'm having a marital crisis and you're over there giving up on footwear."

She retrieves her phone and scrolls through what appears to be her daily message exchange with Marco. Not Alex. *Marco.*

"Alex doesn't care you text his cousin every day?"

"Oh, he *definitely* cares," she says with a shrug that belongs to someone far too pregnant to give a damn. "But Marco was there for me when everything was going sideways. Sure, he annoyed me, but he also helped. Pushed me in the right ways. Honestly? Without him, I don't know if Alex and I would've made it. Plus, pissing off Alex keeps the spark alive."

"Romance, thy name is spite," I mutter, remembering how pushing Rico's buttons went for me. Spoiler alert: not great. Some men need the nudge. Others? They explode. In Rico's case, he detonates, leaves the building, and pretends the fire was just a draft.

"Here," Violet says, spinning her phone toward me. "Marco's been referring to Rico's *'therapist'* in quotes lately."

"That's a suspicious amount of quotation marks." I say with sarcasm, but she clearly doesn't catch on.

"Exactly. He used to say escort when talking about Rico's therapist. Sometimes he'd call her Madame. But he's saying 'therapist' and not even referencing a *her* in there either."

"Madame?" I blink. "Are we talking dominatrix or French art dealer?"

"Don't ask. I've tried digging deeper into Marco logic, and I'm still recovering." She snatches the phone back when she sees my eyes land on a name in the text thread between her and Marco. "You didn't see that."

"Who's Kiera?"

"You. Saw. *Nothing*." Her pregnant death glare is surprisingly effective. I nod in submission and clutch my coffee like it'll protect me from her wrath.

"Okay, so bring this full circle before my brain melts."

"Fine. My theory? He's not seeing her anymore. And maybe he never was. Maybe he said what he said to hurt you."

Something Marco had said to me when I told him I wanted a divorce. But, I refuse to let that flicker of hope damage me again.

"Well, mission accomplished," I deadpan.

"But what if Marco's right? What if Rico didn't cheat on you? What if he's actually seeing an *actual* therapist and trying to get his shit together?"

I shrug, but it feels hollow. "He told me he was with her that night. Point-blank. Didn't even flinch. I know Marco thinks it was just a tantrum—Rico lashing out—but if it was true? Then we're done. End of story. Trust is the minimum, and he burned it with a shrug."

Violet leans in, leveling me with her mom voice. "Just play along. Hypothetically. Say he didn't cheat. Say he's seeing a licensed, degree-holding, couch-having therapist and working through his damage. Not for anyone else—just to be better. Remove the cheating from the equation for one second."

"I'm going to need more Baileys for this level of optimism."

"Think of it as an exercise," she says, all cheery. "You're clearing emotional fog to see what's actually there. Because—if there's even a chance he didn't cheat—what you do with that version of Rico is up to you."

"And if he did cheat?"

She lifts her cup in a toast. "Then we bring snacks and toilet paper to your pity party and start planning a hot girl summer."

"God bless you and your feral energy," I mutter, sipping the now-too-sweet coffee. How much Bailey's does one need to drink before they feel at least tipsy?

Violet's brain is a glittery disco ball—always spinning, occasionally blinding, and once in a while, it smacks you in the face when you least expect it.

"But hear me out," she says, wagging her spoon like it's a magic wand about to rewrite my emotional stability. "In this new and improved scenario, there's no escort. Just therapy. Real, actual therapy. With a couch and tissues and a doctor who probably sighs a lot. Rico's basically the poster child for emotional breakthroughs. If they ever did a mental health PSA, his broody face would be front and center on a Times Square billboard with the caption: 'Got trauma? So does this guy.'"

I groan, dropping my head into my hands. "He's still not signing the papers."

"Exactly," she says, like that's some kind of victory. "You were both forced into this, but that doesn't cancel out the feelings that came after. Are you seriously telling me that falling in love during an arranged marriage doesn't count?"

I open my mouth to respond, only to pause mid-thought and scowl at nothing in particular. "Yes? No? Hell if I know. I can't even tell if my husband cheated on me, let alone figure out how I feel about him."

Violet sips her coffee, annoyingly calm. "All I'm saying is, sure, forced proximity puts everything on fast-forward. But it doesn't make the emotions fake. No one held a gun to your head and said 'Love that man or else.' And no one forced him to love you either. Even if he's yet to say it out loud—which, for the record, I think he *does* love you. He just hasn't read the instruction manual on how to express it."

I shake my head so hard I'm tempted to rattle out the frustration lodged behind my eyes. "It's not that simple, Vi. This was a business deal. A contract. My uterus was the fine print."

She winces, but I power through.

"I've always been a box to check. Marry the girl. Get the heir. Fulfill the terms. And now? Now he thinks staying with me makes sense. Logical. Efficient. But love? That's not logic. That's messy and stupid and impossible to spreadsheet."

"So you think once he's better—like *really* better—he'll wake up one day and realize you were just a placeholder?"

"Exactly." I exhale, chest tight. "He'll be all emotionally evolved and functional, and suddenly the idea of me won't be enough anymore. I don't want to be the starter wife he regrets. I want to be someone's first and final choice—not the safest option on the menu."

"And what about you? Don't you think *you* deserve to be happy?"

I flash a smile. It's weak. The smile you give a stranger in an elevator when they won't stop talking about their dog's gluten allergy. "I do. I think I'm getting there."

And I'm not lying. Not totally.

The restaurant's finally hitting its stride. I've been apartment hunting—actual tours, not just Zillow scrolling at 2 a.m. like some heartbroken millennial. Only, I can't get an apartment until my marital assets are finalized, which would require Rico to sign the damn papers. Clearly, he has the time to text. It would take less time to send those daily messages signing the tabs on the divorce documents.

Then my phone buzzes again.

I don't mean to open the message. But the Bailey's swirling in my bloodstream makes me bold. Or reckless. Hard to tell the difference.

> Rico: There are also now 226 text messages you sent me I never responded to. I plan to make it up to you by sending just as many. Unless you've blocked my number already.

I haven't blocked him.

Thought about it? Absolutely.

But not out of spite. Not even out of that low-grade fury that comes from watching a man who wouldn't share his feelings suddenly transform into Mr. Daily Text.

No, I haven't blocked him because part of me still hopes. And that part? It's stupid. And fragile. And keeps smashing into the reality that this is all happening now.

Now that I've walked away.

Now that I'm not the default option.

Now that he's realized I was never his person—just the contractually convenient one.

So no. I don't text him back.

Because I can't.

This—whatever this is—it's him processing. Grieving. Probably bargaining through the stages of grief. He thinks he needs me, but he'll figure out soon enough that he doesn't. That he never really did.

He never said he loved me.

Not once.

And I'm finally ready to believe that wasn't an oversight—it was the truth.

Eventually, he'll move on. Find someone he wants. Someone who wasn't handed to him in a gilded cage and told to breed.

And when he finds her?

I hope she makes him laugh. I hope she helps him sleep. I hope she gets all the words he's never given me.

He deserves that.

Marco was right—Rico *deserves* to be happy.

And me?

I'll cheer him on from a safe distance.

Even if it leaves me quietly shattered.

Because love shouldn't feel like survival.

And I'm finally done just surviving.

Rico

Every. Fucking. Day.

Karma isn't just a bitch; she's a vindictive, petty, grudge-holding lunatic with a particular vendetta against me.

And right now, she's wearing Marco's face.

Still, I keep going because I don't have a choice. It's the only thing I have left—the sliver of hope that if Allie pressed forward when I gave her nothing to cling to, she might do the same. If I keep sending messages, trying to prove I want her in my life, maybe—just *maybe*—she'll give me a chance.

Or she'll continue to ignore me, and I'll spiral further into the depths of my self-inflicted purgatory. Either way, it's progress.

"I have never in my life seen you this attached to a phone, and honestly, it's making me nauseous," Marco announces from the other side of my desk, his face twisted in melodramatic revulsion. "If this is what personal growth looks like, I'd rather have you emotionally dead inside again, thanks."

I ignore him and check my phone *again*.

Nothing.

Marco leans back in his chair, hands laced behind his head, embracing like the smug bastard he is. "So, is your therapist still that shriveled-up Voldemort look-alike?"

I almost laugh. A real one. And I hate it.

Not because it's Marco, but because it's foreign—an emotion I locked away so long ago that feeling it now is like suddenly remembering how to breathe underwater. I hate I deprived myself, my family, and *Allie* of something as simple as a laugh.

Dr. Dingleberry (his real name is Dr. Lowell, but that's irrelevant) told me to show Allie I care. To let her in since I've done nothing but keep her out and, more importantly, push her away. All of this, frankly, is a fucking mystery to me. How do you show someone you care when you've spent your entire life perfecting the art of apathy?

So, I started texting her. The same messages I would have written on the Post-Its, but digital, because that's all I could think of. Only now I'm more pathetic. Following up, practically begging her to respond. To ask "why" or anything.

She hasn't taken the bait. She hasn't replied at all.

And I deserve that, too.

I ignored months of her texts, her calls, her attempts to speak to me. I did everything I could to push her away, to break her down until she finally stopped trying.

Now she has.

And I hate every fucking minute of it.

I hate waking up, checking my phone like some pitiful, love-sick idiot, only to see the read receipts taunting me.

Now I know how she felt.

To be discarded. To try to and receive only silence. To realize your words aren't worth a response. *You aren't worth a response.*

"That's gotta sting," Marco muses, watching me check my phone again. "She still ghosting you?"

I nod.

"Yeah, see...correct me if I'm wrong, but wasn't that exactly what you did to her your entire marriage?"

I nod again.

"So...what? You think if you just text her enough times, she's going to cave and be all aww, he finally gives a shit and comes running back?" He glances at the envelope on my desk—wrinkled, coffee-stained, and very much unsigned. "I assume you're not planning on signing those?"

I shake my head. "I don't want a divorce."

Marco steeples his fingers under his chin, eyes gleaming with something I don't like one bit. "Why?"

I narrow my eyes. "Are *you* my therapist now?"

"I'm just trying to gauge how far gone you are. Personally, I think you just need a good ass-kicking in the ring, and you'll be cured. But hey, what do I know?"

I ignore him, still staring at my phone, willing a response to appear.

Marco shifts in his chair, and for the first time since he barged in here uninvited, I notice something. He's tense. Marco is a lot of things—chaotic, agitating, unstable, and slightly unhinged—but *tense*? That's not his style.

"What's going on with you?"

His smirk falters. "Nothing."

"Uh-huh."

"You really want to play *who's hiding more shit* with me? Brother, I will win that game."

"I assume not."

"I've got things on my mind." He glances away, jaw stiffening.

"I'd assume so." Marco took on a role most people in this family think he *wanted*. The truth? He didn't. He hates being Don. But he won't walk away—not because he loves power, but because he's the only one stubborn (and ludicrous) enough to think he can change things.

Not really sure how you restructure the mafia, but if anyone is deranged enough to try, it's him.

Dom and Alex walk in, exchanging glances before looking at us. Their eyes flick to Marco, sprawled across from me in a chair that, *yes*, I fucking added to invite people to stay in my office, then land on me, where I'm comfortably ignoring them all from my desk.

"I don't think I'm enjoying this therapy bullshit if it means *this bullshit* shows up more often," Alex says, nodding at Marco.

"There's always a price to pay," Marco snaps, his usual amusement absent. Instead, he looks... bitchy.

Dom drops into the seat next to him. Yes, I added not one, but two chairs. I regret it right now, though. "Time of the month, cousin?"

"Something like that," Marco mutters before pinning Alex with a sharp look. "Why are you here? I thought this merger meant you were permanently chained to your wife's ankle like a well-trained lapdog?"

"I am." Alex shrugs. "Just stopped in to say I'm heading out for the day and to make sure none of you idiots caught some highly contagious illness that requires me to evacuate the building. Rico's entertaining guests, which is suspicious, and you," he gestures vaguely at Marco, "are voluntarily existing in public. Clearly, something is wrong."

Marco rolls his shoulders, exhaling heavily. "I have my own problems to deal with, but instead of handling those, I'm constantly fixing *your* problems."

"Hey," Dom interjects, looking offended. "You didn't help me."

"Oh?" Marco tilts his head. "You let your girl go on a date with Theo Carlyle, and then I had to track him down so you could man up and reclaim her before she realized she had options. Then you handed her your balls on a silver platter. *Again*. For free." His sharp gaze flicks at Alex. "*You* know what you got from me. You're welcome, by the way. I don't even have the patience to list all the ways I carried your ass through your shit with Violet." Then those amber eyes land on me. "And you—I found you the *perfect* wife, one who actually tolerates you, and you still fucked it up. Now you're giving me a headache. You all have officially convinced me there is absolutely no reason to ever get into a relationship. Women are complicated, and they turn grown-ass men into sniveling bitches."

We all fall silent, staring at him.

"What?" he snaps.

Dom's lips curl. "Care to talk about... *her*?"

Marco's eye twitches. "Fuck off. All of you." He stands, buttons his jacket with a little too much force, and scowls at me. "And quit texting her. She won't respond."

I quirk a brow. "How do you know?"

The sound Marco makes is halfway between a groan and the death rattle of a dying bull. Which feels fitting, considering the amount of bullshit coming out of his mouth.

"Why do you think?" he snaps. "She still believes you cheated on her. That you're seeing your so-called *therapist*, which she clearly thinks is code for a weekly appointment with a walking STD in Louboutins. So maybe, just maybe, that's why she's not responding to your soul-baring texts. For fuck's sake, Rico. Clear up the part where you weren't balls-deep in betrayal before you compose poetry about her eyes again."

My jaw tightens hard enough I feel it in my molars. "She *still* thinks I cheated on her? That I'm seeing my escort and not a therapist three times a week?" I ask slowly, biting down each syllable. Feelings are fucking useless. At this moment, they're slapping me hard, and I hate them.

Marco blinks. "Why would she think otherwise?"

I am going to kill him. "Because *you* talk to her. *You* talk to Violet. *Violet* talks to her. All of you talk constantly in your little estrogen-fueled group chat—yet somehow *no one* has passed along the teeny tiny detail that I'm not fucking an escort and haven't since I got married?"

I wave my hand between all three of them. "Not an escort. A therapist. A real one. Framed degree. Office with a ficus. Weekly emotional crucifixions included."

Alex picks at an invisible lint speck on his jacket, unbothered as ever. "Still your mess. Clean it up yourself. Isn't that what your therapist is for? Accountability? Emotional maturity? Or do you just Venmo him to let you monologue into the void?"

Marco rubs the bridge of his nose like my existence gives him migraines. It probably does. I get it. I give *myself* migraines.

"None of it matters," he mutters.

I blink. Again. "She thinks I cheated on her. Which, granted, okay—I may have given her that impression when I implied I was screwing my therapist. I didn't expect her to believe it still because I figured one of you would have blabbed the truth like you do oh so well." I also didn't expect her to leave me, ignore text messages, and weaponize Post-it notes, but here we are.

I breathe through the concrete currently lodged in my throat.

"That assumption's bad enough, but the idea that she still thinks I'm seeing an escort weekly? Still paying a professional for orgasms and validation? And you're saying that doesn't matter?"

Marco drops his hand from his face and levels me with that look.

"Even if she believed you didn't cheat," he says, "she thinks the only reason you want her now is because it's convenient. You don't want a wife. You want a solution. And she just happens to be the lowest-maintenance option on the market. Already installed, preheated, capable of carrying an heir. Congratulations. You've turned your wife into a subscription service."

"That's not how I feel about her at all. It's a lot more than that and you fucking know it."

Silence.

Alex and Dom both gape at me like I just admitted to recreational murder.

"What?" I ask.

Alex opens his mouth, then shuts it. Dom just blinks rapidly.

"So... you're serious?" Dom finally asks, dragging out the word serious like it physically pains him. "Like... actual feelings? *Loooovvveee*?"

And just like that, whatever lingering respect I had for my twin is dead.

"Are you done?"

"Not really," Dom muses. "Might take me a few months to process this."

I roll my eyes, glancing at my phone. Clearly, my current approach isn't working.

Marco groans. "Oh, for fuck's sake." He stalks over, slides my chair out of the way, and starts typing into the search bar on my computer. A few weeks ago I'd kill a man for touching my keyboard. My brothers crowd behind him, leaning over my shoulder like a bunch of vultures circling roadkill.

I clench my jaw but inhale deeply, reminding myself that while this is annoying, it is not worth breaking noses over.

"You want your wife to believe you actually want her for something other than her reproductive capabilities?" Marco scoffs, still typing. "Start here."

We all lean in, looking at what Marco pulled up on the screen together.

Dom raises a brow. "That's... actually, not a bad idea."

We all look at Marco in mild horror.

Marco smirks. "I know. It's disturbing, isn't it?"

His expression shifts, tightening. "Now, if you'll excuse me, I'm going to go handle my shit for once. And no, I definitely do *not* need your help. Your collective relationship IQs are on par with a toaster, and that's insulting to a supremely functional appliance."

Dom holds up a hand. "Wait... *you* have a relationship problem?"

Marco flips him off and stalks out.

Alex shakes his head. "I really pity whatever woman Marco is interested in."

"I pity him," I correct, scrolling through the screen.

They both look at me.

"Think about it," I continue. "Any woman who can rattle Marco has to be the female version of him. And worse. Imagine *that* creature."

Dom visibly shudders. "I'd prefer not to."

We all stare at the screen again.

And then it hits me. The way to prove to Allie that I chose her. That I actually, really, truly want her.

Because *I do*.

Allie

I WAITED UNTIL I was sure Rico would be at work before having Vinnie drive me back to the brownstone—Rico's house, never mine—to grab the last of my things. Most of my stuff was already packed up, neatly folded in my upstair closet, making it easy for Vinnie to scoop and dump it into the trunk.

Unfortunately, I had a few stray items lingering in *his* closet. Which meant I had to venture back into enemy territory.

"I'm gonna grab the rest of my things from the basement," Vinnie says, pointing toward the basement stairs.

I nod. "Yeah, I just need to clear out Rico's closet. Small stuff. No worries."

I shoo him away because, honestly? The man has been living off the same two pairs of slacks, a couple of shirts, and whatever new boxers he bought in a panic after we left. He needs this trip just as much as I do.

Stepping into Rico's closet, I take a deep breath. It still smells like him—cedar, something crisp and clean, and just a hint of whatever cologne he wears that I refuse to Google for the sake of my pride. His side remains perfectly neat, untouched, his limited wardrobe of tailored suits and neutral-toned basics hanging like an exhibit in a minimalist museum. Meanwhile, the seventy-five percent that used to be mine? Bare.

Just another reminder of how easy it was for me to disappear from his life.

Shaking off the thought, I focus on the shelf above. My things. Boxes I'd stored here—keepsakes from Mama, little trinkets from Nonna. Not Nonna Bennetti, but my *real* Nonna, the one who passed away years ago.

I stretch up on my toes, reaching for one box. Can't quite get a grip. I glance around, spot a hanger, and decide to MacGyver the situation—who said that show was useless? A quick swipe knocks the box loose—along with another one I didn't mean to touch.

What follows is a rainstorm of yellow, blue, and orange Post-its, fluttering through the air before the entire damn box collapses in a papery explosion.

The universe hates me.

I pluck one off my head, flipping it over to find *his* handwriting. Perfect. Meticulous. Irritatingly neat.

Rico: I might be born in America, but I still refuse to call soccer anything but football.

My stomach twists as I turn it over, recognizing my handwriting on the opposite side of his.

Allie: I watch SOCCER every Saturday.

Dated. *Three months ago.*

My heart pounds as I drop to my knees, gathering handfuls of scattered notes. Dozens of them. Every single one of his stupid daily facts, neatly stacked and saved. Dated. Like they meant *something*.

Why keep them?

I mutter a string of colorful curse words as I scoop up the spilled Post-it notes from the floor, stuffing them back into the box like I'm loading guilt into a confessional. But one little bastard clings to my jeans, refusing to let go. Traitor.

I grab it, ready to slam the lid shut on this emotional Jenga tower, because I am *not* about to fall apart in Rico's closet while surrounded by his deeply repressed feelings disguised as sticky notes. Nope. Not today. Not when every breadcrumb of hope he leaves me ends with my heart getting demolished.

But then I see it.

No creases. No smudges. No hastily written snarky reply from yours truly. It's pristine, and the blank side stares up at me, daring me to flip it over.

So, of course, I do.

Rico: No one has seen me without a shirt in over twenty years. Once the wounds healed and I no longer had to show them to Mama, Papa, the doctors, or Marco—who was a curious freak about them—I covered them. Permanently. I don't even look at them myself in the mirror. I can't.

My fingers go still.

My lungs forget how air works.

He never gave me this. Never shared it. Just wrote it down, dated it, and tucked it into a box like a time capsule of emotional landmines.

Why?

My eyes shift to the stack, now a rainbow of untold truths. I rifle through them, heart pounding, until I find another one with only his writing.

Rico: I hate clocks. Clocks remind me of how much can change. They're a reminder we're all just waiting for time to tick by until the end. Time is precious, and I don't waste a minute of it. Which is why I hate that new clock you put in our dining room.

I blink. Then blink again.

Because these aren't just random facts. These are pieces of him. *Real pieces.* Scattered in a shoe box instead of being handed to me when I *needed* them most.

Dozens of them.

Thoughts. Confessions. Little windows into that steel-trap mind of his.

He wrote them. Dated them. But never gave me a single one.

What was the plan here, Rico? Stuff every raw thought into a box, die, and let me find it post-mortem? A little bonus content for the grieving widow?

I don't know what's worse—that he hid them, or that he wanted to tell me and couldn't. *Or wouldn't.*

If he had just handed me one... *just one*... maybe I wouldn't have spent half our marriage feeling like I was married to a human brick wall. Maybe I could've cracked through the mortar and seen more of the man underneath. The one I know is hiding in there, buried deep in shadows and sarcasm.

But instead, he locked the door, swallowed the key, and expected me to guess the combination to his heart.

And I would've. I *wanted* to. Not to fix him—I'm not running a rehab center for emotionally suppressed men—but just to *know* him. Just a foot in the door. Hell, half a foot. A toe, even. *Something.*

But no. He handed me silence and locked doors, then acted shocked when I walked away.

I'm halfway through color-coding my heartbreak—orange for trauma, blue for existential dread, yellow for suppressed childhood memories—when a deep voice cuts through the air and snaps me back to reality.

"Looking for something?"

I freeze. Inhale sharply. Then, schooling my face into *I don't care* mode, I stand, placing the box on the built-in dresser and turn to face him. "It fell when I was trying to grab *my* things."

I focus on the actual box I meant to retrieve, not the one that might as well be labeled *Allie's Idiotic Hope and Emotional Torture Kit.* I consider handing it to him, telling him to use it as kindling in the fireplace.

I didn't say I wasn't still bitter.

Broken or not, he broke me. Cheated on me. Used me. Purposely hurt me.

Most importantly, he doesn't love me, and my immature side isn't ready to let that fact go. *You're not loved back by the man you love. Let him go, woman.*

Instead of saying a word, I shove the last of my items into my duffel bag and zip it up, but when I stand—he's there. Blocking the doorway. Arms crossed, watching me like he's waiting for something.

I shouldn't ask. I shouldn't care. But the words slip out, anyway.

"Why...why did you keep them?" I nod toward the box. "The notes." I don't bring up the ones he never showed. Not yet, at least. I need to know why he kept them at all.

He steps forward, just once, as if he's debating whether to close the distance entirely. "Why would I throw them away?"

"Because they were pointless, Rico. Just another loophole for you to meet my request while simultaneously throwing it in my face."

His frown deepens as his gaze flicks to the box. He has to know that I saw some notes he didn't give me. "You thought *those* were pointless?"

"Oh, I don't know. Let's examine the evidence. Rico, who the hell says kale is a government conspiracy and *actually* means it?"

"I do. Seriously. I wasn't making fun of you, Allie. I really think kale has some secret endgame, and it sure as shit isn't making us healthy. Nothing that tastes and feels like cardboard in your mouth can be that good for you. Broccoli? That's debatable."

A laugh nearly bubbles up, but I choke it back because no. He doesn't get to make me laugh. Not now. "But why keep them?"

He shrugs. *That* shrug. The same one he always gives when he's pretending not to care. "It was my way of holding onto something."

My stomach twists. My throat tightens. "Oh? And what exactly were you holding onto, Rico? Because you don't strike me as the sentimental type."

"I'm not."

I huff out a humorless laugh. "No shit."

Zipping my bag, I hoist it over my shoulder and move to pass him—but his hands catch my shoulders, holding me in place.

"Don't you want to know why I kept them?"

"No." Because whatever answer he gives will only make it harder. Because he *won't* mean it. He's trying to win me back. His logical solution. I cannot give in.

He angles his head, eyeing me. "Why not?"

"You made it clear," I say, keeping my tone flat even though my insides are throwing furniture and lighting metaphorical curtains on fire, "that anything you said before wasn't real. Just a box to check. Give me what I need so you can collect your prize at the end of the arranged marriage obstacle course."

I step in, narrowing the space between us.

"And let's be honest... what you needed sure as hell wasn't me. Any woman could've played the role. Wore the ring. Shared the bed. Did the whole smile-for-the-family routine. Right?"

His jaw tightens, that familiar tic making an appearance. Good. That means I struck something—probably that black hole he calls a heart.

I should walk away. It would be the smart thing to do. But I've never claimed to be smart where Rico Bennetti is concerned.

"Why didn't you give me the other notes?" I ask, voice quieter now. A part of me already knows the answer, but I want to hear it from him.

Rico takes a slow step back, his usual blank expression cracking just a hair. "I... I tried to. About a week after you moved into my room. I wrote something that felt... heavier. Something that mattered. I even placed it on the pillow while you were sleeping, but picked it back up."

His eyes flick up to the ceiling like he's searching for divine assistance. "I couldn't put it on the pillow. I starred at it for an hour and then shoved it in the box."

"Why?" My voice shakes now, and it pisses me off. "Why couldn't you just give it to me?"

"You know why."

I nod. *Because I do.*

He didn't trust me. Not enough. Not with the parts of him that actually mattered. I was good enough to share a last name with. Good enough to screw. But trust? Respect? Real vulnerability?

Apparently, those had to be earned with a decoder ring and twelve levels of emotional gymnastics.

And that's the painful truth, isn't it?

I would never win this game.

Because Rico Bennetti never let me play in the first place.

"How's your *therapist*? Knock her up yet?"

His brows lift, and I'm positive I'm hallucinating from weeks of shitty sleep, because he almost looks amused as he answers me. "*Him.*"

My brain stutters. "You..." I blink. "Wait. *What?*"

"You think I like men?"

Then the *asshole laughs*. A real, deep, head-tipped-back, stomach-clutching laugh.

It's beautiful.

A sound I've never heard from him before.

And my *traitorous* ears soak up every second.

I hate him.

"I'm missing the joke."

"If you saw him, you'd see why that's funny." His lips twitch. "For fuck's sake. He's an *actual* therapist. A real, certified, Ph.D.-level shrink. The kind normal people see when they're trying to, you know, *heal*."

I open my mouth, then shut it.

Because...what?

"But that night," I finally manage. "You said you were with *her*."

His expression darkens. "I was with *him*. Not in the way you thought. Not in the way I *let* you think."

"Why would you do that?"

He exhales slowly, stepping closer, his fingers tilting my chin up. "Because I'm an asshole. One who pushes away anything that could make me happy. I was mad—at myself, at you for changing me. So I lashed out. I won't say it was okay, because it wasn't. It was wrong." He hesitates. "And worse...I knew you loved me, and I couldn't say it back." His jaw rocks back and forth. "I couldn't say it back."

"Yeah, we covered that last time. Remember?"

His face tightens. Good. At least he remembers *that* conversation—the one where he shattered me into pieces.

"I didn't mean it."

I let out a sharp, humorless laugh. "Well, that makes one of us."

Ignoring him, I adjust the strap of my duffel bag, shifting my focus to something—*anything*—that isn't Rico standing there with that look in his eyes. The one that threatens to pull me apart all over again.

"Allie..." His voice is rough. "Do you want to know why I'm in therapy? *Real* therapy?"

No. I can't handle it. Not now. Not when I've spent weeks trying to build a wall around the exact thing he's about to bulldoze.

Instead of protecting myself, my mouth opens, and the word comes out, anyway. "Why?"

"To fix myself. For *you*."

My stomach tightens, but I don't let my face betray me. "So...not for you. Not to actually heal. Just to become a version of yourself you think *I want*."

He studies me, waiting, searching for something I refuse to give him.

"You don't fix yourself for someone else, Rico," I mumble. "That's not how it works."

"So trying to be better for my wife doesn't matter?"

"No. Because one day, you'll resent me for it. And if you sign the damn papers, I'd no longer be your wife."

He flinches. Just slightly. But I see it.

I press on, voice firm. "It's too late, Rico. Say you *didn't* cheat. Say you *are* getting better. None of it changes you *not* choosing this marriage. Neither of us did. You never wanted this. And when you finally get better, you deserve the chance to find someone you love because you *actually* love them, not because you think you *should* just because they love you."

His lips part, but I lift a hand before he can speak.

"Don't you dare say you love me." My voice is steady, even as my heart cracks in half. "I filed the papers. Marco gave them to you. Sign them."

I step around him—*Operation: Dignified Exit* in full swing—but then his fingers close around my wrist.

"Allie..."

I stare straight ahead. If I look at him, I'll cave. And I'm fresh out of duct tape for my poor, gullible heart.

He doesn't just stop me here. Instead, he tugs the duffle off my shoulder, then reels me into his chest.

His jaw rests on top of my head. His arms lock around me with a grip that says *mine*—which would be cute if we weren't in the middle of a slow-motion emotional car crash.

"Don't give up on me."

The words are low, rough. Broken, even. If he were anyone else, I'd swear there were tears brimming behind that thick wall of stoicism. But this is Rico Bennetti. A man more likely to bench press his feelings than actually *feel* them.

I should pull away. Run, sprint, crab walk—I don't care. Just *go*. But my traitor of a body decides now's the perfect time to melt. The scent of him wraps around me—spiced woods, clean soap, and something annoyingly addictive. His chest rises and falls in this unsteady rhythm, his heart pounding loud enough to echo in my ears.

He *frowned* earlier. He *smiled*. He *talked*.

Don't be an idiot, Allie.

Maybe he is healing. Maybe the universe hit "update software" on his emotional range. Good for him. I genuinely hope he finds peace, hugs his brothers more, maybe even gets into journaling or goat yoga.

But me?

I was the shortcut. The simple answer to his family deadline and the looming expectation of baby-making. I wasn't a choice—I was a checkbox.

If I let him in now, I'll never stop wondering if I stayed because he needed *someone*, or because he wanted *me*.

"Rico..." I try, my voice already betraying me.

But then both his hands are on my face, cradling it like I'm the most fragile thing he's ever held.

His amber eyes lock on mine. Glossy. Intense. A little unhinged.

"Do you want to know a secret?" he whispers.

Rico

DR. DINGLEBERRY—I'M SURE OUT of respect I should use his real name, but let's not pretend names matter when your job is to dismantle the human psyche like it's a LEGO set—has been dissecting my brain three times a week for nearly a month now. That's twelve sessions. Thirty-six hours. Two mental breakdowns and one regrettable metaphor about emotional constipation.

He says I'm making progress. Points to the chair I added in my office, the one I haven't actively threatened anyone to sit in. Apparently that's character development. I even acknowledged two of the "dude bros" from the merger without fantasizing about pushing them out a window. Growth.

But here's the truth: the one thing that might actually make a difference is the one thing I haven't said. To anyone. *Not* to my therapist. *Not* to Marco. *Not* even to the parents who watched me practically bleed out that night and decided the best response was to act like nothing happened.

They know the bullet points. Kidnapped. Held in a basement. Retrieved. The end.

What they don't know is what happened between *taken* and *rescued*. The part of the story that doesn't fit neatly in a police report or whispered over a glass of scotch.

That part? Only three people knew. And two of them are now fish food at the bottom of the Hudson.

I know I need to talk about it. Process it. "Own my trauma," as Dr. Dingleberry so helpfully phrases it, usually while gesturing with a pen I want to stab into my eye. But every time I try, my throat closes up like a bank vault. Emotions, it turns out, are not only inconvenient—they're also suffocating.

Someone should've printed that on a warning label: *Feelings* may cause *spontaneous oxygen deprivation and general loss of will to live.*

I've avoided it for years. The retelling. The remembering. Because once you put words to horror, it becomes real. Tangible. Something people can poke and prod and pity. And I don't want their fucking pity. I didn't want forgiveness for what I became afterward.

But now?

Now I'm sitting in the closet of a house I didn't want but can't bear to leave. Holding a woman I didn't deserve but somehow ended up loving so completely it burns.

And she's leaving.

All because I refused to give her the one thing I gave no one else: the truth.

Not the cleaned-up version. Not the bite-sized chunks. The whole bloody, unfiltered truth.

I could let her walk. But if she walks out that door, she won't come back. And I'll go back to being the same emotionally vacant ghost I've always been—only now, I'll know what I lost.

So I do the one thing that terrifies me more than my past.

I sit down.

Right there, on the carpeted closet floor, pulling her with me until she's straddling my lap. My hands settle on her hips. She's warm and soft and grounding. And for one second, I forget the words. Forget everything except the weight of her and the echo of my heart hammering against a ribcage that's been sealed for years.

She blinks down at me, uncertain, but she doesn't go to move away from me.

I could joke. Say something flippant about this position and the number of ways it's distracting. But this moment? It deserves more than my usual armor of sarcasm and avoidance.

It deserves honesty.

Because for the first time in my life, I want to be known. Not by a paid stranger in a leather chair, but by *her*.

The little thief who stole my heart while I was too busy guarding my scars.

"When I was thirteen," I start, my voice bone-dry, "two men pulled up while Marco and I were at the park. They asked which one of us was Marco Bennetti. I told them it was me."

Allie's brow furrows, and I can already feel her reaction coming before she says a word. But I continue, because once you pull the thread, you either unravel or you get it the hell over with.

"Marco, at that age, had the self-preservation skills of a housefly. He'd land on the burner and wonder why the world hated him when it lit up. So, I took his place. Figured I had a better shot at survival." I laugh, but it's not amusement—it's bitterness—dark and cracked around the edges. "Joke's on me, I guess."

"They blindfolded me the second I stepped into the van. I didn't see anything again until they strapped me to a chair in some godforsaken basement that smelled like mildew and piss."

She seems completely unfazed by my pre-teen kidnapping.

"You knew?"

She shakes her head. "Marco said you took his place, that you were kidnapped. But he never told me what happened once they had you."

Of course he didn't. Marco doesn't know what happened during my temporary relocation. He saw the aftermath. He saw what they did to me—and worse, what it did *in* me.

I tuck a strand of her soft, dark hair behind her ear.

"I didn't even realize it was two days until I was released. Could've been two weeks, could've been two hours. Time didn't exist. Just the chair. The silence. And the occasional visit from pain with a side of humiliation."

My throat tightens, but I push through. Because if I stop now, I won't start again.

"Uncle Tony taught us early—don't talk, don't break, don't give them anything. If they keep you alive, they want something. As long as you don't give it to them, you've still got leverage. Hope. Whatever the hell you want to call it."

I pause. My fists are clenched so tight my nails bite into my skin. Then I feel her—her fingers sliding through mine. Warm and steady.

"Go on," she whispers.

"When fists didn't work, they got creative. Cigarettes. Knives. Small things at first, like they were playing. One of them enjoyed it too much—he had this wheeze when he laughed. I still hear it sometimes when the room gets too quiet."

I glance away. The memory burns hotter than the cigarette tips ever did.

"I didn't scream. I didn't talk. I just started focusing on details—mold in the corner of the room, the way it turned from green to black the longer I stared. I named the colors in my head. Gave the shadows personalities. Described the peeling paint like it was a fucking Monet. It was the only way to survive. Distraction therapy, trademark pending."

I don't know why I toss out the sarcasm. It's my shield, and an ineffective one at that. She squeezes my hand, encouraging me to go on with the story.

"When the cuts got deeper, I stopped pretending it didn't hurt. But I still didn't talk. Didn't look at them. I stared at a rust stain on the ceiling like it was a roadmap out of hell. I obsessed over the ticking of the clock just outside the door. That fucking clock. Every second a gunshot in my ears. *Tick, tick, tick*—like life was counting down, and I'd already missed the deadline."

My heart's pounding as if it's trying to punch its way out of my chest, and my throat—yeah, that's a lost cause. Dry. Tight. Every swallow sticks halfway down, useless as an umbrella in a hurricane. But I have to finish. I have to say this. At least once in my miserable life, I should try telling the truth.

"I think at some point, my brain just...fried itself out. Not in a fiery, sparking kind of way. No. It was quiet. Surgical. Like someone unplugged the wires behind my eyes and left me on standby mode."

I stare past her shoulder, not because I'm avoiding her—though, let's not pretend I'm above that—but because if I look at her while saying this, I'll never finish.

"They were laughing. Talking. Whispering things I'm sure were meant to scare me, but I didn't hear them. Just saw shadows. They lost their faces. Became outlines. Human noise pollution. The pain stopped registering, too. Even when I felt the blood—*my blood*—running in warm lines down my stomach, I couldn't feel it. My eyes stayed on the concrete walls. The cracks in them. The discoloration. I gave the mold names just to keep my mind from focusing on what was really happening. Fear, pain, hope... all of it vanished when I stopped acknowledging it."

I flex my hands without realizing it, the memory crawling under my skin. Her fingers close around mine, anchoring me. Her hands are warm. Mine are cold. Cold and dead, like the whole of me.

"Some guy showed up, eventually. Apparently, he was a rival of my Uncle Tony's. Classic organized crime twist, right? He walked in, saw me, figured out I wasn't Marco—because let's face it, Marco would've been crying and spewing answers to questions they asked by then—and he shot the two bastards torturing me. Just like that. No warning. No words. Just two gunshots and a man adjusting his cufflinks like he was late for dinner reservations."

I pause. Swallow. Swallow again.

"They dropped at my feet. I remember the blood more than anything else. It soaked into their clothes. Pooled across the concrete. Thick, dark red. The smell hit first. Metal and rot. I didn't realize blood had a smell. Not until it was everywhere. Still hits me sometimes."

"Red. That's why you hate the color red?"

I nod once.

"For a while, I couldn't even look at it. Couldn't drive past a stop sign without gripping the wheel so hard my fingers went numb. But then... remember that gallery night? You wore a red dress."

Her eyes widen, and I hold up a hand.

"You didn't know. You couldn't have. But here's the thing—I saw you in it and I didn't panic. Didn't break out in a sweat. My fists didn't curl. My mind didn't spiral. All I could think was that I wanted to tear it off you. Not because I hated it... but because it made me feel something. For the first time in years, I wasn't disgusted by the color. I was attracted to it."

I don't tell her that it scared the shit out of me. That seeing her in that dress triggered something so deep and raw it nearly choked me. Because if I do, she'll blame herself, and she shouldn't. That wasn't her burden to carry. It was mine. Still is.

"I came back different," I say, my voice dropping. "They left me in an alley like a bag of trash someone forgot to take out. And something in me stayed there. Something important. I don't know what. A piece of color, maybe. A light switch. Whatever it was, it didn't come back with me.

I remember standing in front of the mirror after. Lifting my shirt. Staring at what they'd done. I counted the scars. One, two, three... nineteen in total. Some deep. Some small. Some shaped like cigarette burns. I thought if I memorized them, I could own them. But they owned me. I didn't talk about it. Not really. Not to Marco. Not to my parents. Not to any therapist who scribbled in their little notepads and asked me how I *felt*.

I stopped trying. What was the point? Nobody could fix it. Nobody could rewind it. All they could do was offer me pity—and I didn't want it. I still don't. I don't want a hug. I don't want absolution from sins I never committed."

I meet her eyes now, and mine sting as tears claw their way out.

"I took Marco's place, and I've spent the last twenty-four years regretting it. Not because I got hurt. But because I survived and turned into this. And worse, I regret taking his place. What would my life be like if I hadn't, and he was taken? Who thinks that way? Who wants someone else to suffer? A horrible person. I hate myself for thinking that way."

There's something stuck in my throat. Not figuratively. Literally. A boulder of words I've been too cowardly to cough up for two decades. It burns. Scrapes. Lodges itself behind my sternum like it belongs there—because maybe it does. Maybe pain is the only thing I've ever really earned.

Despite that, I don't stop.

"If I hadn't taken Marco's place that day, who knows? He could've died. Or maybe he would've come out of that basement smiling and emotionally intact—like he does everything else. Maybe he would've been fine. Or maybe he'd be just as fucked up as I am, only prettier about it."

I laugh. Dry. Ugly. One of those sounds that dies halfway up your throat.

"I hated myself for even thinking it. For daring to wonder if it should've been him instead of me. What does that make me? A monster? A coward? The answer doesn't matter, because it doesn't change the math. I stepped in. I paid the price. And then I had to live with the consequences."

A tear slips down my cheek. I don't bother wiping it away. Let it fall. Let her see the wreckage.

"For years, I used to think it would've been better if they'd killed me. That would've been easier than watching Mama flinch every time I ignored another therapist. Or Papa, trying to hide the guilt in his eyes when I came home with another busted lip or broken knuckle. If I were dead, they could grieve. They'd move on. But broken? Broken is inconvenient. Broken sticks around."

My hand moves hers, pressing it over the scar on my side. The one I gave myself.

"After they gave up on the shrink parade, after the family decided ignoring it was synonymous with healing, I started figuring out my own coping strategies. Boxing helped. Pain has a funny way of organizing rage into neat, punchable packages."

I pause, throat tightening again, but this time I shove the words out, anyway.

"And when boxing didn't cut it? I did. Myself. Over and over. Because I figured if I had to live with scars, I'd rather they be mine. Something I chose. Something I controlled. But even that got old. Turns out pain doesn't cancel pain—it just multiplies.

I started pulling away. From everyone. Because if I didn't talk, I couldn't hurt anyone. And the more I disappeared into myself, the more they all seemed... fine. Happy, even. Marco became Don. Dom softened. Alex found balance. Mama laughed again. Papa relaxed. And me? I stayed in my corner and made sure no one had to look too closely."

I shrug, but it feels more like a collapse.

"Somehow, I convinced myself that silence was a form of love. If I stayed quiet, stayed out of the way, then I wasn't infecting them. I wasn't poisoning the family with my shit. And maybe that would've worked forever. Maybe I would've lived my life as a well-dressed ghost, haunting the marble floors of that sterile house. But then..."

My voice falters. My chest cracks wide open.

"Then you walked in. And you pushed. You spoke. You saw me. And I hated it. Because you didn't let me be invisible. You demanded more. And it scared the shit out of me, Allie."

Another tear. Another reminder that I'm bleeding in front of her, and there's no taking it back.

"I fought you every step of the way. Sabotaged us before we ever had a chance. Because I didn't believe I deserved you. And if I don't deserve you, I don't get to keep you. That's how it works, right?"

Her thumbs sweep under my eyes wiping away the tears.

"I've spent my whole life avoiding feelings. Now I'm drowning in them. Chest tight. Eyes stinging. Throat wrecked. But you know what? For once, I don't hate it."

I glance up at her, a bitter smile twitching at my lips.

Her hazel eyes fix on mine, wide and unblinking, and the silence between us stretches so long I start to wonder if I've accidentally overloaded her with all of my truth.

No gasp. No tremble. No awkward *"thank you for sharing."* Just... nothing.

Not even a damn squeak.

Excellent. I've officially trauma-dumped myself into emotional bankruptcy, and she's sitting there with the expression of someone watching a high-speed car crash in slow motion—morbidly fascinated but maybe regretting her front-row seat.

Can't blame her. Most people run from fire. She just found out I am the fire.

And still, she doesn't look away.

I almost wish she would.

Because now she knows. Not just the headline version—kidnapped, tortured, survived. No, she has the director's cut. The scars under the scars. The parts I've never said out loud, not even to the walking notepad who charges me three hundred dollars an hour to nod empathetically and pretend he understands.

She has it all now. My ugliest truth. My sharpest edges.

Congratulations, sweetheart. You've just become the only person alive who owns every piece of me worth stealing.

Allie

I KNEW *SOMETHING* HAPPENED to Rico. You don't end up emotionally mute, allergic to eye contact, and functionally dead inside because you suffered a mild inconvenience during your childhood. But this? This was... more.

Even coming from a world where kidnapping and torture are just another Tuesday, I wasn't ready for this. I didn't expect to be sucker punched by the weight of it all—the guilt, the trauma, the years of silence that festered into something jagged and broken, only to glue back together and become who Rico is now.

The worst part? He blames himself. For living. For existing. For not dying in someone else's place. And now I see it—how the world didn't give up on him. He gave up on himself first. Because no one taught him how to heal. Just how to hide.

"Can you say something, please?"

His voice barely makes it past his lips. His amber eyes are scanning my face like he's bracing for impact. Like I might run screaming. I don't. I just stare, still trying to stitch my feelings back together with emotional duct tape.

"I—I don't know what to say," I admit, my hands cradling his face. "Rico... I'm so sorry. You didn't deserve any of that. But you *do* deserve to be happy, and that doesn't make you selfish."

His lips twitch, but not in a smile. More like a flinch. "I've spent twenty-four years holed up in my own mind. I think I've selfishly hoarded enough solitude to call it a personality trait."

I shake my head. "No. You didn't do that for you. You did it so no one else had to carry your pain. That's not selfish. That's self-inflicted martyrdom."

He goes still. Even his breathing pauses.

"You hid because you didn't want to make other people uncomfortable. You shoved everything down so deep, you forgot what it even felt like to exist outside of survival mode.

You didn't choose you, Rico. Not once. Not when you were thirteen. Not when you were twenty. Not even when you married me."

His jaw flexes. "No one would understand."

"No one ever fully will," I say gently. "But they don't have to *understand* to care. You don't need pity—you're right. You don't need the world to wrap you in bubble wrap, but people love you. They would stand beside you, if you'd let them."

His eye roll is legendary, and I'd find it endearing if I weren't already drowning in the ache of it all.

"You protected everyone from you," I whisper. "Even me."

He swallows hard.

"Please don't leave me, Allie."

God. It's not a plea—it's a gut punch wrapped in gravel and grief.

"Rico—"

His lips crush into mine before I can say anything else. The kiss is all heat and desperation, a battle cry in disguise. His hand tangles in my hair, angling my face just the way he wants it. His other arm pulls me tight like he's trying to weld us together. Tongue, teeth, breath—I taste every broken promise, every unsaid word, every locked door he's slowly been opening.

And it's... a lot.

Too much.

Because this isn't what he needs. Not right now. And as much as I want to drown in this—want to rip off his shirt and claw at all the demons crawling under his skin—I can't.

He doesn't need sex to feel seen. Something he used to hide more than anything else.

He needs to *choose* himself first. He needs to pick *Rico* before he can ever choose me.

So, I pull away.

"Rico—"

"I love you."

Well. That'll derail a train of thought faster than a raccoon in the pantry.

I blink, pulling back just enough to look him in the eye. And for once—*for once*—he's actually giving me *eye contact*. Full-blown, no-blinking, lock-you-in-and-steal-your-breath eye contact. Which, if you know Rico, is basically a marriage proposal, and a sonnet wrapped in a neat package.

And damn it, he means it. I can feel it in every tense line of his body. But now I'm realizing love wasn't the problem—it never was.

"Rico," I say, my voice soft. "I love you too. Which is *exactly* why I'm about to say something that's going to suck for both of us. So I need you to listen. No interruptions. No eye-rolls. No smartass comments. Just... listen."

He nods once.

"You didn't choose what happened to you. Not really. You protected Marco, yes. But you didn't choose what came after. Those men, that basement, the pain, the silence—it was all forced on you. And ever since, you've lived your life trying to keep everyone else safe. Happy. Comfortable. Wrapped in a big, sparkly bubble of 'let's pretend Rico's fine.'"

I reach out, gently cupping his jaw, because I need him to *see* me.

"That makes you a good man, Rico. A good *person*. But it also means you've spent every second of your life thinking about what's best for *everyone else*. Never for you."

"But..." he says, jaw tightening, "you've got a '*but*' coming. I can hear it."

"But, you need to choose *you*, Rico. Not me. Not the version of life that seems easiest. Not the plan that keeps the peace. *You*."

His gaze drops, but I tip his chin back up.

"You're only just starting to open up, to untangle everything you've buried so deep it practically fossilized. You're finally getting help, and I'm so proud of you. But you're still in the middle of the mess. And I don't want you picking your forever while you're still wading through it."

He exhales through his nose. "So what? You think I told you the worst thing that's ever happened to me *because* I'm unsure about you?"

"No," I say, trying not to smile at the fact he's actually *feeling* something, even if that something is anger. "I think you told me because you *do* love me. And that means you're finally waking up. But loving me and choosing me are two very different things."

He stares at me.

"I want you to keep healing. Keep seeing your therapist. Keep figuring out what *you* want—what actually brings you joy. Then, once you've got your footing, once you can breathe without feeling like you're choking on the past... then choose. Choose your life. Your future. And if I'm part of that? Amazing. I'll be here."

He's quiet for a long beat.

"Fine," he mutters. "But I'd *prefer* if you waited here. Naked."

A real smile spreads across his face—crooked, devastating, and entirely unfair. Rico Bennetti smiling should come with a warning label *and* a fire extinguisher.

He pulls me into his arms, wrapping me up like he's afraid I'll disappear. And for now, I don't fight it.

We sit like that—tangled up in each other, hearts beating out their own awkward rhythm, breathing in silence that finally doesn't feel so heavy.

For once, we're not falling apart.

We're just... here. Together.

And maybe that's enough for now.

Rico

WE SAT IN THE closet for hours. No talking. No more crying. Just her curled in my lap and my arms caged around her like I could keep her here just by not letting go.

She didn't try to fix me. God, that was the worst part—she didn't try. She just *was*. And it gutted me more efficiently than anything a cigarette or a blade ever had.

When she finally peeled herself off me, slow and soft, she pressed a kiss to my mouth like a period at the end of a sentence. Final. Clean. Unapologetically certain.

She didn't say the words, but I heard them anyway.

Pick yourself first.

I wanted to tell her not to bother waiting. That the choosing part was already done. *I choose you.* Loud and clear, over and over. With fists and blood and pain. With every breath I didn't deserve.

But I understood what she meant, even if I hated her for being right. Choosing her while I still hated myself would be the equivalent of proposing marriage while actively digging your own grave. A bit of a mood killer.

So she left. And I let her.

Then I did what any man with decades of unresolved trauma and a questionable moral compass would do—I went to therapy.

Yes. *Therapy.*

I told Dr. Dingleberry—because no way in hell am I calling him by his real name—the whole sordid story. From the moment the van door slammed shut to the very last blood-stain on the concrete floor. I unloaded it all like a confession to a priest who charges by the hour and thinks emotional progress is best measured in "assignments."

"I want to be better," I told him. "Not just for her. Not just for my family. I want to stop waking up every morning and loathing the air in my lungs. I want to not hate the guy in the mirror."

He smiled. That knowing, smug little *I'm about to assign you journal prompts that'll make you cry in a Target parking lot* smile. I should've walked out. But I didn't. Because apparently, when you hit rock bottom, you collect gravel like its currency.

That was a week ago.

Since then, I've texted Allie every morning. Pointless facts. Personal confessions. Random bullshit I used to scribble on Post-Its, except now it's digital and pathetic. She texts back. We talk at night on the phone like love sick teens who can't stand to be away from one another. I purposely stay up just to call and tell her goodnight.

I wait up for her to get home. *Her* current home, which, by the way, is Kai's house.

I'm not saying I want to burn it down.

But I'm not *not* saying it either.

"How the fuck do *you* know about a custom ring maker?" I deadpan, side-eyeing Marco, who's currently slouched over the glass counter about as enthusiastic as if we were shopping for lightbulbs.

He doesn't even bother to look up. "You're welcome."

This—this *shop*—was his idea. Dragged me here like I'm a groom picking out cufflinks, not a man crawling back to the wife he never properly asked to marry him in the first place.

Also, let's not pretend this is new information. He pulled up the jeweler's website on my laptop *in front* of my brothers. The same laptop I used to hide several offshore accounts, and occasionally Google things like "how to stop wanting to burn down your life for fun."

I knew what he meant. *Everyone* knew. My original sin, laid bare in 4K.

Allie's wedding band had come from here. From me. Custom-designed, rushed, and delivered like a damn pizza. Only I never told her because that would have required me talking to her, then trying to explain why the fuck I felt the need to get her a custom wedding band, but not bother with the engagement ring.

Marco bought the engagement ring. I didn't even *propose*. Just married her because duty and legacy demanded it. Love, apparently, was a footnote I forgot to write.

"Do you want the new ring to match the band you got last time?" the sales associate chirps. Courtney. Young. Cheerful. Unaware she's playing jeweler to a man who would rather be waterboarded than say *I love you* out loud. I'm in therapy, but that only cures so much.

She recognized me, of course. Hard to forget the emotionally void gargoyle who bought a wedding band while looking like he was planning his own funeral.

Marco grins. "So you *did* get it here."

"Uh huh. Does Allie know?"

"No."

"She will now." He pulls out his phone like a tattle-tale in Armani.

I sign the order form, adding an extra twenty grand to expedite it. Because *of course* I'm rushing. Not because I'm impatient. But because I want my wife *home*. In my house. In my bed. Wearing my ring. Maybe screaming my name, if I'm lucky.

"She doesn't need a ring to come home," Marco mutters.

I shoot him a look. "Are you still in your tantrum era?"

"Are you going to propose or just toss it at her and hope she doesn't duck?"

"I have a plan."

"You *have* a plan?"

"I'm working on it." I give him a once-over. His whole storm-cloud vibe is throwing me off. Normally, Marco looks like he's two seconds away from breaking into an illegal poker game or strangling someone with a silk tie. Now? He's just... tense. Brooding. It's unsettling. I almost miss the chaotic bastard version of him.

"Are you going to tell me who's pissing you off, or should I guess based on your blood pressure?"

"Vi should help," he mutters. "I'm sure she has a scene or three in one of her smutty epics about grand romantic gestures."

He's not wrong. We've both read them. But we're men, which means we'll both die before admitting it out loud. Death before book club.

"Your ability to dodge the question is pathetic," I say.

"Says the man buying a second engagement ring for his *wife*."

Okay, fair.

"Can I at least get a hint?"

He turns to me slowly. That's when I get it—the look. The Don look. The one that strips the bullshit from your bones and makes your soul flinch. The one that says, *if you press this, I will make you regret it in ways that rhyme with body bag.* Pretty sure that look is why he reigns supreme.

"Leave it," he growls.

Charming.

"Wow," I deadpan. "Maybe you need a therapist."

"You'd be the expert. What's Voldemort think about your proposal plans? Did you get daddy's blessing?"

He pouts. *Actually pouts.*

I resist the urge to punch him. That's growth. My therapist should give me a gold star and a juice box.

My phone pings.

"Seriously?"

Marco shrugs like a smug little gremlin. "You need a distraction or you'll keep poking the bear. You're welcome."

> Violet: OMG yay! I can't wait to help you plan this. When can we meet? Oh hell, this is even better. I'm coming to lunch with you. Can you believe this is the first time I've ever texted you? I didn't even have your number!!! We are going to spend so much time together.

Well. That's a horror film title waiting to happen.

Marco claps a hand on my shoulder, all gleeful menace. "Have fun."

"You know payback's a bitch, right?"

"Nope. That's karma. And she's projectile vomiting all over my life right now, so I'm good."

I sigh, glance down, type.

> Rico: As much as it physically pains me to say this—yes. I need your help, Vi.

> Violet: I'm just thrilled you pulled your head out of your ass. Also, good news—I already planned the whole proposal.

> Rico: For fuck's sake. Is this in a book?

> Violet: I plead the fifth.

Fantastic.

Exactly what I need—my proposal idea written by a woman whose last male lead had a praise kink and a secret yacht.

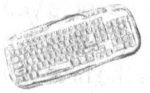

Rico

THIS IS A STUPID idea.

Which I have voiced. *Repeatedly*. To an audience that has no one listening to me.

"She doesn't want me," I growl, adjusting the cuff of my tuxedo—the same one I wore at our wedding. A suit that once symbolized my winning the game of life. Now? It feels like I'm suiting up for a slow, humiliating execution, courtesy of the woman who stole everything, including my dignity and soon my literal life with a very sharp, well-balanced butcher knife she has in that kitchen of hers.

Violet stands in front of me, hands clasped together like she's watching a toddler tie his shoes for the first time. I'm half expecting her to coo. She lives for this. My misery. My downfall. The moment I went from the cold, untouchable enigma of the family to a love-sick idiot groveling for his wife.

God, I am my brothers. I have no self-respect left.

Who am I kidding? I lost that the moment Allie walked into my life. The woman has my balls, my heart, and probably my ability to make rational decisions. She's like some master pickpocket, except instead of cash and jewelry, she swiped my entire soul without me even noticing.

"She doesn't want me, Violet. Not yet. I'm not fixed enough. This is a bad idea."

"Nooooo," she singsongs, rocking on her heels. "She said you need to choose *yourself*, then *her*."

I pinch the bridge of my nose. Therapy was a mistake. All it's done is make people feel comfortable enough to spew their nonsense at me.

"That. Is. The. Same. Thing," I grind out.

"No, it's not," she chirps, undeterred. "She said that *you* need to choose *her*."

Are we all experiencing the same conversation?

I turn to Sienna, hoping for a rational human response, but she's nodding so enthusiastically I'm convinced her head is about to pop off. "Yup. It's true."

"I *want* her. She doesn't want me yet. Not until I'm new and fixed and shiny." Not sure when the fuck that would be, considering I've been told by the Doc I have a lot of work to go.

"Ohhh, and when did you prove that to her?" Violet taps a finger on her lips, an expression so pompous I want to hurl myself into traffic. "Was it when you proposed?" She gasps dramatically. "Oh wait, you didn't do that."

I hate the sound of her laughter. That shit is straight out of a Disney villain's playbook. I would know. I've watched enough of those hell sessions with my nephew.

"Was it when you responded to her text messages like she was a person?" She tilts her head. "Oh, right, didn't do that either."

"Or when you showed up at her debut night?"

Kai's voice cuts through, and I scowl at him. He shrugs, leaning against the booth, arms crossed, gleaming.

"Stay out of this," I warn.

"Hard to do, considering you need *my* help."

I hate him.

"Maybe you're the reason my wife left."

It's a cheap shot, but I'm desperate. Apparently, I've become some hybrid between a caveman and a lion—a territorial, snarling, irrational mess. And the worst part?

Lions are just big, oversized house cats, and you know what cats are? *Pussies.*

Not the fun kind.

Kai holds up a hand, and I grumble, already knowing what's coming.

A countdown.

Why do people do this? As if I need a visual breakdown of their idiocy. Just give me the damn bullet points and be done with it.

He lifts a single finger. "*First,* she left because you told her you didn't love her and, oh right, *cheated on her.*"

A second finger joins. I consider breaking it, but unfortunately, I still need him for my *get my wife back mission,* so I let it slide. For now.

"Second," he continues, looking far too entertained for my liking, "your wife—despite being very attractive—does not possess the parts that interest me."

I blink at his two outstretched fingers.

Well. I guess we can be best friends.

Fuck me, I'm Dom now.

When did that happen?

"We square?" Kai asks, looking far too pleased with himself.

We *were* best friends, but I cannot associate with someone who uses a shape to define a relationship.

I nod, clenching my teeth so hard my jaw might fracture.

I can punch him *after* I get my wife back. Priorities.

Even though Doc hasn't cleared me to use a punching bag—because apparently, violence is *not* the answer—I have been assigned a different form of self-expression.

Journaling.

Yeah, that's right. Writing my feelings and expanding on them like some emotionally maimed teenage girl. I have a leather-bound notebook and everything. All that's missing is a pink fuzzy pen and a playlist of sad indie songs to really complete the aesthetic.

I'm still a man. I think. Therapy has blurred the lines. Testosterone? Unclear. Might've been replaced by pure estrogen at this point. I wouldn't be shocked if I woke up one morning and found myself debating throw pillow arrangements.

"Are we clear on the plan?"

Violet's voice yanks me back from my staring—which, unfortunately, was directed at Kai. The man who claims he has zero interest in my wife's anatomy.

Which is a shame. Because I have seen it. Experienced it. Had an out-of-body, religious moment while inside it. Okay, maybe not religious, per se—I'd rather not get struck by lightning for blasphemy.

Note to self: check with Mama on candle supply. Preferably have her light an entire cathedral's worth.

"It's been three weeks, Vi. Maybe she's moved on. Accepted the fact I'm too broken."

"She hasn't," says the man who claims to be disinterested in vaginas. I ignore him.

"Rico, it's been three weeks because, one—that custom ring took a while, and two..."

Oh, God. Here we go. Another countdown. If this entire night is going to be narrated in a list format, I'm out.

Okay, I'm not.

Because I'm pathetically whipped.

I *need* her back. I *need* her in my bed. Hell, I *need* her wrapped around me so tightly I can't tell where she ends and I begin. I don't even care if I become her emotional support human. She can drag me around like a damn security blanket if it means she's mine again.

My dignity? Gone. My pride? Obliterated.

I think my manhood is currently tucked into the back pocket of her jeans.

She can keep it—so long as I get her.

Oh, how far you have fallen, my friend. There's no saving you now.

"And if this backfires horribly, I can blame all of you?" I point at every single idiot in the room who had a hand in this disaster of a plan.

"Sure," Violet says far too quickly.

I don't trust her.

She's shifty. She's too smart. And she writes romance novels for a living.

Never trust a romance writer.

They will use everything you say as material.

Case in point: me.

You think this complete debacle will not end up in one of her books?

Yeah. You'd be wrong.

"So, can we get this over with?" Kai looks painfully bored.

I'd like to wipe that look off his face. Preferably with something soaked in disinfectant. Or my fist. Either works.

"Fine," I grit out.

Violet is practically vibrating on her toes, her ridiculous twin-filled belly bouncing along for the ride.

Kai claps his hands together like he's summoning a genie.

I could use three wishes right about now.

One: this entire situation disappears and my wife is magically home, forgiving and preferably naked.

Two: I'm buried inside said wife and never have to remove myself again.

Three: ...honestly? Probably should leave one in the vault for emergencies.

"It's showtime!" Sienna practically dances in place.

I exhale slowly, leveling them all with a look.

I should have asked my brothers for help.

Allie

Friday nights are grueling.

Why is it that Friday night seems to summon the absolute worst customers humanity offers? Oh right. They leave their offices after a long week of micromanaging their poor employees and immediately start hunting for their next victim—tonight, that is me.

Too cold. Too hot. Not enough sauce. Too much sauce. Too bland. Too spicy. Why is it so spicy?

I'm one complaint away from launching a ladle at the next entitled jackass and reenacting Carrie, but marinara style and not blood.

Sure, I carve meat for a living, but actual blood? Hard pass. Yes, I realize I grew up in a family that literally paved the way *in* blood, but that doesn't mean I enjoy bathing in it. I prefer my stains of the tomato variety. Thank you very much.

Kai saunters toward me and I know from the look on his face there's another patron requesting my presence.

"No. Absolutely not. You deal with it," I declare before he even opens his mouth. "I'm not going out there to kiss the ring of another entitled asshole just because they don't know how to use salt properly."

His eyebrow arches.

"It's not my week." Understatement of the year, but whatever. Who's keeping track?

"This one you *might* want to see," he muses, pinning me in place with one of those *we both know you need this* looks. "They're not here to complain. They want to thank the chef. And I know you could use a little praise."

I could use a lot of things, but sure, let's pretend a "great job" from some overfed Wall Street reject is going to soothe my deep existential rage.

"You go," I grumble, wiggling free from his entirely unnecessary grip. I'm not in the mood for praise. Or complaints. Or human interaction of any kind, honestly. Yeah, I've officially turned into my husband. And yes, I can still call him that because the tenacious ox hasn't signed the divorce papers. No, instead it's like we are dating. Getting to know one another while he heals himself. It's all so confusing and unfinished.

So legally, we are still one.

One entity.

One unit.

One catastrophic mess.

And it's left me in a sour mood.

"They were quite specific." Kai's smirk is a little too smug. "Asked for Chef Bennetti."

And there it is. That last name that cuts me deeper every time someone says it to me.

"I don't like you," I groan.

He glows. "I can live with that."

"You realize we're in a kitchen full of very sharp objects, right?"

"Oh, I'm aware. I hear they cut clean."

"And that I am specifically trained to use said sharp objects?"

"I heard a rumor."

"That I grew up in the mafia and definitely know how to make bodies—or at least body parts—disappear?"

"Should I be shivering?" He does a very fake, very dramatic shiver.

"I hate you."

"I love you too." He has the audacity to rub his knuckles against my hair like I'm some kind of scrappy little sibling before steering me toward the dining room.

Annoyed and exhausted, I yank off my apron, smooth out my chef's coat, and check my reflection in the mirror.

Yikes.

No makeup. Purplish-blue splotches under my eyes. Cheekbones so sharp they could cut parmesan. I look like the human equivalent of death warmed over.

Time to meet my public.

I step into the dining room, and the low hum of conversation doesn't change. Tables are full. People are eating. No one is paying attention to me.

Until I walk.

Then *everyone* is looking at me.

Smiles. Nods. That weird half-smirk people do when they think they know something you don't.

Fantastic. I might as well be on display behind glass. Observe the estranged wife in her native setting—sipping coffee, pretending to be fine. Thrilling stuff. Bring snacks.

Spotting Nina at the host stand, I tug her aside.

"Which table asked to see me?"

"Oh, table four."

I nod and scan the room, weaving through tables while entirely too many eyes follow me. Seriously, what the hell is going on tonight?

VIP section. Back corner.

That's table four.

Except when I get there?

Every single VIP table is empty.

What. The. Hell.

The lights dim.

No one gasps. No hushed whispers. No dramatic murmurs.

Except me.

Because, *obviously*, I have to be the only one concerned about a potential electrical issue in a fully packed restaurant.

"So sorry, folks! I'll fix the lighting," I call out, even though not a single person seems worried. Last thing I need is some influencer nicking themselves with a butter knife in the dark and blaming me for their inability to function as an adult.

The room is cloaked in near darkness, and—because tonight clearly wants to see me lose my mind—Nina didn't light a single candle in this zone. Apparently, her hopes for a raise and future employment are circling the drain.

Then, without warning, the lights flick back to full brightness, making me blink rapidly, my brain pulsing from the sudden assault like a migraine threw on strobe lights for fun.

And that's when I see him.

A shadowy silhouette in front of me.

Not just standing there.

On one knee.

In a tux.

My...*husband*.

My mouth opens. No words come out. I glance around wildly, expecting some hidden-camera prank, but nope—every single person in this restaurant is riveted.

"Rico?" As if I have another husband out there.

He smiles. A full smile. Not his usual grin or that barely there lip twitch he thinks counts as an expression. No, this one is the kind that makes knees weak, steals breath, and melts panties right off. *My* panties, to be specific.

Hell.

"I choose you," he says, his voice smooth but firm. "And I have wanted you for longer than you probably realize. The day I met you, you didn't flinch at my family, which, frankly, is a miracle. When you asked for my reset button. When you pushed me. Teased me. Fought with me. When you responded to my notes instead of tossing them. I took every bit for granted, but not because I didn't want you."

My lungs forget how oxygen works.

"Yes, we didn't meet the way we should have. I didn't propose the way you deserved. But that doesn't mean I didn't love you. It means I was an idiot." He pulls a small box from his pocket, cracking it open.

A diamond.

With pearls.

Pearlina.

I bite my lip. My chest tightens.

"You are the reason I started fixing myself," he admits. "But I didn't just do it for you. I did it for me. For us. For the future I want—with you. I wanted you long before you said 'I do.' And I wanted you even more after you left. I wanted you in my bed—throw pillows and all." His lips twitch in amusement, and it takes everything in me not to faint.

"But," he continues, his voice dropping an octave, "I never asked you and that wasn't fair. So, I'm asking now." He exhales sharply, his amber eyes locked onto mine. "Will you marry me, Alessandra?"

A collective gasp ripples through the room. *Oohs* and *aahs* follow, but all I can focus on is him.

Rico.

On one knee.

In public.

Using words.

Smiling.

I should be furious that he pulled this in front of a crowd. But I'm not. Because he's here, doing this, saying this—in the most *Rico* way possible.

I look down at the ring. Then back at him.

"What if I need time?" My voice wavers.

His throat bobs. "Then I'll wait. No matter how long you need."

He stands, but my hands fly out before he can stand up. "Yes."

His brow lifts. "Yes?"

"I'm not saying it *all*."

"You should." He tilts his head, his smirk deepening. "Would be cute. I am, after all, in a tux on my knees. I know you clean these carpets, but still, c'mon."

I roll my eyes, exhaling dramatically. "Fine. Yes, I'll marry you."

He's up in an instant, arms wrapping around me, lifting me off the ground before I can so much as blink. Behind us, claps and cheers explode, but all I hear is him.

His heartbeat.

His breath.

His quiet, relieved "Hey."

I smile. "Hi."

His forehead presses against mine. "Can I kiss my wife?"

"Fiancée," I tease.

"I'm not doing another wedding," he mutters. "But I will give you a honeymoon."

I pretend to think about it, but before I can answer, he grabs my face and kisses me.

And just like the first time, like our wedding kiss, it starts slow. Controlled.

And then?

It burns.

Like a full-body ignition. Like the chemistry we always had—the chemistry we *never* lost— exploded in the middle of my restaurant.

By the time he pulls away, I'm breathless. He's breathless. And only then do I see his family behind him.

His entire family.

"For the record," he murmurs against my lips, "I only invited Vi and Sienna. The rest... well, you know."

I snort, pressing a kiss to his mouth. "And Kai?"

His playful growl makes me laugh.

He brushes my hair back, his fingers lingering on my jaw. "Does this mean you'll move back home?"

"To my room?"

He shakes his head. "I moved my stuff up to *our* room. On the second floor." His voice softens. "Down the hall from where, I hope, one day... we'll have kids."

I open my mouth—to argue, to question, to make sure this isn't just about that—but he cuts me off with another kiss.

"And that doesn't have to be soon or ever. I *choose* you. The rest is a bonus."

Epilogue

Rico

ANY TIME SOON TURNED out to mean one month.

One. Fucking. Month.

Leave it to karma to not only screw me over, but to wait—lurking like a sadistic little gremlin—until I proposed to my wife properly, had one incredibly mind-melting night of makeup sex (which, if I'm being honest, I'd fight her every damn day just to relive), and boom—pregnant.

And not just pregnant.

Twins.

Apparently, I have super sperm. My brothers are smug as hell, saying things like *"Told you, stress-free equals fertile AF"* while I plot their premature demises. I might be improving in group settings—slowly, in small increments, not all at once—but I will die before I admit they're right.

I talk more now. Not a lot. Just enough to be human. Most of it is reserved for my wife—*yes, my wife*—who somehow cracked the impenetrable steel vault that was my emotional bandwidth. My family benefits from my newfound communication skills, but the downside? It invites them to drone on about diapers, teething, and whatever allegedly impressive feat Amelia performed that, spoiler alert, is mildly interesting at best. But I listen. I nod. I pretend I'm engaged. Because soon enough, I'll be the one spamming group chats with baby's first smile like some sleep-deprived lunatic.

Which brings me to my current predicament.

"I didn't do it on purpose!" I grip Allie's hand like it's a lifeline, because at this moment, it is.

"Do you see this?!" She waves wildly at her very, very prominent belly.

Yes. Yes, I do. It's impossible to miss, considering my children have overstayed their welcome inside her for forty-two weeks. At this point, we're approaching squatter's rights.

She's fucking terrifying.

I've seen some serious shit in my lifetime. Been in situations where most men would piss themselves and beg for mercy. But my very pregnant wife? This is next-level horror movie shit.

I would not be shocked if one of these kids comes out with a full set of teeth and horns.

And honestly? I can't even pretend to be surprised she got knocked up. Considering how literally inside of her I was for days after I proposed, it would have been more shocking if she hadn't gotten pregnant. My only genuine memory of our honeymoon is her naked in every position known to mankind.

I think there was a beach at some point, but honestly, that part's fuzzy.

Now I get why my brothers were way too enthusiastic about pregnancy sex. It was a full-time job keeping up with her hormones, and I gladly clocked in. Twice a day. Three times during peak hours.

But now?

Now, I'm enemy number one.

And if these babies don't come out soon, I have a feeling I won't be the father of twins—I'll be a cautionary tale.

"They're coming now, baby," I murmur in what I hope is a soothing tone. But really, it's for my balls, because I'd like to keep them intact. Preferably attached to my body.

She groans, gripping my hand with a force that suggests she's aiming for permanent damage. My fingers crack. She's actively breaking them. But sure, *she's* the one in pain.

Also, why does she get an epidural, and I get nothing?

Unlike my brothers, I now hold the ultimate trophy. The first Bennetti twins—one boy, one girl. Take that bitches. Not that I can say it out loud, because the more I talk like them, the more I hate myself.

Insert the bitches comment from earlier.

"Do you have names picked?" the doctor—a *man*—asks while, and I cannot stress this enough, he is elbow-deep in my wife's favorite body part of mine.

I glare at him. "I thought we discussed you not making conversation while your hands are in my wife's vagina?"

I also hate that I have to say vagina like we're in a medical documentary instead of real life. But I'm not about to ask why he's in my wife's pussy. That would make it weird.

I glance at Allie. Yeah. Her eyes? Not full of love. Nope. Those are murder eyes. Eyes that say I could kill you right now and sleep like a baby afterward.

And honestly? I don't blame her.

My balls, sensing imminent danger, attempt to retreat into my body. *Cowards.*

"I don't blame them for wanting to stay where it's warm and wet," I mutter, glancing at her belly.

Yeah. She did not appreciate that comment.

"Rico," she growls through a contraction, her breathing all Lamaze and aggressive—which, honestly, looks like hyperventilating with extra spite—before she turns to me.

"If these babies don't come out soon..." She pauses to crush my fingers like a hydraulic press. "I. Will. Kill. You."

And you know what?

I believe her.

"Head's out!"

The man—whose actual profession should be way more regulated if you ask me—shouts like we're at a damn football game. Which, fun fact, we are *not*. We are in a sterile, too-bright, aggressively scented medical room where my wife is currently trying to expel our offspring like a possessed demon in an exorcism scene.

And me?

I am now witnessing the horror that is childbirth while actively trying to unsee it at the same time.

"Which one?" Allie groans, throwing her head back like she's debating whether she can just tap out of this entire situation.

Like I know which one. I am neither the baby catcher nor the owner of the vagina in question. I was just standing by her side like a supportive husband should, but then, against my better judgment, I looked over the doctor's shoulder.

Which was a mistake.

A catastrophic mistake.

The mistake that will haunt my subconscious for the rest of my natural life.

"One more push, and we'll find out!" The too enthusiastic baby catcher chirps, as if my wife isn't seconds away from committing premeditated homicide.

A moment later, a loud wail fills the room.

"It's a girl!"

Stunning observation, Sherlock. Considering she just made her grand entrance without a penis, I figured.

Before I can even process the information, the nurses steal my child—*my child*—before I can get a proper look at her.

What is it with women and taking shit from me?

I follow them across the room, because if anyone is taking my kid, it's me. The first thing I see? A head of dark hair, tiny fingers curled into delicate fists, and two kicking feet that already scream *fighter*.

Then she cries.

And just like that, something unhinges in my chest.

It's a foreign, terrifying sensation—like someone took a crowbar to my ribcage and let in the light.

They wrap her up in one of those ridiculous baby burrito blankets and finally pass her to me. I look down at this tiny, perfect creature. Her little face scrunched in indignation like she's already had it with this place.

Yeah, same, kid.

"Got a name picked out?"

Both Allie and I freeze.

Right. *That.*

The one thing we should have settled by now. Except, we haven't.

Because every single time we discussed it, it turned into an all-out war where neither of us walked away victorious. And then, just for fun, my brothers had the audacity to steal all the good family names before I could even get in the game, leaving me with a list of rejects.

I glance at my wife, who is looking at me like I should be the one to answer.

"I told you, I like Clover."

I stare at her.

She's clearly delirious from labor exhaustion.

Clover? CLOVER?

Like the weed? Like a lawn infestation?

The nurses shift awkwardly, probably debating if they should report us for attempting to name our kid after a garnish.

"Pearl." I look back at Allie, waiting for the inevitable argument. But instead of fighting me, she bursts into tears.

Shit. "Okay, not Pearl."

"No..." she chokes between sniffles and what I think are hiccuped sobs. "It's perfect."

Well. I was prepared to fight to the death, but okay. This is...progress.

Before I can bask in my insignificant victory, the doctor—who is still in my wife's personal space—pipes up like he's part of the conversation. "And the boy?"

Oh, right.

Our other spawn.

Still hiding like he's waiting for an engraved invitation. Honestly, I respect the hell out of it.

Allie, however, does not.

"Marco?"

My head snaps up so fast, I almost give myself whiplash.

"Hell. No."

Has she lost her mind?

Of all the names in the universe, she wants to name our kid after *Marco*?

The last thing that egomaniacal lunatic needs is another baby in this family, with his name.

"Have you seen his ego? It was at Thanksgiving. Floating over the parade. Big and shiny. Gave children nightmares."

Allie groans, her head dropping back onto the pillow with an exhausted sigh. "Fine. Not Marco. But you better have a damn name ready, because if I push one more human out of my body and we're still arguing, I'm legally changing it to 'Revenge.'"

Fair.

My son—who I already know is going to be the biggest pain in my ass—finally shows up. There's a lot of commotion, more shouting, and another wail. I don't even have time to see him before the nurses swipe this one away, too. Fantastic. Two kids and I've gotten zero time with them before they're being poked, prodded, and handled by people I will run background checks on later.

"What's the name?"

I look at Allie. She looks at me. Then at our daughter in my arms, who is happily snoozing without a care in the world, and finally to the screaming newborn in the doctor's grasp, already giving the world hell.

I smirk. "Roman."

She tilts her head, considering. "Like the empire?"

"No, like the guy who's going to drive us insane for the next eighteen years."

Allie rolls her eyes but doesn't argue, which means I win. Again.

Roman and Pearl.

Pearl stole my heart. Roman will rebuild my peace.

Allie stole every last part of me, and I'm letting her keep it.

The doctor hands me my son, and for the first time in my life, I hold everything I never knew I wanted.

Two babies. A wife who should hate me but somehow loves me, anyway. And a future that doesn't feel like a ticking clock to self-destruction.

"You happy?" Allie murmurs, exhausted but glowing like she just conquered the entire world. Which, technically, she did.

I glance at our kids, then at her. My wife. My constant. My entire damn universe.

"I have you. And you're stuck with me forever." I press a kiss to her forehead. "So yeah, I'm happy."

She snorts, her eyes already drifting shut. "Better not start ignoring my texts again."

I grin. "Not a chance, thief."

Acknowledgements

Writing a book is never a solo endeavor—unless you count the many hours spent alone in front of a screen, mumbling dialogue to yourself and surviving solely on caffeine and donuts (true story). But even in that madness, I'm lucky to be surrounded by the best people.

To my incredible beta readers—thank you for your time, your feedback, and your tolerance of my cliffhangers and emotionally stunted characters. You help shape these messy drafts into something worth reading, and I am forever grateful.

To my OG beta reader, Shannon: how are we still friends after three books and *another* last-minute change? (Don't answer that.) Your patience with my process—aka my inability to not make impulsive edits—is saint-level. You deserve snacks, a nap, and perhaps an emotional support llama. Does Amazon sell those?

To my audiobook narrator—you already know this, but I'm saying it for the people in the back: you are not just the voice of these books, you're my behind-the-scenes therapist, hype squad, and idea wrangler. Thank you for helping me fine-tune the ending when I was spiraling in twelve directions. Also, sorry in advance for whatever chaos I write next... you're stuck with it.

To my cover designer—thank you for not blocking me when I changed my mind (again) and for turning my vague "I want it to be pretty, but with coral and not too pink" into actual art. You're magic.

And finally, to every single person who reads and reviews my books: you're the reason I get to keep doing what I love. Your support helps my stories reach new hearts. You make this wild dream real and your support is valued more than words could ever express.

Also by Everly Summers

If you're new here—*hi, welcome, I bring snacks and emotionally unavailable men who fall hard and fast once they get over their trauma. Okay, that's just Rico, but still...*
If you're returning—*welcome back, you beautiful glutton for angst.*

The Bennetti Boys Series:

Pretending to be His – Alex and Violet's story (a billionaire fake dating that is also in duet on Audible!)

Playing House – Dominic and Sienna's story (the control freak meets rainbows and glitter neighbor and, well, you can guess the rest...)

Coming this Fall (if the stars align and the espresso flows):

Marco's story (the Don, the myth, the sarcastic legend). A full-circle finale to the Bennetti Boys series.

Want to stay in the know about release dates, bonus content, spicy sneak peeks, or just hear me spiral about fictional men at 2AM?

Come hang out on Patreon – you can follow *for free* to stay updated or join for exclusive perks, early chapters, bonus epilogues, and chaotic writer brain dumps.

www.ingramcontent.com/pod-product-compliance
Lightning Source LLC
Chambersburg PA
CBHW012001120726
47901CB00012BA/2506